LAST

GW00786652

ROBERT F BARKER

1

First published as an ebook in 2015

First published in paperback in 2016

Text Copyright @2015 Robert F Barker

All rights reserved. This is a work of fiction. Names, characters, places and incidents are used fictitiously. Any resemblance to actual events, or persons, living or dead, is coincidental. All rights reserved. No part of this publication may be reproduced, or transmitted in any form or by any means, electronic or otherwise, without written permission from the author.

By Robert F Barker

The DCI Jamie Carver Series

Last Gasp (The Worshipper Trilogy, Book#1)
Final Breath (The Worshipper Trilogy, Book#2)
Out Of Air (The Worshipper Trilogy, Book#3)
Family Reunion
Death In Mind

Other Titles
Midnight's Door

A Killing Place In The Sun - An Action-Packed International Thriller

Find out how it all started

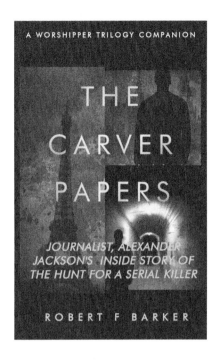

Sign up for the author's V.I.P. mailing list and get a free e-copy of, *THE CARVER PAPERS,* the series of articles that kick-started it all - as feature in LAST GASP

To get started, visit:-
http://robertfbarker.co.uk

To Carol, for your endless patience

To Christina, for your endless enthusiasm

To the talented members of the Vale Royal Writers Group, for your endless support

To everyone at Harrogate's Theakston's Old Peculier Crime Festival, for your endless inspiration

Prologue

The man in charge of the operation is worried. He senses something is wrong. He can't yet say what it is, it's just a feeling. But he's had it before.

He interrupts his pacing to check the screen around which his strike team are hunched. Two men and a woman, they are staring at a second woman, framed in its centre. Perched on a chair, her legs are crossed at the knee, hands resting, almost demurely, in her lap. If she is anxious, she does not show it - which is remarkable considering she is waiting for someone who may be coming to kill her.

The man checks his watch. Her visitor is twenty minutes late. In that time, tension within the team has risen to the point where they can no longer hide their nervousness. One drums fingers on the table. Another cracks his knuckles. The female member clicks her nails. Meanwhile the man in charge paces, and worries. The apartment they are using as the Forward OP faces directly across from hers. She sits no more than twenty yards away. Yet he fears that when the time comes, it may be too far.

It wasn't his choice.

From the start, he'd argued they should be secreted

somewhere in her apartment. But she would have none of it, pointing out that apart from the two bedrooms, her apartment is open-plan. 'If he opens the wrong door, you'll be blown.' Again, when he tried to push it, 'You're only across the hall. How long would it take to reach me? Five seconds? Ten, max. I'll be fine.' He wishes now he had stuck with his instincts. A lot can happen in ten seconds.

The radio next to the screen bursts into life.

'He's here.' There is a general shuffling as they all come on alert, then, 'He's in the lift. Going up. Over to you.'

The man reaches forward, presses a button on the console. 'He's on his way. Thirty seconds.' Then he adds, 'How're you doing?'

The woman looks up to the camera concealed in the light fitting. 'I'm fine. Stop fussing.' She even manages a smile, though it seems a little forced. Not for the first time, he marvels at her self-control, but then thinks, *What else should I expect?*

Half a minute later, as the bell's double-chime sounds, tinny but clear through the speakers, four pairs of eyes lock onto the screen.

The woman in the chair hesitates, then rises. As she makes her way to the door, the black satin robe she wears over her work-attire billows behind. The clicking of her heels on the wood floor echoes round the apartment. Her pace is measured, as if her visitor's arrival holds no fear for her. But as she reaches the door she stops and they see her take a deep breath.

'Right,' she says, just loud enough for the microphones to pick up. 'Here we go.'

Reaching up, she releases the latch, unhooks the

chain, turns the key. She opens the door. A man stands there, but she is between him and the camera, shielding his face.

'You are late.' Already in role, her tone is strident.

His mumbled apology is too indistinct to hear.

For what seems longer than necessary she leaves him there, confirming the order of things. Eventually, she takes a step back, moves to the side. 'I suppose you'd better come in.'

Head down, his reply is also lost.

As he steps through, the onlookers strain to get their first sight of him in the flesh. His hair is dark, as expected, but his stooped posture makes it difficult to gauge his height. His dress is smart-casual. Black leather jacket, blue shirt, dark trousers. But his face stays hidden as he keeps his head bowed, in keeping with his part.

'Is it him?' the female member of the team says. 'He looks different from the photograph.'

They all look to their leader. Any decision is his.

The man in charge takes his time, weighing the visitor who seems to be taking in everything about the apartment. Suddenly the newcomer lifts his head and appears to stare directly into the camera, as if sensing the watchers' presence. But after a few seconds his gaze moves on, elsewhere.

'It's him,' their leader says.

To his colleagues, he seems calm again. No sign of the hand-wringing of earlier. Almost as at ease as the woman herself. What they cannot see however, is the turmoil inside. They cannot know that already he is struggling with the instincts telling him that something is wrong. That his bowing to her insistence that this is

3

the right way to play it was a mistake. That he should have made her see things his way. And now-.

'Is someone here?' the man asks. He speaks with the deep, northern vowels that fit the profile.

As he finishes, he lifts his gaze to meet hers in a way that almost challenges the protocols she'd begun to assert the moment she opened the door. Seeing it, the man in charge's concern deepens. It is not what he'd expect from a novice. But the woman shows no sign of being fazed and returns him a cold stare.

'No. And even if there were, it would be no concern of yours.'

As if satisfied, the man reverts, mumbling some response that fits with her rebuke.

Relieved, the man in charge nods. He even grants himself a wry half-smile. She is good at this.

For the next few minutes the pair play-out the unwritten script that governs such encounters. She is haughty, dismissive; he fawning, obsequious, eager to please as she admonishes him, again, for his tardy time-keeping.

But the man in charge still worries. For a supposed first-timer, the visitor's responses seem well practised. In his head, a warning bell sounds. 'Something's wrong.'

The others turn.

'Seems okay to me,' one of the men says, before returning his gaze to the screen.

His female colleague follows suit. 'Isn't this how it's supposed to go?'

He doesn't answer, struggling to convey the instincts that come from the sorts of experience he knows they do not have. Anxiety growing, he returns his attention to the screen. The scene is still being played out behind the

4

front door. The rules of the game dictate that she will not admit him further until she is satisfied he is properly, 'in role'. Even as they watch, that moment arrives.

Turning on her heel, she crooks a finger, beckoning him to, 'Come this way.'

This time they hear, clearly, the, 'Yes Mistress,' as he moves to follow her.

But it is a feint. As she strides away he makes a quick reverse, turning swiftly and silently back to the door. Reaching up to the latch, he does something with his hands, the sound covered by her clicking heels, before returning to scurry after her so that he is where he should be as she turns to address him from the middle of the floor.

The watchers lean in, alarmed.

'What was that?' one man says.

'What did he just do?' says the woman.

At first the man in charge does not answer. Like them, he is stunned by the unexpected development. His mind races to interpret the significance of what he's just witnessed, how it affects their plans. Finally, he voices what they already know.

'He's snicked the lock and set the chain.'

'Shit,' is one response.

'Fuck,' another.

'What do we do?' the female says. 'Do we abort?'

For a moment he hesitates, torn between wasting many weeks' effort – others' as well as their own – and risking the safety of the woman who is unaware that her visitor has just blocked the only route by which any needed rescue would come. In fact, the decision is an easy one. But even before he can voice the instruction, matters are taken out of his hands.

Careful to proceed as she would with any client, the woman has already adopted the classic stance in front of the sofa, hands on hips, legs slightly apart, face stern. But as she makes ready to deliver the lecture that will progress things to the next stage, the visitor makes his move.

Taking two determined strides forward, he punches her, hard, in the middle of the face. The mics relay the 'crunch' of the contact. The force of the blow sends her reeling back onto the sofa's thick cushions from where she bounces off onto the floor. Before she can even begin to raise herself, he is on her. The scream dies in her throat as his hand closes round it. As he lifts his other arm, high, the camera picks out the vicious-looking hunting knife he is already brandishing.

But the watchers do not see it. They are already charging out through the door and into the brightly-lit atrium that distinguishes this particular luxury-apartment building from the many others that have sprung up around Salford's quays the past decade. And while there is no shouting, no sense of panic among them - they know exactly what they must do – they are under no illusion as to the difficulty of their task. They were all present when the woman who had entrusted them with her life described the care she took to check things out before signing the lease. It included making sure that the sturdy, metal-framed front door with its five-lever mortise-lock was up to providing the degree of protection someone in her line of business needs. They also know that the several contingencies catered for within the Operational Plan that regulations demand be posted before an operation of this sort, were all based on one assumption. That the front door would remain unlocked and with the chain off, so they can gain swift entry any time they wish using the key the man in charge now holds, firmly, in his hand.

And of the many thoughts racing through his mind as he reaches her door, one stands out.

It'll take more than a damned key to get us through in time to save her.

PART I

Deja Vue

CHAPTER 1

DCI Jamie Carver stared through the iron gates and up the drive at the house half hidden by the trees that lent it their name; 'Poplars'. He'd been staring since he'd parked up opposite the sandstone gateposts five minutes earlier. Part of him was conscious of what his passenger would be making of his silent vigil, the questions it could prompt. He didn't care. The reasons behind it were complex. They boiled down to one word. Fear.

It wasn't the house itself scared him. A fine looking property in the Georgian style, it was far from the sort of Gothic pile which, in films and books, house knife-wielding psychos. Nor was he over-worried about meeting the woman they'd come to see. He'd been preparing for that for days. His fear came from his imagination; thoughts of what may come after, where it would lead. He even knew what was fuelling it. When it comes to painting scary scenarios, the past provides a rich palette.

He was still staring when a voice said; 'Are we just going to sit here all day admiring the view, or shall we get out and ring the bloody bell?'

Carver turned to face the young woman he'd heard

people referring to lately as his, 'partner'.

The expression on DS Jess Greylake's face was one he'd seen before, usually when she had a point to make. Or was impatient, or bored, or all three. Like right now. He could imagine her thinking, *What the fuck's his problem?* He could tell her, but there wasn't time. For long seconds he stared into the bright hazel eyes some said reflected a keen intelligence, others, more earthy qualities.

'Er... Hello?' She waved a hand before his eyes. 'Anyone home?'

He blinked. Blinked again. Came out of it.

Get a grip.

He took a deep breath, reached for the door handle. 'Right.'

'Hoo-ray,' she muttered.

One of the gateposts housed an intercom. The plate next to the button read *Press and Wait*. Jess pressed it. She gave it a minute and was about to try again when a squawk of static issued from the grill. It was followed by a tinny, 'Hello?'

'Megan Crane?' Carver said.

'Who is it?' The voice was shrill.

'It's the police, Mrs Crane. Detective Chief Inspector Carver and Detective Sergeant Greylake.'

A pause, then, 'What do you want?'

They exchanged glances. 'We're from Warrington Police, attached to the Operation Kerry Inquiry. What the media call The Worshipper Murders? We'd like to talk to you about some matters we think you can help us with.'

There was another pause, longer this time. *Weighing her options.*

The grill squawked again.

'I need to see some identification. Show it to the camera. Over here, next to the other gate-post.'

Carver saw it. Secured to the gate's iron frame, the small black box was discreet enough not to be noticed unless looked for, and was pointing at them. Crossing to it, he took out his warrant card, held it up to the lens.

Eventually the voice said. 'Come up to the front door.'

There was a buzz and a click, and with a jerk, the gates started to swing inwards. They stepped through.

As they crunched their way up the drive, birdsong echoed in the trees. The midday sun cast dappled shadows. Ahead, a grey squirrel startled in its foraging, darted under a spreading rhododendron.

'Jesus,' Jess said. 'She lives here? And she's into this stuff?'

Carver shrugged. 'It's perfect if you think about it.'

'Maybe. But it still seems out of place.'

As they skirted the trees and he got his first full view of the house, Carver's first impressions were confirmed. The Poplars was, indeed, a substantial property. He could imagine it once being home to people of influence in the village. Retired military types. Bankers. A Country Lady or two. Tea parties on the lawn, that sort of thing. The thought came as to what sort of parties it might witness now. He shook his head, forced it away.

Most of the front was covered in ivy. High up, part of the side wall had been cleared around a yellow alarm box. Beneath the eaves, lights and sensors pointed down. The solid oak front door was adorned with heavy, black door-furniture. They waited. After a couple of minutes, the sounds of bolts being drawn and chains unhooked filtered through. It opened with a judder as its bottom edge caught on the step-guard. As it swung back, Carver got his first glimpse of the woman who'd rarely been out of his thoughts the past two weeks.

The face peering round the door did so from under a white, towel-turban. A neat oval shape, the reddish glow suggested she'd just stepped from the shower. A matching bathrobe that was way too big covered everything apart from the fingers gripping the edge of the door and the painted toes peeping out from a pair of gold mules. Carver's first guess put her some years older than Jess. Fortyish, maybe. From under immaculately plucked eyebrows, dark, piercing eyes regarded them with undisguised annoyance.

Not best-pleased about being dragged from her shower, either.

Even without make-up, Megan Crane was striking. Not quite as tall as Jess, but then Jess's five-ten was above female average. But as he noted the well-defined features, the high cheekbones, Carver wasn't certain he could match her to the picture in Jess's document case.

'Mrs Crane?'

'Show me your identification again. Your hand was shaking.'

Most times, Carver found people who make a point of showing they're not intimidated, 'just because it's the Police', irritating. *What're they trying to prove?* But he said nothing, and dug out his warrant card again. This time as he held it up, the shake was barely noticeable. Nevertheless, a thumb and forefinger, nails painted to match the toes, emerged from the folds of white to pinch the leather next to his and steady it. For several seconds she went through the motions of comparing him with his photograph. Standing there, he was conscious of the tableaux they presented. She presumably naked or nearly so under her robe; he, smart and formal in his suit and tie, the two of them frozen like statues, fused together by the flimsy piece of leather. It was an image that would return to him over the coming weeks.

Eventually, the hand withdrew. She nodded her satisfaction.

Carver motioned to Jess. 'And this is Detective Sergeant Greylake.'

For the first time, the woman turned to her.

'Would you like to see my identification as well?' Jess said.

'That won't be necessary. But thank you for offering.'

Carver sensed that the polite smile that came with it could as easily have been a smirk. And the way the two women stayed, staring at each other for longer than the brief exchange merited, he wondered if he was missing something. Eventually, the gaze transferred back to him.

'Well-well. The Police no less. And what, exactly, is the nature of your business?'

Carver didn't hesitate. 'We'd like to talk to you about your listing in a journal called DOM.'

Beside him, he heard Jess's intake of breath. *What the hell.* After two weeks trying to flesh out the little they'd been able to discover about her, he was tired of pussy-footing.

But the woman remained as impassive as if she had never heard of the magazine. Her head tilted back, until she was almost looking at them down her nose. 'And just how is an entry in a journal relevant to your enquiries? I wasn't aware such publications break any laws?'

Carver stifled his impatience. But her reaction was only what he'd anticipated. He stuck to the script. 'If you'd care to invite us in Mrs Crane, we can explain. Unless you'd rather we discuss the matter here on the doorstep?'

It was an old ploy, one that works well with those who like to maintain at least a show of respectability, for the neighbours. But the woman in white wasn't about to be rushed. She continued to look at him as if she were weighing her options.

Eventually, in a voice dripping boredom, she said, 'I'm not sure I want policemen and policewomen traipsing through my house. But I suppose if I stand here like this, I'll catch my death of cold. You'd better come in.' Taking a step back, she swung the door open, but stayed mostly behind it.

As Carver stepped through she caught his eye. 'And it's *Ms* Crane, Detective Chief Inspector. Not *Mrs*. The kitchen's straight through. Make yourself a drink while I finish dressing.'

Carver paused long enough to meet her gaze, before passing down the hall. *And so it begins.*

As Jess followed after, he heard her say, 'And may I remind you we're all Police *Officers* these days, *Ms* Crane. We don't refer to Police *Women* anymore.'

Inside, Carver grimaced. Jess had seven years under her belt now. In that time, she'd have met plenty who fitted the term, 'different'. He doubted any would match Megan Crane. She would learn. As he reached the kitchen, he heard the front door close. Soft footfalls signalled her mounting the stairs. Somewhere above, a door banged.

The kitchen was large, gleaming and modern. The

only item disrupting the sweep of black work-top was a coffee pot, warming on its plate. An oak table rested close to one wall. He crossed to it, pulled out a chair and sat down. He checked around. Three doors led off the kitchen, four counting the one they'd just come through. One, half-open, down left, led through to what looked like a living area. A back door in the far right corner gave onto the garden. Halfway down the right-hand wall was a third door, which was closed. He turned to see Jess leaning against the worktop, arms folded, glaring at him. She opened her mouth to say something but he got in first.

'First impressions, *Ms* Greylake?'

She paused. 'Um, I think you would have to say she's... interesting.'

He nodded. 'Interesting... Good word.' He stood up. 'Are you sorting coffee?' She raised an eyebrow, gave a pointed look. With a shrug, he pleaded guilty, and headed through the door into the living area.

As he came through into a room that was spacious and square, he felt his shoes sink into the cream carpet's deep pile. It was furnished comfortably, but simply. A bright red sofa and matching chair were arranged in front of the biggest television screen he'd seen outside of a sports bar. French windows looked out onto the garden. Floating shelves on the wall opposite contained some books, a few vaguely-oriental ornaments, a photograph in a silver frame. As he crossed for a closer look, he checked to make sure his shoes weren't trailing dirt from his walk up the drive.

The books were innocuous. A couple of travel guides – France and Italy - a clutch of crime-thrillers, some celebrity-chef cookbooks. Nothing that gave anything away. He studied the photograph. Against a blue-sea-and-sky back-drop, the woman they'd just met was standing with her arm around the waist of a tall, bearded man. Both were dressed in sunglasses, shorts and singlets and sported deep tans. Something about the man sparked Carver's interest. He leaned in. Taken from about twenty feet away, the face lacked the detail needed to make it out clearly. *Nevertheless…*

'COFFEE.'

Giving up, he returned to the kitchen.

Jess was holding the fridge door open for his inspection. 'She either lives on fresh air or takeaways. I'll bet the mice get food parcels from the Red Cross.'

Dipping to see, he noted the container of skimmed milk, tub of low-fat spread and three tomatoes resting on a plate. A couple of wines, a Sauvignon-Blanc and a Prosecco, rested in the door shelf.

'Maybe she's on a diet.' He returned to the chair. 'It's the same through there. Clean, but bare. Reminds me of a show-house. Looks great, but it's not a home.'

Jess handed him his coffee before taking hers over to the window. As he drank - it was scorched and bitter, but drinkable - he mused over what the house's sparse contents said about the woman soon to join them. Something about order, he thought. And, presumably, control. Which figures. Rising, he went to join his partner.

The early afternoon sun was high over the trees at the bottom of a garden which he was surprised to see badly neglected. The lawn was long overdue mowing, and the sparsely-stocked borders looked like they hadn't been dug over for weeks. *Not into gardening either.* At that moment an image swooped in, from where he wasn't sure. It was of a man, naked apart from leather briefs and a collar, pottering around, weeding and planting things. For the first time in weeks, Carver came close to breaking a smile.

A noise behind made them turn.

Megan Crane was framed in the doorway.

As he took in the sight, Carver's heart skipped several beats and he had to juggle his mug between finger and thumb to stop it slipping from his grasp.

CHAPTER 2

Corinne Anderson is in her seventh heaven. She loves Kubu like a second home and relishes the regular trips she makes to the famous Manchester corsetière to replenish her already bursting wardrobe. Not that she really needs much more in the way of corsetry. Her collection of the exquisitely-handmade satin, velvet and leather garments is one of the finest in the country, or so Evelyn tells her.

Evelyn Merryweather is Corinne's, 'Kubu Personal Shopper', and a real treasure. She seems, quite genuinely, to look forward to Corinne's trips and Corinne always makes a point of ringing beforehand to make sure Evelyn is available. After enjoying the woman's impeccably-mannered services over many years, she often wonders what she would do without her. Evelyn always seems to know her requirements even better than she does.

Having worked in the family-run business's shop long before Corinne discovered it, Evelyn is an expert in the mysteries and mythology of corsetry. She can tell immediately, which type of garment best suits a customer's body shape.

Take Corinne for instance. According to Evelyn,

Corinne is, 'pear-shaped'. Slim waist, wider hips. Not at all the classic, 'hour-glass' figure most women covet. Nevertheless, under Evelyn's guidance Corinne has discovered the right types of garment to wear and, more importantly, the right way to wear them so as to achieve the effect she is looking for.

But Corinne Anderson is not particularly interested in the amazingly detailed technicalities, or the often bizarre history of corsetry - despite the running commentary Evelyn maintains throughout her visits. She simply enjoys the experience of browsing through Kubu's stock, leafing through the catalogues, running her hands over the items on display, and generally immersing herself in what she refers to as, 'The Kubu Experience'.

It is such a pleasurable, not to mention sensuous, way of passing her time she always makes a point of allowing herself at least three - sometimes four - trips a year. Even if she chooses not to buy any of the more elaborate and expensive garments, the staff are always attentive and polite. They never seem to mind if, after a couple of hours browsing the shop's three floors, she ends up spending only a few pounds on hosiery or other inexpensive items. Not that that happens often. More usually, with or even without Evelyn's help, she manages to spot some new, exotic design, or something sufficiently different to attract her interest. As she has this very morning.

Of course, she likes to try on her choices before buying. In fact she usually tries on several before settling for the one she's had her eye on all the time. That is part of the fun. There is something uniquely satisfying about the process of trying on a new corset, especially in an environment such as Kubu. The Victorian décor and the old-world values the staff show towards their customers, respect, patience and courtesy, mixed with just the right amount of deference, combine to create an atmosphere which, on the face of it, is impeccably, 'correct'. But below the surface run *frissons* which Corinne finds intensely arousing.

In fact, as she discovered during her early visits, the act of being laced into a corset by a relative stranger but an expert in the technique, while she holds onto the brass grab-handles provided for the purpose in Kubu's plush, velvet and leather dressing suites, is not too dissimilar to some of the scenarios she occasionally plays out. Though at home of course, the erotic element is rather more to the fore.

It is a strange paradox. For while she is the customer, and therefore the person being 'served', either by Evelyn or one of Kubu's expert 'dressers', it is the dresser who is in charge of the situation. It is she who places the customer's body in this position or that; gives the commands, 'Hold tight Madam,' 'Stand up straight Madam,', and pulls the lacing tight, winding the loose ends round the customer's waist several times before tying them off in the regulation bow. It is, Corinne thinks, symbolic. And more than a little suggestive.

But Corinne doesn't allow herself to dwell long on such things. She just enjoys the experience for what it is. As she has been doing for most of the morning.

As always, Evelyn is right. The black and scarlet satin over-bust with the black lace trim - a recent addition to the, 'Belladonna', range - docs indccd look wonderful on her. Just what she has been looking for in fact. Something special for her forthcoming rendezvous.

Something to mark the occasion as the new departure she hopes it may be. An opportunity to expand her horizons, for the relationship to take on a new significance perhaps. Something that has been missing from her life for too long now.

But even as her thoughts turn to the evening to come, she cautions herself. She shouldn't let herself get too carried away. Things must be allowed to take their natural course. Nevertheless, she is hopeful.

'Will this be all Mrs Anderson?' Evelyn says as she lovingly places the garment, wrapped in swathes of tissue, into one of the black and gold boxes that are reserved for Kubu's most valued customers.

'I think so Evelyn.'

As always, Corinne savours the woman's reverential attentions. She has often wondered how she might react if Evelyn ever slipped up and referred to her, not as, 'Mrs Anderson', but as, 'Mistress', - as she knows she has come close to doing a couple of times.

Of course, Evelyn would have guessed her secret long ago. But she is sure she is far from the only one of her kind Kubu counts amongst its regulars. How many, she has often wondered? Perhaps one day she will ask Evelyn outright. It would be interesting to hear what she has to say on the subject.

'I take it you would like me to update your account Mrs Anderson?' Evelyn says.

'If you would Evelyn, thank you.'

That is the other nice thing about Kubu. The words, 'money' and 'payment' seem to be regarded as being somehow vulgar; insulting even. As though the business of monetary exchange is of secondary importance to the shop's main purpose, which of course is to give pleasure to their customers. Something at which they excel.

Evelyn picks up the bags containing her charge's morning purchases and steps from around the counter. But before handing them over she remembers to ask, 'Would you like some assistance to where you are parked?'

'No thank you Evelyn, that won't be necessary.' Corinne isn't done shopping yet, and the bags aren't too heavy. Besides, she enjoys walking around the city bearing the evidence proclaiming she only shops at the most exclusive outlets. She wouldn't be seen dead carrying Marks and Spencer.

Evelyn hands her the bags. As the exchange takes place a small, plain-white envelope finds its way, discreetly, from Corinne's hand to Evelyn's from where it disappears, as if by magic, into her suit jacket pocket. 'Thank you Mrs Anderson.'

'Thank *you*, Evelyn, you've been a great help, as always.'

Evelyn accepts the brief but no-less genuine compliment with the slightest of nods. She knows that the contents of the envelope - which she won't open until she gets home that evening - will speak louder than words. 'I hope your evening goes well,' she says.

Evelyn speaks entirely without irony, and Corinne doesn't need to check that she isn't wearing a knowing look. The woman is the model of discretion, and even if she has an inkling of the sort of evening Corinne has planned, she would never show it. She could be referring to a dinner engagement. Nevertheless, she flashes Evelyn a brief, conspiratorial smile before turning away and heading for the door.

As she nears the front of the shop, a tall man in a

dark suit, appears from a doorway to her right, as she'd been expecting he would. In his fifties with greying hair and a moustache that hides his upper lip, he is gushing in his manner and wears a broad smile as he takes the hand she proffers him.

'Have you had a successful morning Mrs Anderson?' Always keen to demonstrate to his staff the standards he expects, he speaks a little louder than necessary. Bowing at the waist, he brings her hand to his lips, making ready to bestow on her his formal farewell.

'I have indeed James, most successful. Please thank everyone for me.' The smile she sends him is one of her warmest.

'I will indeed, Madam.' His lips brush the back of her hand. But he holds it there for a fraction longer than he needs to and, still bent over, raises his eyes to hers. In a voice that is barely more than a whisper and which he knows will not carry, he says, 'Mistress is most welcome,' and gives her a respectful look.

'Thank you James.'

She also speaks in a low voice, but her smile makes clear how much she appreciates his personal attention. It is a ritual that has become a feature of her visits. It makes her feel a little special. And she knows he enjoys it too.

With a final bow, he opens the door for her and she steps out into the street.

As she gives him one last nod of farewell, she thinks about where she has to go next. Ah, yes. Shoes. There's a new shoe shop, so she has heard, just opened up in The Exchange Building. She sets off down Deansgate towards the Royal Exchange.

As she heads away, James Ollerenshaw, Kubu's long-serving sales-manager, watches her, admiringly. It always fascinates him the way women such as her manage to walk so gracefully in their heels - and despite the pencil-skirt that in this case sheathes her fine legs. As she disappears round the corner, his wistful look begins to fade. But before turning from the window he allows himself one last, self-satisfied smile. He relishes the luck that brought him to a position where he can spend a good part of his day serving women such as Corinne Anderson. If only he could do so more often, and on a more permanent basis.

Still, you never know, he thinks as he finally turns away. If his plans work out, the dream may just come true, one day.

CHAPTER 3

Carver thought that if he tried hard enough, he could probably recognise the woman in the doorway as the one who had greeted them earlier. Just. In the fifteen minutes since, an extraordinary transformation had occurred. While the woman in white had been striking, she wouldn't have stood out in a crowd particularly. Especially if the crowd were well-to-do and fashionably dressed. But the woman now before them would have turned heads at a Hollywood reception.

Slim about the waist, Megan Crane had a figure that would fit well within the covers of the sort of top-shelf magazines that are becoming increasingly rare nowadays . Her shining, coal-black hair was cut just above her shoulders in a bob that perfectly framed the oval of her face. Her makeup was sparse but effective, highlighting her prominent cheekbones, the dark, almond-shaped eyes. Her lipstick was a shade of red which, on someone else this time of day, might have seemed out of place. Only on her it wasn't. The black bodice with three-quarter length sleeves was tucked into shimmering-white leggings that emphasised the length and shapeliness of her legs. A gold belt with a round buckle encircled her waist. Standing tall in a pair of gold, strappy heels, the effect was what Carver could imagine certain members of his team describing as, 'Sex On Legs'.

And Megan Crane knew it.

'There you both are.' The smile was the sort she might wear to greet old friends. As she came around the breakfast bar, her heels click-clacked on the tiled floor. 'I see you've found the coffee. Give me a moment, then you can tell me what you've come to talk to me about.'

As he watched her move, gracefully and purposefully, around the kitchen, Carver wondered if this was Megan Crane's normal daytime look, or if she'd dressed to reflect the credentials he'd alluded to, briefly, at the front door. Whichever, in the setting of a domestic kitchen on a bright sunny afternoon, the effect was unsettling. As he watched her frothing up a cappuccino with an electric hand-whisk she'd conjured from somewhere, he felt Jess's stare. Turning to his left, he caught something that reminded him of the look on his mother's face that day she chanced upon his stash of adolescent 'reading material'. About to throw her a, '*What*'? their hostess interrupted, purring, 'I'm ready for you now.' Instead, he sent Jess back as neutral a look as he could manage, mindful that if the woman was aiming to make an impact, it was working.

'Come through to where we can be comfortable and you can ask me your questions.'

As they followed her cat-like saunter back into the hallway. Carver was conscious that so far, almost her every word had taken the form of an order. He threw another glance at Jess, only to find her staring again. This time he saw what he read as a hint of concern. It made him wonder, w*ho for?*

The woman led them through to the spacious front sitting-room. It was dominated by two cream sofas and a matching chair. They were arranged around a huge ceramic coffee table, the top of which rested on stone-plinths shaped as dragons. Other furnishings were few and simple, and blended with the simple colour scheme. She indicated to them to take one of the sofas, and settled herself in the chair. As she waited for them to start, she sipped at her cappuccino.

As Jess settled next to Carver, she took the opportunity to check out the woman opposite. Her sense was that beneath the perfectly composed exterior, their hostess was enjoying some amusement. Unzipping her document case, she took out the folder she carried with her almost everywhere these days and passed it to her boss. Placing his coffee down, he began rummaging through it. Whether intentionally or not, Megan Crane mirrored his action, leaning forward to place her mug in line with his, then sat back with her hands clasped in her lap. It made Jess ponder on how she seemed able to convey a mood by the subtlest change in the way she carried herself, or shift of expression. It also made her wonder just how much of what she was seeing was the real Megan Crane. As she waited for Carver to begin, she realised the woman was subjecting him to a more detailed appraisal than the one she'd given him on the doorstep. As her eyes narrowed, Jess had the impression she was gauging him in some way. She was wondering why such interest, when suddenly the gaze switched and she found herself staring into two deep pools that held her and refused to let go. Jess returned her the sort of quick smile people use to cover embarrassment, but forced herself not to look away. For what seemed minutes but could only have been seconds, it was as if the woman was inside her brain, poking around memories, learning secrets, noting fears.

The spell broke as the eyes moved away, only to be replaced by another as the searching gaze now travelled down her body to her feet, then back again. The open scrutiny reminded Jess of how she'd felt that first day when she'd walked into the Major Incident Room and Chris Metcalf, one of those DCs who thinks he's God's gift, had turned in his chair to ogle her, quite blatantly. As he stared at her, she'd felt him, mentally stripping away layers until she was sure that in his mind, she was standing naked before him. She'd hated him for it, but got her own back that night at Evita's, when she'd responded to his drunken groping by thrusting a hand between his legs, and squeezing hard, at the same time smiling a warning to keep his hands to himself.

But Megan Crane's inspection was different. On this occasion Jess felt less invaded, than buoyed by the thought that someone whose lifestyle was, by all accounts, 'unconventional,' seemed to find her so interesting. Nonetheless, Jess was uncomfortably self-conscious - the second time since they'd met - and shifted in her seat. Uncrossing her legs, she leaned over to see how Carver was doing, just as he began to speak.

'As I mentioned Ms Crane, we're investigating the series of murders the media are calling the Worshipper Killings.' The woman's eyes narrowed. 'We're following up a line of enquiry which may involve your posting in this.'

As he dropped the A5-sized booklet onto the table, Jess again found herself caught out. She'd been expecting he would spend time loosening her up before getting to the potentially embarrassing matter of her listing. She hoped it was the right approach.

Megan Crane threw only the briefest of glances at the magazine, with its single-word title, 'DOM!' emblazoned in thick, black script across the top, before returning to meet Carver's gaze. Staring out from the front cover was an exotic-looking red-head. Pictured from the waist up, she was wearing a black bustier that pushed her ample breasts up and out. Between her hands she was flexing a crop-whip. Retrieving her coffee mug, Megan Crane sipped at it.

'Go on.'

He opened it at a point marked by a paper clip. The page was divided into segments. Each contained a photograph of a woman posing and dressed in a way that was in keeping with the cover. Each picture was accompanied by a few lines of text. Carver pointed to the bottom-right segment.

'This is you, I think?'

She didn't even bother to look. It showed her dressed in a black basque made of some shiny material, cut away to expose her breasts. A studded collar was around her throat and she was holding a crop similar to the one on the cover. Looking directly to camera, the expression on her face was stern, yet at the same time, Jess had thought when she first saw it, inviting.

For a brief second, the tip of Megan Crane's tongue darted, snake-like, from between the glossed lips. And though she'd done little to merit it, Jess couldn't resist. *Got you, you cocky bitch.* Like Carver, the difficulty Jess had been having matching the picture to the woman who greeted them at the door had disappeared the moment Megan Crane appeared in the kitchen. And Jess didn't need to re-read the text accompanying the photo to remind her of what it said. By now she knew it by-heart.

'Experienced, independent, lifestyle Mistress, (n/s), willing to administer to the needs of discerning, (and deserving), gentlemen and/or ladies who have already discovered their true natures. Owns a fine collection of dramatic outfits and a range of equipment and accessories designed to heighten the experience. If your intentions are honourable then write, with photograph, describing your preferences, interests, and circumstances.'

An identifying code, 'DW12987', was printed beneath the photograph.

Megan Crane crossed one leg over the other and clasped her hands over her knee. 'And if it is me?' She couldn't have been less self-conscious were Jess and Carver selling insurance and they were discussing levels of cover.

'You're a dominatrix.' He said it the way a traffic cop might tell her he'd caught her doing forty in a thirty zone.

She pursed her lips. 'I'm not sure what the term, 'dominatrix' means to you, Chief Inspector.'

Her use of his official title reminded Jess that he hadn't yet invited her to, 'Call me Jamie,' the way he usually did. Nor had he given her first name when he introduced her as, 'DS Greylake.' Megan Crane continued.

'Admittedly, I pursue a lifestyle that some might consider... unusual. And yes, it sometimes involves themes of sexual domination and submission.'

'But you usually take the dominant role?'

She thought about it. 'Not always, but mostly.'

'Do you advertise yourself in ways other than this magazine?'

She frowned. A first outward sign of impatience. 'May I ask what this has to do with these-' She paused, as if reluctant to acknowledge a connection. 'The murders you referred to?'

Carver sat forward. 'There've been four murders over the past fourteen months. We've discovered that all the victims were listed in editions of this directory.' He pointed down at the booklet. 'Their postings were similar to yours. We think the killer may be selecting his victims from it. We think he could be intending to target you next.'

Her response, when it came, was in keeping with the image she'd been working hard at portraying. She stared at him for something close to half a minute. Then, uncrossing her legs she rose and, with slow deliberation, crossed to a drinks cabinet that stood against the far wall. As she moved, the material covering her legs made a silky, 'swishing' noise. From a crystal decanter, she poured a measure of amber liquid into a tumbler then tossed it straight back. As she did so, her hair swung, smoothly, around her shoulders before settling back, not a strand out of place. For several seconds she remained facing the wall, letting the injection do its work, before turning round.

'Okay, Chief Inspector, you've succeeded in scaring the shit out of me. Now tell me. Why would I be a target for this... this lunatic?'

Suddenly Jess felt guilty for having revelled in the woman's earlier discomfort. When it came to being murdered, it seemed Megan Crane was no different to any potential victim. Confused. Scared. She sensed the need for a lighter touch and threw Carver a glance. He nodded.

'You fit the victim profile, Ms Crane. And you live within the area where he's been operating. Basically the Northwest around Liverpool and Manchester. As Jess spoke, the woman returned to her seat. 'We believe the killer may be approaching his victims through this magazine, posing as a prospective submissive. We think he probably arranges an encounter, possibly more than one. At some stage it appears that he takes on the dominant role, at least we are assuming he does, then he kills them.'

Megan Crane looked at them askance. 'I find that a little hard to believe. Some tops do switch of course, but not with someone they've only just met.'

'We're not sure how he does it. So far we've found no signs of any sort of struggle, and the way he leaves his victims suggests they were compliant, at least in the early stages. It's something you may be able to help us with.' Jess paused then added, 'It's possible he may already have tried to make contact with you'.

Megan Crane looked from Jess to Carver and back again, as if gauging if they were exaggerating things.

'If he is-.' Her voice cracked. She started again. 'The magazine is only available on direct subscription. If he's using it then surely you must have his details, or something?'

Carver stepped in. 'It seems the magazine is popular in certain circles and gets passed around a fair bit. It wouldn't be that hard for him to get hold of a copy. We only found out about the connection recently and again, we've found no trace of any correspondence at the victim's homes. We're assuming he removes it after.'

'But what about the people who run the magazine? Can't they tell you anything?'

Carver shook his head. 'They simply forward on the envelopes that come in addressed to the subscriber's code.' He pointed down. 'In your case, DW12987. As you know, they don't check to see who, or where it's from. They claim to be hot on privacy. All they do is record that they've forwarded correspondence.'

She gave a huffy look. 'Yet they gave you my details.'

'Yes, well,' He glanced at Jess. 'In your case, they didn't really have much choice.'

Jess suppressed a smile, remembering their visit to the cramped office above the industrial unit on a business park south of Birmingham. To begin with, the older of the two women, the matronly one who looked like she'd been around a bit, stalled, going on about, 'Client confidentiality,' and her, 'duty of care' to subscribers. Carver had turned to Jess and said, 'Ring it in. Organise a search warrant,' before talking about seizing files and computers and taking maybe a couple of months to find what they were looking for before they could be returned. He wasn't at all threatening, but Matron got the message straight away. Crossing to one of the grey metal filing cabinets that had seen better days she produced the information they were looking for in seconds. He thanked her for her cooperation and promised to tell her clients she'd been forced to disclose their details. But as they were leaving, he'd stopped. 'I'd advise against contacting any of them before we speak with them. It might be bad for business.' This time the threat was clear. Jess knew now it was the way he sometimes worked. Soft, then hard. A variation on the old, good-cop-bad-cop routine everyone's heard of. But he did it all on his own. Jess remembered his promise.

'To be fair, they only gave us your details under threat of being closed down.'

'Really?' Megan said. 'You could do that?'

Carver broke in. 'Let's say it wouldn't do business much good if it leaked out that their subscribers were being murdered.'

'But if you are speaking to people like me, then they'll know anyway won't they? And you've still not said how you know he is choosing his victims from the magazine. It could just be coincidence, couldn't it?'

As Carver cleared his throat - it was a sensitive area which he and Jess had discussed at length. - Jess realised that she'd been wrong. Megan Crane wasn't behaving like many victims might - in such a panic they're happy to do anything the police say. She was searching for a hole in the logic. Unwilling to give herself up so easily.

'Knowing about DOM is the only advantage we have at the moment. If we approach too many people, it could leak out, and he might change his methods. We're focusing on those whose entries most closely match his previous victims. Like yourself. As for how we know he's using the magazine, we've trawled all the other avenues people like you use to advertise your services-.' At this point her left eyebrow arched a fraction. Jess wondered if he'd caught it. 'And 'DOM!' is the only one that lists all the victims. Let's just say it's an educated guess. But don't bank on it being wrong.'

As Megan Crane sought to buy time by finishing her coffee, Jess thought she didn't have many options to consider. But her last question, about the magazine connection, reminded Jess of how, around the investigation team, the uncovering of the 'DOM' link was still something of a mystery, even to her. The envelope in which it had arrived - addressed personally to 'DCI Jamie Carver' and with a central London postmark, gave no clue as to who had sent it, or why. Nor had Forensic come up with anything that might identify the sender. But as soon as Carver spotted Tracy Wilcox's entry, enquiries with the magazine and a review of back issues quickly established that the other three victims had also been featured. It was one of several aspects of the inquiry that, to Jess, were still a bit 'grey'.

There was a short silence, then the slump of Megan Crane's shoulders seemed to point to her capitulation. For all her dominant airs and graces, when it came to being murdered, maybe she was like other women after all.

'What do you want from me?'

Carver sat forward again. 'We think that with your experience, your knowledge of this area, you may be able to help us identify the killer. As DS Greylake, Jess, says, for all we know he may have already made contact with you. According to DOM's records, they've forwarded on several contacts to you over the past few months.' Carver hesitated, before uttering the words that changed everything. 'We need details of all your clients.'

CHAPTER 4

Later, Jess would recall thinking that maybe he was using some interview technique she hadn't come across. One that involves making someone angry as hell, before employing some subtle means to bring them round again. Certainly, from what she had seen of Megan Crane, her reaction to Carver's words came as no surprise. Her face coloured and for long seconds she regarded him as if he were guest speaker at some Woman Of The Year Lunch who'd just told the most appallingly-sexist joke. When she eventually spoke, her voice which previously had been melodic, beguiling even, was cold, almost contemptuous.

'You don't know much about people like me, or the life I lead, do you Chief Inspector?'

His reply seemed aimed straight at her heart and made Jess gasp.

'What's there to know? You provide sexual services to perverts through a contact magazine. What I need from you are their details, because one of them may be killing people. At the moment he's targeting women like yourself. Eventually he'll move on to other women.'

Jess could hardly believe her ears and threw him a concerned glance. But his gaze stayed locked on the woman opposite.

Megan Crane remained still and silent for several seconds, as if working to keep a grip on her composure, before replying. 'I assume you mean other, *respectable*, women?'

The shoulders of his jacket lifted with his shrug. 'I didn't say that, but if that's how you want to interpret it-'

Jess felt like something had taken a grip of her stomach and was squeezing it. If he was aware of how offensive he was being, it didn't show. But though she had no idea how he was going to turn things round, she had seen enough of him to be confident he would. As the silence lengthened, she wondered if they were communicating telepathically. *Come on Jamie, just reel her in. She was there for the taking a minute ago.*

But it was Megan Crane who spoke first, sitting back in her chair and folding her hands in her lap.

'Whatever you may think of me, *Chief Inspector*, or whatever you are, I am not a prostitute. Nor do I take kindly to the inference that I consort with, how did you put it, 'perverts'?'

'Whether you charge for what you do, Ms Crane is, frankly, immaterial. I-.'

'Oh but it is material.' she interrupted, letting her anger show. 'I don't have-.' She spat the word out. 'Clients. What I have are close and dear friends, none of whom I would ever dream of describing as perverted. They are people I respect, and with whom I share an interest in things that your narrow police brain is probably incapable of understanding.'

His voice rose to match hers. 'You'd be surprised what I'm capable of understanding, Ms Crane. I'm aware of your so-called alternative lifestyle, and the way people like you live your lives. But the fact remains, we need to know who these people are. One of them could be a killer.'

'Listen,' she hissed, leaning forward and dropping any reference to his rank. 'I only have relationships with people I trust, and I take time to get to know them first. I've known some of these people for years. None of them could possibly be the person you are looking for.' She paused. 'Besides, some of my friends are in positions where they wouldn't want their details given to the police. It's out of the question.' She sat back, point made.

For a long time the only sound was the ticking of the gold carriage clock on the mantelpiece. It was Carver's play but for reasons Jess couldn't fathom, he wasn't coming back as she expected. She wondered if something was going on she wasn't party to, and resisted the temptation to enter the fray for fear of ruining whatever ploy he was using. When he did speak, his line surprised her again.

'You know we could get a warrant and seize what we want?'

A scornful look spread across her face. 'Hah. I don't keep files on my friends. Or notes, or diaries, or anything else of that sort. I don't think going away and coming back with a warrant would be very productive, do you?' As she taunted him his eyes narrowed and his lips merged into a single, straight line. 'Of course you could always try torturing me for the information.' Her lips curled into a wicked smile. 'The only trouble is, I might enjoy it.' She paused before adding, 'So might you for that matter. Then where would we be?'

When he answered, Carver's tone was more

measured. But Jess could hear the suppressed anger.

'This isn't a game, Ms Crane. We came here today to try to save lives, yours as well as others. We can't force you to help us. But you might regret it if you don't.'

To Jess's surprise he started gathering his papers. Surely that's not it?

'Think about it.' Rising from the sofa, he began to march towards the door.

Caught off guard - it was becoming a habit - Jess looked across at Megan Crane and wondered if what they had told her had frightened her in any way. If it had, it didn't show. Her plucked and pencilled eyebrows were raised as if to say, *Was there something?* Jess held her gaze a few seconds to show that she was neither impressed nor intimidated – untrue on both counts - then stood up to follow after her boss, already at the front door.

As she headed after him down the drive, and for the second time that day, she could feel Megan Crane's eyes burning into her back. So much so she had to fight against the urge to break into a sprint. It wasn't until she reached the iron gates she heard the front door slam behind.

CHAPTER 5

The Golf rocked and kicked as Carver threw it round the winding country road taking them back to the motorway. Jess hung onto the grab handle, casting uneasy glances in his direction. Carver was oblivious. At that moment he was consumed by a single train of thought.

You stupid, spineless bastard. You knew what you were walking into and you still let her get to you. You weak, useless, piece of-

'WHOA,' Jess cried, almost falling into his lap as the car hurtled around another bend. 'TAKE IT EASY.'

Glancing left, he saw the concern in her face. 'Sorry,' he murmured. Forcing himself to relax his grip on the wheel, he eased off the accelerator. The car slowed, and steadied.

'Thank you.'

But Carver didn't hear it. He was already back in his silent world.

As much as anything, he was embarrassed. Okay, he hadn't been looking forward to it, for reasons he'd barely let himself think about. But he should never have let her get to him the way he had. It was unprofessional. And if there was one thing he prided himself on, it was his ability to remain profession... Then he remembered Angie, and the thought withered.

A 'School Ahead' sign recalled Jess's concerned look. He slowed again, and checked her out of the corner of his eye. But she was turned away, staring out of the window, ignoring him. Apart from her appeal to slow down she hadn't said a word since they'd started back. She didn't need to. He knew what she was thinking.

He'd fucked-up.

Big Style.

Jess had never felt as uncomfortable in Carver's presence as she did right then. A flurry of questions swirled in her brain but each time she was about to say something, she found she couldn't stop it sounding like, 'What the FUCK happened back there?'

One thing was certain. Whatever the problem was, it was of his making. Sure, Megan Crane was an unusual woman, and needed careful handling. Someone like her would be bound to be wary about getting involved with the police. But from what Jess had seen, there was nothing about her that couldn't be overcome by a few well-chosen words. She couldn't understand why they hadn't come.

She had seen him in action and knew what he was capable of. Damn it, he had even used it on her a couple of times and, like a schoolgirl, she'd fallen for it. During that first after-work gathering in the Red Lion, she'd found herself opening up to him like she hadn't with any man except her father, never mind one who was still all-but a stranger. She'd even told him things about herself she hadn't told Martin yet.

But she had seen none of it used on Megan Crane.

Not even a half-hearted attempt. She wondered if, deep down, he was some sort of closet puritan, but then dismissed the idea. Given what she knew of his past, that was hardly likely. It reaffirmed the thoughts she'd been having the past couple of weeks. Contrary to her early impressions - like the others who'd applied for the Operation Kerry Victim Analyst post, she'd read everything about him she could get her hands on before the interview - she was beginning to realise the man was a mass of contradictions.

Remembering the all but silent outward journey - she couldn't bear the thought of a similar return - she stretched out a finger and pressed 'play.' The car filled with the sound of a woman's voice, singing what sounded like some mournful, Spanish melody. This time she knew what it was. Fado he'd called it. Some sort of Portuguese folk music. An image of his flame-haired girlfriend, Rosanna, came to her. They'd met only once, but she wasn't the sort you forget in a hurry. In places, the strangely-vibrant music reminded her of an old film her father used to enjoy re-watching every couple of years. What was it? The Thin Man? Third Man? Whatever, it fitted the mood.

It didn't help it was Friday afternoon, the roads and Motorway full of POETS traffic. By the time they turned into Warrington Central's crowded yard, Jess was ready to Piss Off Early herself, whatever day Tomorrow was, and looked forward to finding someone to talk to. As they climbed the back stairs to the CID suite in silence, she checked her watch. They would catch the end of week de-brief after all. Leaving that morning they'd prepped for a late return, imagining being ensconced with Megan Crane into the evening hours, going over things. So much for that idea.

At the door to his office, Jess didn't stop but kept going towards the main office further along the corridor. About to turn in through the door she looked back. He was leaning against the door-frame, hands in pockets, head down, staring at the floor. She barely recognised the man she had been working with the past six weeks. Then his head lifted and she saw the self-doubt in his eyes. But then, as if spurred by the look in her face, he seemed to remember who, what, he was. Taking a deep breath, he squared up, and suddenly he was back, ramrod-straight, shoulders broad. For the first time since they'd left The Poplars, he managed to string a sentence together.

'I guess that wasn't one of our more productive days, was it?'

She shook her head. For a moment she thought he was going to invite her in to go over it. She was wrong.

'We'll talk about it Monday,' he said. He tried to give something approaching a smile. 'Don't worry, I'll sort it. See you in de-brief.'

He turned into his office and the door closed. She remained staring that way for several seconds then, with a final shrug of her shoulders, headed for the Briefing Room.

As she approached, she heard the buzz of the assembled detectives and thought about how she would respond to the inevitable questions about their visit to see, The Woman. But as she walked in, her bright smile was in place, as always.

CHAPTER 6

Carver sat at his desk and cast his eyes over the mass of job sheets, folders and statements littering its surface. Some he'd left there that morning, others were new. Two items drew his eye.

Top of the pile was a yellow sticky-note. He recognised Alec Duncan's heavy scrawl. It read, 'Jackson rang. AGAIN!!! Wants you to RING HIM BACK!!!'

Carver sighed. The Scottish DS's exclamation marks were becoming hard to ignore. But he wasn't in the mood for reporters. Certainly not Jackson. Even now, years on, those who liked to make mischief still occasionally referenced the Sunday Times Magazine feature article that Carver was yet to live down. It wasn't long ago some bastard even left a copy on his desk. If he knew who, he'd shove it up their… He put Alec's note to one side, but where he could see it.

The second item was a bright white envelope with clean, sharp edges. Drawing it from the pile, he recognised the distinctive typescript showing his full name, title and station address. He tore it open, and digested the single-page letter's contents in one quick scan.

His appearance before the Promotion Interview Panel was set for 10.30am on the twenty sixth of the month following. He calculated. Four weeks yesterday. *Wonderful*.

He stared at it for several seconds, before letting it slip from his hands to float down onto the desk. He turned his chair left, ninety degrees, so he faced the window that looked out onto the dull, grey-slate roof of what used to be the station's grand Parade Room, but had long since been converted into extra office space. Another time, Carver may have looked forward to it. Even allowing for the hiccup he could never forget, the route mapped out for him years before by a certain Chief Officer to help chart his upward progress was still on track, more or less. But right now the timing couldn't have been worse. It was nobody's fault but his. When he'd applied for the Board appearance three months ago, it seemed like the right thing to do. He'd realised since how much his decision was influenced by those whose support he welcomed, but whose drip-drip encouragements had steered him down a route he wasn't certain he was yet ready, even willing, to travel.

'If you're not careful, you'll miss the boat.'

'Superintendent by forty. That's the benchmark if you want to hit Chief Officer.'

'Now's the time. You're over what happened, and they only have to look at how you're running things here to see you're back on song.'

He turned to check the date on the letter again. Eight weeks was the widely-accepted minimum prep time for a, 'board' appearance. 'More like three months,' according to Richard Dunning, the most recent of his peers to have negotiated the process. Four-weeks-less-a-day when you're helping to run a series-murder inquiry was laughably short.

'Bollocks.'

For several seconds he let his mind roam, seeking an option that would enable him to give it a decent shot, whilst not detracting from his role as Deputy SIO to the largest investigation the force had seen in a generation. Eventually he realised. There wasn't one.

He checked his watch. Six minutes to debrief. After the afternoon's shambles he needed to focus on the job in hand, not what may or may not happen four weeks from now.

Turning his chair a further ninety degrees, he faced the white board behind his desk. Its ink-scarred surface was all-but-hidden under a montage of felt-pen scribble, stick-its, photographs and papers held in place with magnets. It was his Personal Investigation Log and had grown over the fourteen months since Kerry Martin's death. As often happened when he needed to focus, he found himself staring at one particular photograph. It showed Kerry on her knees, bound to a post by ropes wound round her upper body, waist and thighs, her ankles crossed and tied behind. Her arms were extended out in front, tied at wrist and elbow. Her palms and fingers were super-glued flat together. As many commented at the time, apart from the lingerie, heels and black silk ribbon wound tightly around her throat, she might have been praying - hence the media's 'Worshipper' Tag. Three others had followed Kerry since, though he hadn't felt compelled to add their photos. There was no need. Scattered across the board, almost randomly it seemed, were circled question marks, reminding him of the scale of the task they still faced. Apart from making him forget about board appearances, they also made him aware of how much tighter the knot in his stomach had grown since that morning. At that moment, an image of Megan Crane, as she had appeared in her kitchen doorway, glossily-perfect, ambushed him. He tried pushing it aside but quickly realised, he needed help.

'Fuck it.'

Rising from the chair, he snatched up the briefing-file that was ever-present on the side of his desk, and headed out.

CHAPTER 7

As usual on a Friday, the briefing room was fuller than other days. Everyone liked to make a special effort to be present for the SIO's weekly, 'State Of The Inquiry' address. As Carver entered at the back, a big man with close-cropped greying hair rose to his feet from the middle of the three chairs set out at the front. At once, a wave of silence washed over the assembled throng, cutting through the jokey-chatter.

Detective Superintendent John 'The Duke' Morrison was dressed, impeccably as always, in his trademark shiny-grey suit. Seeing his deputy coming through, Operation Kerry's Senior Investigating Officer pulled himself up to his full six-feet-five.

'Right Ladies and Gents. Let's make a start.'

Behind, in the chair to The Duke's right, a slim, dapperly-dressed younger man came upright and alert as if he thought that by doing so he was setting an example to the rest of the audience. As Carver took the left-hand chair, he glanced across only to find the other man waiting for it. As their eyes met, the younger man sent over a wink and grin that said, *I've had a great day. How was yours*? Carver held his gaze, but kept his expression neutral. Whatever his thoughts about his fellow Assistant SIO, he was obliged, in public at least, to treat DCI Gary Shepherd as his equal. Turning away, Carver gave his attention to the figure in front. Having gained everyone's attention, The Duke was taking a moment to scan faces. Carver knew he would be noting absentees to mention to him after, along with the superfluous request that Carver update them as soon as the opportunity presented.

As he stared at the broad expanse of back, Carver noted, as always, the ease with which the man in overall charge of the Kerry Investigation asserted his authority. It wasn't just to do with his size. Though his nickname, 'The Duke', referenced the birth surname name he shared with the old cowboy-actor, John Wayne, as well as his rolling gait, his record as an investigator was known to all. Eventually his gaze settled on a paunchy, middle-aged man, halfway down on the left. Back to the wall, he was drinking from his favourite Celtic mug.

'Alec, perhaps you can start by telling us where we are up to with the silver Astra?'

Detective Sergeant Alec Duncan spluttered a mouthful of tea back into the mug and muttered under his breath. Though the Glaswegian's oath carried to those nearest, they stifled their amusement, wary about getting marked as, 'next'. The former Lothian Police detective from long before Police Scotland days reached behind for a sheaf of papers on the windowsill. Coming as straight as his paunch allowed, he began speaking in his distinctive burr.

'Reet Guv'nor. For those who missed it, werr' talkin' aboot the silver Astra that was seen outside Jeannette Fairhaven's house an' which featured in the Crimewatch recon. We've traced it back to a bloke called Hamilton, from Ormskirk who works on a North Sea gas rig. On Monday, Geoff Conway and I will be....'

As the old-sweat DS set about describing the process through which he and his partner hoped to finally eliminate the vehicle that had been the cause of so much speculation and, they all suspected, wasted effort, Carver began to relax, grateful for the opportunity to focus on, 'normal stuff'. While he wasn't expecting anything dramatic – if there had been any developments he'd have heard straight away - he prided himself on keeping up with all aspects of the investigation. Senior to Shepherd in service and experience, though not rank, he was the enquiry's 'Designated Deputy'. As such he saw it as his responsibility to spot the often-camouflaged links between lines of enquiry. Experience taught him that if he didn't, there was a good chance no one else would.

For the next thirty minutes, The Duke went from team to team, eliciting updates, posing questions. Carver listened mainly in silence though now and again, he would raise a question or zero in on a particular point. On these occasions The Duke always checked back with him - 'Okay Jamie?' - before moving on. Sometimes the reason behind Carver's query was obvious, as often, not. One by one, the various lines of enquiry were covered.

The white nylon rope used in the last three killings?

'It's made for B&Q. You can get it in any of over 300 branches anywhere in the country.'

The smartly-dressed man seen in the vicinity of Vanessa Wilcox's home near the time of her murder?

'The Mormons have finally confirmed they *were* working in the area after all. They're sending us a list.

We think he'll be on it'.

The efforts to verify the alibis given by Trevor Hargreaves, the Salford University Rapist released on license the month before the killings began?

'His solicitor-girlfriend has confirmed he was on holiday with her in Ibiza the week Anna Davis was killed. We think she's telling the truth this time.'

And so on.

Most of it was routine, though Carver sat up when The Duke turned to the team whose task it was to follow up on the 'Blond Hairs' link. Of all the outstanding enquiries and potential leads, it was the one they all knew could yield the break-through they longed for. Barry Swift, the DS running the team rose to his feet. Even before he opened his mouth, his low-key body-language told Carver all he needed to know.

'Not much to add since last time, I'm afraid, boss. The DNA has come back on the two blonde women we traced last week and who were known to be past friends of Tracy Wilcox and Kerry Martin. They don't match the hairs from the scenes and they're both alibied to the hilt for the dates in question. We've still got another name to follow up on. She's a girl Kerry used to knock around with, but we think it was before she got into the S-and-M stuff. Don't hold your breath.'

The Duke nodded his thanks, but remained up-beat. 'Okay Barry. But let's all stay focused on this. The blond hairs are still the only common link between the scenes. They belong to someone. Remember that everyone when you're knocking on doors.'

At the back of the room, a DC, Jack Rowe, spoke up. 'Any further thoughts on whether this blonde, whoever she is, is a suspect or just someone who happens to have known each of the victims and visited their playrooms, dungeons, or whatever?'

Carver came upright, nodded to The Duke. Since the link came to light after the second murder, he'd been monitoring progress almost daily. The Duke nodded back.

'We still can't say. If we accept the possibility the killer is female, then obviously she'd have to be a suspect. But we're still waiting on Doctor Cleeves's, assessment on the likelihood of a female killer.' Ewan Cleeves, visiting Professor in Forensic Psychology at the University of Manchester was the enquiry's allocated 'profiler'. 'When we first raised it he seemed doubtful but we're keeping an open mind. She could still just be a common contact we haven't yet been able to trace. The bottom line is, we won't know 'til we find her.' The party line delivered, he sat back in his chair. He hated fence-sitting, but in the case of the blonde hairs it was all they could do.

From that point, and as it continued, Carver found it increasingly difficult to focus on the updates. Despite his best efforts, images of Megan Crane, her dramatic appearance and mocking smile kept coming. At the same time, snippets of his conversation with The Duke before they'd left for their abortive visit to Calderton that morning still lingered. The Kerry Inquiry was into its second year, and was rapidly becoming 'hot'. As The Duke had said, unless there was a breakthrough soon, the Joint Chief Officers Board – the panel of Deputy and Assistant Chief Officers charged with overseeing the inquiry on behalf of contributing forces, and fuelled no doubt by an impatient media - would start looking for scapegoats. Thankfully, John Morrison was one of a rare breed, a career detective, but one with enough political nouse to fight his corner. The prospect of a JCOB-inspired witch-hunt wouldn't cause him to lose sleep, nor Carver for that matter. They both knew that with an investigation like Kerry, success was only ever a phone call away. But concern over when, not if, they would be presented with a new victim, troubled them both. It was now three months since Anna Davis had become the killer's fourth victim. The series profile put the murders at roughly four-month intervals. If the breakthrough they were hoping for didn't come soon, it could be too late. They'd both had high hopes for Megan Crane, though in Carver's case, other factors impinged. He squirmed in his seat as he thought again on the possible cost of his failure. But then he remembered his last, bullish words to Jess. *I'll sort it.*

Carver turned his attention back to his boss just as the big man turned to his fellow ASIO.

'Gary, perhaps now's a good time to bring everyone up-to-date with Cosworth?'

Nodding vigorously, Shepherd rose to his feet and stepped forward. Lively and business-like, he never flinched from an opportunity to be seen and heard. Opening a folder he'd been holding throughout, he began passing out photographs and briefing sheets to people at the front to hand around.

'This is a photograph of William Cosworth. It was taken by the Surveillance Unit before he clocked them.' He paused while the copies circulated. 'As you can see, it's a bit grainy but it's the best we've been able to get so far. The briefing sheet gives his personal details and vehicles we know he has access to.' He waited again, letting his audience catch up.

Carver used the lull to weigh the younger man some more. A product of the Accelerated Promotion Scheme, word was Gary Shepherd was destined for greatness. Carver's take on it was that if true, it wouldn't be in CID. And he wasn't alone in seeing Shepherd's appointment as ASIO to the inquiry as nothing more than a career-broadening exercise - as opposed to recognition of the 'Leadership and Investigative Qualities' he'd seen mentioned in a Headquarters Memo on The Duke's desk one day. Nevertheless, Carver had to admit that Shepherd's vital, athletic look - gained from pounding the treadmills at the five-star Park Royal Hotel's fitness centre out at Daresbury - lent him a confident air of authority, even if it didn't match his experience - or detective skills.

Shepherd turned to hand copies of the picture to Carver and The Duke. Carver studied it. It showed a slim man, around forty, dressed in jeans and a white T-Shirt, getting into a black Porsche Carrera parked in front of a high-rise apartment block. The picture had been taken with a long-distance lens from somewhere overlooking the car park. But it was blurred, indistinct. Carver wondered why Shepherd hadn't produced a better one. Surely the SU had managed to get a better picture than this?

'As some of you already know,' Shepherd continued. 'Cosworth's name has come into the frame only recently. He's a fashion photographer who specialises in the fetish end of the market. A few years ago he escaped a conviction for raping one of his models. She withdrew her complaint so as not to ruin her career.'

The Duke sat up. 'I think you mean that was a *possible* reason for her withdrawal Gary?'

Shepherd missed the hint. 'Technically, that may be true, but I've spoken with her and she insists it was because her agent told her she would be committing professional suicide if she went ahead.'

Alec Duncan's hand went up and The Duke nodded.

'Sorry if I've missed something boss. But why's he of interest? People escape rape convictions every day.'

'Good point, Alec,' Shepherd said, warming to his theme. 'For those of you who weren't here last week, I'll recap. Six years ago Cosworth produced a feature for a fetish magazine called 'SkinTight'. Ostensibly it was a fashion-shoot for fetish-wear. The leather and chains look. Latex, boots, that sort of thing. The pictures were based around a bondage-submission theme. They showed the model tied up and being threatened by someone stretching a ligature. The set-up appears to mirror our murder scenes in several respects, including the way the subjects appear to be praying. If anyone wants to see the pictures they're in my office.' As a forest of hands went up, The Duke 'harrumphed' to show the humour was misplaced. They came down again. Shepherd continued.

'It's possible he may have taken his scenario a stage further, and moved on from rape to murder.'

Carver checked the audience's reaction. Some of the older detectives were looking openly sceptical. He wasn't surprised. A killer would have to be pretty stupid to use an MO that could so easily be linked to him. He'd been doubtful when Shepherd first voiced his theory. He'd heard nothing since to make him think differently. But he also knew that when it comes to crime investigation, any theory is a good one until disproved.

'Cosworth is highly surveillance-conscious. Twice

he's clocked the SU within minutes of them picking him up. That raises the question of what it is he wants to hide."

Or maybe he's just observant and likes his privacy?

'We're still doing background but when we're ready we'll be looking to lift him and bring him in for a closer look. In the meantime, myself and DI Frayne-' he paused to indicate the stocky Surveillance Unit Team Leader at the back of the room, '-are monitoring his movements as best we can. We'll keep you informed of any developments. Until then, you all need to bear Cosworth, and his vehicles, in mind.' As Shepherd sat down The Duke stood up.

'May I remind you, ladies and gentlemen, that what you have just heard is strictly confidential? Cosworth's name must NOT be mentioned outside these walls. And I don't want to read anything in the papers about the Worshipper-, the Kerry Inquiry, having a possible suspect. Clear?' Murmurings of, 'Yes Boss,' sounded round the room.

Satisfied, The Duke turned to Carver.

'Finally, Jamie. You've been to see a potential victim? How'd it go?'

Carver got to his feet but didn't waste time on preliminaries. What he had to say would be brief enough.

'Jess and I visited a woman over in Calderton earlier today. She fits the victim profile but she's reluctant to cooperate just yet. We've left her to think things over and we'll be speaking to her again soon.' He sat down.

For several moments The Duke stared at him, shrewd eyes narrowed, as if trying to guess the story. Getting nothing, he turned to where Jess stood amidst the throng of detectives. But at that moment it seemed like she had found something at her feet that needed her attention. Freed from Morrison's gaze, Carver stole a glance in Shepherd's direction. He was doing a bad job of holding back a smirk.

A few minutes later, de-brief over, Morrison spoke the usual words of thanks and encouragement he liked to close with, before bidding those who weren't working the weekend, 'Enjoy your break,' then adding, 'And keep your phones on. Mr Shepherd and his team are weekend cover. If there are any developments, they'll text or call.' He turned to Carver. 'Got a minute?'

CHAPTER 8

Back in his office, The Duke was straight to the point.

'What's the story?'

Carver hesitated, thinking on how much to share. He respected The Duke as much as any man he knew. But it was complicated, the week was nearly over and it had been a long day.

'Like I said, she isn't ready to co-operate yet. I think we caught her off-guard and she was embarrassed. She'll come around once she's thought things through.'

The Duke gave him a hard look. 'I hope so. We need her onside.'

Carver didn't need reminding, but nodded. *Noted.* But he'd done enough thinking about Megan Crane for one day. 'What's the crack with Cosworth?'

For a moment, The Duke looked like he might probe further - Carver had hardly been forthcoming - but then with a sigh, let it go. He dropped into his chair and started flicking through the messages his PA had left during de-brief.

'I think we share similar views about friend Cosworth. But-'

Carver waited. The Duke was old school. He never criticised members of his team openly, not even to

Carver.

'He can't be ruled out, and God knows there's enough weird shit there. I'm giving Gary his head.' He paused before adding, 'I need you to concentrate on this Crane woman.'

Carver nodded again.

Morrison hesitated, looked up at him.

'What?'

Morrison sighed. 'You probably already know this, but I'm going to say it anyway. Gary wants a collar like a dog on heat. You know what he's after and he thinks this inquiry can give it to him.' Carver said nothing. 'Whether he's right or not, he sees you as the opposition. If there's any chance of an arrest, he'll want it to be his.'

Carver gave a weary sigh, and met The Duke's gaze. 'He can have whatever he wants. I couldn't give a toss. I've even tried giving him a few steers myself. Not that he listens much.'

The Duke nodded. 'I can believe that, but Gary wouldn't. He's as likely to think you're trying to set him up. I'll say no more. Just watch your back.'

'I will.'

'Speaking of which. I believe the board dates are out?'

'Just got the letter. I'm set for four weeks yesterday.'

The Duke tutted. 'That's tight, the way things are.'

'Tell me about it.'

'You could ask them to put it back?'

'I know.'

'But you won't.'

'Would you?'

'Point taken.'

The conversation over, Carver rose.

But Morrison wasn't finished. 'One more thing.'

Carver stopped. 'What?'

'Do me a favour and ring that reporter back who keeps leaving messages all over the place. Apart from Alec Duncan giving me grief, the ACC rang this morning. Looks like someone with clout told the Press Office you're avoiding him. The Chief wasn't best pleased. He thinks a positive spin might help keep the heat off.'

Carver gave The Duke a straight look. 'Someone needs to tell the Chief I'm a detective, not a fucking poster boy.'

The Duke made a soothing gesture. 'Take it easy. I'm not suggesting you put yourself through it all again. Just speak to the guy. Give him some titbits, that's all.'

'It's not titbits he wants, John. He'll be after doing another bloody feature. "The Man Who Brought Edmund Hart To Justice – Five Years On." Well he can piss off. He can find himself another Sherlock.'

'Just play him, Jamie. That's all I'm saying. If something breaks we may just need the press onside.'

Carver counted to three. But whatever his take on it, The Duke was right. There's never anything to be gained rubbing the press up the wrong way, whoever it is.

'I'll ring him, but that's all. If we met I'm not sure I could trust myself not to strangle the bastard.'

The Duke sighed. 'Like I've said before, he wrote what he wrote in good faith. It's not his fault some saw it as you blowing yourself up. There's jealous bastards in every organisation. We're no different.'

By now Carver had had enough and wasn't about to argue. 'Is that it? Can I go now?'

'Yes. Piss off. Enjoy your weekend, while you can.'

As Carver reached the door The Duke said, 'By the way, are you still seeing your Dad this weekend?'

Carver turned and nodded. 'It's their ruby wedding anniversary tomorrow. We're doing dinner. Some restaurant outside Ripon.' As an aside he added, 'If we all make it.'

'Well if you get there, remember me to him.'

'I will.'

Back in his office, Carver slumped in his chair, reflecting on his day. Leaning forward, he rubbed his fingers into his temples where a dull pain had grown during the course of the afternoon. He spotted Alec's note about Jackson. Picking up the desk phone, he dialled the number.

It answered on the third ring.

'Jackson.'

'This is Jamie Carver.'

'Jamie. Thanks for coming back to me. You got my message?'

All of them. 'Yes.'

'Okay. Good. So… does this call mean you're ready to meet me?'

It means, who the fuck rang my ACC? Carver remembered The Duke's request. 'I can't right now, but give me a shout next week. Monday- no, make that Tuesday. We'll sort something. It may only be over the telephone. There's a lot happening here.'

There was a pause, then, 'Of course. I can imagine how busy you must be. But I'd prefer if we could meet. His tone said, *is this just another string-along?* 'I'd promise not to take up too much of your time?'

Carver shook his head down the phone. The man was a pro, and as persistent as he remembered.

'We'll speak next week.'

'Great. See you.'

Carver hung up.

He checked his watch. Going on Seven-thirty. It was an hour into Manchester this time of evening. Still time to make it. About to rise, Shepherd's face appeared round the door. The look of concern wasn't convincing. Carver came on guard.

'Everything okay Jamie? Shame the Crane woman wouldn't come on board. Any particular reason? Would you like me to have a go?'

Carver bit back his first response. 'Thanks, but no thanks, Gary. Jess and I will sort our Ms Crane out. You've got your hands full with Cosworth.' Rising from the chair, he reached for his keys off the desk. Blind as ever, Shepherd slipped further inside.

'Speaking of Jess, how's she doing? I have to say I was a bit surprised when you chose her. She worked for me once on a rape case. A bit lacking in experience, I thought.'

Carver knew the case. Alec Duncan was the first CID on the scene. His account of how Jess, then a uniform sergeant, had dealt with the hysterical victim and preserved the scene, was in his mind when he interviewed her. 'She's doing fine. What she lacks in experience she makes up for in common sense.' *Unlike some.*

'Glad to hear it. Mind you, she's not a bad looker either. I hope you're making sure to give her the benefit of your… experience?'

About to head for the door, Carver froze.

Straightening, he stepped back, looked Shepherd straight in the face and folded his arms. 'Scuse me?'

Whatever his failings, Shepherd knew when he'd overstepped. His swagger faded. 'Whoops. Sorry, Jamie. That's my mouth running away with itself again. Don't worry, everyone knows you're straight down the line.' Along the corridor, a telephone rang. He hung out the door. 'Calls coming in. Needed in the MIR. Have a good weekend. You look like you need it.'

Carver listened to Shepherd's footsteps receding. 'Prick,' he muttered.

Checking his desk one last time - it would still be there Monday - he pulled his jacket off the back of the chair, sending it spinning. As he strode out he was looking forward to his first proper break in weeks. But his inner voice was telling him, 'And pigs fly.'

CHAPTER 9

From the window in the main CID Office, Jess watched Carver's Golf slow at the gate, before gunning forward and left into a gap in the streaming traffic. She followed its departure down Arpley Street. A voice close behind made her jump.

'How're you enjoying the big time then, Jess?'

She spun around. Shepherd was right on her shoulder, way too near. Avoiding his gaze, she weaved past him and headed back to her desk.

'I'm enjoying it fine, thank you. Sir.'

'That's good.'

He sauntered after her, eyes wandering the room, fingers flicking, randomly, through papers on detectives' desks. They were alone, the others either left for home or grabbing refs.

Sensing something, Jess was wary, and set about tidying her desk. To her dismay, Shepherd settled himself on the edge of the neighbouring desk, lifted a foot and rested it on the edge of hers, hemming her in. She caught a whiff of something musky. It hadn't been there when they'd passed in the corridor following debrief.

'You know Jess, this inquiry could be good for you.

You're showing promise for this sort of work. I mentioned it to The Duke and he agrees. Keep it up and I'm sure there'll be a permanent job when this is all over.'

She managed not to laugh. 'I appreciate that, Sir.'

There was an awkward silence before he continued. 'So what do you think of this Crane woman thing? It's not just Jamie looking for a bit of a diversion, is it?'

Unsure what he was getting at, she said, 'That's not for me to say. But Mr Carver's confident she can help.' As she picked up her shoulder bag and stood up, Shepherd chuckled in a way she found strange.

'He would be.'

Jess was intrigued, but wasn't about to start talking about her boss in his absence. Before applying for the job she'd heard the rumours of course. But she'd avoided digging, preferring to take things, and him, as she found them. Turning, she skirted the back of her chair to avoid his leg-barrier. But he moved swiftly to catch up, traversing between the desks to come alongside her as she neared the door. Suddenly his hand was on her elbow and she stopped. His boldness surprised her, as well as his stupidity.

'There's something I think you should be aware of.' She waited. 'I know you and Jamie are working together, but... Well, it's just that he has a reputation for sometimes getting a bit, you know, *involved* in this sort of thing? You need to be careful.'

As shock joined with the surprise, Jess wondered where it was coming from. Jealousy or genuine concern? He *seemed* sincere. 'What are you trying to say?'

He attempted a warm smile. 'Just a friendly warning.

This sort of inquiry, it can suck you in if you're not careful. I wouldn't want it to happen to you.'

'Thanks for the heads-up. I'll bear it in mind.' She turned away.

But he wasn't finished. 'A couple more things.' Stopping again, she almost sighed in annoyance. 'Firstly, we've worked together before, so let's cut out the 'Sir' business, ok? My name's Gary, right?' She inclined her head, *anything you say*, but stayed on alert. 'Second, I've still got a vacancy on my team. I'd like someone like you to fill it. I feel we could work well together. With your help I- we, could nail this guy. You know, this Cosworth link is stronger than some people are giving it credit for. You might want to give some thought to swapping horses.'

Jess let her face show both her disappointment, and lack of interest. It didn't put him off.

'We could talk about it over a bite at Henry's if you like?'

The station's closest eatery, Henry's Wine Bar did good business out of being the most trouble-free venue in town.

Jess was so taken aback she struggled to reply. She'd learned long ago how to deflect advances with a smile and light remark. It was easy enough to make enemies in this job without having to worry about men - and women - with grudges. But she'd always imagined that people like Shepherd -on the fast track- would be careful about leaving themselves open to a harassment charge.

'I'm sorry, *Sir*. I was under the impression you're Duty SIO this evening? I'm not sure it would be appropriate for you to be seen dining out with a junior officer? In any case, I think that any discussions about my future should take place with Mr Carver present.' She let him digest it and then turned to leave, searching for a way past. But he reached out and took her elbow, again, not too heavy, but enough to pause her.

'Listen Jess.' He gave her the sincere look again. 'Just because he's had some media attention, don't expect to ride the crest of any wave that comes along. Your boss isn't as squeaky clean as you might think. Don't be surprised if you find a skeleton rattling around his closet someday. When that day comes some may assume you're tainted as well. It would be a shame to ruin a promising career.'

Jess had heard enough. Time to be out of here. She looked down at the fingers gripping her elbow. 'If you would like to give me my arm back, I'll be on my way. *Sir.*'

With a final smirk he let go, and stepped aside.

As she crossed the room, Jess was conscious of a feeling similar to the one she'd had as she'd walked down Megan Crane's drive that afternoon. She didn't look back, and was relieved when she turned the corner, out of his gaze.

CHAPTER 10

Corinne Anderson turns sideways, admiring the way her most recent Kubu purchase disguises the stomach she's never quite managed to restore to pre-Tom and Betsy condition. At forty-four, Corinne is proud of the figure many younger women would envy. Still, she is glad she decided on her shopping trip that morning.

Dragging herself away from the dressing mirror - she can still see herself in the one over the dressing table if needs be - she crosses to the bed where the tools of her trade are laid out. She runs her hands over them, thinking on how best she might use their different textures, the imagery associated with them, to get the most from her forthcoming engagement. Like an artiste preparing for a performance, she is aware of a feeling of excited anticipation. She knows that only those closest to her have an inkling of how seriously she takes her favourite pastime.

Corinne Anderson was thirteen when she first started to become aware that her interests lay in different directions to those of her celebrity-obsessed friends. In the years following she sought to understand the nature of the urges that grew strongly within her. In the years following her doomed marriage – Michael could never come to terms with his young wife's emerging preferences – she read widely. Titles such as, 'The Ties That Bind' and 'Different Loving', striving to grasp the complex psychology that underpins the range of activities encompassed by the acronym, BDSM – Bondage, Discipline, and Sado-Masochism.

But after many years, Corinne concluded that trying to explain why as many as eighty percent of people - some studies put it higher - and of both sexes, find the idea of dominating a partner, or being dominated, a turn-on, is as misguided as trying to explain why some prefer music to sport. *It's the way people are*, has come to be Corinne's philosophy on the subject. She gave up searching for any deeper meaning years ago.

This particular evening, her choices are informed by the contents of the letter resting on her bedside table. Thorough as always, she reaches for it to double check she hasn't missed anything.

The typescript's first page is headed, '(Respectful) Suggestions for Mistress's Attire' and she has already checked that her outfit matches the specification.

Black collar. Red / Black corset, (Satin preferred). - Her new Kubu purchase is perfect. *Seamed stockings, (black). Black stilettos, (four-inch heel, minimum). Opera/Evening gloves, (Black.)'*

It is the classic, 'Dom' look. Corinne has worn it often, and is comfortable with it. She turns the letter over, skipping over the fawning, introduction in which the writer emphasises that the contents are only suggestions, and that, *'if Mistress chooses to ignore them, then that is, of course, Mistress's prerogative'*. She reads on.

'At our last meeting, Mistress demanded that her

unworthy slave write, describing how the scene may progress...' She skipped further down. *'When unworthy slave arrives, Mistress may wish to be dressed as per'* Blah-blah-blah... *'...may choose to invite slave into her beautiful home... Conversation will be polite, cordial.... Eventually... will find slave's manner offensive... will become angry... will slap slave's insolent face... will place a collar about slaves insulting throat ...will then drag slave to her Playroom.... Punishment will begin...'*

She reads it all again, making sure it is embedded within her memory. It is quite well written. More so than many such she has received over the years. And she knows how important it is that the scene be played out exactly as specified.

As well as her figure and expertise, Corinne prides herself on her ability to make sure that her relationships are based on *mutual* pleasure, unlike a professional whose only interest is in extracting her 'tribute'. For that reason, she believes it important that the details agreed beforehand meet *both* their needs. And for all the letter's submissive tone, its writer is as entitled to dictate how things are to proceed as she. Once the scene commences however, that is another matter.

That said, apart from one or two interesting and original little touches - the procedure with the electric toothbrush is one she hasn't tried before - there is little within the first act that is new. She has all the necessary props, and where the letter isn't specific- Well, she is certain her experience will see her through.

But it is the second part of the script that intrigues her. It's a variation she hasn't tried before and is interested to see if it can work. Her first thought was to reject it as altogether too contrived - not to mention contrary to her natural instincts. But curiosity has since taken over, and she has begun to think that, with a bit of imagination, it might just work.

It depends, of course, upon trust. Absolute trust. And she has thought long and hard on whether they know each other well enough. But the last couple of sessions have proceeded more smoothly than she anticipated. They both responded well to each other's signals. In fact at this early stage, she feels more at ease with this particular 'unworthy and undeserving slave' than she has with any of the others. It would certainly be different. And if it doesn't work, well, it will be back to business as usual.

Satisfied with her preparations, she sits at her dressing table, pouting into the mirror, turning her head this way, then that, thinking about hair and makeup. Now, what sort of look for what is planned? Hair up, or down? Up, she decides. And make up? The usual, or something darker, more dramatic? Perhaps a darker look might actually sit better with the variation - if things happen to go that way.

Opening her expansive makeup box, she peers in, reminding herself of the many options available within its nooks and crannies. As she considers the myriad possibilities, the dampness between her legs reminds her of how the elaborate preparations are almost as enjoyable as the scene itself.

She closes her eyes, savouring the moment.

CHAPTER 11

The girl sniffed quick and hard and the line disappeared up the rolled-up twenty. Sitting up straight, she tossed her blonde-streaked main back and tweaked her nose, sniffing again to make sure every grain was absorbed into the sensitive nasal tissues.

'WOO-HOO! FUCKing ayy-ONE,' she declared in her New York twang. Within seconds she felt her system beginning to respond. She lifted her voice. 'THAT'S FERKIN GOOD CANDYCAINE LOVER. Sure hope you got more o' this somewhere.'

In the bedroom off the main living area, William Cosworth paused in his packing to poke his head round the door. Her face was already flushing. The good stuff works so quickly these days. He frowned. Petra's cravings were definitely getting worse. She was becoming flaky, and that was a problem. Life was complicated enough. Her reliance on him – and what he provided - meant she served his purposes well. She actually seemed to enjoy the work and there was nothing she hadn't been willing to try. But as her dependency increased, so did her tendency to talk. Twice recently he'd caught her just as she'd been about to describe some of their recent work to her friends.

After the business a few years ago, he couldn't afford more rumours, even if most people had forgotten all that by now. Amazing how these things blow over, eventually.

Time was coming he would need to do something about her. But he'd have to be careful. If she got wind of anything in her present state, she would blow. Probably run off to that faggot hairdresser of hers - wassisname, Damien? - and tell him everything. A normal person would assume she was making it all up, but not that cock-sucking idiot. He was stupid enough to believe her. And if he started talking - as he no doubt would - the proverbial-fucking-cat would be out of the proverbial-fucking-bag.

Returning to his packing, he stuffed straps, cameras and other items into the big leather holdall in which he kept everything he needed for his, 'shoots.' As he did so he considered his options. Apart from the obvious, there were a couple of possibilities that would be tidier and less risky. If he started now, made a couple of calls, he could be rid of her by the end of the week. She would never realise - until it was too late. The only thing she needed right now was to know where her next fix was coming from.

He'd have to remember not to get the next one hooked so quickly. Girls willing to do his kind of work were hard to come by. And while the money was good, he couldn't afford to burn them out too soon. One in particular, Lisa, had been in his mind lately. The more he saw of her, the more he was certain she would be ideal. She'd been getting plenty of work recently and might be hard to convince, but there were ways. And a reliable supplier counts for a lot in this business.

Bag packed, he pulled the zips and carried it through to the living room. Petra was high now, in the active phase of her hit, picking up items of clothing and trying them against her reflection in the wall mirror. The old Prodigy hit, 'Climbatise' was booming from the B and O and she ducked and weaved to the heavy beat. Seeing the bag, she stopped.

'We goin' out hon?'

Picking up the remote, he turned the volume down. He looked round for his car keys. 'I'm going out babe. You're staying here'.

Disappointment crowded her features. 'You mean you're leaving me here? Alone? Again?'

Her voice was a hurt whimper and he knew he had to be careful. He didn't have the time to deal with her if she went off, and he was already late.

'It's only a small job. Just got the call this afternoon,' he lied. 'Anyway, you're out of it for the night. I told you to lay off that stuff. You're no good to me in that state.'

The eruption was instantaneous. 'You BASTARD,' she screamed. 'You line me, then tell me I'm out of it? I'll show you who's FUCKING out of it.' The manic eyes searched about her. A heavy glass ashtray rested on the coffee table. But even as she bent for it he moved, fast. Grabbing a fistful of hair, he pulled her head back. At the same time his other hand took her wrist and twisted her arm up her back, forcing from her a scream of pain. He pulled her round so her face was inches from his and when he spoke his voice was full of menace.

'Don't start Petra. I'm not in the mood. I'm going out and you're stopping here. If you fuck me about, I swear, you'll regret it.'

But she was angry too. Despite the pain she was about to start struggling when she saw his eyes. The drug hadn't fully dulled her senses yet. There was something in them she'd seen more and more recently during their fights and spats. A chill ran through her, and the fear she'd felt coming on the past weeks – and which she kept telling herself was groundless – surfaced again. She stopped struggling and waited, bearing the pain rather than risk angering him more. He looked deep into her eyes, then pressed his mouth to hers, kissing her, hard and rough so her bottom lip caught against her teeth, before pulling away, sneering.

'That's better. Now you just wait, nice and quiet, and I'll be back later. If you've been good, I might just have something for you.'

He pushed her down onto the couch were she lay, nursing the pain out of her arm, running her tongue over her bloody lip. Picking up the bag, he threw her one last look of disdain, then left the apartment, slamming the door behind him. As he headed down the corridor, a muffled sob echoed behind.

Ignoring the lift, he took the stairs, using the exercise to dissipate his anger. He'd laid it on a bit – so she'd get the message – but was surprised how close he'd come. As he reached the ground floor and headed for the lobby, he allowed himself a final, 'Fucking bitch,' then shook his head, purging himself of her.

By the time the tall man in the long, grey coat turned to see who was approaching from behind, William Cosworth, Fashion Photographer, was back in character; his normal, charming self.

"Evening, Wilson,' he said.

With a deferential nod, the old concierge pressed the button that released the door lock and stepped forward to pull it open. As he did so, a gust of damp wind stirred the bottom of his greatcoat.

'And good evening to you, Mr Cosworth-Sir. Have a pleasant evening.'

'Oh I will, Wilson,' he said, merrily, as he stepped out. 'I will. Goodnight.'

'And goodnight to you to, Sir.'

As he reached the pavement, Cosworth paused and pressed the button on his key ring. Thirty yards away, the lights of the black Porsche flashed brightly and a loud double clunk echoed across the car park. He glanced back up at the lobby, checking to make sure that Wilson, boring, fuddy-duddy Wilson, was watching. Sure enough, he was staring through the glass, shaking his head in admiration. Satisfied, Cosworth turned and walked, briskly, towards the car, already looking forward to the pleasures the evening would bring.

Up in the lobby Wilson raised his bright eyes to the ceiling and shook his wise old head.

'What a pillock.'

CHAPTER 12

As Jess watched her three friends falling about laughing over the latest, awful pun on the subject they'd been doing to death the last ten minutes, she wished she had never mentioned the word, 'dominatrix.' Earlier, their incessant badgering – 'Why so quiet tonight Jess?' 'Is something wrong?' - had lured her to mention a meeting with someone a bit 'unusual', and that it had not gone well. It was a mistake. They all knew of her involvement with Kerry. The media couldn't get enough of it. Normally tight-lipped, Jess's uncharacteristic reveal was enough for them to fall on it like wasps on jam.

'What do you mean, 'unusual'?'

'Was it a suspect?'

'You'll have to tell us. Whoever it is, they're obviously on your mind.'

She'd thought that if she could put the day's events behind her, she might be able to get on with enjoying her night out with friends she saw less and less these days. She told how she'd met a 'lifestyle' dominatrix. But when she realised that was about all she could share, she recognised her error. It triggered a torrent of questions, the first from Abi, the youngest. 'What's a domin-itix?' What followed was proof enough - were any needed - that when it comes to 'laddish' humour, women in drink are no different to men. She then spent the next twenty minutes denying she was holding back on some earth-shattering secret that her friends had every right to know - 'Remember, it's us who pay your wages.' Eventually she called, 'Enough' and suggested they find another topic to fixate on. It didn't work. Cut off from their source, they resorted to squeezing every drop of humour they could from the information they'd been given. The string of puns and double-entendres that followed covered everything from handcuffs to interview - read 'interrogation' - techniques, and looked set to continue. The last, from birthday-girl Lou herself, was typically inane. A telephone call from the woman in question apologising for not being able to help with Jess's enquiries because, 'I'm tied up today.' It was the last straw. Jess was still smarting over the afternoon's shambles, and her friends' behaviour struck her as not just disproportionate - Charlotte looked like she was about to wet herself for God's sake – but crass in the extreme. They'd obviously forgotten that the subject they were laughing about connected to a string of brutal murders.

Close to saying something she knew she may later regret, Jess grabbed her purse and slipped from her stool. 'That's it. If you've not found something else to talk about by the time I get back, then I'm out of here.'

But as she headed for the Ladies, the digs followed.

'I like it when she gets all dominant.'

'Get her another drink. That'll whip her into shape.'

'Feeling a bit ropey are we?'

'Just joking Jess. Not.'

As always on a Saturday night in Jasper's the Ladies was jammed. Jess had to queue for a cubicle. When one came free, she was in it like a rabbit down a hole. Locking the door, she leaned back and took a deep breath. Then she sat down and put her head in her hands.

When she'd arrived home that evening, following her creepy-but-revealing encounter with Shepherd, she had little time to reflect on her day. Already an hour late for her meeting with the girls, she'd been desperate to try Martin again. She showered, changed and saw to her hair and makeup in record time. Through it, she was conscious of questions lurking in the back of her mind, waiting to be dragged out and pulled apart. Mostly, they related to their failure to recruit Megan Crane to their cause. Jess didn't do blame, but her sense was that if she did, she wouldn't be pointing any fingers at herself. With an effort, she'd turned her thoughts away from the afternoon's events, grabbed her mobile and tried Martin.

The 'unavailable' signal she'd been getting all week sounded again.

'Damn it Martin, Where the hell are you?'

Two weeks earlier, as he'd left for his trip to somewhere in Eastern Europe – Azerbaijan? – he'd warned that communication might be a problem. 'The way things are out there right now there's no guarantee there'll be a decent signal so don't worry if you don't hear from me for a while.' He'd also spoken about spending, 'a fair bit of time in the mountains, where the rebels are holding up.

Jess knew nothing about Azerbaijan. She wasn't even clear as to what the television documentary he'd been commissioned to produce was about. Something to do with Human Rights abuses, she thought. But she could imagine mobile phone coverage being spasmodic, at best.

It wasn't that she was missing him, exactly. Before Martin, she'd lived alone long enough it didn't bother her. But this particular night, she'd have been interested to hear his take on Megan Crane. Instead, all she had were The Three Degrees out there, who were no use at all. *How can a grown woman not know what a dominatrix is, for God's sake?*

Sitting there, Jess felt the day's frustrations rising again, though who to focus her anger on she wasn't sure. Carver? Herself? Her piss-taking friends? It didn't matter. Whoever the rightful target, it fed her ruminations.

They should have persevered; she knew that now. If she'd been able to talk with the woman on her own, she was sure she'd have… Which is when the idea came

Her first thought was to reject it outright. He would never approve. But the thought stayed, and the more she considered it, the more certain she became. He couldn't say anything if it worked. And it would show him what she was capable of.

Leaving the cubicle - too noisy - she returned to the bar but steered away from where her friends looked like they were still enjoying her absence and made her way outside. Slipping round the corner away from the bustle, she took out her mobile and brought up the number she'd got off the woman in the DOM office and which she'd added to her contacts, 'just in case.' It was late, but something told her she wasn't the early-to-bed sort.

After a few rings it picked up and an unmistakeable voice said, 'Yes?'

She took a deep breath. 'Ms Crane- Megan. This is Jess Greylake, the Detective-'

'Jess!' The gushing tone made it sound like she was hearing from a long-lost friend. 'So lovely to hear from you. I was wondering when you would call.'

CHAPTER 13

Carver entered at the back of the Royal Northern College of Music Concert Hall, just as the woman on stage hit the soaring highs of *Povo Que Lavas No Rio*. As he settled into his seat, the hairs on the back of his neck rubbed against his collar, just as they had the first time he heard it.

Rosanna Nogueira looked stunning in the glittering white dress that fitted her like a glove and which she'd anguished about buying for weeks before he'd finally told her 'Buy the damn thing. I'll pay. You know it'll look great.' And as he'd told her the several times she'd tried it on since, he was right.

After the day he'd had, Carver was tempted to close his eyes and let the music transport him back to the smoky depths of Barco Negro, but he resisted. He rarely got to see her perform live. Barco Negro was the Lisbon nightclub where he and Gill had fetched up on the last night of their final, make-or-break holiday in Portugal - break as it turned out. The memory of the flame-haired *fadista,* as he later learned the term, singing a type of music he had never heard before but which sent shivers up his spine, was all that stayed of that abortive week. When he chanced across her again three years later, at a

Liverpool music festival to which a lady Police Doctor friend dragged him in an effort to force him back into the real world, he was glad it had.

Checking around, he gauged the hall was two-thirds full. Not bad considering the limited audience for Fado in the North. At least it was enough she would feel it had been worthwhile. The past two weeks she had been checking the website's ticket sales daily. For the thirty minutes remaining of her set, her voice did something he'd tried to do many times the past few weeks but failed – wipe away thoughts of murder, dominatrices, past misjudgements and, more recently, Megan Crane. After her closing number and the obligatory encore, she joined him in the basement Camerata Bar. He had a large Rioja waiting, alongside his pint. She was eager for his opinion.

'Fantastic,' he said. 'As always.'

And though she pressed him for detail – 'How did it sound?' 'What did you think of the dress?' 'Was the volume right?' his critiquing skills weren't up to the job.

'Fantastic.' 'Great.' 'Amazing.'

'That's all you ever say.'

'That's all you want to hear.'

She tossed her hair and laughed the throaty laugh that always did it for him.

Over the next half-hour they drank and talked through the concert – as much as he'd heard. She was surprised but glad he'd managed to get there at all, and teased him about, 'showing her gratitude,' later. He hoped he would be up to it, and tried to act like he knew what he was talking about when he mentioned the hall's 'great' acoustics and the clarity of the guitars. 'Guitarra,' she corrected. In reality they were both aware that if he knew a tenth as much about music as he did football – like his father, he was die-hard Liverpool fan – he would sound more convincing. It didn't matter. They both knew that the fact they were polar opposites – she a cultured artiste with a taste for fine wine, he a beer-swilling detective whose only real interest apart from her was football - was one of the reasons the relationship worked, so far at least. Eventually there was a lull. As she sipped her wine, she regarded him over the glass's rim.

'How did it go today?' She tried to make it sound casual, like it wasn't a big deal.

He gave her a long look, thinking on how much to tell. Right from that first night in Liverpool when he introduced himself and told her he'd seen her perform in Lisbon and talked her into dinner, Carver had resolved not to repeat the mistakes he'd made with Gill. It meant sharing more about his work than he was used to. Rosanna knew he hadn't been looking forward to his meeting with the Crane woman. She even knew some of the reasons why.

'Not too well. But we're not giving up. We'll try again next week.'

'And your Jess? What did she think?'

He thought on it. 'Difficult to say. I don't think she'd met anyone like her before. She said she was, 'interesting.'

'What about you? Do you think she is, 'interesting'?

He checked her face. It was giving nothing away. 'She's a possible lead. Of course she's interesting.'

Rosanna pulled her chair closer to his, cupped her hand to the back of his head. She stared deep into his eyes, as if searching for something. *What?*

'You must be careful, Jamie Carver. Some women, they are bad for you.' She paused then added, 'You know this.'

He nodded, thought he could joke himself out of it. 'Like you, you mean?'

'You know what I mean.' But then she lightened. 'I, on the other hand, am very good for you. This, you also know.'

As they held each other's gaze, he felt her other hand on his thigh. And as she leaned in to press her lips to his, he felt an unexpected stirring. Driving into Manchester, all he'd thought about was how he'd messed up, what he needed to do to make it right. He'd worried it would cast a shadow over their whole weekend. But as he returned the kiss, he thought, *Maybe not.*

CHAPTER 14

Corinne Anderson jerks as the flogger's stinging tails rake across her back. Again it is harder than she thinks necessary. It adds to the concerns that have grown within her the past few minutes.

To begin with, the scene had played out strictly as per the script. Her 'dutiful slave' had obeyed her every command, without question. But the last couple of lashes have been heavier than expected. It makes her wonder if it is inexperience that is the problem, or something else. Either way she decides, if her next instruction isn't obeyed, precisely, she will issue the safe-word and bring this part of the encounter to a close. Time for a stern reminder.

'That was too much,' she says. 'I told you, I am not to be marked.' She waits for the whimpering apology the rebuke demands. Silence.

'Do you hear me?' She lifts her voice to signal her anger, tries to twist round. But the ropes securing her to the post are tight and the way her wrists and arms are secured in front and above her, restricts her movement. She waits, unsure whether her slave's lack of response is due to fear at having upset, 'Mistress', or the need to indulge in some strictly-forbidden self-relief - which will itself require punishment. Whatever the reason, the lack of response means it is time to re-assert herself.

'Red.'

Nothing. She tries again.

'Red. Do you hear me? I've given the safe word. Release me at once.'

Still no response. Corinne is shocked. It is unheard of.

For experienced players such as Corinne, the safe-word is sacrosanct. In all her years of acting out scenes, she has only ever known it be ignored once. She never saw that person again. For the first time, she feels the stirrings of unease.

Just a few minutes before, her slave had seemed the same, natural submissive she had come to know during their previous meetings. And it was her co-player's compliance with her commands during those meetings that had convinced her she could play out this element of the scene safely. That her slave will bend to her will on command. She hopes she hasn't miscalculated.

The answer comes in the form of another blow, the hardest yet - across her buttocks this time.

'OOOWWWWW. Red. RED!' The stinging pain ripples through her body. But before she can remonstrate further, she feels a hand balling in her hair and her head is yanked back, hard.

A voice, breathless and menacing, whispers in her ear. 'You can shout, 'Red' as much as you like, *BITCH. I'M* in control here now, not you.'

The vicious tone and the threat implicit in the words are enough for Corinne to realise. This is no momentary aberration. *I've been set up.*

Icicles of fear radiate through her as she realises her

vulnerability. If the whole thing has been a contrivance, then what else lies in store for her? Feelings of panic begin to well up. But she doesn't say anything. Her instincts tell her she is no longer, 'Mistress,' and it will do her no good to try to act the part. Too late, she admonishes herself for being so gullible.

But she isn't allowed to ponder on it long. A red ball-gag appears in front of her. Before she can react, it pushes hard into her mouth, behind her teeth, making it impossible to spit it out. She shakes her head, violently, to no avail. She feels the strap being buckled behind, tight. Her former sub is making sure their roles are well and truly reversed. More rope is wound about her legs, lashing them to the post. To her horror, she feels something soft draw tight about her neck. She tries to call out through the gag, but her cries are cut off as it tightens even more, choking off her efforts.

The combined effect of fear, the gag, and whatever is now about her throat, forces Corinne to gasp for breath. She squeezes her eyes shut. When she opens them again, she finds herself gazing into two dark pools. Earlier, the eyes had been respectful, compliant, underpinned with the submissive's desire to obey. She had put her trust in those eyes. Absolute trust. Now they are cold, clinical, reflecting nothing but … what? Hate? Her fear spreads. It is the sort of fear a mother experiences when her child is away from her care and she sees a policeman walking up the path. She knows something bad has happened, but doesn't yet know what.

She tries to ask, 'What are you going to do?' But the words come out a meaningless jumble of 'Wha''s and 'oo's.

In response, her captor's face closes on hers. She feels hot breath on her cheeks. The chilling voice rings in her ears once more.

'You're under *my* control now, *Mistress*. And we are going to play the game the way *I* want to play it. Understand, *Mistress?*'

Terrified, Corinne Anderson can only nod. Whatever the game is, she hopes it won't last too long, or be too painful. She dare not even think of another possibility, which is even worse. Far worse.

It is years since Corinne has cried from fear. She does so now, tears running down her cheeks, dripping off her chin and onto the shelf the entwining ropes have formed from her jutting breasts, as her former sub goes to work.

CHAPTER 15

It took Carver's mobile several rings before it penetrated the depths where he dreamed these days enough to register. As his hand groped over the bedside table, Rosanna stirred beside him.

'Wh- Who is it?'

'Shhh. S'alright. Go back to sleep.' Finding the source of the annoying buzz, he checked the screen. His eyes weren't focusing yet. 'Tch.' He jabbed a finger at the green circle. *First bloody weekend off in months...*

'Yes?'

'Jamie. It's Rita.'

It took him a moment. 'Rita. Whassup?' He prised himself onto an elbow.

'I'm at Carnegie Avenue. You need to come.' Her dull tone told him it wasn't for debate.

He swung his legs out, sat on the edge of the bed, mind clearing, rapidly. 'What's happened?'

'Kayleigh's stabbed Stuart.'

'WHAT?' *Shit.* 'Is he-?'

'Dead? No. But it's a right mess. Your people are here. I need you.'

He checked the clock. 03:05. He stood up.

'Thirty minutes.'

Carver saw the blue flashing lights reflecting the length of Carnegie Avenue long before he got anywhere near number twenty-five. Along the approach he counted two ambulances, several Police cars, a couple of plain, CID cars. Someone had hit the button hard on this one.

He parked behind the last police car and got out. As he headed for the house that was once a pair of semis until the project converted them into one, he was already working scenarios. Then he remembered where he was. Turning, he pointed his keys back at the car and waited while the lights flashed. Nearing the house, he saw every window was showing a light. Likewise the houses either side, and opposite. *They're used to it.* The front door was open. There was shouting coming from inside. Several voices. A young policeman was on point at the garden gate. Beyond him, further down the street, dark figures roamed. Not all were in uniform. Carver hoped none were press. He needed to get a lid on, fast.

"Morning, Mr Carver.' the PC said, as if it were a nice sunny one.

Carver nodded. "Morning, Matt.'

As he turned up the path, the shouting got louder. Some from upstairs, some down. Stepping into the hallway, two things struck him. First, there was carpet on the stairs he'd only ever seen bare. Nothing fancy, just a plain mid-brown. But it was an improvement. The second thing was the smell of fresh paint – another first. He remembered an email a couple of weeks back, something about a local decorating company offering sponsorship. To his left was the main living-room, directly in front, the stairs. He was about to go up when a voice he recognised came from his left.

'SIT DOWN RUSSELL.'

He turned to it, then realised something else. He was looking at a door. It was back on its hinges. Checking up the stairs he confirmed what his sub-conscious had registered as he'd come in. The upstairs doors had been re-hung as well. When the project started, they'd found all the internal doors stacked in the back garden amidst all the stolen motorcycle parts. It had taken many weeks and much bridge-building before the older kids told how they'd taken them all off so they would have early warning of their Dad's approach. As he entered the room, Carver saw the night-CID DS, Paul Hill, nose to nose with Russell Lee. A uniformed PC stood off, watching, ready.

At seventeen, Russell was the oldest of the family's nine siblings. With a history of showing violent aggression towards the police, he had been the hardest to bring on board. It wouldn't have happened at all without Kayleigh. To Russell's credit, the way his fists kept jerking up into the 'ready' position then dropping, Carver could see he was fighting against the instincts telling him to show the man in his face he was no longer a kid. On the couch behind him, Billy, fourteen, was watching wide-eyed, waiting to see which way things would go. The door into the kitchen was shut. Women's voices drifted through.

Hill had his back to Carver, but must have seen the change in Russell's face as he came in. Hill turned. When he saw his DCI he looked relieved.

Russell didn't waste a second. 'Mr Carver, this twat's just assaulted me.' He pointed to somewhere on his face. As long as Carver had known him, it had always been a patchwork of battle-scars.

Hill spun round on the youth. Carver could see he

was close to losing it. 'If I'd assaulted you, you wouldn't be shouting about it, you little shit.'

'Thanks Paul,' Carver said. As the detective turned back to him Carver threw him a meaningful look before turning to the youth he'd been berating. 'Russell. Calm down and do as you're told. I'll speak to you in a minute.' He didn't wait for a response but said to Hill, 'Where's Rita?' Hill nodded towards the kitchen. 'Ok. I'll see you outside in a few minutes?'

Hill got the message. As he turned to leave, he gave Russell one last warning look.

Russell mouthed, 'Fuck off,' before dropping into the couch next to his brother.

The kitchen was full of women and kids. Most were in tears. The mother, Paula Lee, was sitting at the far end of the long table Rita had scrounged off Social Services weeks before so the family had somewhere they could all get around for family conferences. It was still too early to hope they may one day use it for eating together. A big woman with greasy hair, Paula's saggy arms were draped around a couple of the younger girls who were cuddling into her. There were tears and sobs a-plenty. Kayleigh, herself was stood off to her left, leaning against a worktop, hands cupping a steaming mug. She was wearing flowery-patterned pyjamas. The top was stained with dark red patches.

At fifteen, Kayleigh was the eldest of the five girls. Slim and dark, like her father, her black hair was growing out of the punkish style she'd worn the last time he'd seen her. As Carver entered, she turned him a resigned look that seemed to say, 'Here we go again.' He could see she'd been crying, though right now she seemed in control. Good. Whatever she'd done tonight, he would need her if they were going to sort this lot out.

To Carver, Kayleigh was still something of an enigma. When the Government launched their 'Problem Families Initiative', the Lees were number one on almost every agency's list; Police, Local Council, Social Services. And it quickly became clear to all that if the Lee Family Project was to ever achieve its aims, Kayleigh's part would be vital. One of those kids whose existence seems to run contrary to both sides of the nature/nurture debate, she was the one family member everyone else was prepared to listen to. Mature beyond her years, intelligent and committed to the project from the start, she'd brokered truces from stalemates on several occasions, both within the family and with the 'participating agencies'. During early case meetings, Carver had mused on how, if it weren't for the slightly weaselled features that echoed her father, he'd have put her as the product of one of her mother's once-notorious sexual escapades. There had been times the past six months when, seeing her in action, fighting to hold together a family who sometimes questioned both her motives and loyalty, he'd felt like taking her by the hand and leading her out of the nightmare that was the Lee household. Now, as he noted the calm-but-sad expression that said she was resigned to whatever outcome fate had in store for her this night, he felt it again.

At the end of the table, her back to him, a colourfully-dressed black woman with an abundance of braided hair turned as she heard him come in. Seeing him, Rita Arogundade, Lead Case Worker for the Lee Family Project, rose from her chair.

'We need to talk,' she said, motioning to the back

door.

The lack of greeting didn't surprise Carver. Rita always preferred action to words. He following her out into the garden, closed the door. They could still see by the light through the kitchen window. She got straight to it.

'I hope you're going to be able to sort this.'

Her expression was serious and Carver returned her a neutral one. What she'd meant was, 'You *are* going to sort this.'

'Give me the story, then I'll tell you if I can. First, where's Stuart and how is he?'

'He's upstairs with the paramedics and a couple of yours. He's got a hole in his stomach which they think is probably superficial but can't be sure. He's refusing hospital. They're trying to convince him.'

'Good luck to that,' Carver said. Since childhood, Stuart Lee had trained himself to never cooperate with anyone wearing a uniform.

Over the next two minutes, Rita summarised what she'd learned since she'd answered the phone at two-o-clock to hear Kayleigh's quivering voice saying, 'I've stabbed me dad.'

The previous evening, Stuart and Paula had argued over Benny, the youngest boy, four, continuing to see the child psychologist. 'Stuart hates her guts,' Rita offered. 'You know what he's like.' Carver nodded but said nothing. Losing the argument with Paula, as he always did, Stuart had reverted to norm and taken himself off to The Cricketers. There he'd proceeded to fall off the wagon, returning home at midnight drunk out of his skull and high on something. When Paula saw the state he was in, it all kicked off like it used to in the old days. The kids got involved and, as always happened, the family divided along gender lines. The girls blamed Stuart, the lads sought to defend him. Kayleigh tried to call a conference, but by then Stuart was too far gone to listen, so were most of them. Things spiralled out of control and eventually Stuart just blew and went for Paula. He put his hands round her throat and pushed her down into the kitchen table. The kids tried to prise them apart but couldn't get him off. Stuart was wiry, but strong. Paula began turning blue. Kayleigh thought he really was going to kill her this time.

'She picked up a knife and tried to warn him. When he didn't stop, she stabbed him.'

'Where?' Carver said.

Rita pointed up and under her right ribs.

Carver sucked air. 'Lucky he's still alive.'

'She says she only pricked him enough to get him to pay attention.'

'Let's hope so. But he needs to be checked out properly.'

'He's saying he's not going anywhere until he knows no-one's going to take Kayleigh away.'

'So he's come round a bit?'

'Oh God, yeah. The neighbours called the police and I got here just as your guys did. He was like-' Rita affected Stuart's nasally whine. It was remarkably accurate- '"It's all my fault. Kayleigh was only protecting her ma. If you want to arrest someone, arrest me. I tried to kill her." Tears. Pleas for God's forgiveness. The lot. I don't think your people know who to arrest. That's why I called you.'

Carver nodded. 'Thanks.'

Rita lowered her voice. Carver knew what she was thinking even before she said it.

'If we don't get this right, Jamie, the whole project could go down the pan.'

He nodded again. 'How's Paula?'

'She's got a nice set of finger marks round her throat, but she doesn't want to make a complaint either.'

'Great.' Carver tipped his head back to look up at the sky. It was cloudy. No stars.

The one thing Carver didn't have right now was time to spend trying to keep the project afloat. Rita was the most dedicated Case Worker he'd ever come across. But if things went bad, she would need his full support in getting them back on track. He turned back to her. 'Stay with the girls. I need to speak with Stuart.'

He found Stuart Lee in the front bedroom, sitting on the marital bed that people quipped ought to be doing time for all the trouble it had caused. He was still resisting the efforts of the two paramedics, a man and woman, to let them take him to hospital to get checked out. They both looked pissed off. A uniformed sergeant and another detective were doing their best to lend weight to the paramedics' pleas. As Carver entered they all seemed to take a step back.

'I tell you. I'm fucking okay. It's only a scratch.'

The slurred speech and wild expression told Carver he was still under the influence of whatever he'd taken. It wasn't going to be easy.

Seeing Carver, Stuart renewed his resistance. 'T'ank God you're here, Mr Carver. Tell 'em I'm okay. I don't need 'em.'

Carver leaned in, saw the blooded tee-shirt on the floor, the dressing the medics had managed to put over the wound in his side. It was still seeping. 'You need to go to Hospital, Stuart. If you slip off the plate, Kayleigh will be in big trouble.'

Anguish flooded his dark features. 'No-no-no. It wasn't her fault. She's a good girl.' He appealed to Carver. 'You won't let them take her, will you Mr Carver? Your boys want to lock her up but I told 'em, "No." She was just looking after her Ma, that's all.' He tried to stand, shrugging off the medic's efforts to help. He turned towards the door.

Carver stepped forward and raised his voice. 'Look at me, Stuart.' He managed to grab his attention. 'My boys will do what I tell them to do. Right now I need you to behave. If you go to the hospital, I'll sort things out here.'

He calmed some, eyes narrowing as if gauging how far he could trust the man who'd arrested him more times than Carver cared to remember. Not that pissed then, Carver thought.

'Do you swear, Mr Carver? Swear you won't let them take my Kayleigh away.'

Carver looked him in the eye. 'I promise I won't let them take Kayleigh away.'

'In that case I'll go. But I want to speak to me family first.' Turning to the door he shouted down the stairs. 'I CALL A CONFERENCE.'

Carver groaned, inside. 'Now's not the time Stuart. We need to get you to Hospital. You can do all that when you get back.'

He sat back down on the bed. 'I'm not going anywhere until we've had, a FUCKING CONFERENCE.'

Carver checked the medic's faces. They looked

bewildered. He wasn't surprised.

The right to call a Family Conference was one of the project's key underpinning principles. Any family member, kids included, could do so at any time. If one was called, everyone else was obliged to attend. He weighed options. If Stuart's injuries were serious, a struggle could see him off. Right now he appeared to be holding up. He gave an exasperated shrug.

'Okay. But it'll be short. Then you're off to hospital.'

Ten minutes later Carver stood in the kitchen, watching, with the same sense of disbelief as always, the weird phenomenon that was a Lee Family Conference.

Twelve months ago, if someone had suggested that a family like the Lees would one day sit round a table talking about their problems like some debating society, Carver would have called them crazy. Now, as he listened to Stuart Lee baring his soul and seeking his family's forgiveness for the behaviour that had brought the Project closer to disaster than at any time since it began, he wondered how much stranger things could get. As amazing as the actual 'conference' itself, was the fact that despite the events of that evening, they were still, largely, playing by the rules. At that moment, Stuart was holding up a green plastic card. It meant he had the floor, and while the card stayed up, no one could interrupt. Around the table Carver could see at least two other members of the family, Billy and Izzie, the next eldest girl after Kayleigh, holding up orange cards. At the head of the table, Rita, acting as chair, nodded to show that she had noted their wish to speak.

Carver still had no idea whether Rita's novel approach to sorting out the family's deep-rooted communication problems had anything more than a snowball's chance in hell of continuing in the longer term. Part of him still suspected that what he was seeing was simply the rational response of a group of devious individuals who recognised that as long as they showed they were willing to 'play the game,' they would continue to receive the support – and associated benefits – that came with inclusion in, The Troubled Families Programme. He often wondered what sort of mayhem erupted after the likes of Rita and he departed. That said, according to Kayleigh, conferences had taken place with only family present - and more or less according to the rules.

When Rita had first outlined the concept, everyone - family, other agency staff even Carver himself, though privately - had derided the idea. Carver's first thoughts were that it was just another example of the sort of liberal theorising social workers come up with from time to time. The disasters that were Rita's first attempts at 'family conferencing' supported that view. But then, over the space of a few weeks - Rita was unshakeable in her belief she could get it to work - Carver was amazed to see changes taking place. As the family as a whole started to grasp that in order to stand any chance at all of addressing their own problems - emotional, practical and financial - they had to learn to communicate. And they had to do it in a way so that everyone, from eldest to youngest, had a voice. He'd confessed to being 'gob-smacked' the day he turned up at Carnegie Avenue to find everyone apart from Russell - away doing his Community Service - sitting around and holding up coloured cards as they waited their turn to speak. Of course there were some - mainly those not directly involved with the Project - prepared to state that the whole thing was a, 'load of crap' and that the Lees were merely acting out a charade to keep the Police and combined Social Services off their back. Time would tell. For now, Carver was willing to go with anything that kept things on any sort of even keel.

At that moment, having spent the last five minutes describing the pressure he'd felt himself under these past few weeks, Stuart Lee paused in his mea-culpa and lowered his green card. Rita nodded to Izzie, who raised hers.

'I want to say, it's not just you, Dad that's under pressure. Mum's under pressure too. She's the one has to argue with you every night to stop you going out and getting pissed.'

Stuart half-rose and started to open his mouth to respond, but Rita stopped him with a raised finger. 'Ah-ah.'

As Stuart sank back, Carver shook his head. Incredible. Izzie continued.

'And that applies to the rest of us as well. We've all been trying hard.' She turned to send her eldest brother a pointed look. Her voice lowered. 'Even him.'

'What's that mean?' Russell said, trying to sound innocent.

'You know,' Izzie said, her tone accusing.

On the surface, relations between the older kids – boys and girls – seemed much improved. But Carver was aware of the undercurrents. Some of the old tensions were still there. He had his thoughts on their origins, but resisted probing. There were enough bags of worms as it was.

'And I just want to say that if Kayleigh hadn't done

what she did, Mum would be dead right now.'

The other girls joined in a chorus of, 'Yeah's.

As Izzie lowered her green card, Rita nodded to Billy.

'You've all got to stop having a go at Dad. He's the one who said we should do all this in the first place.'

Or face prison, Carver thought.

'We've all said things are better now than they were.' Billy turned to Kayleigh. So far she'd said nothing. 'I don't blame you for what you did to Dad. You had to do something.' He turned to look round at Carver. 'And if the Police try to have a go at you, it just shows what I've always said. They'd rather just see us all put away.'

Carver stayed silent. As an outsider he had no voice. But Billy was right. Carver knew plenty who thought exactly that.

As Billy lowered his card, silence fell for the first time since they'd gathered. Carver knew why. They were waiting. He knew what for. Eventually, Kayleigh cleared her throat. About to speak, she remembered, and lifted her card.

'Billy's right. Everyone's been trying really, really, hard. But there's still too much sniping going on. I know why, and I understand it.' At this point she stared, hard, at the table, as if to stop herself looking at certain faces. 'But that's all in the past and none of us want to see it being dragged up again now.' Carver shot a glance at Russell. His face was puce. 'The bottom line is, if we want Rita to keep doing what she's been doing.' Her eyes flicked towards Carver. 'And Mr Carver too, then we have to try harder to help each other when we know someone is struggling. Like Dad tonight. We should have called a conference before he went out, not after.'

Stuart Lee started nodding, suddenly sage-like. 'Whatever happens now we've all got to stick together. There are those will say that what happened tonight was typical Lees. Always trying to kill each other. They'll try to use it to close us down. We mustn't let that happen.' She turned to her father. 'I'm sorry for what I did to Dad, but I don't regret it. I'll always defend any member of my family, even if it's from other family. And for all that's been said, the police haven't arrested anyone, and I don't think they're going to. Are you Mr Carver?'

As every head turned to see Carver's response, his thought was, *You crafty little bugger.*

Carver slid the hand-written document bearing Kayleigh Lee's signature into the buff folder containing the statements that had been taken from the other family members, and sat back in his chair. He checked his watch. Ten past six. Too late to think about going back to bed. He rubbed at his eyes. Nearly done. When he opened them again he found Kayleigh's steady gaze, waiting. For several seconds he returned her stare, letting her see he had nothing to hide. Carver thought that by now, Kayleigh was close to believing she could trust him. Probably around ninety percent. The missing ten was the legacy of what she and her family had received from the police over the years. He would love to see the scale reach the hundred mark, but there was a limit to what he could do. Only time and experience would bring that about. Tonight would be a big test. Eventually he saw her take a deep breath.

'So you're saying, that's it? There'll be no come-backs after tonight?'

He nodded. 'No come-backs.'

'Don't you have to report it to someone? The CPS?'

So on the ball. 'They'll go with my recommendation. They're part of the project as well, remember'

'And my Dad won't be done for attacking mum?'

'So long as your mum doesn't want it.'

'And if she changes her mind?'

He gave a reassuring smile. 'If she did, I think that would be the end of it all, don't you?'

She thought about it. 'S'pose…'

He waited, giving her time. 'Anything else?'

She thought again. 'No. I guess not.'

He made to rise.

'Are you married?'

He stopped.

'What?'

'Are you married? Like, are you with someone?'

He frowned, not annoyed, just puzzled. 'I'm not married, but yes, I'm with someone.'

'Boy or girl?'

He gave a half-smile. 'Girl. Why?'

'Just wondered.'

'Anything else?'

She shook her head.

He rose again.

'Where do you live?'

He looked down at her.

'Over the river. A place called Pickmere.'

'I know it. There's a lake there isn't there?'

'Yes.'

'I went swimming there once. With some friends.'

'Right.'

'Is it nice? Living there I mean?'

'I like it.'

'I bet it's a lot nicer than here?'

He smiled at her, feeling the tug again. 'I think you know the answer to that.'

She thought about it. 'I guess...' He turned to go. 'Mr Carver?' He turned back. Her eyes bore into his. 'Thanks.'

Something about the way she said it prompted him to glance across at Rita, sitting in as 'responsible adult'. Rita's eyes were narrowed, as if she'd just seen something ever-so-slightly worrying. He turned back to the fifteen-year-old girl who was looking at him in a way that was suddenly making him feel uncomfortable.

'No problem.'

CHAPTER 16

Jess sat at the kitchen table where twenty-four hours earlier they'd waited for Megan Crane. This time she was watching her brew coffee. The break in conversation had given Jess the chance to flesh out her sketchy impression from the day before, and she was determined to make the most of it. When the woman produced a bottle of brandy, seeking Jess's approval to, 'Add a splash, just to liven things up,' Jess nodded and smiled. Brandy wasn't her favourite, but right now anything that might keep things ticking along better than last time was fine by her.

When she'd arrived, she hadn't been surprised to find the woman looking as immaculate as the day before. She guessed that the cream, silk top, yellow skirt and pearls combination was probably Megan Crane's idea of, 'casual'. It was Saturday after all. The gold stilettos were gone, but only in favour of a cream pair that matched her top. Only their second meeting, Jess already felt confident enough to predict the woman didn't do slippers - not unless they were the sort with four-inch heels. It was another fine day. The sun streaming into the kitchen bounced off its shiny surfaces and sent sunbeams dancing through Megan Crane's hair in a way that made Jess wonder about her own care-regime.

She was already seeing her host in a different light. The day before, she'd have summarised her impression in two words. Cold Bitch. Today, she was all warmth and smiles. It had begun with the friendly-but-firm handshake and ready smile which Jess read as, 'Let's start again.' She reinforced it when she invited Jess to, 'Please, call me Megan.'

'And I'm Jess,' she'd responded, already sensing the anxieties that had gnawed at her on the way there draining away. It continued over coffee and the chocolate cake Jess suspected she must have bought that morning from somewhere and which made her wonder, *Why?* When Jess began with a rambling expression of regret for any 'misunderstanding' that may have taken place the day before - in reality a disguised but clear enough apology for Carver's crassness - the woman waved it away.

'I'm used to it. People often find it hard to put their thoughts into words when they meet me for the first time. Considering my interests, it's not surprising they sometimes get the wrong idea.'

It was one of the few nods she'd made to the side to her character that had brought them to her door. So far, most of the conversation had been of the, 'getting to know each other,' variety. Prompted by Megan's questions, Jess had shared more about herself than she normally did with those she met through work. She hoped her description of her conventional Sussex upbringing hadn't sounded too, 'Jolly Hockey Sticks', though she had to admit that the learning curve since joining the police had probably been steeper than most.

She was more guarded, or tried to be, when conversation turned to Carver and she found herself defending him.

'Actually, Jamie's very open-minded. Yesterday wasn't like him at all.'

But while the 'Jamie' was deliberate, she realised she may have overplayed things when Megan Crane gave a knowing smile. 'You sound like you're his biggest fan. Are you two…?'

Jess was quick to scotch the idea - 'Definitely not' - but tried not to over-react to something the mischief-makers on the team liked to put about now and again.

For her part, Megan spoke of her own, more worldly upbringing. Born in Cheltenham, of a Welsh mother and French father, she'd spent much of her school years in Paris, where her father ran a cabaret club in the Montmartre district. Returning to England in her late teens, she'd worked as a dancer and model before meeting, 'Someone who changed my life forever.' At this point she also became guarded, eventually turning the conversation back to the reason for Jess's return visit. By now Jess felt sufficiently at ease to press on.

'Whatever impression we gave yesterday, we're only interested in your safety. Yes, we hope you can help us, but we're also trying to stop more women being killed.' She made sure to avoid the, 'like you,' phrase.

When Megan reached across and laid her hand, softly, on hers, Jess felt it like an electric charge. Personal contact was the last thing she'd expected. She hoped her blush wasn't too noticeable, but didn't move her hand away.

'I believe you,' Megan said. 'But please, understand. It's hard for me to open up to others in the way you ask.

The things I do, the people I spend time with. These are very private matters. My friends value that privacy highly. The idea of me working alongside the police raises all sorts of possible complications.'

Jess wanted to ask, *What complications*? *Who are these 'friends'?* What she said was, 'Believe me Megan, Jamie and I understand that. We'd be sure to be discreet.' She hesitated, not sure whether to mention it. 'If it helps, I can tell you Jamie's got experience handling cases like this. He was involved in one before that was quite sensitive and got a lot of publicity. He does understand your concerns.'

At first, Megan Crane looked doubtful. But then her face began to change, slowly, as if something was dawning on her.

'I read an article in a magazine a few years ago. I think it was one of the Sunday papers. It was about a police investigation into some murders. I think they were- escort girls?' Jess nodded, seeing an opening. 'It was all about the detective in charge?'

Jess nodded again. 'He wasn't actually in charge but he played an important part.'

At once, Megan's face reflected interest. 'Oh my God, was that him?' Another nod from Jess. 'I remember it now. Some people I know were scared out of their wits at the time. There was a killer... I'll remember his name in a minute. Hunt? Something like that?

'Hart. Edmund Hart.'

'That was it. And your Jamie was the detective who caught him?'

'Yes.'

'Good God. I see what you mean now about him being experienced. And wasn't there something about another case before that one?'

'The Ancoats Rapist.'

'Yes,' Megan Crane jumped in. 'I had friends who lived there. We followed that one as well.'

'They both got a lot of publicity. That's why the papers were interested. The article was supposed to be about running a major police investigation. But as time went on it focused more on Jamie.'

'How interesting. And I assume he did well out of it, career-wise I mean.'

Jess shook her head. 'He hated the whole thing. In fact I'd suggest you don't mention it. He's still sensitive about it.'

'Why? From what I remember it was quite complimentary about him.'

'Hmm…Too much so, some thought.'

'What do you mean?'

Jess was conscious they were drifting into an area she'd rather avoid. But having said as much, she felt she had to see it through. 'There were some who thought it played up his role at the expense of others.'

'Ah.' Megan lifted her head and gave another of the knowing looks Jess was becoming used to. 'Jealousy.'

'Maybe.'

'If there's a subject I know a lot about, it's jealousy.'

Jess gave a wry smile. 'I can believe that.' She was beginning to sense that beneath the gloss was a woman it would be interesting to get to know. But she'd also noted that Megan hadn't balked when she'd spoken about maybe meeting Jamie again. Another good sign. Time to make the pitch. But before she could carry on Megan Crane rose from her chair saying, 'Before we go any further, I need another coffee.' Which was when

Jess took the chance to expand on her impression of her from the day before.

A few minutes later, as Megan returned to the table with freshly-charged mugs, she was wearing the same smile as the day before when she'd sat on the sofa, waiting for Carver to begin.

By now Jess felt confident enough to ask. 'Why the smile?'

The look changed to a guilty one. 'I'm sorry, I know I shouldn't, but I find it amusing when I know someone is trying to figure me out.'

Jess almost spluttered a mouthful of her coffee back into the mug. 'Was it that obvious?'

The light touch again, her arm this time. 'Don't worry. I'm used to it.'

'I'm sorry, it's just that-'

'You've never met someone like me before?'

'No, I haven't.'

'I get that a lot.'

Not sure where the conversation was heading, Jess decided it was time to get down to business. 'Can we go back to where we were yesterday, before-?' She left it unfinished. 'Is there anything I can do that will reassure you that you've nothing to fear from us?'

Megan Crane lowered her gaze to her mug. She stayed like that for almost a minute. Jess waited, wondering what sort of thoughts, fears maybe, were going through her mind. Eventually she lifted her head, and their eyes met. For long seconds Jess held her gaze. Again, she had no idea what she was thinking, or looking for, but this time she was determined not to look away, despite the strange sensations the woman's scrutiny was again triggering inside her.

Eventually Megan Crane sat back. In a wary voice she said, 'If I did agree to help. How would it work?'

Later Jess would look back at that moment and wonder how she managed to stop herself punching the air.

CHAPTER 17

Out in the smoking area at the back of the restaurant, Carver waited with the whiskies as his father lit his post-dinner cigar. He knew what was coming. Sure enough, as Peter Carver blew smoke away over his shoulder, he fixed his son with the stare Carver imagined he used to use on his old Command Team when he wanted them to think he knew something they didn't. As Carver handed him his drink he said, 'How's Kerry coming along?'

Carver was grateful. At least he'd waited until after dinner. He'd sensed his father champing the moment they'd arrived. A six-years-retired Chief Constable, he always asked after his son's cases. It wasn't always professional curiosity. From the day Carver was appointed constable, his father was settled in his view that his son should one day rise to the same dizzy heights as himself. Not that he ever put it as openly as that. Next to The Duke, Carver Senior was the slyest operator Carver knew. Still unsure how much to share, Carver lifted his glass and checked the malt's colouring. Eventually he said, 'Slowly.'

His father nodded. 'What's it been? Four months since the last one?'

Carver sipped his drink. 'Three and a half.'

Another nod. 'Remind me of the intervals?'

'Four months. Roughly.'

'Hmmm.'

Carver waited. It was like being tied to a railway track, watching the train approaching.

'Last time, you mentioned something about a possible lead? Some photographer?'

Carver nodded. 'We're still looking at him. I'm not convinced. I could be wrong.'

Carver senior pointed at him. 'That's good. Always keep an open mind.'

'Thanks, Dad. I'll remember that.'

The flash in the older man's eyes reminded Carver how his father hated being patronised. Another reason why his ambitions would probably never match his father's. *What happens to their sense of humour?*

'Any other developments?'

The question Carver had hoped wouldn't come. His father was the one person he could never lie to.

'We're looking at potential victims. Seeing if they can tell us anything.'

The glass stopped halfway to his father's mouth.

'How are you identifying them?'

Knew it. 'There's a magazine. One of those contact journals. We think they're in it.'

'You *think* they're in it?'

'They're in it.'

'So are you… Have you approached any of them?'

'Actually, I met one yesterday.'

His father's head lifted, slowly, as if he'd just been told something significant. 'And… how did it go?'

Carver met his gaze head on. 'She wasn't expecting

us.'

'I should bloody well hope not. How was she?'

'Undecided. But I think she'll come around, eventually.'

'Is she one of these… dominatrices?'

Carver nodded.

They sipped their whiskeys

'Everyman's fantasy, I suppose?'

'Not everyman's.'

'Yours?'

Carver looked at his father over the rim of his glass. He could barely believe he'd asked. 'No.'

In the silence that followed, Carver thought about heading back inside. Rosanna had met his mother and older sister once before, but this was her first time with Sally – the family's problem child. But he decided against. Best deal with it now.

After a while his father said, 'What makes you think she'll come round, 'eventually'?'

'Because she'll realise it's in her interests.'

'How will that happen?'

'I'll convince her.'

'*You'll* convince her?' His eyes bore into his son's face, searching for information.

Carver sighed. 'Me. Or someone else. It doesn't matter.'

'Maybe someone else would be better.'

'Stop it, Dad.'

'Stop what?'

'You know.'

'I'm only thinking what's best for you.'

'I know you are, but-'

'We don't want another episode like-'

'DAD.'

The older man jumped so he almost spilt his drink.

'What?'

'Leave it. It's nothing to do with you.'

Carver senior opened his mouth to say something, but saw the look in his son's face and stopped. For long seconds the man for whom one successful career would never be enough stared at his son. He changed the subject. 'Any news on your board date yet?'

Carver gave a wry smile before replying. Their team's biggest match in Europe in a decade was three days away, and still all he could talk about was shop.

'Next month. The twenty sixth.'

'That's a bit short notice.'

'Tell me about it.'

The older man hesitated, as if sensing his son's mood. 'If I can help with anything, just let me know.'

'I will. Thanks.'

Carver Senior stubbed out his cigar and drained the last of his whisky before turning to his son.

'All I'm saying is, be careful.'

'I intend to be.'

They headed back inside.

Later, back at the converted farmhouse his parents had moved to after his father's retirement, Carver looked up from his undressing to find Rosanna sitting up in bed, giving him, The Stare. They were in the room his mother liked to call, 'Jamie's Room', though he'd never lived there.

'What?'

She swept her hair back off her face. In the low light he could see why his father said she reminded him of the old Italian actress, Gina Lollobrigida.

'What did you and your father talk about?'

Carver hesitated. 'Guess.'

'The case?'

He nodded, then shook his head. 'He never changes.' He stepped out of his trousers.

'He worries about you.'

'I know.'

'I worry about you.'

He sat next to her, took her face in his hands. 'I know.' He kissed her on the lips, lightly.

She searched his face for signs. 'Remember, Jamie Carver. You are a good man.'

'You think?'

'I think.'

'Tell him that.'

'He doesn't need me to tell him. He knows already.'

As Carver drank in her beauty, the feelings that were never far when they were together stirred. Shifting position, he buried his fingers in her hair, luxuriating in its thickness. He kissed her, again, deeper. As she responded, he threw back the duvet, and they fell back onto the bed. Suddenly she stopped, pulled her mouth from his.

'They will hear,' she whispered.

Carver stopped, listening to the silence. His parents' room was down the corridor, a bathroom between them.

'Fuck 'em.'

About to start again, his mobile beeped a message alert. He stopped. *Fuck.* He leaned over to the bedside table, checked the screen.

It was from Jess. *Can you speak?*

Turning to the woman still half under him, he made

a, 'sorry' face. She rolled her eyes, dramatically. He slipped off her, sat on the edge of the bed.

He had Jess on speed dial. As soon as she answered he said, 'What's up?' Hearing her take a deep breath, his thought was she was about to tell him there'd been another murder. He was wrong.

'Sorry to disturb you so late, Jamie, but I went to see Meg- the Crane woman again this afternoon. We talked. She's prepared to come on board. But she wants to see you, asap. Like in, tomorrow?'

Carver stared at the floor. Behind him, Rosanna lay, waiting. But the only thing registering in his brain at that moment was the echo of the words, *she wants to see you.*

'Jamie? Did you get that? I said I went to-'

'I heard. What happened? You two have a girly chat?'

'Something like that. What do you want to do?'

He checked the time. Just gone midnight. He turned to Rosanna. She was already reading him. His heart sank at the thought of yet another weekend cut short. But he couldn't risk a change of heart.

'I'll see you at the nick at eight.' He checked back with Rosanna. Read her face. 'Make that nine. You can tell me about it on the way.'

'Right.' There was a pause, then, 'You don't mind I went to see her do you?'

He hoped the hesitation before he answered was brief enough she didn't notice. 'No, I'd probably have suggested it anyway.' And he couldn't tell if the noise he heard was a relieved sigh or just static on the line. 'I'll see you tomorrow. And Jess?'

'Yes?'

'Well done.'

She hung up.

Carver stared at his phone. For twenty-four hours, he'd managed to keep all thoughts of Megan Crane at bay. Now her face hovered before his eyes, mocking, alluring. Inviting.

Jess had said she was willing to cooperate, which meant the door to her world was about to open for them. Where would it lead, he wondered? Deep down, another memory stirred. Despite his efforts, he couldn't stop it breaking through.

A crowded court room. In the dock a tall figure, resisting the flanking security officers trying to drag him down to the cells. A look of hate, aimed squarely at Carver. The shouted words that reflected that hate in every syllable. 'YOU'RE DEAD, CARVER. YOU AND THAT OTHER BITCH. WHATEVER HAPPENS TO ME, YOU'RE BOTH DEAD.'

And as the memory of Edmund Hart's cursings echoed in his head - they'd been doing so more and more of late - the knot inside Carver's stomach tightened another notch. Closing his eyes, he forced himself back to the present. He turned to Rosanna. He opened his mouth to speak but she placed a finger across them.

'Don't.'

Her eyes sent their message. Forcing his mind back to where it was before Jess's message, he slid his arms under and round her. She wrapped her legs round him and their mouths melded, tongues, playing, probing. He felt himself responding again.

Thank God.

He never gave a thought as to why Jess had left it so late to call.

CHAPTER 18

Thirty minutes in, Carver thought his second meeting with Megan Crane was going a whole lot better than the first. Conversation was cordial, if not exactly friendly, and she seemed better disposed towards their mission than at the end of their last encounter. So far everything seemed to bear out what Jess had told him on the way there. That whatever the reason for Megan Crane's turn-around – she'd given no clue - she was now willing to help their cause as much as she could, within reason. There was just one problem. Every time he looked at her.

By now, Carver was certain that her decision to take the sofa directly opposite, rather than the chair where she'd sat last time, was a calculated one. The same for the above-the-knee black skirt that went so well with her blouse. Each time he looked up, he couldn't help but notice what it wasn't covering. He suspected it was a test. So far, he thought he'd done a fair job of not failing it. No wandering eyes. No knowing looks or half-smiles. No jokey-allusions of the, 'view from here' variety. She would take any of those as a sign of weakness. A susceptibility to being manipulated. And the last thing he needed was her thinking she could manipulate him.

He focused again on the matter under discussion.

'This 'wide circle of friends', you mentioned?'

'What about it?'

'Dare I ask, how many is 'wide'?'

There was a hint of a smile. 'You can ask, but I won't say.'

Great. But it was within the rules. At the beginning he'd agreed they wouldn't press for details of what she referred to as her, 'circle,' unless there was good reason. That reason was yet to show itself.

'Fair enough, but we do need to know about any new or recent contacts. One of them could be the killer.'

'Define 'recent''

He thought about it. 'The past twelve, maybe fifteen, months.' He was tempted to say longer, but it would do for starters. She would be more willing to reveal recent contacts.

Like him, she thought on it. 'There are a couple. I'm happy to give you their details.'

'Good. What we need is-'

'Before we go further, can you explain something?'

'If I can.'

'Out of all the listings in the magazine, you seem to be focusing on me. Why is that? Presumably the killer could choose anyone?'

Carver turned to Jess, nodded. Reaching down, she fished in her case for the magazine, handed it to him. Carver sat forward, conscious that by doing so, his view was considerably improved. He spread it open on the coffee table between them. She leaned forward. He pointed at one of the photographs. Next to it was a star, penned in red.

'Do you know her?'

'No.'

Flicking through the booklet he stopped at another photo, also starred. 'This one?'

'No.'

A third. 'Her?'

'No.'

He nodded. 'They're the last three victims. The first was in an earlier edition.'

Megan Crane's hand went to her mouth. Some of her colour drained.

'You saw the stars?'

She nodded. The 'Yes' was barely a whisper.

He turned to her picture again. This time he made sure she saw the star next to it.

'The only photos that are starred, are the victims, and you. This is a copy of the original magazine that came into our possession. It's now with our forensic people. The stars were already there.'

Her eyes widened. 'Oh my God.'

He waited, letting it sink in. Then the questions began to tumble out.

'How did you come by it? Did the killer send it to you? What does it mean? Why me?'

He tried to reassure her, explaining how the magazine had arrived through the post, addressed to him personally. 'We don't think it came from the killer. Why tell us how he's choosing his victims, who he's thinking of targeting next? More likely it was sent by someone who is close enough to him or the circle he moves in to know, or at least suspect, something.'

'So whoever sent it could have got it off the killer?'

'Possibly. Or someone is trying to second-guess him

and wants to tip us off.'

'But why would the killer, or someone else, pick me out as a possible victim?'

'We can't answer that. All we know is that on the face of it, your entry is similar to the others. It's one of the things we hope you might be able to help us with. You may even know or be connected with the victims in some way.'

She shook her head, slowly, staring down at the booklet, mind working. 'If I am, I'm not aware of it. I certainly don't know any of them.' She looked up, caught Carver's eye. 'I'm sorry,' she said.

Carver squashed his disappointment. But there were still other ways she could help.

'If you can take it, I'd like to show you how the victims died. It may mean something to you.'

Her eyes widened again. She swallowed, gave a cautious nod. 'Okay.'

'I have to warn you. It's not pretty.'

She gave him a square look. 'I've seen plenty of things most people might find hard to stomach.'

'Violent death?'

'Staged, yes. But not real.'

'What I'm about to show you is very real.'

She took a deep breath followed by a good slug of whiskey. 'I'm ready.'

Carver opened the folder on the table so she could see. Amongst the papers was a booklet of photographs. He picked it up and was about to pass it across when he hesitated. Showing photos like these to someone outside the investigation was normally a no-no, for all sorts of reasons. He'd done it only once before, during the Hart case - another parallel. To his right, he could sense

Jess's breathless stare. They both knew it was a risk. But they'd agreed. He handed the booklet across.

'These show the victims as the killer left them. As you'll see, it's all *very* 'staged'. Tell us if any of it means anything to you.'

As Megan Crane opened the booklet and her eyes lit on the first picture, she didn't so much react as simply freeze, to the point where it was hard to tell if she was even breathing. As Carver watched her staring down at what, for all he knew, might be the first dead body she'd ever seen, he found it impossible to gauge what was going through her mind. Her face was a blank mask, lips slightly parted. There were none of the facial reactions - anguish, horror, fear - most people exposed to such images for the first time might register. But then Megan Crane wasn't 'most people'. Nevertheless, he noted the tiny movements above her jaw. She was grinding her teeth the way some do when they are trying to mask emotion. Slowly, she turned to the next picture. There was one sharp intake of breath, then she resumed her almost detached, perusal. For a full ten minutes there was only silence. As Megan Crane studied the photographs, Carver and Jess watched for signs of recognition or insight. None came. After giving the last picture the same lengthy study as the rest, Megan Crane closed the booklet and placed it back on the coffee table. Lifting her head, she closed her eyes and took several long breaths, as if purging herself of contamination from looking at the booklet's repellent contents. Eventually, she returned her gaze to Carver.

'The way- The way they are posed-' Carver waited. *Anything would be good.* 'It's not dissimilar to the sort of thing you find in fetish magazines, or thousands of web sites.'

Carver's heart sank. Her words were no surprise. Like others, he'd done the research. But he'd hoped that being an, 'expert', she might offer *something*.

'That said-'

'Yes?'

'The way they are posed, as if they're praying. I assume that's where this 'Worshipping' thing comes from?'

Carver read her face. 'You've seen it before?'

'I'm not certain. It *feels* familiar, but I'm not sure why, or where from.' She looked at them, both. 'Tell me about the hands.'

They said it together. 'Superglued.'

She nodded, as if confirming something in her mind. 'I seem to remember either hearing or reading something. It would be a few years ago now. It was about using glue as a restraint, in place of rope. And how it could be dangerous because it can cause burns. I think someone had tried it and were talking about how long it took to un-stick themselves. It wasn't recommended.'

'I can imagine. Can you remember who you heard it from, where you read it?'

She closed her eyes, searching for it. 'It's not there. But give me time. I'll probably remember the moment you leave.'

Carver gave her a cautious look. So far she'd managed to avoid naming any of her 'circle'.

'I swear, I'm not holding back. Believe me, if I can remember who it was, I'll tell you.'

He nodded. 'It could be important.'

She pinned him with a look. 'If I promise to do

something, Jamie, you can count on me doing it.'

He returned her gaze. *Message received.* But he noted one thing. For the first time, she'd called him by name.

As they continued, Carver sensed things becoming more relaxed, the bottle of single malt she'd opened soon after they arrived, also playing its part. Over the next hour, he revealed more about the four murders than he had to anyone outside the enquiry team. Personal information about the victims, their habits and interests, details of the killer's MO. When he mentioned the black-ribbon garrotte, she nodded again.

'It's another common motif in BDSM. I've seen it used many times. Sometimes unwisely.'

'In what way?' Jess said.

Megan looked at them. 'I take it you know about erotic asphyxiation?'

'We do now,' Jess said.

'To practice it safely, you've got to know what you're doing. You also need to know your partner. I've met subs who like to be taken right to the edge, to the point where they black out. To do that they need a partner they can rely on to stop before damage occurs. I've known plenty who would love to take things further, a lot further, if they were given half a chance.' She gave Carver a direct look. 'They're the sort who end up killing someone. You've probably met some.'

He nodded. 'A couple.'

There was another short silence. Jess broke it. 'So our killer is likely to be someone like that? Someone who doesn't know when to stop?'

Megan held Carver's gaze another moment, before turning to her. 'Possibly, but it doesn't necessarily follow. I'm sure you must have someone… one of those… What do you call them? They're in all the TV crime dramas...'

'Profiler?' Jess said.

'Forensic Psychologist,' Carver corrected.

'Them. What does your profiler say?'

Carver hummed, careful not to sound disparaging. 'He's keeping his options open.'

'Can I ask if the killer ejaculates? That would give an indication.'

'It would, and from a DNA point of view it would be a big help if he did. But so far we've found no fresh traces of body fluids of any sort. If the killer ejaculates then he does a good job of cleaning up after, or he takes it away with him.'

They talked further about what, if anything Megan could draw from the killer's method. But she was wary about speculating too far.

'It could just be a show. What if the killer is staging the whole thing to cover up something else?'

'Like what?'

'I don't know. Maybe he just hates dominatrices and likes to make them suffer.'

'We've considered that as well.'

'Of course you have. I'm sorry. I'm not being very helpful.'

'Don't worry,' Carver said. 'I'm sure you will be. In other ways.'

They turned their attention to DOM magazine, its contributors, subscribers, circulation. Jess had a question.

'I thought all this contact stuff is done online these days? Why use a magazine that relies on snail-mail that can take weeks, when you can make contact with someone right away?'

Megan gave a patient smile. 'People like me aren't interested in casual, short term, relationships. Like I said, I'm not a prostitute.' She said it so matter-of-factly, Carver was happy it wasn't a dig. 'The internet is full of time-wasters. People who just want sex, or who've got something to hide. That's why it's so dangerous. DOM is for those who genuinely want to meet someone they can develop a relationship with. Someone you can get to know, and trust. It requires openness and honesty. You're more likely to find that in someone who's willing to write a letter and give a name and address. No, the internet is too easy. Too anonymous.'

Jess nodded. 'Sounds logical.'

'Some of the subscribers are professionals of course. You are right about that.' Carver made sure not to look smug. 'But most are simply interested in finding like-minded individuals. Without having to stoop to payment, or run the risk of being discovered in a place of ill-repute.'

Carver quashed the impulse to smile, saw Jess doing the same. There were times when her phrasing was almost puritan.

As the afternoon drew out, Megan rustled up a platter of sandwiches and they talked over it. Carver returned to the subject of her recent contacts. 'I know you're reluctant, but I am going to have to ask for their details.'

For what seemed like minutes, Megan's eyes bored into his. He hardly blinked. She seemed to be going through the same decision-making process as the day before. 'Wait a minute.'

Rising, she went through to the kitchen. A door opened, then closed. Carver and Jess waited in silence. When she returned she was clutching a handful of papers which she cradled in her lap, protectively. Carver remembered her assertion of two days before. *I don't keep records.* Nice bluff.

'Let me be clear. I won't give you copies of anything unless you force me to. I mean, legally.' Carver nodded his agreement. She took a deep breath. 'You might want to make notes?'

Jess took out her notepad and sat, poised, like a secretary at a board meeting.

Megan Crane talked, guardedly at first, but then more freely. For the most part, the detectives listened in silence, interrupting only where some detail needed clarifying. Jess noted names, places, details. Occasionally, Megan referred to the papers in her lap, but mostly spoke from memory. Jess scribbled to keep up. They had been talking for close to thirty minutes when Megan gave a name that struck Carver like a thunderbolt. He didn't flinch and Jess managed to keep writing without pausing.

The light dimmed as the afternoon gave way to early evening, then a grey dusk. Jess switched on the table lamp next to her so she could see. For a long time it was the only light in the house.

Carver never gave the view from the sofa another thought.

CHAPTER 19

By the time Alec Duncan poked his head round The Duke's door, the fireworks had died down and the meeting was in the throes of breaking up. The six participants had already split into pairs, discussing what had emerged.

Carver was talking to Mike Frayne, the Surveillance Unit DI, about requirements for the meetings that were to be set up between Megan Crane and her would-be 'companions'

Shepherd, still agitated over Carver's startling revelation concerning William Cosworth had gone straight for The Duke, though the big man was having none of it. He'd agreed with Carver's assertion that arresting Cosworth just because he'd contacted Megan Crane through the pages of 'DOM!' would be premature, and, most probably, counter-productive. As Carver had argued, 'Evidence-wise it doesn't mean anything and unless we know we can get something on him when we arrest him, we would simply be letting him know we are looking at him. If he's our man, then it'll only make him harder to catch in the future.' Despite Shepherd's offer to, 'Bring him in and bleed him,' The Duke had agreed with Carver. Letting him meet with

Megan, like the others, offered the best chance he might show his hand – assuming he had one to show. Frustrated, Shepherd had spent the rest of the meeting twiddling a pencil around his fingers like some practising cheerleader, and drumming them on the table.

Jess had been cornered by Doctor Ewan Cleeves, the team's sometime 'Profiler'. The visiting Professor in Forensic Psychology at Salford University showed up now and again to offer what 'insights' he could into those the inquiry considered, 'of interest'. He had seemed particularly interested in Megan Crane and was eager to hear more. Like The Duke, Carver's expectations of what Cleeves could bring to the team weren't high, and so far he hadn't disappointed. He thought Cleeves's analysis of Cosworth was particularly bland, with nothing in it he couldn't have come up with himself. To Carver it was just another nail in the coffin of the much-over-hyped role of the Criminal Profiler people read about in books or see on TV. That said, Carver never ruled anything out. If Cleeves was to come up with something that sounded promising, he'd be more than happy to run with it. He'd just be surprised was all.

Jess was wondering if Cleeves's interest in the dominatrix was as academic as he was trying to make out, when the sound of the door opening behind made them all turn.

Alec Duncan's face was grave.

Everyone stopped talking.

'There's been another one.'

CHAPTER 20

Even before Carver descended the steps leading to Corinne Anderson's cellar, he knew they'd been wrong. Megan Crane had not been next on the Worshipper Killer's list after all. His instinct was to thank God, but then realised what that meant for the poor woman who was, and felt awful. When he saw what awaited them, he felt even worse. About to give the scene his full attention, he paused to glance across at Jess. Her face was pale, a hand over her mouth.

'Okay?' he said.

She nodded, slowly.

Carver knew what she was going through. A detective's first murder scene is always the worst. You struggle to look like you're in control, when what you really want to do is get the hell out. Everyone goes through it. He wasn't worried. What he'd seen of her, she would handle it, though in this case it may take a while.

Corinne Anderson's body was as it had been found that morning, tied to the post, and posed in the manner now so familiar. Squatting next to her was a portly figure with thinning, silver hair and wearing thick-lensed glasses. Long past normal retiring age for those in his line of work, Howard Gladding, was the Senior Home Office Pathologist for the Northern Region. Assigned to the investigation following the second in the series, Jeanette Fairhaven, this was his fourth Kerry scene. In Carver's book that made him, an Authority. And he was glad to see Howard wearing a paper suit. It wasn't that long ago it had taken a telephone call and follow-up letter from the Home Office to get him to fall in line. Last in a long line of HO Pathologists who wear their eccentricities like a badge, Howard Gladding was definitely, 'Old School'. He was also the best.

Right now he was testing skin texture and tone, pressing a wooden spatula against the victim's arm, and noting the result in a spiral-bound notebook. Earlier Carver had watched him examining the petechial-haemorrhaging around the eyes and lips that would inform his estimate of time of death. Every now and then Howard instructed the young woman who was today assisting Robin Knight, the Force's Senior Crime Scene Manager - to take a photograph. Carver didn't interrupt to ask what of. He'd get a full briefing after the PM, by which time Howard would have assembled all the pieces of the jigsaw that was Corinne Anderson's murder - he hoped.

The cellar was roughly twenty-foot square. Despite the makeover - carpeting, panelled walls, recessed lighting - traces of the dank smell that characterises cellars the world over still lingered. As in the other cases, it had been kitted out with the usual sex-dungeon paraphernalia. St Andrew's cross; bench, frame, anchors, etc. Carver had already made a mental note to remind the search team to look for receipts. So far they'd found no link between those who supplied the victims with their equipment or fitted out their 'Playrooms.' But that didn't mean there wasn't one. As the pathologist continued working round the body, Carver thought on what they knew so far.

Corinne's body had been discovered by a neighbour who'd called around to see why Corinne hadn't showed for a planned coffee morning. The Family Liaison team were with her now, scoping what they were facing. Corinne lived alone in the smart, Edwardian mews-terrace, close to Chester City Centre. There was an ex-husband over in Derbyshire somewhere, and two children who lived away, a boy in Liverpool and a girl in Telford. Carver didn't look forward to the time when he, or someone, would have to explain to them how their wife/mother had met her death. The families of three of the four victims had been totally ignorant of their mother/sister/daughter's involvement in SM. Given the shocked state of the neighbour who'd found Corinne, Carver suspected the same applied. As soon as Howard was finished, the Forensic Specialist Team would begin its painstaking examination of the scene. And though it had been videoed before Howard arrived, Carver was glad the Chester DI who was first on scene recognised the MO in time to make the call to the Kerry MIR before the scene got too-spoiled.

Like all detectives, Carver knew there is something about being at a scene early, that video can never replicate. It allows an investigator to experience things as the killer left them. There is only ever one opportunity. Once the body has been found, things start to change. Doors that were shut are opened. Drawers that have been left open get closed. Lights are switched on, or off. Items of clothing or other articles are moved.

He'd never forgotten the mantra from his early CID training. 'At a murder scene, stay HIP,' – 'Hands In Pockets'. But no matter how experienced the investigators, how often people are reminded, 'Don't touch anything', they do. In the case of Corinne Anderson, the process had already begun. Less than three hours had passed since she'd been found. By Carver's count, ten people had been in the cellar since then. As well as the five now present, there were the two uniformed officers first on the scene and their Sergeant. They were followed by a local DC and her DI. He had no way of knowing what, if anything, they had picked up, fingered, put down again – in a changed position. He hoped it wasn't much. Even Howard was doing it. He'd already seen him move some loose ropes lying next to the body - albeit he'd photographed them first. He'd also swept some of the victim's hair off her face to examine her. Worst of all, he'd altered, slightly, the angle of her head when he examined the ribbon-ligature around her neck. Carver hoped it wouldn't prove important. Which is always the trouble. There's no way of telling which small changes may come to deceive the investigators, sending them off chasing red herrings. All because some ham-fisted busy-body couldn't keep their hands in their pockets.

Carver concentrated. He'd already had a good look around the room, but seen nothing that told him anything new. As Howard moved round to the other side, he stepped forward and squatted in the space just vacated. Starting with her ankles, he examined the way she had been posed, casting his eyes over the ropes, the bindings, the positioning of her limbs. After a couple of minutes, he checked back over his shoulder to see how

Jess was holding up. She was scribbling in her notebook. He was impressed. It had taken him a long time to get to the point where he could make notes at a murder scene. He resumed his examination.

As far as he could tell, Corinne Anderson's death-pose mirrored the others, the rope-work exactly the same. He checked the tying-off at the wrists. As always, the ends of the rope had been tucked down, neatly, out of sight. The resinous smell of the superglue was strong this close and he saw the hardened, glossy film between her palms. He looked at her fingers, noticed something, moved closer.

'What do you make of this Howard?'

The pathologist stopped his note-taking to peer round at where Carver was pointing. He came round to squat next to him. The little fingers of both of Corinne Anderson's hands were bent under on themselves, so that only three fingers of each and the thumbs were straight. Carver joined his hands in like fashion. It felt awkward.

'Interesting,' the pathologist said. He probed at the fingers with the end of a spatula. 'I've not seen that before.'

'Did the killer leave them like that do you think?' Carver said. 'Or did she do it herself for some reason?'

The pathologist probed again. 'All I can say is they're not glued. But given how the palms and fingers are fixed, they wouldn't need to be to stay in that position. They don't look broken either, though I can't be sure until I get back to the mortuary and separate the hands. If they're not broken, then it's unlikely to have been done post-mortem.'

'In which case the question is, why?' Carver said.

For the first time since she'd entered the cellar, Jess spoke up.

'If I'm not mistaken, one of the Buddhist religions pray like that.'

Carver looked across at her and noticed she looked flushed, breathing heavily. It was warm in the cramped conditions and he remembered how he'd felt at his first murder scene.

'If it has any religious significance, it could be she was trying to tell us something. We need to find out if she had any religious leanings.' He gave Jess a look so she would know he was offering her an excuse. To his surprise, she took it.

'I'll get on it,' she said. Taking one last look at Corinne Anderson's lifeless body, she turned and headed back up the stairs.

As he heard her gain the floor above, Carver set himself a reminder to give her some positive feedback. She had done well for her first time.

CHAPTER 21

As Jess burst out into the hallway, she had to swerve to avoid colliding with the slightly built young woman wearing a paper suit who was coming through the front door. She was carrying a chrome-steel examination box. Jess recognised her as Claire Trevor, the head of the Forensic Team assigned to the Kerry cases.

Seeing Jess, Claire began, 'Hi Jess, I-'

Jess didn't stop but went straight out into the street.

At the front, black metal railings surrounded the cellar bay. Leaning over, Jess gulped fresh air. Conscious she was in view of those who had already started to gather – a couple of reporters, some neighbours, other gawpers - she fought not to throw up.

Even as she'd followed Carver down the steps, Jess had felt her heart pounding. She'd seen plenty of bodies in her time but this was her first Worshipper scene. As she stepped around her boss's sturdy frame and saw Corinne Anderson, the pounding increased. Her breathing soon quickened to the point where she was in danger of hyper-ventilating and she had to consciously work at slowing it down. The urge to turn and run back up the steps was so strong it surprised her. She had to work on it for a good few minutes before it went away.

During that time she hoped she'd managed to give the impression she was coping, conscious that Carver would be noting her reaction. After a while and in order to distract herself from the dark thoughts running through her head, she took out her pocket book and pretended to take notes. She hoped Carver would never ask to see the meaningless scribbles.

Next to her father's funeral, Jess's first Worshipper scene had been one of the worst experiences of her life. She already knew it would take some getting over. It wasn't so much the body. She'd witnessed death enough times it no longer bothered her. It was coming face-to-face with the tableaux she'd only seen before in photographs and on video that got to her. She'd always known the first time was going to be difficult. Her early reactions to the photos had told her that. Even so, she wasn't prepared for the assault on her senses that hit when she saw Corinne Anderson's lifeless face, her bulging eyes, the swollen tongue, the ribbon wound tight round her throat.

Things started to go wrong almost immediately. Though she knew she shouldn't, she couldn't stop thinking about how Corinne had died. She began to mentally reconstruct the scene, letting it play over in her mind like a video-loop. Time and again she imagined a dark figure, indistinct but menacing, standing behind Corinne, pulling the ribbon tight. And she had imagined the woman's terror, tied helpless to the post, as the life was wrung out of her. To begin with it was like watching some by-the-numbers TV drama. Chilling, but not particularly involving. But after replaying the scene several times, and without any warning, her perspective suddenly switched. Suddenly *she* was the woman bound to the post. She actually found herself holding her breath as she imagined her air being cut off. She had to force herself to start breathing when she realised she was becoming light-headed. It was then she started scribbling, desperate to divert her over-active imagination away from the awful facts of Corinne's death. It hadn't worked. The harrowing scene continued to play. She'd begun to panic, thinking there must be something wrong with her, that perhaps she wasn't cut out for this sort of work after all. She'd been on the point of turning to flee back up the steps, when Carver mentioned the fingers. It was then - God knows how - she remembered her trip to India.

It was years ago, before University. She and her mother had joined her father on one of his work-trips and he'd taken them to some temple outside Delhi. She remembered the priest showing them the 'correct' way to pray, with their little fingers bent under, pressing against each other. The memory had come like a lifeline to a drowning woman. It probably gave Carver the impression that her mind was functioning rationally. She wondered if she would ever be able to tell him the truth.

Revived, a little, by the fresh air, Jess forced herself back to the present. Looking round she saw the young PC by the front door whose job it was to log everyone in and out. He was watching her, a sympathetic look on his face.

'Bad in there, is it?' he said.

She shook her head, shuddered. 'Not good.'

On shaking legs, she walked down to where her car was parked. Thank God they'd travelled separately. She needed some space. But as she reached it, her stomach spasmed. Leaning over the wheel arch, she heaved the remains of her lunch into the gutter.

Several pairs of eyes, peering out from behind lace curtains and slatted blinds, witnessed Jess's distress. It would give rise to a rumour - which would persist for weeks - that the scene of Corinne Anderson's murder was as gory and blood-spattered as they come.

At that moment, Jess couldn't have cared less.

The Pathologist's examination complete - Howard had found nothing that signalled anything significant - Carver craved fresh air himself. So far he'd managed to keep other distracting thoughts at bay. But now other memories, Megan Crane amongst them, were starting to intrude.

It was clear now she hadn't been the killer's next planned target after all. Corinne Anderson had already been cast in that role. How long ago, he wondered? And what did that say about the stars against the entries in the magazine? What did it say about Megan Crane? Did it mean anything, or was someone playing games, in which case, who, and why? He didn't let himself dwell on it. Okay, they were too late to prevent Corinne Anderson's death, but Megan Crane might still point them in the right direction. This latest killing meant that whatever urges were driving the killer, they were likely to have been sated – at least for the time being. In most series, the intervals grow shorter as the killings continue. Even so, it was a reasonable bet it would be at least several weeks before they needed to start worrying again about who may be next. It meant they had time to dig deeper, to get to know more about Megan Crane, and the strange world she inhabited.

As he mounted the steps taking him out of the fantasy world where Corinne Anderson had played and died, Carver felt the familiar, conflicting emotions – eager anticipation and a dread foreboding - taking root once more.

CHAPTER 22

The Duke sat at his desk, Carver facing. The 'DOM!' magazine lay between them, open at the page showing Megan Crane's listing. The Duke's face was grave.

'So do these bloody stars mean anything, or is someone fucking with us?'

Carver hesitated. He'd been asking himself the same question all the way back. 'There's no way of knowing. It could be whoever sent it, simply got things wrong-'

'Or?'

'Or like you say. Someone's fucking with us.'

'The killer?'

Carver shrugged. 'Right now, your guess is as good as mine.'

'For fuck's sake, Jamie. It was you who said we needed to focus on the magazine in the first place. What are you saying now? It may be a load of bollocks?'

Carver ignored the accusatory tone, shook his head. 'I'm saying, on what we've got, we can't say one way or another. We need to keep an open mind.'

'An open mind,' The Duke repeated, more evenly. Carver sensed his frustration. 'Great.'

Still, Carver waited. The Duke was playing catch-up. In reality nothing had changed, apart from someone else had died.

'Was she listed?' The Duke said.

'Just a photograph and a reference, but she was there. Some of the longer standing subscribers don't always put a full entry in every reprint. Just enough to show they are still active.'

The Duke mused on it. 'That might cause us a problem.'

Carver nodded. The thought had occurred as he'd watched Howard Gladding going about his business.

After discovering the link with 'DOM' they'd met with the ACC overseeing the inquiry. They'd talked about whether to contact all of DOM's two hundred-plus entrants, or just those starred. He'd argued that contacting them all risked alerting the killer. They might lose their only advantage, and there may not be another. Eventually he'd got his way. The decision to contact only the starred entry - Megan Crane - was recorded in the Inquiry Policy Book under The Duke's signature, and ratified by the ACC. It was a calculated risk. The sort SIOs often have to take. On this occasion it hadn't paid off, and Corinne Anderson had died. Of course, if and when the next Six-Week Review fell due, it would find that the decision had been taken only after all possible consequences had been properly weighed. No blame would attach to Carver, or any of them, over Corinne's death, though he could already hear the words, 'with hindsight', ringing in his ears.

But Carver's mind was still clear. 'We've got to stick with it John. 'DOM' is still the only thing we've got.'

John Morrison took a deep breath. For a long time, he said nothing. As SIO It was his decision. But nothing had changed and they both knew it.

Eventually he gave a slow nod. 'Okay.' He thought a few moments more then added, 'But if Cleeves is right, then all bets are off. This one was earlier than expected by a good few weeks. Now that the killer's broken his schedule, he thinks he might start diverging from his MO in other ways. If that happens, everything could change.'

Carver nodded. He'd read Cleeves's Interim Assessment. The psychologist had prepared it as soon as the bare facts of the latest killing had been relayed back to the MIR.

'So long as he's using DOM there's a good chance we'll pick up something, either through the Crane woman or someone else. She still matches all the victim profiles remember, including Corinne Anderson.'

The Duke gave his deputy a long look. He'd dealt with plenty of murder cases, but Carver had more experience with series. When it comes to enquiries like Kerry, conventions around rank and seniority don't always count for much.

'You know this stuff better than me. And Cleeves. What're the chances he may change his MO? Choosing his victims at random or snatching them off the street?'

Carver got up and walked over to the window. The Duke's questions actually hid another. How far could they depend on Pinnacle? He, of course, would say, 'all the way'. But then, he'd invented it.

Carver developed what had since become known as the, 'Pinnacle Inventory', in the wake of his experiences in the Ancoats Rapist case - his first 'series'. After days and weeks spent trawling the web, looking at 'repeat offending' studies, one thing in particular had struck him. Almost all sex-crime 'repeaters' are motivated by a single, driving fantasy – the 'Pinnacle', as he coined it, of what they hope to achieve through their crimes. It led to him devising his, 'Pinnacle Inventory', basically a questionnaire that collects data about repeat-crimes and the victims, as well as a wide range of circumstances leading up to, during and after the crime itself. Properly analysed and compared, crime by crime, the data could reveal enough about an offender to lead to identification – or so Carver believed. To his knowledge, Pinnacle had been used in five 'live' investigations; two in the US, three in Europe. In two cases, the SIOs were on record as saying Pinnacle was of significant help in identifying the offender. A third felt it had been, 'little or no value whatsoever'. The remaining two were undecided, but would consider using it again. From an evaluation point of view, the jury was still out. But Carver's gut told him that, used properly, his 'PI' was as good as any other tool available to an SIO - and better than many. As he mused on The Duke's questions, staring out of the window at the grey day, he thought on what it had revealed so far about the Kerry series.

'One of the killer's drivers seems to revolve around getting his dominatrix victim to switch, to submit to being restrained. That initial consent seems to be a vital element in what he does. I can't see that changing. Not yet. The only alternative would be to start targeting prostitutes…,' he tailed off as his words triggered a train of thought.

'But?' the Duke prompted.

When Carver turned, his face was set.

'There's something about the way he kills. The mind games are important. He needs the victim to be a willing participant, not just someone who's doing it for the money. Otherwise he could have gone for pros to begin with and spent less time gaining their confidence.' He thought on it some more. 'As long as he doesn't know we've sussed out the 'DOM' connection, he'll stick with it.'

The two men looked each other, both thinking the same.

They were flying blind now, basing decisions on instinct and gut feelings rather than evidence or facts. During the months they'd worked together they'd come to trust each other's judgement. Still, The Duke spoke for them both when he said, 'I hope to God we're right on this.'

'So do I.'

For several moments there was only silence. Then The Duke said, 'You'd better get on with setting things up with the Crane woman.'

CHAPTER 23

Returning to his office, Carver took out his mobile and brought up Jess's number. About to dial, his office phone rang. He snatched it up.

'It's Claire,' the familiar voice said to his greeting.

Carver brightened. An unsolicited call from a case Lead Forensic always held out the promise of something. He made a quick calculation. She would still be at Corinne Anderson's.

'Wassup Doc?' It was an old joke. A play on her PhD. They'd first met on the Ancoats job. Back then she was just one of the team.

'We're just finishing up here. Thought I'd let you know.'

Carver sat up. 'What?' Even before she said it, he guessed.

'Blonde hairs.'

Carver's pulse quickened. 'Like the others?'

'Same shade and length. I've prioritised them for DNA and we'll know for sure tomorrow. But I'm prepared to bet right now they'll match.'

'Jesus,' he said, and lapsed into a thoughtful silence. Blonde hairs. Again. That made all four scenes.

'Still there, Jamie?'

'Sorry Claire. Anything else?'

'Not right now. We've got plenty of swabs and traces, but then it's a sex-dungeon. We'll see what comes.' Then she added. 'Sorry. That was accidental.'

'Thanks Claire. Speak tomorrow.'

He rung off, tried Jess. She answered at once.

'Where are you?'

'I'm on my way back from seeing Corinne Anderson's ex in Buxton'

'And?'

'He's in the clear. They only see- *saw*, each other a couple of times a year. Kids birthdays, that sort of thing. He didn't even know she'd become a full-on Dom, though he wasn't too surprised. It was why they broke up.'

'How'd he react?'

'Devastated, I'd say. He was holding onto the hope they might get back together.'

'No pointers then?'

'None. And he insisted he wants to tell their kids without any police present. Which I suppose lets me out.' She paused. 'So what's next?'

Carver told her his next step was to ring Megan Crane and tell her about Corinne Anderson and that they now had permission to go ahead as they'd all discussed the day before. There was a Press Conference planned for an hour's time, after which he and The Duke would be briefing the team.

'Do you need me there?' Jess said.

'Not especially. Something you got to do?'

'I'll struggle to get back in time. My mother's dropping in on her way to my aunt's in Newcastle. I haven't seen her for months.'

'That's okay. There's not much else you can do on the victim side tonight anyway.'

'Thanks Jamie. If it'll save you a job, I can ring Megan and fill her in?'

'That'd be good, thanks. Besides, I've been called to attend a Lee Family Case Conference after. I sense a late night coming on.' On their way to The Poplars the day before, he'd told her about his call-out to Carnegie Avenue.

'That'll be fun,' she said.

He harrumphed down the phone. 'See you tomorrow.'

After ringing off, Carver stared at his phone, tapped the desk. It wasn't like her to duck out of press conferences and briefings. He hoped he wasn't missing something. That said, she'd just had her first scene, and what was no doubt a difficult meeting with the victim's husband. A bit of family time might do her good, even if she had seemed fine the last time he saw her. About to go looking for the Press Officer who was around somewhere getting things set up, he remembered he'd forgotten to tell her about the blonde hairs.

It'll do tomorrow.

CHAPTER 24

As she ended the call, Jess let out a long breath. It was the first time she'd consciously lied to him. She hated herself for it. But right now press conferences weren't uppermost in her thoughts. Turning to her right, she stared at The Poplar's iron gates.

She still wasn't sure why she had diverted here on route back from Buxton. All she knew was that since escaping the horror that was Corinne Anderson's basement, she hadn't been able to stop reliving the experience. All afternoon the images had kept coming, even through her difficult meeting with Corinne's ex. The cold, stone steps leading down. The dungeon setting. Poor Corinne, bound to the post. She deserved a medal for managing to stay focused enough to show the compassion that was needed when she broke the news to Kevin Anderson, and dogged enough to get what she needed to eliminate him as a suspect. And though she could have given in to his request that she tell him exactly how his wife had died, she spared him. For all that relatives insist they need to know, there are occasions when it's better they don't. But she was grateful when Corinne's former husband said he wanted to break the news to his children himself. It left her free to do what she needed to do, which was get her head straight. Her first instinct was that the best place to do that was home, on her own. But her route back took her past Macclesfield, not far from Calderton, and, somehow, she'd ended up here. She was actually sitting looking across at the gates, wondering what the hell she was doing, why she'd come, when Jamie had rung. Now she had the perfect excuse.

About to get out, she hesitated. In the time she'd been there, she'd seen no sign of life and though it was now well into evening, no lights showed. Best check first. She rang Megan's number. It rang out several times, then cut off. No voice mail option.

That's that, then.

She started the engine and was about to pull away when a light came on downstairs. She stopped. A moment later her phone rang. The screen read, 'Megan Crane'. She hit the accept button.

'Sorry I missed your call, Jess. I was busy.'

'No problem, I was just-'

'-Ringing to tell me there's been another murder?'

'Actually, yes. How did-'

'The TV news is reporting a murder in Chester. They keep mentioning the Worshipper Killings, but say it's not been confirmed yet.'

Jess tutted to herself. They should have rung her earlier. 'It will be. There's a press conference in the next hour.'

'Will you be there?'

'No, I'm-' She hesitated, conscious of how it might sound. 'The thing is, right now I'm sitting outside your house. I was just on my way back from-.'

'Tch. You should have said. I'm just changing. Give

me a few minutes. I'll open the gates. It's getting dark so you'd best drive in.'

Ten minutes later Jess waited on the sofa as Megan mixed them both drinks. Tonight she was draped in an oriental-style black and gold lounging robe. Fastened up to the neck and floor length, Jess thought it looked gorgeous and wondered if and when it would be appropriate to ask where she'd bought it. Her guess was, not The Trafford Centre.

Returning to the sofa, Megan handed Jess her drink then sat down at the other end. They chinked glasses. 'You look like you need that.'

Jess cocked an eyebrow and made a half-smile, but said nothing. She drank it down, and gave a little cough as the liquid burned its way down her throat. It had been a while since she'd tasted whiskey this good. They drank in silence. Jess sensed Megan waiting for her to begin. She felt awkward.

'What are they saying on the news?'

'Just that a woman's been found dead at her home in Chester, and that officers from Operation Kerry had been called in.' As she spoke she adjusted her position so she came round to face Jess more. At the same time, she bent her legs under and sat on them. Her arm fell so it was draped across the back of the sofa. Despite what they were talking about, she looked relaxed, glowing. Done up in the black robe as she was, Jess was put in mind of a sleek, black panther.

Over the next few minutes, Jess confirmed the details, describing what they'd found in Corinne's cellar. When she mentioned Corinne by name, Megan shook her head.

'I can't say I've ever come across her. Was she listed

in DOM?'

Jess nodded. 'Not as prominently as you, but she was there.'

When Megan asked if Corinne's entry had been starred, she confirmed it wasn't, then repeated the conversation she'd had with Carver about its significance, or not.

'Does this undermine your theory about what the stars mean?'

'Not necessarily. We still think the killer is using the magazine to choose his victims.'

'What does Jamie say about it? Does he still want to go ahead as we discussed?'

'Absolutely. His view is, it doesn't change anything. We're carrying on.'

Megan nodded. 'And do you agree? That we should carry on I mean?'

Jess wondered what, if anything, lay behind the question. She nodded again. 'God yes. I think it's more important than ever.' By now she was conscious that Megan was staring at her, closely. As during that first meeting, she seemed to be weighing her. Her next question surprised her.

'Will you be okay if we carry on?'

Jess gave a quizzical look. 'I'm not sure what you mean. Why shouldn't I be okay?'

Megan took a deep breath. 'If you don't mind me saying, you look like you've been through hell since I saw you last. Would I be right in thinking that today's been a bit of an ordeal?'

Jess stared at her. 'Let's just say it's not something I want to repeat any time soon.'

Megan nodded. 'I can imagine. Most people find sex

dungeons unsettling at the best of times. When it's the scene of a real-life murder, it must be horrific.'

'It was. Though-'

'What?'

'I was going to say yes, it was a horrific sight. But it's not so much that that's bothering me as-'

'As what?'

Thinking on what she was trying to say, Jess looked up to find herself staring into the dark pools she remembered from that first encounter. She also became aware that Megan seemed to be sitting closer than she had been, though she hadn't seen her move.

'-As what led up to it.'

It was Megan's turn to look puzzled. 'How do you mean?'

'What I mean is, since I joined this investigation, I haven't been able to get my head around what it is these women- women like you, do. These games you play. The whole fantasy role-play thing. I guess this morning just brought it all to a head.'

A knowing look crept into Megan's face. 'Ah.'

But Jess wasn't finished. 'This whole sub-dom thing?' She gave Megan a sheepish look, conscious how naïve she must sound. 'I don't understand how intelligent, attractive, confident women like you can expose yourselves in such a way. It doesn't make sense. Why do they do it? Why do you do it?'

Megan cocked her head but said nothing.

Jess sipped her drink. 'I sometimes think-' She stopped, fearing she'd said too much. More than ever, she was conscious of Megan's stare.

For a couple of minutes, neither spoke. Jess drank and fidgeted, embarrassed at having revealed herself, unsure what to say or do next, or even why, exactly, she had come.

Reaching across, Megan took Jess's glass then rose and went across to the drinks cabinet for a refill. When she came back, she handed it to Jess but didn't return to her seat. Instead she stood over her, looking down. After several seconds she said, 'Would you mind giving me a few minutes? There's something I have to attend to.' Before Jess could say anything she left, closing the door, firmly, behind her.

Lifting her glass, Jess gulped its contents down. Suddenly she worried what she was doing, why she was there at all. Part of her thought she should leave. Right now. But another was telling her she was imagining things, that she was just wrung out from the events of the past twenty-four hours.

How long she wavered, Jess was never sure. It seemed a long time, but was probably only minutes. Eventually, the door opened and Megan Crane came back in. But it was a different Megan Crane to the one that had left. Jess sucked air and her heart started thumping in her chest.

This Megan Crane was the one whose picture she had seen staring out of the pages of DOM! Her torso was squeezed into a shaping, black corset, supporting matching black stockings. Round her neck was a leather collar. The heels of the knee-length boots were about the highest and spikiest Jess had ever seen anyone manage to walk on without toppling over. She wondered how she had changed so quickly, then realised. She'd been wearing the outfit under her robe all the time. Megan stalked towards her, the cat-like eyes locked on their target. Jess's stomach flipped somersaults. Then she was standing over her again, hands on hips, appraising her, like a teacher weighing a pupil before a difficult test. While she'd been gone she had done something with her make-up. She looked different somehow, and not just because of the outfit.

Jess's first instinct was to get up and leave, right now and without saying a word. But something - the impulse that had driven her to come in the first place? - stayed her. She remained frozen in her seat.

Megan bent towards her and Jess tensed, the way she might if someone was about to attack her. But she simply took Jess's hand and pulled her, gently, to her feet.

'Come,' she said.

She led her through to the kitchen. The door halfway down the right-hand wall was open. It led into a short passageway at the end of which was a stout, wooden door with heavy, iron hinges and a lock with a large, round, black handle. As Megan took hold, and turned it, a loud click echoed in the bare passage. Jess's nervousness increased as Megan pushed the door open and ushered her through.

Spotlights, set into the ceiling lit the large room. The walls were mostly bright white, lending it a clinical appearance, though one area, over to the left was finished in what she'd come to think of as 'dungeon stone'. It was equipped, like other places she'd seen including Corinne Anderson's cellar, with the usual items of 'furniture'. Harnesses, chains, ropes, and other accessories were set into, or hung from the walls and ceiling.

But while all of this registered in Jess's brain, it was not what drew her eye the most. As she turned her head, taking it all in, she looked to her right, where her gaze fell on the strangest sight she'd ever seen in her life.

On their knees and facing the wall, were a man and woman. They were both laced into face-hugging leather hoods, their wrists locked behind in leather cuffs which were attached by short lengths of chain to similar restraints around their ankles. As Megan and Jess entered, the pair shuffled round. Apart from their hoods and collars, they were all-but naked. The woman wore a body-harness with straps that framed her modest but firm breasts and the small 'v' of blonde hair between her legs. The man was wearing a skimpy, black-leather jockstrap. Their stifled grunts suggested that under the masks, they were also gagged. Thin chains ran from their collars to metal rings set into the wall.

Megan led Jess into the centre of the room, then returned to the couple. Bending down, she unzipped eye holes in their hoods which Jess hadn't noticed before. Seeing the visitor, they both became agitated, turning from Jess to Megan and back again, swaying frantically, mewing and grunting into their gags. It was obvious that Megan had given them no warning of Jess's arrival.

Jess's stomach squirmed with embarrassment, both for the couple and herself. She didn't know which way to look. But each time she thought of turning away, she felt her gaze being drawn back to the strange tableaux she had been brought to witness.

'Quiet,' Megan said, her tone stern.

Immediately, the pair fell silent and became still. It reminded Jess that there was a side to Megan Crane she had not yet seen. Certainly, her willingness to spring such a surprise on the couple hinted at a capacity for cruelty that, up to now, she'd kept well hidden.

As the pair calmed, heads bowed, Jess used the opportunity to take a closer look at them. Without seeing their faces, it was difficult to guess their ages. The woman's body was tanned and toned, pointing to someone yet to reach forty. The man however looked older. His greying chest hair and mottled skin suggested someone of more mature years, sixty maybe? She wondered if they were a couple, or just two of those Megan Crane counted amongst her, 'friends'.

At last, the reason for Megan's delay in answering her phone was clear. Jess had indeed called at an inconvenient time. In fact she was surprised Megan had bothered to answer at all. Before she could pursue the thought, Megan turned to her and made a sweeping gesture.

'Mistress Jessica. May I present my devoted servants, Slaves Arthur, and Tracy.'

CHAPTER 25

The man with the distinguished-looking head of steel-grey hair turned to look down at Carver, seated at the far end of the table. In the clipped tones Carver always found mildly irritating, he said, 'For the sake of clarity, can I ask, whose decision was it to make no arrests for what appear, *prima facie*, to be two incidents of grievous bodily harm, if not attempted murder?'

Carver sighed and bowed his head to look down at the table's beech veneer. Ninety minutes gone, and they were still going round in circles. When he looked up, it was to find Spencer Wright, the Crown Prosecution Service's Deputy District Prosecuting Solicitor, still waiting, eyebrows arched, expectantly. He tried to keep the disappointment, and impatience, out of his voice.

'As I've already said Spencer, it was my call. I was there and I was satisfied I had all the facts I needed to make it.'

Wright made a point of casting his gaze round the room, as if it might gain him backing.

'But by doing so, you prevented anyone else from having a say. For all you knew, one of us may have felt that under the circumstances, due process should have been followed. I'm sure I don't need to, but may I remind you of the fact that Kayleigh is still a juvenile after all?'

Carver felt the sting, but stifled the impulse that made him want to get up, walk around the table, grab the solicitor by the throat, stare into his frightened face and say, 'Correct, you don't need to remind me. I saw her in her pyjamas, the ones stained with her father's blood. Where the fuck were you at four o'clock that morning when it was all kicking off?' Right now the aim was to get them to do what was needed – endorse his decision and move on. And much as he'd like to, throttling Spencer Wright wouldn't help. Checking to his right, he saw Rita Arogundade staring across at Wright. The look on her face suggested that at that moment, she was feeling the same mix of contempt and anger as he was. More than any others of the eight agency representatives comprising the Lee Family Project Steering Group, Wright was the one who still seemed to have most difficulty with the principle of rapid decision-making. God knows but when they began, there was plenty of evidence to show how red tape and bureaucracy was contributing to the family's problems. Instead of issues being resolved quickly, delay and organisational dithering were encouraging the family to believe that 'the authorities' weren't only uninterested in their plight, but were, in fact, The Enemy. In truth, they weren't wholly wrong. It was why the Joint Memorandum Of Understanding that underpinned the project allowed for decisions to be made outside the frameworks that would normally kick in when individual family members came to notice. It was also why those seated around the table occupied relatively senior positions within their organisations.

After weeks and months of long, often fractious, meetings, most now accepted that by dealing with problems straight away, even if a decision was later shown to be 'wrong', the benefits outweighed the disadvantages. Six months on, there were definite signs that trust between the Lees and the organisations in whose sides they had long been a thorn, was growing. Things were actually getting done. And to its credit, the family was beginning to take control of their lives in ways none of the Project Group had ever seen before. It had taken time, but as the most telling statistics showed, unauthorised school absences were down to single figures.

Carver made sure his voice was even as he made his reply to Wright's challenge. 'You're right, Spencer. I don't need reminding. In fact it was Kayleigh's situation I had most in mind when I made my decision. If I'd opted for a full-on investigation, we'd have had to remove her. That would have been bad for her, and bad for the family. The family would have split down the middle and everything we've achieved the past six months would have gone down the toilet. As it is, they've all made up and things are back on track.'

But Wright wasn't convinced. 'I'm sorry, Jamie, but we've only your say-so on that. How do we know-'

'For fuck's sake Spencer, give it a rest will you?' All heads turned to Rita. She looked ready to blow. 'While you were playing golf, or whatever it is you do weekends, I was at Carnegie Avenue, mending fences and building bridges. I was there as well, remember? And I can tell you, Jamie's dead right. If you want to turn the clock back to when we were all spending half of our day dealing with problems coming out of number

Twenty-Five, then just veto Jamie's decision and tell him to go back and run a full investigation. But don't forget, that would also involve arresting Stuart for what he did to Paula. And possibly other members of the family as well. And when that happens we may as well just pull the plug and go home.'

She stopped to cast her gaze around the table, making sure to have eye contact with the seven others present – two members having sent apologies. No one came back at her. Carver could tell Spencer wanted to, but knew better. Not for the first time he thought on how Rita Arogundade would make an excellent lawyer – or detective - had she chosen a different path.

'Right,' she said. 'If no one's got anything else to say, can I suggest we take a vote, record the result then piss off home. I've promised my Nigel a curry tonight.'

Leaving the Council Offices, Carver lingered to let Rita catch up.

'Thanks for that show of support.'

'No need to thank me. Besides, you didn't need my support. You were right and everyone knows it apart from that dick-head. I just didn't want to see blood on the table. Had enough of that recently.' She paused. 'Something I need to mention though.'

'Go on.'

'You do know Kayleigh's got a crush on you, don't you?'

Carver stopped dead. 'What?'

'Might just be she sees you as the father figure Stuart never was. Either way, you need to be aware of it. I've seen too many professionals end up in trouble over young girls.'

Carver cast his mind back, remembering his most recent visits to Carnegie Avenue, occasions when he'd seen her looking at him in a way he suddenly realised he should have thought about more. He thought about the feelings he had when he saw her doing her best to keep her family afloat. They were the sort of protective, fatherly feelings most men would have when they see a kid struggling through a difficult situation. Then his stomach flipped, and suddenly he was scared.

'Oh, fuck.'

'That's what I thought when I saw her looking at you the other morning.'

Carver's drive home took forty minutes. They passed in a blur.

CHAPTER 26

The next day the press was all over everything, working themselves up to a frenzy that the Worshipper Killer had claimed another victim. Even before Corinne Anderson, Carver's plan was to call the journalist, Jackson, and get him off his back. But now he felt a face-to-face meeting would be better. Less risk of any, 'misunderstandings'. But inviting him into the station risked stoking rumours of the, 'Courting Media Attention Again' variety. For that reason he arranged a meet in The Causeway Inn, half-way between Warrington and Stockton Heath. A large, traditional ale house and not a regular police haunt, The Causeway is the sort of place you can easily get lost in.

Jackson was already there, seated at a table at the back, a pint of Carver's favourite Bombardier next to his own Balvenie. After exchanging stiff-ish greetings, Carver sat down, took a long swig and gave the man across the table a hard look that said, *Listen closely.*

To his credit, Jackson, leaned forward to give Carver his full attention. Younger than Carver by several years and slightly built, he was wearing the same mismatched grey, herring-bone jacket and jeans Carver remembered. He also still sported the designer-stubble Carver saw as part of the, 'who-gives-a-shit crumpled look' Jackson liked to effect. Carver had learned long ago not to be lulled by it all.

'Before we start, let's get a couple of things straight,' Carver said. 'First, I'm only meeting you because I've been asked to.' Jackson nodded. 'Second, I'm not going to give you any more about what we're investigating than what's in the official releases. Including yesterday's.'

'I wouldn't ask you to.'

'Third, if you print anything that tries to show me, or anyone else as anything other than just a small cog in a big machine, two things will happen. First, I'll come round to that nice flat you've got in Knutsford and beat the crap out of you. Second, no detective in the country will speak to you, on or off the record, again. You know what I'm saying?'

Jackson gave a wary nod. Carver had no way of knowing what he'd been expecting when he agreed to the meeting, but it probably wouldn't have included being threatened with violence.

'And I don't give a fuck if you're taping this or not. The same applies.'

A hesitant smile crossed Jackson lips. Taking up the mobile he'd placed on the table as Carver took his seat, he played with it, then showed Carver a screen showing a button labelled, 'Delete Recording?' He pressed 'Yes', and put it away.

'Right,' Carver said. 'What do you want to talk to me about?'

Jackson took a slug of whiskey. 'I'm being pushed to do a follow-up on our last piece.' Seeing Carver's look he added, quickly, 'Sorry, *my* last piece. But I've already told them it's a non-starter. Not after last time.'

'So why are we here?'

Jackson looked around, as if expecting eavesdroppers. 'I'm still interested in the questions that remain un-answered after Hart's suicide.' He eyed Carver, warily. 'It was suicide, I take it?'

Carver stared at him. 'That was the coroner's verdict.' *If you think I'm going to make this easy, think again.*

'Of course. It's just that, I didn't ever feel it was properly explained?' He put on an innocent face. 'I'd be interested to hear your take on it?'

Carver supped his pint, then stared into the glass. Eventually he lifted his gaze to meet the other man's. 'When someone talks of modern-day sex-killers, who you think of?'

Jackson thought a moment. 'Nilson. Black. The Wests. Hindley and Brady if you want to go back that far.'

Carver nodded. 'Hart was worse than all of them. Far worse. There was a lot that didn't come out during his trial. Stuff we found after he was arrested. I won't give details but let's just say that in several people's opinion, including mine, Hart was the most extreme sexual-psychopath we've seen in this country. Think of a deviation that involves sexual violence, torture, sadism. He was into it. We know, mainly because he told us, that his plan was to go on killing and torturing for a long time, using a range of methods. For the Escort Girls he used a knife. But they were to be just the start of it. If we hadn't caught him when he did, he'd have begun targeting other types of victims. Using other techniques. Other deviations. The point is, he was addicted to this stuff the way a junkie is to their drug of choice. When he was put away, he couldn't stand life without the thing that had driven him for so long. Suicide was the easy way out. In fact, it was probably his last big hit.'

Jackson nodded. 'I've heard of that, but never come across it.'

'Sexual suicide is more common than most people think. Coroners tend to go for accidental death for the benefit of relatives.'

Jackson became thoughtful. 'Jesus.' He finished his whiskey, pointed to Carver's empty glass. 'Can I get you another?'

Carver hesitated, then nodded. 'It's not often I get to charge to an expense account.'

When Jackson returned, he was ready to change tack.

'The other thing I'm interested in-' He paused, as if needing Carver's permission.

'Go on.'

'There was talk at the time that Hart may have had an accomplice.'

Carver gave another nod.

'Did you ever bottom it?'

'We could never prove it one way, or the other.'

'So… it's still possible there *was* an accomplice?'

'Depends who you ask. Some believe he worked alone, others not.'

'You?'

Carver took another long swig. 'Off the record?'

'Off the record.'

'I tend to go with the accomplice theory.'

'Why?'

Carver gave a non-committal shrug. 'Small things. There was a lot of blood at the scenes. We never found traces in his car, yet we know he used one to get to and from at least some of them. Either he had another car we never found, which is unlikely, or someone else dropped him off and picked him up after. Also, before and after some of the killings he made telephone calls to a mobile we never traced. Which begs the questions who was it, and why? Then there's the Black Merc.'

'Black Merc?'

'On the nights of two of the killings, cameras picked up a black Mercedes close to the victim's homes. Both times it was on false plates, different ones each time. We couldn't connect it to the scenes but it's a hell of a coincidence. As far as we've discovered, Hart never owned or had access to a Mercedes, black or otherwise.'

'And you think that's enough to show there must have been an accomplice?'

'It is for me.'

'In which case whoever it was- is, you must believe they're still out there, somewhere?'

Carver gave Jackson a hard stare. 'Yes.'

Jackson stopped his glass halfway to his mouth.

'My God.' He paused. 'So...'

'What?'

'So is anyone doing anything about it? Is anyone- are you, still working on it?'

Carver shrugged. 'The file's still on my desk.'

'So is that a, 'Yes'?'

Carver chose his words carefully. 'The Hart investigation was officially closed after the court case. To my knowledge no one is working on it. Officially.'

'Unofficially?'

Carver held Jackson's gaze. For long seconds, it was as if they were the pub's only customers. 'I'm hopeful that one day something will happen that will allow me to put the file away.'

Jackson's eyes narrowed. 'Why so circumspect? Presumably your bosses know your views on all this?'

Carver lifted his glass and stared at Jackson, hard, as he took a long swig.

'Fuck,' Jackson said, but quietly. Realisation showed in his face. 'They told you to drop it.'

Carver said nothing.

'But why? Surely, if there's a possibility someone else was involved, then the investigation should have continued, shouldn't it?'

'That would seem logical.'

'But it didn't.'

'No.'

'So I repeat, why?'

Carver breathed deeply. 'You'd be better putting that question to others. I can't answer it.'

'You must have a theory?'

Carver took a long breath. He'd been over it so many times. 'When Hart was arrested, certainly after his conviction, the media presented it as a success story. A victory for 'local policing'. You'll remember. You were part of it.'

Jackson nodded, 'I was, but-'

'At the time there was lot of politicking going on. Police reorganisations. Force amalgamations. All the crap the Home Office digs out every few years whenever there's some sort of policing crisis and they think they can convince everyone the answer is to get rid of a load of Chief Constables.'

Jackson leaned forward, as if sensing something. 'You're going to tell me it involves The Black Quintet?'

Carver acknowledged the man's insight with a slight

nod. But then Jackson would be more aware than most of the other, Big Police Story of the time.

The media frenzy that followed the discovery of a conspiracy amongst the Chiefs of the five biggest forces outside the Met had lasted for weeks, not to mention the accompanying Parliamentary hoo-hah. According to a disaffected, whistle-blowing Chief Superintendent, The Black Quintet, as they were quickly dubbed, had been meeting in secret for years. By pulling strings within ACPO, as it was back then, as well as Whitehall and elsewhere, they made sure the service presented a united front in the face of the various Police Reforms successive governments wanted to force through.

Jackson saw the link. 'The Home Office was trying to use the scandal to drive through force amalgamations.'

'Right. But the Hart case was being championed as the counter-argument by a lot of police spokes-persons. Their line was that Hart would never have been caught if a local detective, working for a local force, hadn't been able to use his initiative.'

'The 'local detective' being you.'

'Right.'

'And they used my feature to do it. The perfect example of local policing coming up trumps.'

Carver pointed a finger.

'Fuck me. How did I miss this?'

'Good question.'

Jackson looked at him for a long time. 'Jamie, I'm sorry, I never-'

'Forget it. It's in the past.'

'Yes, but-'

Carver gave him the look again. 'I said, 'forget it'.'

Jackson fell silent. Carver waited, finishing his drink, giving him time. Eventually the man across the table picked up the thread.

'It was in their interests to forget that Hart might have had an accomplice.' Carver stayed silent. 'It wouldn't have been such a success story. In fact, some might have said the opposite. That it was a failure, because there's still a killer out there, waiting to be caught.'

'Some *might* say that.' Carver said.

'I'm beginning to understand why you might not have been returning my calls-'

About bloody time.

Jackson became animated. 'I've got it.'

Carver looked up.

'These latest killings-'

'What about them?'

'You think they're the work of Hart's accomplice.'

Carver shook his head. 'But don't think I haven't considered it. We've looked at it every which way. Profiled them all, up, down, inside-out. There's nothing about the Worshipper series that matches what Hart was doing in any way.'

'So you think it's an entirely separate series?'

'That's how we're seeing it.'

Jackson seemed disappointed.

'So where is he now?'

'Who?'

'Hart's accomplice. What's he doing, right now?'

Carver drained the rest of his pint. 'I haven't a clue. But he'll come. One day.'

'How so?'

'Someone'll give him up. Or he'll come forward and

confess his sins. Or he'll get picked up on something else and we'll make the connection. All I know is, he'll come. I'm sure of it.'

Jackson looked doubtful, but said nothing.

For several minutes neither man spoke. Carver waited.

Eventually Jackson said, 'So how much of this can I use?'

'None of it.'

'WHAT?'

'Like I said. Off the record.'

Come on Jamie. There's got to be some angle I can use.'

'If there is, I can't give it to you. Besides, you said you just wanted to do a follow-up piece on me?'

'I do, but-'

'In which case the story is I've recovered from it all, moved on and now I'm involved in a new investigation.'

'Involving a killer who's as twisted, if not more so, than Hart himself.'

'That's a story isn't it?'

'Yes, but not as-'

'-Good as the one you'd like to tell.'

'Right.'

Carver stood up. 'Life's a bitch-'

Jackson gave a wry smile. 'Then you die.'

They finished their drinks.

Eventually Jackson rose, held out a hand. 'Thanks for seeing me.'

Carver hesitated before taking it. It was as dry as he remembered. 'Like I said, it wasn't my idea.'

'Even so. Can we meet again? If I can come up with an angle, I mean? One that's acceptable to you?'

Carver thought on it. 'Maybe.' He left Jackson standing by the table.

Walking towards his car his thought was, *Maybe he's not that sharp after all.*

Then, behind, he heard, 'JAMIE.'

He turned. Jackson was jogging towards him, animated again. *Spoke too soon.*

'These spokespersons you mentioned. The ones who wanted to make a big thing out of the Hart case.'

'What about them?'

They included your Chief Constable at the time.'

'So?'

'He was your father.'

PART II

Like Minds

CHAPTER 27

A break in the clouds allowed the full moon's silvery light to fall through the open window and onto the bed where the couple lay, entwined in each other's arms. At that moment the man cupped the woman's jaw in the cleave between fingers and thumb and they kissed, deeply. Turning the back of his hand to her neck, he slid it down, over skin that was slick with sweat, over her breasts, her stomach then onto her thighs, before doubling back to rest in the dampness between her legs. He nuzzled into her neck, tasting the bitter traces of her musky fragrance, drawing from her purrs of pleasure. After a few seconds, she slipped out from under him, and turned him over so their positions were reversed. From there she began to move down his body, planting kisses on his neck, chest, stomach, and onward. As she worked her way down, her flaming tresses trailed in her wake and he gathered them to his face, luxuriating in their bouquet. A moment later urgent fingers dug into his shoulders, pulling him down to meet her hungry mouth once more.

For hours it seemed, they had explored each other this way, delving, caressing, tasting, as their mutual rhythm built to the point where each would bestow on the other the release they craved. As the man raised himself onto an elbow, another burst of moonlight revealed the spill of her hair across the bed, the graceful curve of her neck and shoulders. The light waned again but the image stayed, spurring him to even greater efforts.

Suddenly, the hoot of an owl drew his eye to the open window. A shape, indistinct and fleeting, but vaguely human flashed across his line of vision. For a moment he was disoriented. He cast his gaze about but detected no movement other than the lace curtains billowing in the breeze, the moon-shadow of their lovemaking, projected onto the wall next to the bed. He looked back at the window, where the branches of a tall beech tree swayed in the wind. In the dark they could easily be mistaken for the arms of a human figure, waving. He relaxed. Nothing to be alarmed about. He turned back to her, ready to lose himself once more. But something had changed.

Where before she had been naked, her sweat mingling with his, now she was wearing hose and stiff lingerie. Previously her neck had been bare, but now it bore a length of ribbon, the ends of which lay in his hands. Instead of her arms being around his neck, she was spread-eagled beneath him, wrists and ankles anchored by some unknown means to the bed's corners. His mind raced to make sense of what was happening. To his horror, he became aware of a dark shape at the head of the bed, looming over them. Paralysed with fear, he could neither speak nor move, as the intruder clamped its hands about his wrists and began to draw them apart, taking up the slack in the ribbon so it tightened about her throat. He tried to let go, but for some reason his fingers wouldn't respond, nor could he resist.

Choking noises came from her throat and her body bucked and strained beneath him as she pleaded through gritted teeth. 'STOP. Please, YOU'RE HURTING ME.'

He tried to resist the pressure on his wrists, but his attempts seemed puny, pathetic. And though the figure's face was shrouded in darkness, he knew that were it not, he would see a mocking smile. The woman's face creased in pain and she gasped, desperately, for air. But the crushing ribbon denied her efforts. Bit-by-bit, her struggles weakened. Her body arched upwards in one last, gasping spasm that lifted them both into the air. Then she collapsed to lie still, lifeless eyes staring up at the ceiling. Hands suddenly free again, he shook her, vigorously, but she didn't respond. Unable to comprehend what had happened he looked up. The figure was gone. He turned back to her and as he realised what he had done, anguish and horror overtook him and he cried out into the darkness.

'Nooo!'

A voice called out, 'JAMIE. JAMIE !'

Her voice. But it couldn't be. She was dead. He cried out again.

'NOOO.'

The voice came again, urgent now, frightened. 'JAMIE, What is it? JAMIE.'

Then he was sitting up, shaking, Rosanna beside him, cradling his face, calling to him.

'Wake up Jamie. You are dreaming.'

He turned to her, gasping. 'Rosanna? Oh Christ, Rosanna.' He fell into her arms.

She pulled him to her. 'It's alright. I am here. Your Rosanna is here. Hush my love.'

As his breathing steadied, she began to croon a gentle, Fado lullaby. Slowly, he relaxed, sinking into her, letting her voice lead him towards a new sleep, one he hoped would take him far from the terror that had besieged him. And as the darkness reclaimed him, the last thing Carver saw was the soft skin over her larynx vibrating to the gentle rhythm of the Fado as it banished, for the time being at least, Edmund Hart's mocking grin.

CHAPTER 28

The Shropshire Union Canal winds its way through Chester's City Centre. The "No12" restaurant stands on its North Bank, close to Northgate Locks. A striking, red-brick building, it was once the city's main cotton-trading warehouse. Nowadays it is regarded as one of Chester's trendier eating houses. Inside, the varnished-wood and brass 'Upper Saloon' hangs, suspended above the circular dining floor. The alcoves dotted around the outer walls, which were once trading booths, are now cosy, semi-private dining areas, popular with lovers, romantics, and those who prefer that their conversations remain private. In one of the booths, a man and woman were sitting back in their chairs, wine glasses in hand, as the waiting staff finished clearing away their dinner plates.

From his vantage point across the room, Carver was thinking that Megan Crane looked as alluring as he'd seen her. The sheer black dress, split to the thigh had been drawing glances all evening. The bling adorning her wrists, ears and throat lent her more than a hint of Old-World Glamour. Earlier, her appearance at the top of the stairs leading to the Saloon Bar had caused a noticeable lull in conversations, and heads turned as she cast about, seeking out her date for the evening. Several pairs of eyes followed as she strode, confidently and purposefully, across to a stocky, middle-aged man sitting at the end of the bar. Thrusting out a hand she'd said, 'You must be Maurice. I'm Megan. Thrilled to meet you. I'll have a Martini.'

Seconds before her dramatic appearance, Maurice Clarke had been about to despatch his third whiskey since he'd arrived fifteen minutes early for his rendezvous with the woman with whom he hoped to - What, Carver thought? Enter into a sub-dom relationship? Enjoy an occasional rendezvous? Set up for a kill?

Whichever it was, Maurice Clarke looked unprepared for the vision that came striding towards him. And as she offered him her hand a look of something close to panic seemed to spread across his features, as if suddenly realising that the woman with whom he had exchanged letters might be way out of his league.

Not that Megan Crane gave any sign that was her view. In fact, judging by her smiles, tactile behaviour and all round enthusiasm, an onlooker could be forgiven for thinking that, the balding, overweight man in the plain grey suit was some Hollywood heart-throb in disguise.

At that time, Carver and Jess were sitting on the sofa opposite, where they'd settled after following Clarke up to the bar. From there they'd watched him down two whiskeys before ordering a third. Witnessing Clarke's discomfort following her very public arrival, Carver turned a wry smile on Jess. Her response was to carry on sucking on the straw embedded in the pink, nonalcoholic concoction she'd ordered, and let her face show her feelings.

Within twenty-four hours of commencing background on Clarke, Jess had declared herself convinced that he was not, could not, be their man. A travelling Operations Manager for a water-utility company, she couldn't imagine for a second that he was the sort Megan Crane - or any of the victims - would entertain as a prospective play-partner. Nor did he come close to fitting the profiles - psychological, physical, behavioural - from Cleeves and his ilk. As Jess kept pointing out during the period leading up to their meeting, it rendered the whole enterprise a waste of time. For his part, Carver wasn't so sure. Besides, along with the rendezvous they'd observed the week before - a university lecturer by the name of Greg Trueman - it provided a benchmark that could prove useful when it came to the next - to which Gary Shepherd, was especially looking forward.

Now, two hours later, sitting directly across from where Megan and Maurice appeared to be enjoying each other's company, Carver was feeling some sympathy for the man. He would, no doubt, be interpreting Megan Crane's smiles and mild flirtations as evidence that she was as interested in him as he was in her. Carver was also listening, hard. What had passed between them so far was more notable for what hadn't been said. But as the waiting staff went about their business and the pair lapsed into silence, Carver sensed a change coming. Pressing his finger to his ear-piece, he focused. He didn't want to miss a word of anything that might follow. It was Clarke who broke the silence, leaning forward the moment the waiter and waitress had departed.

'So... Is this where you tell me you're not interested and that I should get lost, or what?'

Megan Crane put down her glass, and eyed her companion through long lashes.

'Well, Maurice,' she began. Propping her elbows up on the table, she rested her chin on the backs of her hands. 'You *seem* very nice.' Clarke beamed, but managed to contain himself. 'And you have been, *very* charming.' She paused, stringing it out. 'So you tell me. What is it, *exactly,* that you are looking for?'

This'll be interesting, Carver thought. *Not a mention of anything for two hours, and now she tells him to spell out his fantasies.* Carver couldn't resist. Dropping his head to shield his gaze, he peered across.

All evening. Megan had been playing Clarke like he was on the end of a hook. But now, as she waited for the man opposite to make his pitch, she seemed to turn the, Do-You-Think-I'm-Sexy-dial up to melting. Her face took on a slightly dreamy look and the tip of her tongue emerged to run round the glossy red lips. Not for the first time, Carver experienced the pangs he had been doing his best to ignore since the moment he'd seen her greet her dinner-partner with an exchange of kisses and a smile that was a lot warmer than any she'd shown him. It also reminded Carver of how little they really knew about Clarke. The usual checks - credit, tax, digital profile - had revealed nothing more than motoring offences and a caution for Class C Possession at a rave-bust in his twenties. Divorced - amicably as far as they could make out - and with no recorded history of violence, Clarke was a father of two teenagers, both living with their mother. On the face of it, he seemed no more than what he purported to be, an unattached man looking for someone with whom to share his interests in BDSM. On the other hand, there was nothing to say he wasn't a psychopathic killer.

But if Megan's request that he spell out his fantasies had caught him off unawares, Clarke hid it well. Pausing only to glance round at the other diners - no one seemed to be taking an interest - he leaned forward.

'I wish to be able to worship a beautiful, dominant, woman.'

Though Carver picked up on the word that had become associated with the inquiry, he didn't rush to react. In Megan's fantasy world, the notion of 'worship' was common. It didn't necessarily signal anything. Clarke continued.

'I wish to be enslaved, totally. I want to be made to do my mistress's bidding. Housework, cooking, cleaning, that sort of thing. Foot-worship as well, if that is acceptable. I don't enjoy complete restraint, such as sensory deprivation, or severe pain, though I can take a light caning and being chained up, preferably, at your feet.' He paused, but when she didn't respond he carried on. 'I'm not twenty-four-seven. I'm just looking for someone I can get to know, as a friend, as well as a Mistress. Someone I can see maybe... once a month to begin with?'

Carver waited. It sounded right. Clarke's job meant he travelled the country. He glanced at Jess. Her mouth was hanging open. Then it snapped shut, as if she'd sensed his gaze. 'He looks so normal,' she said. 'Who'd ever believe it?'

'C'mon Jess,' Carver said. 'You should be used to it by now.'

'Yeah, but so far it's all been behind closed doors. But tonight? In this place?' She looked around, as if half-expecting that diners might suddenly start tearing their clothes off and whipping each other. 'It just seems, *weird*.'

Carver was surprised by her apparent wide-eyed innocence. By now they'd been working with Megan Crane, on and off, for close to three weeks, helping her plan and set up the series of meetings with prospective 'play-partners'. In reality, his and Jess's input had been minimal. Megan had drafted the responses to the various letters herself, and "No12" was her choice. Reading them, Carver had been impressed the way she dangled the prospect of a relationship, while making clear that nothing would happen unless she was entirely satisfied they were genuine. As Jess had said, 'She'd make a great politician.' But as he'd come to know her more, Carver had begun to suspect that motivations other than self-preservation and a sense of public duty, were driving her. She even seemed to be relishing the role of 'bait', to the point of offering to test her 'suitors'' intentions by engineering scenarios he worried would put her at risk if one did turn out to be the killer. On one occasion, when he'd pointed out that it was his job to protect her, *as well as* catch the killer, she'd turned coy, fluttering her lashes and expressing mock-gratitude for his gallantry. Despite himself, he'd smiled. Jess also seemed to find it amusing, though looked a little less certain. Tonight was the second of three arranged meetings. By now, Carver thought, surely Jess would have heard most, if not all of what there was to hear? Nevertheless, he followed her gaze as she stared at the couple across the room whilst waiting to hear Megan's response.

Eventually she said, 'That sounds fine Maurice. But tell me. Are you totally sub, or do you ever switch?'

His face registered distaste. 'I tried topping once, but it didn't work. I don't think I have a dominant side, sexually I mean.'

Picking her words, she raised the topic they had rehearsed her through.

'What if I asked you to switch? You top, me bottom. How would you feel about that?'

He looked confused. 'Me, dominate you? I… I'm not sure…? I thought you are a-' He paused. '-Mistress? Why would you-?'

She leaned forward, patted his hand. 'Don't worry, Maurice. I'm just checking. Some men say they want one thing, but are really interested in something else. I just need to know if you would ever ask me to switch?'

The confused look faded. He shook his head. 'For me the fantasy lies in putting my Mistress on a pedestal. It wouldn't work if I knew she had a sub side. The answer is no.'

For the first time, Megan turned towards Carver and Jess's' table. He nodded across, confirming he'd heard.

For the next few minutes the pair discussed their preferences, though Megan seemed to be talking less freely now, reluctant to disclose more of herself. Clarke seemed to sense it, and leaned forward.

'Well then, what's it to be? Will I see you again?'

She showed affront, as if shocked by his impertinence. 'I never make a decision straight away Maurice. I need to be sure. Let me think about it. I have your number.'

The disappointed slump of his shoulders was visible

across the room. But Clarke knew better than to push.

'If that is your wish.' He paused, then, like a young boy who has finally plucked up the courage to approach the girl of his dreams and needs to get the words out said, 'But for what it's worth, can I just say you are the most magnificent Mistress I have ever come across. I would give anything to be able to honour you.'

The look Megan gave back bordered on affection. 'Don't be too disappointed Maurice. I didn't say, 'no', and there's still wine in that bottle. Let's get to know each other some more.' She smiled, and his face lit up again.

Like throwing a switch, Carver thought.

Over dessert, Clarke was like a pupil out to impress his favourite teacher. He poured her wine and hung on her every word. Carver still had the impression Megan was going through the motions, but letting him down more lightly. The power she wielded was fascinating. Eventually, she made to bring things to a close.

'Thank you for a lovely evening Maurice. We may do it again.' She didn't offer anything towards the bill and after the way she'd encouraged him, Carver wondered if they would witness a burst of petulance. But Clarke seemed resigned to the inevitable. During the last half hour his submissive persona had come out. By now he was at the point where he wouldn't dream of doing anything that might offend her.

'Mistress?' he said as she rose.

'Yes Maurice?' There was a haughtiness about her. Like Clarke, she was in role.

'May your humble servant give Mistress a, kiss?' As the words tumbled out, he cast his eyes down, avoiding her gaze. For a split second, a smile flitted across her face and her expression softened. Clarke missed it and when he glanced up again, she was back in character.

'Although this is only our first meeting, I will allow it. But don't think I make a habit of letting people I've only just met kiss me.'

'Of course not Mistress. Thank you Mistress,' he gushed. Standing up, he leaned forward, brushing his lips against her cheek. But as he broke contact he froze, his face an inch away from hers and Carver both saw and heard him breathe deeply, savouring the essence of the woman he hoped to one-day serve. When he sat down again, he wore a contented look.

'Goodnight Maurice', she said.

'Goodnight Mistress. Thank you Mistress.'

As he watched her go, along with those others who were in a position to follow her graceful meander out to the reception area, Carver spoke into his hand-mike.

'She's off and running. Heading home.'

Mike Frayne, the surveillance team-leader, came back immediately. 'Roger. We have eyeball.'

Carver sat back. For the first time since they'd arrived, he even managed to relax. He was looking at Clarke, but remembering her exit.

Jess broke into his reflection. 'So, what do you think?' But before he could say anything she held up a hand. 'What's that?'

It took him a few seconds to work out what she was talking about, but then he heard it as well. A soft humming accompanied by a quick-tempoed, drumming. He pressed a finger to his ear-piece and looked across at Clarke. He was sitting back in his chair. His eyes were open, but they seemed, dull, unfocused. His hands were under the table and he was making a humming noise that was too low to carry above the general hubbub. Suddenly his mouth started to hang open and Carver realised what the other sound was. Jess realised at the same time. Her eyes widened.

'He's, not-? Surely he isn't-?'

'He is,' Carver said. Even he was shocked.

Clarke's face tensed, his shoulders lifted, held, then dropped. Carver checked the diners closest to Clarke's table. No one seemed to have noticed.

Coming to, Clarke fumbled under the table with a napkin then straightened himself. He poured the remaining wine into his glass and drank it down.

Carver shook his head. 'I guess we can safely say we've seen everything now.'

Jess tried to look suitably disgusted, but he could see she was struggling to suppress amusement.

'Not *everything,* thank goodness.'

CHAPTER 29

'So what do you think?' Megan said. 'Does my theory hold up?'

They were sitting in a corner of the otherwise-deserted 'Arkle Lounge' in Chester's elegant Grosvenor Hotel. As he thought on what she'd said, Carver was conscious of her stare. Nestling in the brown leather sofa opposite, with her legs tucked under, - she'd actually kicked off her shoes - she was nursing a glass of Cointreau as she waited on his response.

He ran his hand over his face and reached for his Jack Daniels. It had been a long day and he wasn't sure he was up to getting his head round the more subtle aspects of sub-dom dynamics, but he was wondering if she might have hit on something. A role-reversal scenario in which the submissive asks to suffer the ultimate humiliation - being 'forced' to dominate his mistress – could explain how the killer gets his victims to let him restrain them. The dom-victim would think she was still in control, until her 'sub' revealed his true intentions - by which time it would be too late. But he wasn't sure he could see an experienced Dom falling for it, and said so. 'More to the point,' he added. 'Would you go for it?'

Megan hesitated. 'At first, I thought it would be too contrived. But the more I consider it…. If I *thought* that I would still be in charge of things, then, yes, I might.' Seeing his doubtful look she shrugged. 'You said yourself, there's no evidence he overcomes them by force.'

He nodded, took another drink. Eventually, he said, 'Okay, let's go with it for now. It's certainly something we can start looking at.'

She looked pleased. 'Does this make me a detective?'

Carver tried to not respond to the smile he knew now was infectious. 'I'll think about it.'

As they sipped their drinks, Carver was conscious it was the first time they'd been alone together. After de-briefing Megan on her impressions of Maurice Clarke, Jess had excused herself and bid them goodnight. Since Corinne Anderson's murder they'd been working almost round the clock. They all needed to catch up on sleep.

During the debrief, Megan had shown doubt over Clarke being their man. To her, he came across as a genuine sub - 'Nothing more, nothing less.' But Carver knew his early impression of Clarke had been off. Not as tongue-tied or nerdish as he'd first seemed, he was wary about writing him off too soon.

Megan broke the silence. 'So what happens next?'

Carver put his glass down. 'We'll keep our Mr Clarke on ice while we get ready for your meet with Cosworth. It may produce something more positive.'

'Just a minute,' she said. 'You've just said, I'm not a detective yet. That means I'm allowed some sleep even if you're not.'

This time he couldn't stop the smile. There were times he found her genuinely amusing.

'Don't worry. I think we've done enough for one night.'

'I'll drink to that.' She raised her glass.

A minute later, Carver was about to make a move when she suddenly said. 'Do you know, I've just realised something?

He stopped. 'What's that?'

'You know all about me, but I know nothing about you. Who are you really, Jamie Carver? You never seem too shocked by what I do. Why is that?'

He recognised the feeling that comes when a man thinks a beautiful woman is taking an interest, and reminded himself to be careful. She could get inside a man's head before he knew it.

'What's there to know? I'm just an ordinary copper investigating some murders. Simple as that.'

An eyebrow lifted. 'But you're not an ordinary copper, are you? I believe you're famous?'

Dammit Jess, what have you been saying? But he was careful not to let his wariness show. 'I was involved in a couple of cases that got some media interest. Nothing special.'

It didn't work.

'But according to one article I read, you are, how did they put it? "Britain's Foremost Serial Sex-Crime Detective"'?'

For a moment he was so surprised he forgot to respond. How the hell had she got her hands on that particular article? He tried to laugh the label away. 'Well there aren't that many. This isn't America.'

'But it said that if it wasn't for you, that man, Edmund Hart was it? He would have killed more women. It said the investigation was going nowhere until you arrived. That you were able to work out how he operated, or something. How was that?'

Inside, Carver squirmed. Edmund Hart. A little research and, bingo. Maybe she *should* be a detective. He sensed things getting out of hand and hoped he didn't look as uncomfortable as he felt. He tried to sound matter-of-fact.

'I'd just done some work in the US. With the FBI. I had some insights the enquiry team didn't. You shouldn't believe everything you read.'

Her response hit him like an express train. 'But didn't I read somewhere that you had some inside information?'

Stunned, he reached for his glass, buying time. He was certain there had been no mention of a source in anything that had been made public.

'Where did you read that?'

'Ohh… somewhere. I can't remember now. What sort of inside information was it?'

His mind raced, wondering if her questions were as innocent as she was making them sound. Or did she know something? Unable to see how she could, he blanked her.

'I'm sorry. I can't talk about it.'

She was immediately contrite. 'I'm sorry, Jamie. I didn't mean to pry.' Her voice softened. 'But from what I remember reading you had a hard time of it. Didn't this Hart make some threats against you or something?'

It was as if someone had pressed 'play' on a video. The court scene he couldn't stop remembering played again. He shut his eyes, trying to draw across the curtain that seemed to be becoming flimsier by the day. He waited a moment. 'Let's just say it wasn't pleasant.'

A look of what might have been sympathy came into her face, but he was glad when she didn't probe further. Time to go.

He knocked back the remains of his drink, but for some reason didn't move. For what seemed like minutes but was only seconds, they regarded each other across the low table. He, trying to give the impression her questions hadn't rattled him and reluctant to rush off in case she guessed they had. She eyeing him like a cat watching a mouse.

Megan broke the silence. 'I think there's more to you than you are letting on. In fact, I think you are rather…' She drew it out. '…Interesting.'

He was thinking about another diversion, when she stirred. Uncoiling herself, she swung her legs off the sofa, reached down for her shoes and purse then straightened up, ready to go. He breathed a sigh of relief. But she had one last move.

Bending to him, she cupped his chin in her hand and brought her face close to his. Their gazes locked.

'I think you and I have a lot to talk about sometime, Jamie Carver.'

Her perfume surrounded him and her hair brushed against his cheek. He was conscious of the feelings she was triggering within him, at the same time remembering what she was capable of. He knew how close he was, and not just physically. But then her expression changed and the open, friendly smile broke through.

'Thanks for looking after me, Jamie.' She kissed him on the cheek, light and quick. 'Goodnight.'

Then she was heading towards Reception, shoes dangling from one hand, purse from the other. She didn't look back as she rounded the corner towards the lifts.

And as she disappeared from view, Carver knew why he hadn't made too much of Maurice Clarke's unorthodox way of bidding Megan Crane, 'Goodnight.'

CHAPTER 30

It was late evening when Jess climbed the stairs leading back up to the CID suite. Several phone calls - including a thirty minute one from Martin, at long last - had interrupted her work on the file report of Megan's meeting with Maurice Clarke. It hadn't helped that she'd had to use one of the Typing Bureau computers as hers was playing up. As she reached the CID landing she was looking forward to grabbing her things and getting off home. But about to push through the double-doors giving onto the main corridor, she stopped.

At night, the station's lights operated through a press-timer mechanism. Through the window set in the door she could see that the corridor and all the offices off it save one, were in darkness. The one was Carver's office. The door was ajar no more than an inch or so, a green-tinged glow leaking from it. She knew at once it was the light from his desk lamp. That evening Carver had, unusually, finished early - for him, at least. Something to do with picking Rosanna up from a recital in Liverpool. He was a bit OCD about switching lights off. Her instincts kicked in.

Opening the door carefully, she slipped round into the corridor, easing it shut so it wouldn't bang. The

198

corridor was silent, but for a tinny-sounding murmur. Tiptoeing to Carver's office, she peered in. Gary Shepherd was sitting in his chair, angled away from the door and facing the white board. He was holding something at ear level. The noises she'd heard were coming from whatever was in his hand. It took a moment, but as she saw his hand move and the murmur stopped, then started again, she realised. Shortly after Jamie had gone, Julie, the typing supervisor had brought up the transcripts of the taped conversations between Megan and Clarke at the restaurant. Jess had told her to leave them on his desk, which Julie did – along with the micro-recorder into which he'd copied the audio file for transcribing. Shepherd was listening to the recording, re-playing the part where Megan asked Clarke to spell out his fantasies, and she'd responded, kindly. Seeing the vacant look on Shepherd's face Jess felt her skin crawl. It wasn't too different from how Clarke had looked as he'd fumbled under the table. It wasn't all. Open on his lap she could just make out a manila folder. She knew at once what it was. Jamie usually kept it locked in his bottom desk drawer. It contained everything they'd learned about Megan Crane. Personal details, contacts, associated pieces of information. At that moment, Shepherd turned to look at it. In his other hand was a pen. She watched as he made a note of something. Browsing further, he pulled out a document, then turned to face the window where he continued to give whatever it was his full attention.

Angered by Shepherd's snooping - not just his invasion of Jamie's office; the greater part of the folder's contents was the result of her work - Jess was about to barge in and confront him, when something stayed her.

It would do her no favours if she made an enemy of Shepherd, which is what would happen if she embarrassed him outright. Similarly, until you need to confront suspects with everything, it's always better to let them think you know less than you do.

Retracing her steps, she opened the fire doors, loudly, hit the light switch then strode, purposefully towards Carver's office. As she neared, she heard the rustle of papers being shuffled, the 'clunk' of a drawer closing. Walking straight in, she switched on the main light then stopped, effecting what she hoped would pass for a surprised expression. Shepherd was standing over the desk, looking flustered, already starting to redden. His hands still lingered over Julie's typed transcripts, the recorder next to it. She tried to sound innocent.

'I'm sorry, sir. I didn't realise you were here. I didn't mean to disturb you.'

He shifted uncomfortably. 'Er, hi Jess. I'm, er… looking for something. Didn't realise you were still about.'

'I'm working downstairs,' she said, matter-of-factly. 'I just need some of Mr Carver's notes.' She pointed behind where he was standing. 'They're in the drawer.'

Looking down, Shepherd's face registered dismay. However he got into the drawer, he wouldn't have had time to re-lock it. He stepped aside to let her pass.

'What is it you are after?' she said. 'Can I help?'

Recovering rapidly, he had a story ready.

'I need a picture of the Crane woman. I'm about to brief the surveillance team for tomorrow's op. I thought Jamie has some somewhere.'

'He does,' she said. Reaching up to the white board next to them, - right where he'd been looking as he sat in the chair - she detached one of the head-and-shoulders photographs from the magnet holding them there. It was the one SOCO had taken especially for use by the surveillance teams. The one Megan had provided was, as Jamie put it, 'not suitable.' SOCO had had to make several more copies than were usually needed for such operations. For some reason they kept disappearing.

'I thought the SU had all they needed, but you can have one of these.' She handed it to him. As he took it, she saw his eyes narrow, suspicious now. 'Anything else, sir?' Ready in case of another excuse, she gave up trying to hide her scepticism.

Trapped, he became surly. 'No. Thanks.'

He gave her a vindictive stare then, with one last glance at the drawer next to her, left the office.

Watching from the doorway, she waited until he'd disappeared round the corner towards the MIR, before returning back inside.

As expected, she found the drawer unlocked, a dent in the wood above the lock. He must have used a knife or something similar. Right on top was the folder. Across the front in Carver's distinctive scrawl were the words, 'Megan Crane – Personal'. Pulling it out, she placed it on the desk, opened it.

The A4-size photograph stared out at her. He hadn't had time to put it back in the envelope Carver had glued to the file's inside back cover where it would be safe from prying eyes. It wasn't the photograph she'd just given Shepherd. This was a portrait. One of Megan's. The one she sometimes sent to her friends, to remind them of who, and what, she was.

It showed her posing, dramatically, in full dominatrix mode, much as she'd revealed herself to Jess that night.

She was made up in the glossy, movie-star way Jess was now familiar with and was wielding a bullwhip, the end of which lay in coils at her feet. Looking directly into camera, her expression was stern. It was a powerful image, and one that for Jess, stirred memories.

Megan had given them the picture during one of their meetings. Jess hadn't seen it since. Now, alone in Jamie's office, wondering about Shepherd's motivations, it raised in her a strange mix of emotions. Discomfort. Fear. Awe. Even some excitement. She wasn't sure whether the discomfort related to the connotations within the picture itself, or other feelings which she didn't want to analyse too closely. She thrust it back in its envelope.

As she did, she noticed a sheet of paper which also looked like it had been disturbed. She remembered the note Shepherd had made. Pulling it out, she recognised the list of names, addresses and telephone numbers - Megan's and some of her contacts. Towards the bottom, Jamie had added other names and numbers, which meant nothing to her.

'Now then Mr-DCI-Gary-Shepherd. Just who were you so interested in?'

CHAPTER 31

William Cosworth studied the photographs spread out on the table and congratulated himself. These were much better. It was the lighting that made the difference, he thought. But then, with each shoot he was gaining greater insight into what he was aiming for. He was definitely improving.

'Pour me a drink babe,' he called out, then tutted at his forgetfulness. Petra was gone of course, never to return. It hadn't been so hard after all.

But it was a shame he hadn't been able to talk Lisa round yet. She had balked when he first approached her, but he was sure she would come good, eventually.

He focused on the photograph showing the side profile. The camera hadn't quite picked up the finer detail of the rope-work, and the contrast with the darker flesh tones wasn't what he'd been looking for. He wasn't used to his new Canon yet, but was resisting the temptation to give up and go back to the Olympus. The technology changed so quickly these days, and he needed to keep up with it. He made a mental note to do some test shoots before his next assignment. Thoughts of his project aroused him and he popped another pink. He didn't want to crash too soon. He dropped into the couch, thoughts drifting to what lay ahead.

He was looking forward to meeting 'Mistress Megan' with growing excitement. From her photograph, the one he'd framed and placed on the mantelpiece, she certainly looked the part, even more so than the others. He was already energized at the prospect of what might be – provided he could get her to play ball.

He thought about how he would approach it. It was so important to get things right at the outset. If you fluffed it, women like her rarely gave you a second chance, not willingly at any rate. It was easy to say the wrong thing or give the wrong impression and, considering how they offered themselves, they were so choosy. He wondered, sometimes, if the man, or woman, they were looking for really existed, or whether they were as prone to fantasy as the people they met with. Still, he hadn't done badly so far.

Her letter still lay on the table next to the sofa and he reached for it. He brought it to his face, breathing in her delicate traces and the hint of the fragrance he had – after much searching –finally identified. He closed his eyes. The photograph and the minute but tangible traces in the paper, were all he needed to imagine her there, right now, acting out the role he'd assigned to her.

He imagined how things would be. The look on her face when she learned of his ambitions. But he was sure that, as long as he dealt the cards right, she would play along. After all, the others had.

CHAPTER 32

By the time Carver made it to Shepherd's office, his fellow ASIO was in full flow. When he'd taken his colleague's call summoning him to a meeting to hear, 'something important,' Carver was in the middle of briefing Mike Frayne on the following night's op. Clearly, Shepherd hadn't felt inclined to wait.

Shepherd was stood facing The Duke, Jess, Cleeves and Alec Duncan who were fanned out before him on chairs, as if they were a judging panel. At the back were two of his team, DS Tony Taylor and DC Colin Webster. Shepherd was holding up a couple of items for his audience's inspection. In his right hand, open at the relevant page, was the edition of 'Skin Tight' magazine containing the photo-shoot that seemed to presage the murders. In his left, was a head-and-shoulders photograph of an attractive young woman with mousey-blonde hair. Artfully-lit, and with its soft-focus and careful framing, it was the sort of thing an aspiring model might tout around agencies. As Carver entered, Shepherd barely paused in his delivery.

'.... thanks to excellent work by Tony and Colin-' He motioned to the two men at the rear. 'We've identified her as a Dutch girl by the name of Katelijne Mertens.

She came to Manchester to do some modelling and from there got into glamour work, eventually progressing into porn. By the time she did these-' He tapped the photos with a finger. '-She was already established around the fetish scene. You can still find some of her stuff on the usual porn sites.'

Carver thought about interrupting to ask what they were, but decided against.

'A year or so after this shoot she dropped off the scene altogether. We think she moved back to Holland but that's not confirmed yet. Tony and Colin are still working to track her down, but no luck so far.'

The Duke picked it up. 'I take it you've not raised an enquiry with the local police over there yet?'

Shepherd shook his head. 'I thought we should take stock before we do anything else. Which is why I called you all here.'

The Duke nodded. 'Good. Well done Gary, and you Tony and Colin.' He turned to Carver. 'What do you think?'

'If we can't trace her here, Holland's the next logical step. But someone needs to get over there. I can't imagine the Dutch police putting too much effort into tracing a former porn model.

'Agreed. Gary, if we need to do that it'll be you and Tony. Sorry Colin.'

The lowest ranked man in the room hid his disappointment. 'No probs Boss.'

'When's the Crane woman meeting Cosworth?'

'Tomorrow night,' Carver said.

'Okay. Let's get that out of the way, then see where we are.'

Later, alone together in Carver's office, Jess pinned

him with a look. 'Do you think the girl will take us anywhere, assuming we find her?'

Carver returned her stare. 'I'd like to have the option of finding out.'

'I thought you didn't think much of the Cosworth connection?'

'It's Cosworth himself I'm not sure of. He may treat women like shit, but I just don't see him as a killer. That said, there's no denying those photos are damned close. If there is a connection, the girl may point us to it.'

Jess nodded, changed the subject. 'So, how about tomorrow night?'

'What about it?'

'Are you- Are we, ready for it?'

Carver's response was a long time coming and his face was deadly serious when he said, 'I hope to God we are.'

The car park opposite the Museum Street exit from Warrington Police Station is unlit. The light from the street lamps around its perimeter isn't strong enough to penetrate to its centre, which remains a dark pool. In the middle of that pool and square on to the station's gates, a figure in black-leathers and full-face helmet was sitting astride a Yamaha 250cc motorcycle, arms folded, waiting.

Shortly after nine-thirty, a black, VW Golf poked its nose out of the gates and stopped as the driver checked right, down Museum Street. Road clear, it accelerated left and out. At the same time, the motorcyclist pressed the machine's ignition, gunned the throttle and headed for the exit. By the time the Golf paused at the junction with Parker Street, making ready to hang another left down towards Bridge Foot and on out of town, the Yamaha was in the ideal follow position, ten yards behind. From there the rider could hang back or advance, as traffic and circumstances dictated until such time as the Golf's sole occupant reached his final destination for the evening. Home.

CHAPTER 33

Carver was becoming increasingly irritated. He tried showing it by letting out a heavy sigh. It didn't work. Shepherd carried on staring across at the table where Megan Crane and William Cosworth appeared to be enjoying each other's company. Carver exchanged a glance with Jess. She merely raised an eyebrow that said, *Don't look at me. I'm the junior here.*

'*Gary*.' Carver said it low but sharp. This time it had the desired effect. Shepherd snapped his head round, but avoided Carver's gaze. Carver sighed again.

It was the third - or was it fourth? - time he'd caught Shepherd breaking the most basic rule of surveillance. *Don't stare.* Okay, Shepherd's accelerated career track meant his 'Agreed Training Priorities', wouldn't have included formal Surveillance Training. But static observation isn't rocket science. Jess wasn't trained either, but she was managing to make it look like her attention was on her male companions. Not for the first time, Carver wondered if Shepherd's interest was focused on his favoured suspect, or his date.

As with the previous meetings, Megan looked stunning, though tonight's look – hair up in a classy chignon - was one Carver hadn't seen before. The clinging, cream jersey-dress certainly showed off her figure as well as the black numbers she'd worn previously. Satisfied Shepherd's attention was back where it was supposed to be, Carver tuned back in to the conversation in his ear.

Despite Megan's attempts to draw him out, Cosworth was still downplaying his fashion-photography interests. Earlier, Carver was surprised to hear Cosworth pass up the opportunity to mention his fetish-work for magazines such as SkinTight. Under the circumstances he'd have thought it an advantage. But then he wasn't the one being weighed by an experienced dominatrix as a prospective play-partner. More surprising, and strangely disconcerting, was the fact that Cosworth was coming across as both articulate, and charming, not at all the drug-fuelled rapist his background suggested. But then, Carver thought, psychotics often present as rational, caring even. He sent out a mental warning. *Be careful with this guy Megan.*

From the moment they'd witnessed her sashay up to Cosworth in the Saloon Bar and introduce herself, Cosworth had wrong-footed them. Used to the company of beautiful women, he'd maintained his cool. He even gained brownie points when he presented her with the gift-wrapped package which she opened as he ordered her drink. 'Shalimar!' she exclaimed, eyeing the blue, flower-stem bottle with what seemed genuine delight. 'How ever did you know?' He didn't answer, but tapped the side of his nose, mysteriously. Jess's face said that even she was impressed. Chalk one up to Cosworth.

Right now they were talking food, favourite eating places and such. Still at the, 'getting to know each other stage', they weren't yet ready to explore the matters that had brought them together. Bored by the slow progress, Carver settled back and put his trust in his subconscious telling him when they were. In the meantime, he focused on catching Shepherd out again.

Across the table, Jess was having trouble deciding what to attend to most. Megan and Cosworth were her main priority, obviously. But the interplay between Carver and Shepherd was every bit as interesting. Carver was clearly irked by Shepherd's lack of guile. Even she was galled that someone marked as a future Chief Officer could be so lacking in basic operational nouse. As bad, if not worse, was the look that came into Shepherd face each time his gaze slipped back to the table across the room. She was sure it wasn't Cosworth who was triggering it. It confirmed the thoughts she'd been having about him ever since that night he'd tried to lure her into his camp. 'Creepy' didn't do it justice. But something about Carver's behaviour also bothered her, though she couldn't put a finger on it.

Certainly, the 'edginess' that had been growing in him the past weeks was as noticeable as ever. And the way he seemed discomfited each time he caught Shepherd staring, put her in mind of an old boyfriend who hated other men looking at her. She wondered if maybe he was finally responding to her news about Shepherd's late-night snooping, though why he would wait so long to let it show was beyond her. The day after the incident, she'd tried several times to get him to show concern – interest even – and was surprised when he contented himself with a bemused rub of the chin, an ambiguous narrowing of his dark eyes. He wouldn't even speculate as to what Shepherd might have been up to. 'Who knows?' he'd said. 'Gary can be a strange sort of guy sometimes.' *He said much the same about you once,* she'd thought, before giving up, frustrated and not a little annoyed that she had put her head above the parapet to confront Shepherd - and he didn't seem to give a hoot.

What made it worse was having to spend the evening in Shepherd's company. But as Carver had pointed out, Cosworth was Shepherd's man. It was only right he should be part of the eye-ball team. As she continued to switch her focus between the two men and the table across the room, Jess wondered where the Hell the night's events would take them.

Carver had to wait until coffees arrived before talk turned, finally, to what they were waiting for. Megan began by asking how and when Cosworth first became interested in kink. He said it was through a photographer friend, early in his career. 'Things just seemed to develop from there.' Despite the vague answer Megan nodded, as if it was all she needed. When he asked the same, she spoke, equally vaguely, of an experienced, 'former partner' who had led her into it. After skirting round the subject a few minutes more, Megan said. 'Right William. This has all been very nice, but I think it's time we got down to business.' Cosworth nodded and sat forward, readying himself for the expected interrogation. 'But before we do, I need to freshen up.' She rooted in her bag hanging over the back of her chair and took out a small pouch. 'Excuse me a moment.'

Rising, she threw a smile at the young waiter whose eyes had hardly left her all evening and who scooted over to take her chair, before making her way to the Ladies at the back of the restaurant. Cosworth leaned to his left so he could follow her progress. There was the sound of doors opening, the clack of shoes on tile, another door banged, then silence. Carver looked across at Jess.

She rolled her eyes. 'She's hardly going to let you listen to her pee is she?'

By now Megan was familiar enough with how the mic worked - tonight it was fitted into her brooch - she no longer needed Jess's help to switch it on and off. Proceedings interrupted, they relaxed. But only for a moment.

'What's he doing?' Jess said.

Carver looked up in time to see Cosworth unhook Megan's bag from the back of her chair. He glanced towards the Ladies, before starting to rummage through it.

'Oh-Oh!' Carver said. A moment later he was dismayed to see him take out a piece of paper. Checking the toilets again, Cosworth took out his mobile and took a snap of it. Putting the item back he returned the bag to the chair.

Carver shot Jess a glance. 'I hope to God that wasn't her address.' Jess grimaced. Neither of them had thought to check her bag.

A moment later, Megan appeared and re-joined Cosworth. As she sat down she mouthed something to him. They all groaned.

'She's forgotten to turn her mic back on,' Jess said.

Carver spoke urgently, into the mic in his sleeve. 'Alec? Her mic's off. Can you alert her?'

Up in the Saloon Bar, Alec Duncan, the backup-eyeball, appeared at the railing. Looking down on the diners he said, 'I'll try, but she won't be able to do it at the table without making it obvious.'

Though the mic was in the brooch, the transmitter and switch was somewhere under her dress.

A couple of minutes later, Alec sauntered into view, making towards their table as he pretended to be talking on his mobile. As he approached, the pair were deep in conversation. Neither marked him, but once he was passed and Cosworth's back was to him, he lingered, trying to attract her attention, at the same time tapping a finger in his ear. The young couple at the nearest table began giving him strange looks. Eventually Megan glanced up. She stared at Alec for several seconds while managing to not register anything, before snapping her attention back to Cosworth, who remained oblivious.

A few minutes later, responding to something Cosworth said, Megan brushed a hand against a wine glass, knocking it over and spilling its pale contents over the table and her dress. Full of apologies, she retreated to the ladies' once more.

'At least she's taking her bag with her this time,' Jess said.

A minute later, the low hum that kicked in told them the mic was back on.

'Sorry about that,' Megan whispered.

Relieved, they watched her return to the table.

'I'm sorry William. Now, where were we?'

He waited while she settled then said, 'You were about to tell me if you would see me again.'

Megan barely hesitated. 'I don't usually make decisions on a first meeting, but…' She paused. 'But I sense we are on the same wavelength and my instincts are telling me you are the sort of person I can trust. So, yes, I will allow you to see me.'

Carver tensed as Jess threw him a startled look. What had they missed?

Shepherd snapped his head up, 'This is all a bit quick isn't it?'

Concerned, Carver kept his head bowed as he stared across, Shepherd's discretions of earlier now forgotten. As with the others, the plan had been that Megan would use delaying tactics before agreeing to any meeting.

Megan continued. 'Apart from what you've already told me, William, what other sorts of things interest you?'

Over the next half hour the detectives listened, mostly in silence, as Cosworth outlined the various *penchants* for humiliation, restraint and forced submission that fuelled his imagination - particularly his fervent wish to be verbally and physically chastised by a cruel schoolmistress. The images it conjured made Carver squirm inside - for several reasons. Eventually he came to the end of his fantastical musings. He sat back in his chair, waiting.

'That's a very detailed list,' Megan said. 'And I don't think it would be a problem. Just one thing. How would you feel about restraining your Mistress, if I ordered you to?'

'If that was your requirement, then so be it.' His voice gave nothing away and Carver wished he had a clearer view of his face. Megan nodded, slowly, as if contemplating her next move.

'Right then, William. I think we should leave it there for now. I'll be in touch regarding our next meeting. But when we meet again you will refer to me only as,

Mistress, unless I direct otherwise, and you will speak only when spoken to. Do you understand?'

He bowed his head. 'Yes, Mistress.'

CHAPTER 34

Jess could see that Carver was as puzzled as she was.

'I still don't understand why you agreed to see him again instead of putting him off,' he said.

They were back in The Grosvenor's otherwise deserted Arkle Lounge. Earlier, Megan had given her first impressions of Cosworth.

'He seemed quite nice, on the surface,' she'd said, but then went on to describe her feeling that there was, 'Something underneath. Something a bit, well, weird.'

'You can say that again,' Shepherd huffed. It prompted a silence that was heavy with censure. He hadn't spoken since. Jess took pleasure in his discomfort, remembering her own gaff during that early meeting in Megan's lounge at the Poplars. Now she waited to hear what lay behind Megan's hasty-seeming decision to grant Cosworth an 'audience'.

'Well, under the circumstances I thought it was what you would have wanted. I just went for it.'

Carver turned to Jess. She was none the wiser.

'Sorry, I'm not with you. What circumstances?'

'You know. That business about him wanting to worship his Mistress. Praying to her like a goddess, and all that. You've not told me everything about these murders but I had the feeling it might be significant and-.' She stopped. The three detectives were staring at her. 'What?' Her brow creased into a frown, then suddenly her hand went to her mouth and her eyes widened.

'You missed it. It was when the microphone was off. Oh God, I *thought* you were all taking it rather calmly.' She began to redden.

Carver leaned forward. 'Just what, exactly, did he say?'

She took a deep breath. 'When I came back from the ladies the first time, he said something about how people were looking at me, *reverently*, the way they would a Goddess. He said that worshipping a woman as a Goddess was one of his favourite fantasies. That he wanted to be *forced* to worship her, to pray to her.' She paused to look at each of them in turn, conscious of the effect her words were having. 'Everyone talks about this Worshipper thing and I thought you'd want to check it out sooner rather than later. So I agreed to a meeting. Did I do wrong?' She read their faces, and brightened. 'It means something doesn't it? I can tell.'

Carver remained non-committal. 'Anything else?'

Jess could see she was excited now, her usual icy calm temporarily suspended. Megan continued.

'He talked about kneeling in front of a woman and praying for her soul. Or was it *his* soul? I'm sorry, I'm not sure now. Anyway, I've known men want to worship their Mistress, but not in the literal sense. So tell me. Is it important?'

Jess waited for Carver. He was staring into space, lost in thought. Megan was still animated, waiting for a response. But Shepherd could contain himself no longer.

Jumping up off the sofa, he said, 'I'll say it's important.' He looked like he was in a rush to go somewhere.

Carver came to. 'Gary, we-.'

'We ought to call The Duke. Let him know. This is pretty near the mark Jamie. SU can pick Cosworth up when he gets home.' He reached into his jacket for his mobile.

Carver tried again. 'Just-'

'I'll call Mike Frayne and see where they are. If Jess can get Megan's statement, we'll-.'

'HANG ON GARY.'

Carver's words echoed around the room. Through in reception, the night-clerk looked up, bored, before going back to whatever she'd been doing.

Shepherd stopped, mobile in hand. When Carver spoke again his words were pointed. 'It *may* be significant, but on its own it's not enough to tie him to anything. We'll speak to The Duke in the morning. But for the time being, things stay as they are.'

For several seconds the two men glared at each other. Then Shepherd snapped the cover back on his phone, and put it away. He sat down again, stony-faced.

But Megan had read the exchange. 'Is there something about this man I ought to know Jamie?'

Carver breathed a sigh and shot another annoyed glance at Shepherd.

'Some of the things you describe ring some bells. They may mean something, or they might not. Either way, we still need to take a closer look.' He turned back to her. 'There's something else.' She gave a quizzical look. 'May I see your bag?'

'My bag?' She reached out to where it lay on the cushion next to her. 'Certainly, but what's my bag got to do with anything?'

'Would you mind?' Carver held out a hand. She gave it to him and he passed it across to Jess. She delved into it and pulled out an envelope bearing a label showing Megan's address. Carver clicked his tongue.

'It's the envelope from 'DOM!' Megan said. 'The one his letter came in. I brought it just in case. Is there a problem?'

'He photographed your address,' Jess said. 'While you were in the Ladies.'

 She paled, then closed her eyes, pummelling a fist into her thigh. 'Stupid, stupid, stupid. What was I thinking? Why didn't I take the damn thing with me?'

'As of now, we're putting you under full surveillance,' Carver said. His face was set.

Her composure returned instantly. 'You can't do that Jamie.' She was somewhere between imploring and defiant. 'You know I could never allow it.'

Their gazes met and held. So far, Megan had always dismissed suggestions she might need guarding. Her friends would never forgive her if she let them be spied on.

Jess waited. So did Shepherd. Eventually Carver appeared to let go. It had been a long day.

'There may be other options. We'll talk about it tomorrow.'

But Shepherd seemed to feel the need to impose himself.

'I don't think you've got any choice Megan. Unless you want to risk an uninvited visitor.'

Jess saw the exasperated look that came into Carver's

face. They'd learned long ago that trying to tell Megan Crane to do or not do something was guaranteed to raise the drawbridge. Megan started to colour. Carver saw it.

'Let's not scare the lady, Gary. There could be any number of reasons why he wants her address. In any case, if he and Megan are to meet, she'll have to give it him sometime.'

As she witnessed the confrontation, Jess mused on the change in Carver's attitude towards the woman. *Lady, no less.* They'd come a long way since their first meeting. But if there was an innocent explanation for Cosworth stealing her address, Jess couldn't think of it.

Carver stood up, and stretched, signalling 'de-brief over'. He looked down at Shepherd.

'There're a couple of things we need to talk over Gary. If you'll excuse us, ladies.' He set off towards the lounge-bar.

Sullen, Shepherd took the hint. He drained his brandy and, rising to his feet, gave the women a piercing look. 'Goodnight. *Ladies.*' He followed after Carver.

As he rounded the corner, Megan turned to Jess. The flashing eyes showed that any concerns she may have been having over Cosworth having her address were forgotten. At least for now.

'Well, wasn't that exciting? Jamie and Gary do seem to have an interesting relationship.' She patted the cushion next to her. 'Sit here, Jess, and tell me what that was all about.'

Jess rolled her eyes. *Here we go again.* But she recognised the warm feeling of intimacy that comes when friends share secrets.

CHAPTER 35

The Duke shuffled the papers between his spade-like hands, regarding them the way he might if they'd been written in Greek. After several moments he shook his head, let the pages fall to the desk and looked up to meet the gaze of the waiting academic. 'Let me get this straight. You're saying he's working towards something specific?'

Ewan Cleeves tapped the papers in his lap and nodded. 'It's all in my updated profile, Chief Superintendent.'

As Carver flicked through his copy, he caught the Duke's glance. He'd been late joining them due to yet another planning meeting with Jess and Megan. He was still catching up.

'Profiles do nothing for me,' The Duke said. 'Talk me through it. Keep it simple.'

Cleeves smiled, weakly, as if he didn't mind at all having to spell out in words of two syllables, what had taken him three days to put into a precisely-worded, scientific analysis.

'It's to do with the way the victims are *restrained*. With each murder the arrangement of knots and ropes, the positioning of body, arms and hands become more *precise*. More *deliberate*. It's as if the killer is working towards replicating a specific image or scene.'

Carver looked up. 'For example?'

'You see it with Corinne Anderson,' Cleeves said. 'When he bound her arms he used more rope than previously, and applied it more carefully so they would stay in position. And the pathologist's report shows that at some stage he strapped her forehead to the post to hold her steady.'

'The significance being?' The Duke said.

'That the killer's motivation is *obsessive*, driven by something in his subconscious. I would postulate something in his past, an event, perhaps an image that has great significance. Subconsciously, he believes that by re-creating that experience, it will exorcise the forces that are driving him.'

Carver recalled what Megan had said about Cosworth's interest in praying to his goddess.

'What about her little fingers?' The Duke said.

Cleeves sat forward. 'Now that's interesting. They weren't glued in position. I believe that if the killer had folded them under, he would have done so. That he didn't, suggests the victim did it herself.'

'But we know from Jess's enquiries, she wasn't religious,' Carver said.

'Precisely.' Cleeves said. He seemed to be enjoying leading his audience. Just like dealing with college students. 'Given that their position is far from natural, we could conclude-'

But Carver had seen it. 'She was trying to tell us something-'

'-About her killer,' Cleeves finished, almost triumphantly.

For several minutes they reflected on what message Corinne Anderson might have been trying to convey as her life leaked away. But eventually, they agreed that without further information they could only speculate. The Duke moved them on.

'So what happens when this nutcase completes his 'picture' or whatever it is?'

'Killers of this sort don't usually stop, Chief Superintendent,' Cleeves said. 'They get a taste for it. Most likely he will move onto something else.'

The Duke's explosion was instantaneous. 'SOMETHING ELSE? Like what? You mean a different method? Targeting other women?'

Cleeves rocked back. Clearly he hadn't anticipated The Duke's reaction.

'Christ, how would we know it was him? We'd be back to square one with no way of knowing what he might do next.'

By now Carver had speed-read Cleeve's profile. He didn't want to waste time debating its limitations. 'That's why we need to catch him quickly,' he said.

A few minutes later, Cleeves left, taking his papers and slamming the door behind him. Carver suspected he wasn't happy being the butt of The Duke's grumpy reaction to his 'analysis.'

But once he was gone, The Duke seemed to calm, a little. He turned to Carver.

'Where does it leave us?'

'If Ewan's right, and the worshipping thing isn't just window dressing, then we need to dig deeper, try to work out what it's about.' He gave The Duke a pointed look. 'We need to move up a gear, John. We need to trace the Dutch girl in Cosworth's original photographs, and take a more in-depth look at Megan Crane's contacts

The Duke read his look. 'Staff?'

'Two, maybe three more teams?'

Carver wasn't hopeful. For weeks he'd been fielding questions from hard-pressed Divisional Commanders asking how much longer their staff would remain locked into an enquiry that seemed to grow by the week.

But The Duke didn't hesitate. 'I'll speak with the ACC this afternoon. You'll have them by tomorrow.'

CHAPTER 36

The four-year old sat, cross-legged, in front of the television. He pressed the remote again. Nothing happened. He started to worry. It was time for Fleabits. He didn't want to miss his favourite programme. He kept pressing the button and, without taking his eyes off the screen, leaned back, half-turning towards the kitchen behind him.

'IT'S NOT WORKING MUMMY.'

Around the door, a woman's face appeared. Flushed and breathless, straying strands of dark hair, hung from the untidy bun pinned to the top of her head.

'Wha'd you say sweetheart?'

'The thingy's not working again. Fleabits is on.'

Anna Kirkham sighed as she propped the iron on its stand and moved the clothes basket aside so she could come through into the living room. She was only halfway through the ironing and hadn't even thought about putting tea on yet. A couple of mothers had been late picking their kids up from the nursery, and it was gone four thirty before she and Debbie finally closed up. The drive home had been horrendous – Leeds United were playing an early evening game - and it was well after half-five by the time they got in. Now, to top it all, Jason was playing up.

But it wasn't his fault she reminded herself. He had a cold coming on and hadn't slept well the night before. If she hadn't had to open up the nursery she'd have kept him at home. She made up her mind to ring Debbie and tell her she would have to manage on her own tomorrow. One of the mums would volunteer to help out. Jason would be better off in bed. And a day off wouldn't do her any harm.

Reaching down, she took the control off her son and pressed the channel button. The irritating commercial for flavoured crisps, the one with the ridiculous genie, continued to blare out, and she remembered what the problem was. The control needed new batteries and had done for a week now. She *must* put a note on the fridge magnet. Stepping forward she reached under the TV, and pressed buttons on the TV box. Channels flashed across the screen. Eventually a large, fluffy blue animal, of what sort she was never quite sure, appeared.

The boy yelped. 'HOORAY. FLEABITS. Thank you Mummy.'

At once, he was lost in the make-believe world of strange animals and even stranger robotic children. She looked at him, then back at the TV. She and the other mums thought the programme was a bit, well, weird. But the kids loved it.

She smiled down at him, the harassed feeling banished, temporarily, by his childish joy. Leaning in, she hugged him to her - she was low on hugs today – and ran her fingers through his thatch of thick, black hair. But he pulled away from her, the wide eyes that were unusually dark in one so young, riveted to the screen.

For several moments she regarded him through wistful eyes. A normal kid, watching TV, with his mum. A normal mum. A mum with ironing to do and tea to prepare. A working mum with a nursery to run. A mum who could still turn it on, if she put her mind to it.

But not for anyone anymore. Nowadays she was only interested in turning it on for one man. A man who was actually nice to her. A man who'd even stayed after finding out she had a four-year old son. A man with a steady job, who cared for her, and wanted to look after her. More importantly to look after Jason, as well. What was more, if she was reading the signs right, it looked like he might be planning to stay around more permanently in the future. Provided nothing scared him off.

She didn't dwell on the thought. She had known for months that she loved Rob and was sure he loved her too. He just needed a bit of help to realise it. The relationship was as normal as she had ever dreamed she could have. And there was no reason to think it wouldn't stay that way.

She looked about her. The flat was on the small side, compared to what she'd once been used to. But she had made the most of it - with a bit of help from her mother, which itself was amazing. There had been a time she thought her parents had disowned her for good. And though the flat wasn't fully paid for yet, it was hers. A real home. Though she knew it was silly after all this time she allowed herself a tiny feeling of self-congratulation, as she did now and then, over the way things had turned out. It could all have been so different. A moment of whimsy came over her and she gave the boy another hug and kissed him, hard, on the cheek.

'Who's my beautiful baby then?'

'MUM. You're blocking Fleabits.'

She laughed again as she stood, refreshed and ready to face the chores awaiting her.

The chime of the doorbell echoed through the flat.

Checking he was still engrossed, she headed to the front door.

He was tall, slim and smartly-dressed in a grey suit. Not-bad-looking in a certain kind of way. But standing there, on the block's long walkway, he stood out like a chocolate dildo on a wedding cake. Although she had never seen him before, it was so obvious who, what, he was, he might as well have had a flashing blue light fixed to the top of his head. She fought against the panicky feeling that welled up in her.

'Angela Kendrick?'

'I'm sorry. There's no one here by that name.' Old habits. Give nothing away until you know what they want.

He gave her a smart-arsed look. 'Yeah, you're Angela alright. I've seen your photograph. You've not changed much. A bit older, that's all.' She saw the hint of a sneer, the arrogance below the surface. She hated him already.

'Who are you? How did you get my address?'

'DCI Shepherd.' He flashed a warrant card but she didn't need to look at it to know he was genuine. 'But you can call me Gary. I'd like a word Angela. Don't worry you're not in any trouble.'

She debated whether to tell him to go to hell, but he'd got her address and that couldn't have been easy. If he'd gone to all that trouble, he wasn't going to be put off by a door slamming in his face. He would only be back, calling and knocking, harassing until she gave in. She knew what they were like. What *some* were like.

'You'd better come in.'

She led him into the living room, but carried on through to the kitchen. She didn't want Jason to hear.

'Nice looking lad,' he said, as he walked through. 'Got his mother's looks.'

She ignored him. Whatever he wanted, she couldn't bear the thought of him touching their lives, not even to compliment her son. She closed the door just enough to block out the TV noise, but could still see her boy.

'What do you want?' she said.

For a second, he gave her the look, then the smile, as if he might be thinking of turning it on the way they often do before they get to the meat. But her eyes must have told him it would be wasted. He got straight to the point.

'You used to know a detective called, Jamie Carver.'

The bottom dropped out of Anna/Angela's world.

CHAPTER 37

Carver was passing the MIR when he heard Alec Duncan call, 'Boss. Hey, Boss!' He stopped and retraced a couple of steps. Alec was at his desk, pointing at a screen.

'Christ, Alec. It's Monday bloody morning. Can't I get my coat off?' But he was already heading across. The burly DS was clearly animated.

'I've been on CCTV all weekend,' Alec said.

Carver nodded. Soon after the second killing, they had realised that the only way to keep on top of the mountain of CCTV footage that arrived in a steady stream was to pay the teams overtime to view it. They worked a rota system, evenings and weekends. 'What you got?'

'These blonde hairs everyone keeps talking about?'

'Ye-es?'

'Take a look.'

Alec rose to let his boss take his chair. As Carver settled, he ran the video clip.

The snowstorm of static cleared to show a night-time view of a petrol station forecourt. A street corner showed top-right. The time-stamp in the bottom corner showed, '02.47'

'This is from Valley Garage, opposite where Dale Street meets Valley Road. The night Corinne Anderson was killed.'

Carver's heart skipped a beat. Dale Street was where Corinne had lived, and died.

For several seconds it was like looking at a still photograph. Then, from round the railings that skirted the corner came a woman. She was walking quickly. As she turned so she was side-on to the camera, Carver saw the blonde hair that flowed from under her woollen hat and over her shoulders. She was wearing a dark coat that met the top of calf-length boots. In her right hand she was carrying some sort of holdall. It looked bulky. She was in view for only seconds before passing out of shot on the left.

Alec hit 'pause' and turned to Carver, eyes bright with expectancy.

Carver stared at the screen. 'Play that again.'

The way Ewan Cleeves kept swallowing and catching his breath, Carver could tell he wasn't comfortable being pressured like this. But he wasn't going to let up. They were still waiting for the psychologist's assessment on the female killer theory. 'Just putting some final touches to it,' had been his last update. They could wait no longer. It was time he either put up, or shut up.

Carver pressed again. 'We're not asking for a definite yes or no, Ewan. All we need to know is, how likely is it? Is it a possible?'

Across the table, The Duke, Jess and Shepherd focused on the academic. He'd just watched the clip for the second time. Carver could almost hear the cogs

232

whirring.

'Ewan?'

The psychologist blinked, twice, then lifted his head. He looked pained. He would much prefer to give his conclusions on paper, in his own time.

'Of course it's possible. The motivating factors we are assuming could just as easily reside in a female's psyche. And there's nothing about the murders themselves that rule out a female killer. The absence of semen at the scenes tells us that. As for how likely? It's impossible to say. Most repeat killers are male. But there are enough examples of female repeaters that we should not rule it out. Certainly, in a case like this and at this stage, where there is no direct evidence pointing in either direction, we have to accept that our killer could as likely be female as male.'

Carver leaned back in his chair and locked his hands behind his head.

The Duke turned his face to the ceiling.

Shepherd snapped the pencil he had been playing with in two.

Only Jess gave no visible reaction to the words that had just blown so many of their long-held assumptions out of the water.

For several seconds no one spoke. Carver felt the weight of the investigation pressing more heavily than ever.

'Okay,' The Duke said. 'Let's talk about where this leaves us.'

For the next half hour, they discussed possibilities. Carver pointed out several. The woman on the tape may have nothing whatsoever to do with Corinne Anderson. The blonde hairs from the scenes could still be from a common 'contact' who, likewise, has nothing to do with the murders. Or they could, indeed, be looking for a female killer. In which case a good part of the investigation would need revamping. It drew anguished looks.

'There's another possibility,' Jess said.

'What's that?' The Duke said.

'It could be a man dressed as a woman.'

They all stared at her.

Shepherd gave out a guffaw. 'Jesus Christ. Someone'll suggest it's Father-Bloody-Christmas next.'

Carver continued to stare. Then he said. 'It looks like a woman to me. But Jess could be right. We shouldn't rule it out.' He nodded to The Duke, who was taking notes. Shepherd turned to look out through the window. At The Duke's urging, they turned their thoughts to what needed to be done.

The list grew, rapidly. Most of it came from Carver. They needed to check the rest of the CCTV recordings in case the blonde woman showed up elsewhere. The whole team needed to be told to review everything they'd done to make sure they'd not missed any references to a woman. Enquires were to be made with the National Crime Agency and the National Crime Faculty regarding women offenders. Carver would liaise with his FBI contacts over what their databases had on female killers.

The others contributed as well. Shepherd would redouble his team's efforts to trace Cosworth's previous girlfriend. A blonde, she seemed to have dropped off the scene of late. Cleeves would suspend his lectures to review his - previously ignored - profile literature on female-offending.

'I'll run it by Megan,' Jess said.

Eventually the suggestions dried up. Carver was about to head back to his office with Jess to write up Actions when The Duke called him back. Concern etched his features.

'I'm going to have to speak to the ACC again about more staff.' Carver nodded but said nothing. The Duke continued. 'Each time we think we're making progress, something comes up to put us right back. The people upstairs are becoming jumpy.'

Carver wasn't surprised, but gave his SIO an even look. 'I know this will sound like bullshit, John, but... my sense is, we're getting close to something. I feel like I've been here before... But I'm missing something. I just need time to put it together.

'Well I suggest you get on with it, rapido.'

CHAPTER 38

Jess wrote 'Alec D' next to the item on the flip chart that read, "Review remaining CCTV."

'He'll love you for that,' she said.

'Alec's thorough,' Carver said. 'If there's anything there, he'll find it.'

The list now ran to eighteen items. Leaving The Dukes office, it had been ten. As they worked, other things kept popping up. Jess's feeling of despondency was growing.

'How are we going to get through this lot?'

'One at a time,' Carver said. 'As always.'

As he went back to checking his notes, Jess shook her head, gave a wry smile. The video clip with the blonde woman seemed to have restored his focus. More like his old self. It certainly seemed to have taken his mind off whatever was gnawing at him.

His mobile rang. Deep in his notes, he reached for it. When he saw the screen, Jess was surprised to see him come bolt upright. He spun his chair round to face the window.

'Angie?'

The conversation lasted not much more than a minute. As Jess listened to his end, her interest grew.

'No… Okay, just surprised to…No, it's fine… Go on… Who…? He *What?*' There was a longish silence, then, 'Of course… TONIGHT?' His breath came out in a rush. 'I'm not sure… Yes. Yes I understand. Okay... 'Bye.'

He ended the call but continued to stare out of the window. High on his temple a blood vessel pulsed.

A minute passed. Jess waited.

'Jamie?'

No response.

'Jamie?'

He turned. The slightly startled look made her think he'd forgotten she was even there.

'Sorry Jess. Er… Where were we?'

But he was miles away, eyes all over the place. She gave a half-laugh, trying to make light of his distracted state. 'I take it that was something important?'

He tried batting it off. 'Hmm? Just someone I've not heard from in a while.' He lapsed into silence again.

She waited. If he wanted to tell her, he would. About to ask if he wanted to postpone what they were doing he beat her to it.

Sitting up suddenly, as if he'd made a decision, he said, 'There's something I need to do. We'll have to finish this in the morning.'

'That's okay. I've plenty to be getting on with.' Her first thought was to leave it there, but she couldn't resist. 'If you need to go somewhere, would you like me to come with you?' His answer gave nothing away.

'Thanks, but I can manage.'

She didn't press, but headed for the door. About to leave, he called to her.

'Do me a favour?'

She turned. He was going through the motions of tidying his desk. Picking things up, then putting then down. *Who the hell was that?* 'Sure.'

'Ring Rosanna for me? Let her know I'll be late? As in, *very* late.'

'No problem.'

Heading back to the office, Jess was worried. One phone call and he was back to the way he'd been the past week or more. It wasn't just the call that intrigued her. She knew how close he and Rosanna were. She'd been with him a couple of times when he'd rung her to say he'd be late, or to break off some arrangement. He always promised to make it up to her. He'd even spoken of how understanding Rosanna was, compared to his ex. Yet this time, he'd ducked out. Even asked her to make his excuses. It meant only one thing. He didn't trust himself to tell a convincing lie.

Back at her desk, she rang the number he'd given her weeks ago, 'In case of emergencies.'

Rosanna sounded surprised when Jess passed the message. 'Jamie asked you to call?' But even before Jess could explain she continued. 'Is he alright?'

'He's fine. It just that he's involved in something and can't get to the phone.' *Why the hell am I lying?* The silence that followed made Jess wonder if she'd seen through it. 'Rosanna? You still there?'

'Yes, yes I'm here.' She sounded tired. '*Is* he fine Jess? Are *you* fine?'

Jess frowned. 'Yes, like I said, it's just...' She dipped a toe. 'Why do you ask?'

'It's just that, these murders. They are a *nasty* business, yes?'

'Yes, they are. *Very* nasty.'

'And are you- Does it upset you, dealing with a case like this?'

Jess wondered where the conversation was going. 'Sometimes. But a lot of what we do is upsetting. You know that.'

'But do they give you the... the *pesadelos*? How do you say it? The horses of the night?'

It took Jess a moment. 'You mean nightmares.' Another time Jess would have laughed at her tortured English. But murder and nightmares are no laughing matter. 'No. Some nights I don't sleep much, but they don't give me nightmares.' Then she realised Rosanna's meaning. 'Is Jamie having, nightmares?'

'There are times... Sometimes he is... troubled.' Jess waited for her to say more. When she didn't she probed.

'Tell me Rosanna. I may be able to help.'

There was another long pause. Eventually she began to speak. For several minutes Jess listened in silence. The more she heard, the more her concern grew. When Rosanna was finished, Jess did her best to sound reassuring.

'I'm sure it's just the pressure of the investigation,' she lied. But she was at a loss what to do with her new-found knowledge, what else to say. It wasn't like they were close friends. 'Look I'll keep an eye on him at this end. If things don't look any better in a few days, ring me.'

'Thank you Jess. I'm so glad there's someone I can talk to.'

As Jess hung up the phone, she was more worried than ever.

CHAPTER 39

Jess worked on until everyone else had gone except the night-clerk through in the MIR. He wouldn't budge unless there was a big break. Alec was last to leave, stowing the discs he'd been watching in the cardboard box with, 'VIEWED' scrawled on the side. As he passed he reminded her not to stay too long. 'You look tired,' he said. She promised not to.

After he'd gone, she checked the rest of the floor - she didn't want to make the same mistake as Shepherd - before making her way to Carver's office. She closed the door and switched on the desk light, pulling the lamp right down to minimise spill.

It took her the best part of twenty minutes to find Megan Crane's personal folder. Its new hiding place was in one of his filing cabinets – it was locked but she knew where he kept the keys – within a docket marked, 'Kerry Overtime Returns'. She spent another couple of minutes trawling through it before she found what she was looking for - the sheet of paper she'd seen Shepherd pull out and scrutinise. She scanned down it, ignoring the details she was familiar with. At first she couldn't see it, and began to wonder if maybe it was her memory playing tricks. But then, right at the bottom, written in pencil, there it was. The name must have lodged in her subconscious and only surfaced when she heard him answer the phone, 'Angie.' Beside it was a reference; NCA/RI/0427/PS. She copied it onto a post-it note and put the folder back. Then she turned to his computer and switched it on.

Ten minutes later, she swallowed hard and clicked on the 'proceed' flag. As she did so she tried to ignore the Security Warning – an intimidating black exclamation mark in a yellow circle - and its dire warnings about 'unauthorised access' and 'punishable with imprisonment'. Nor did she dwell on the possible consequences of hacking into the National Crime Agency Registered Informant Database using Carver's system-embedded authorities and personal identifiers. It could mean her job. A prison sentence even.

But after listening to Rosanna, she was determined to get to the root of whatever was troubling him. 'Angie' seemed a good place to start.

That Carver had shared with her his PC boot-up passwords that first week they'd started working together was typical of the trust he placed in those close to him. But she knew he'd only intended it as a contingency. In case he wasn't around and she needed to access a file-note or something they'd worked on together. It certainly wouldn't have included her accessing any of the databases and Crime Information Systems that showed on his desktop after she booted up. *VICAP?* Wasn't that something to do with the FBI?

She clicked again. A text-box appeared. 'Source Registration Number'. She entered the 'Angie' reference, hoping she was remembering correctly the demonstration of the NCA Databases – using dummy files of course - she'd witnessed during her Primary Investigator Course. The message that flashed back proclaimed, 'Confidential: Access to Source Handler Only: Authorised NCA User 2192: Enter Password.' An empty text box with a flashing cursor stared back at her.

She had feared as much. His computer's built-in permissions and memorised passwords had got her this far, but a final security feature, personal to him, had been added. She would have to gamble. Knowing how most people use the same password for multiple applications, she tried his desktop log-in. The message came back, 'Password not recognised. Please re-enter.' She tried 'Rosanna' - a long shot, but worth trying she thought. It didn't work. She began to worry about how many failed attempts she would be allowed before alarm bells started ringing. It wouldn't be many.

As she stared at the screen, she sought inspiration. Who was, 'Angie', and why would her name and details be recorded in the Megan Crane file? What connected her with the dominatrix, and the Worshipper Inquiry? Carver had first made a name for himself around Manchester. Was that where he knew her from?

Nothing came.

She thought on what she knew of him. He wasn't a techie. He had little time for computers and used his mobile's features only as much as he needed to. He wouldn't be good with passwords. She could easily imagine him paying little or no attention to the regular implorings from the IT people about the, 'absolute necessity,' for proper password management. In which case... She cast her eyes over and round his desk. No out-of-sight sticky notes. Nothing taped to the side of the monitor or the computer. She cast wider, turning in his chair as she gazed about his office. He wouldn't want to have to leave his chair each time…

She checked the cork notice board by the door. Nothing there. Next, the bookcase behind his desk. Nothing obvious. She turned to his white board, ran her eyes over its familiar details. At first nothing jumped out at her, but then, about to move on, she spotted something. A single word, written in green in the bottom right corner. No dotted lines or arrows connected it to anything else. In the dim light she had to lean forward to make it out. *WentWorth29*

To begin with, it meant nothing, then her heart did a little skip as she remembered. Churchill Wentworth was the name of the Ancoats Rapist. Carver's first serial sex offender. And she wouldn't mind betting he was twenty-nine or thereabouts when he was convicted. She turned back to the screen, typed it into the box, just as it showed on the board, hit 'enter'.

'Yesss.'

The screen that came up was headed, 'Source Personal Details'. And there was a photograph. She started noting details in the notebook she'd made sure to bring with her.

Her name back then was Angela Kendrick, since changed to Anna Kirkham. She was in her thirties, born Manchester, now living in Leeds. The photograph showed an attractive, mixed race woman with mid-length dark hair and a slim face. But there was an edge to her, a certain hardness. 'Pro,' Jess thought, conscious she was stereotyping terribly. At the bottom of the screen was a 'next' flag. She clicked on it. A page headed 'Informant History' contained paragraphs of text, all timed and dated, all attributed to Carver. She began to read.

She'd been right. Angie was, or had been, a prostitute. The early entries related to the Ancoats Rapist Inquiry and detailed the information she provided to Carver about the drug-dealer/pimp, Wentworth, who was eventually convicted of the crimes. The entries also showed details of the informant payments that had been made to her.

The other entries, two years later, concerned the Edmund Hart, 'Escort' killings.

Jess was familiar with the case. Anyone around at the time would be. She'd still been in her probation when they started and people were always referring to them, for one reason or another, on the many training courses she attended. The investigation into the murders of seven, high-class 'Escorts' - for some reason, people shied away from calling them prostitutes - beaten, sometimes smothered, but mostly stabbed to death around the North West was one of the biggest of its kind. Since then, much had been said and written about the inquiry, and the man - Hart - who was convicted of all but one of the killings. More was said after he was found hanged in his prison cell, just when it seemed the police might be getting close to the truth about the outstanding case. Much was also written about the intuitive Detective Inspector who brought Hart to book.

It was one of the first, 'live' enquiries to take place under the full glare of the media spotlight. A TV production company was just starting on a documentary about the Longsight CID when the fourth murder occurred in the district. Overnight, the film-makers ditched their original - hidden - agenda, which was to expose the racism reported to be rampant amongst certain elements within the force's CID, in favour of following the investigation 'fly-on-the-wall' style.

The completed series gave some recognition to the man who led the inquiry in all but name during its final six months, and the last three murders, but not as much as the series of magazine articles one of the Sunday broadsheets ran some months after it did. According to the journalist who wrote them - *Jackson??* - before Carver's arrival, fresh from his stint with the National Crime Faculty's Operation Chain-Link, things had stalled and seemed to be going nowhere. Carver was credited with turning it around.

Now, as she read of Angie's involvement, Jess saw some of how he'd done it. He had someone working on the 'inside'.

By then Angie had come up in the world, operating from a smart apartment in the fashionable Salford Quays area. An entry described her as, 'one of the area's higher-class escorts' There was reference to her specialising in, 'fetish'. Jamie had taken her on as a, 'Special Advisor', guiding him and his team through the shadowy world of the paid escort. It wasn't clear if he'd approached her, or the other way round. The record showed that for several months she'd worked almost on a salaried basis, receiving regular payments of several hundred pounds - a thousand in one case. Jess wondered what she'd done to earn such sums. The last few entries were even more revealing.

Angie had been contacted, several times, by a man calling himself Eddie, who seemed eager to meet her. A 'session' was arranged, but something went wrong – the report didn't say what - and Edmund Hart was arrested in the act of attacking her. The record wasn't clear on the point but the wording made Jess suspect he'd raped her, maybe other things as well. Forensic matched up rope-fibres and wounds on the victim's bodies, with the assortment of restraints, knives and hammers found in the bag Hart had with him. He pleaded guilty to all but one of the killings, though everyone knew he was connected, in some way, with it. There was speculation about a second killer, but it was never proved.

Angela Kendrick was well-rewarded for her assistance, and the risks she'd taken. The last entry referred to a one-off payment of five thousand pounds, and her being given a new name and re-housed in Leeds. The final entry was her new name, and an address.

Jess shook her head. It was clear now why Jamie seemed so at home with some of the more bizarre aspects of the Worshipper Killings. He had seen it all before, been close to it. How close, she wondered? The entries were simply a record of a handler's dealings with his source. But they mentioned covert operations where she and Carver had worked closely together, much as they were now doing with Megan Crane. And Angie only ever dealt with Jamie.

Jess sat back, pondering. She had learned much, but still didn't know what lay behind Angie's call, or why he'd had to rush off. There was any number of possibilities. Some she preferred not to think about.

Checking she had all the information she needed, she clicked on 'Close Record', logged out of the various systems and closed down. Gathering her notes, she switched off the desk-light and left the office, remembering to leave the door open.

CHAPTER 40

As the door opened and he saw the face that was once so familiar, Carver felt a pang of regret. The woman that once had been, was no more. In her place was an unremarkable, though still attractive woman, whose understated appearance proclaimed what she now was - a working mum. But even as he took in the crows' feet around the eyes, the ever-so slightly worn-out look, he could still detect the traces of the woman for whose services some – usually those with money and power - had once been willing to part with large sums. It triggered the thought of what might still lie, stashed away in some cupboard somewhere. It was followed, immediately, by a rush of guilt for even thinking that way. Ashamed, he banished the feeling of disappointment, replacing it with the fervent hope that she was happy with her new life, the reason for his visit apart.

'Hi,' He said.

Angie Kendrick returned him the slightly-knowing smile she'd always liked to use when she wanted to unsettle him. He wondered if she'd guessed what had flashed through his mind.

'Thanks for coming. Come in.'

In the cramped hallway, there was a moment's awkwardness. He made to kiss her on the cheek, but she misread it and turned towards him so he had to pull away quickly as their lips met. At the same time her fingers brushed, briefly, against his. Then she was leading him through into the living room, urging him to sit while she put the kettle on.

'What? No Cointreau?'

'I'm sorry,' she said. 'Would you prefer…?'

'I'm teasing. Coffee's fine.'

He looked around, taking in the simple furnishings, the toy boxes, the children's DVDs under the TV. Above the fireplace were several photographs of Jason. He homed in on the latest. It showed him head thrown back, laughing. It looked to have been taken in a park somewhere. Even out in the sun, his dark features and hair stood out. Like his father. Either way.

'Where is he then?' He was conscious of a feeling like nothing he'd experienced before.

Her head popped round the kitchen door. 'He's stopping over with Debbie, my business partner. I thought it best.' She gave a wan smile. *Please understand.*

She came back in with two mugs, handed him one. He smiled at the cartoon animals on the side. She read his thoughts, and smiled also. For several seconds neither spoke. He took a deep breath.

'So. How you doing?'

Over the next several minutes they caught up with each other's lives. He asked after her, the nursery and, of course, Jason. She told him they were all fine, about how she'd gained her Nursery Attendant's NVQ Level Three and used it to set up the business with Debbie, who she'd met at ante-natal classes.

He marvelled. Five years ago he could never have imagined... Then he remembered. She was no longer that person.

She told him how well Jason was doing, how bright he was. 'Just like his Dad!' He ignored it, though he could hear the pride and love in her voice. She, at least, had no doubts. She mentioned Rob.

'Rob?'

'My boyfriend. He's divorced.'

He wasn't sure how to react so said nothing.

She seemed to sense his awkwardness.

'He's nice. You'd like him.'

'Is it serious?'

She nodded. 'I think so.'

He forced himself to relax. She deserved it. 'I'm glad.'

She asked how he was doing and, tentatively, about Rosanna. He lied of course, telling her he was fine, then more truthfully how he and Rosanna were still together. He left out the 'but'.

'That's nice. How long is it now? Three years?'

He nodded, drank his coffee. Time to move on.

'Tell me what happened.'

She took a deep breath, and began. Shepherd's story was that he was working on the Worshipper Case. She'd remembered hearing about it on the news, but not much. It was away the other side of the Pennines, but it had crossed her mind that Carver might be involved. Shepherd had said he'd been ordered to resurrect her, so she could assist the inquiry through her, 'specialised knowledge of this sort of thing.'

Carver was aghast. He could barely believe the man

would be so stupid. Strict rules govern approaching a dormant informant, the first being that the original handler has to be consulted before any approach. But Carver knew what he was trying to do. Conscious of the role Megan Crane was playing, Shepherd was after an 'inside' source of his own. But that he should try to get one this way, wasn't just against the rules. It was unethical, dangerous, and, potentially, fatal to the investigation. Curious, he asked how Shepherd had tracked her down. She could only repeat what he had told her. Someone 'high up' had passed him her details. She'd known he was lying, right off.

As he listened, Carver remembered how Jess had caught Shepherd rifling his office. Even so, he was puzzled. The only place Angie's details were recorded was the NCA Intelligence System. Either Shepherd had accessed the database, or someone with high-level access had passed him her details. Either way he would need to follow it up. He let her carry on.

To begin with she'd tried to blank him, referring him back to Carver, saying she would only speak to him. But he had given her some story about Carver being 'unwell' and no longer in charge of things. He told her he'd been appointed her new handler.

Carver shook his head. 'How the hell did he ever think he would get away with it?' he muttered, as much to himself as her.

'I got the impression he assumed that because of... what I used to do, I would be too scared to argue, or do anything.'

'Hmm. Maybe.' *In which case he couldn't be more wrong.*

'There's more,' she said. She became sombre. 'When

I held out, he became threatening. He said I had no choice, and that if I didn't cooperate people would hear about the past. He said he knew what happened between you and me, and that if I didn't help him it would all come out. You would lose your job and I would lose the flat, the business, and Jason.' She hesitated and her eyes glistened. 'He said Rob would find out.'

'He doesn't know?'

She shook her head. 'There was no reason to tell him. Was there?'

He hesitated. 'None at all.'

Carver was fuming. Shepherd had used the oldest tactic in the book to squeeze a woman. Threaten her family. He put the question as gently as he could.

'Did he say, *what* he knew? About us, I mean?'

'Not specifically, but-' She hesitated again. She would know how difficult this was for him. 'He said he knew we'd got involved. That Hart might have got off if it had come out during the trial.'

The knot in Carver's stomach doubled in size. He forced himself to stay calm.

'He said something about you having a bad time of it afterwards. That you'd been referred for counselling, or something. He asked me why.'

'Did you tell him?' He hardly dared ask. Her look told him he shouldn't have.

'I just told him you'd had some problems. The pressure of the case, that sort of thing.'

'Did he believe it?'

She shook her head. 'He said I was protecting you. That unless I told him everything it would all come out. He kept saying I had no choice and that as my new handler he needed to know it all. He gave me a week to think about it, then he'd be back.'

Carver pondered on it. There was enough there to sink Shepherd, and then some. But he wasn't sure that was best for either of them right now. He needed to think it through.

'Is it true?'

'What?'

'About the counselling thing?'

He smiled, weakly. 'After it was over, I saw someone a few times. Then I went back to work. Not long after I met Rosanna. She was all the therapy I needed.'

She nodded. 'Do you ever…?'

'It's in the past. I'm over it. Unfortunately it looks like some people would like to think I'm not.'

'But what about what happened… at the end of the trial? Do you ever think about that?'

The curtain in his mind stirred. He managed to keep it shut, but a darkness fell.

'Sometimes. At night mainly.' He was quiet for a while, but then made an effort and brightened a little, for her sake. 'Whatever he said, whatever threats he made, Hart's dead Angie. He can't get at you now. You're safe.'

'But what about Shepherd? Can he harm you, us?'

He was amazed that she could still be concerned about him when her own, new life, was under threat. Then he remembered how things once were. He recalled The Duke's words. '*He sees you as the opposition. Watch your back.*' Until now, he'd not realised the scale of Shepherd's ambition.

'That depends on what he knows,' he said.

For several minutes they sat in silence. He leaned across, took her hand. He rubbed his thumb along her knuckles.

'I'm sorry. This shouldn't have happened.'

'It's not your fault.' She forced a smile.

Suddenly she gathered herself, and sat up straight, clasping her hands in her lap.

'So. What do we do?' She said it as if she expected him to have the answer at his fingertips. For a brief moment, he caught a glimpse of the old Angie. Haughty, self-assured. An image from the past floated into his brain. He thrust it aside.

'Right now, ' he said, '*You* don't do anything. *I'll* deal with Gary Shepherd.'

CHAPTER 41

Megan Crane sat on the edge of her sofa. She was bristling.

'I'm telling you. It won't work. It doesn't happen like that.'

Carver took in the flashing eyes, the colour that had come into her cheeks. This wasn't going to be easy. He glanced at Jess next to him, but she was staying tight-lipped, keeping out of the debate. He was on his own.

Megan was right of course. Even he knew that no Dom would allow herself to be exposed during a first session in the way he was suggesting. But time was against them. They either needed to get something on Cosworth, or eliminate him. He needed to show that he understood her concerns.

'You're right Megan. I'm sure that it would normally take three, maybe four sessions before you'd trust a partner well enough.' She granted him a slight nod, acknowledging his grasp of things. It was a start. 'But these aren't normal circumstances and this isn't a normal session. You're never going to have a relationship with Cosworth. We just need to see how he reacts if he's given a chance to top you. Remember we're trying to stop people getting killed.'

She looked into her glass, swirling ice. They waited.

'What about the others I told you about?' she said. 'Where are you up to with them?'

Carver spread his hands. 'We've looked at them, but they all seem to live exemplary lives.' He paused before adding, 'At least they do until they meet you.'

The look she shot him reminded him he still needed to be careful.

'And Maurice?'

'Same story. We've been watching him since the night at No12, but he's not shown interest in anything else apart from you'

She fell silent, out of questions. Eventually, she said, 'If I go with it… Where will you be?'

'Twenty seconds away. Maximum.'

She fixed her gaze on him. 'Shall we make that ten?'

As he re-read the letter, William Cosworth's excitement mounted. At their first meeting he hadn't been sure if she was being straight about seeing him again, which was why he'd taken her address. But now here it was. A letter inviting, no, *demanding* his presence the evening after tomorrow. Just enough time for him to prepare. He didn't expect things would fall into place so quickly, but there was no harm in being prepared - just in case.

He picked up her photograph and, as he had done several times, wondered if she was going to be, *The One*. She was certainly the most photogenic so far. *A perfect picture.* If he had only found her years ago, he could really have done something with her; could have made her famous, them *both* famous. But it was too late for all that now. He had moved on to other things, and if she had been interested in becoming an icon, she'd have done something about it long before now. After all she couldn't help but be aware of the effect she had on people.

Well you never know, he thought. By the time he was finished, maybe she would be an icon, of sorts.

CHAPTER 42

Carver sat on the sofa, reading by the dim light of the table lamp. It was sometime after one o'clock in the morning. He was alone. It had become a habit.

Rosanna had gone to bed hours ago. As she'd closed her book and risen from her chair, she'd confined herself to a simple, 'Will you be long?' before heading up the stairs. She didn't challenge his promise that he would join her, 'soon', though they both knew it was a lie. Carver was grateful. He hated the accusatory looks, the pointed questions inferring something was wrong if he needed to stay up half the night just to keep on top of his statement reading.

He couldn't say when separate bedtimes had become a habit. The real worry was, he was no longer trying to kid himself it was just a temporary thing, brought on by the influx of statements and other gumph that flowed from Corinne Anderson's murder. The truth was he couldn't remember the last time he'd brought statements home. Most nights he wasn't even reading, though tonight he was.

The final draft of the Operational Order setting out arrangements for the following night's op ran to twelve pages. If asked, he couldn't have said how many times he had read it already. Not even just that evening. Double figures somewhere, starting with a '2'. As he came again to the section towards the end headed, 'Debriefing Arrangements,' he put the papers down and reached for the glass on the table at his shoulder. If the operation got to that point without whatever he was missing becoming apparent, it wouldn't be critical. But everything before that was.

As he savoured again the single malt's reassuring mellowness, he was conscious that he was way-past the point where it was actually aiding his concentration. He knew damned well he'd be better joining Rosanna and beginning again in the morning, refreshed, awake. Only he couldn't.

Of course, he couldn't be certain he was missing something. In fact, given the number of people who had poured over the paper as he was now doing and declared themselves, 'satisfied', he would have been justified in concluding the opposite. That all the bases had been covered. All the possibilities considered. That the various contingencies catered for within the document were enough to meet every likely, and unlikely, eventuality. But he couldn't bring himself to do it. He'd done that once before and been proved wrong. He wasn't going to let it happen a second time.

Deep down, Carver knew he was wasting his time. 'Failing to plan - planning to fail', the saying goes. Only it isn't always true. With an operation such as this, it simply wasn't possible to anticipate everything. Too many imponderables. Too much to go wrong. Last time it was as simple as a door lock. Who knows what it might be this time?

Over the last week, Carver had felt the burden of

responsibility for keeping Megan Crane safe growing as each day saw some new addition to the, 'What-if?' list. At least he knew that this time, if something went wrong, it wouldn't be a locked bloody door. The debate about how and where they would monitor her session with Cosworth had been lengthy, and at times fractious. At first, she was vehement in not letting them set up their Surveillance Control Point inside the house. But over time, as Carver countered her arguments and dealt with her concerns by pointing out that there was actually only one objective – her safety - she seemed to realise that for once, he wasn't going to let her have her own way. Eventually she offered one of the attics at the top of the house. He'd have preferred one of the bedrooms on the first floor but, for the sake of keeping her onside, he took it. What she wouldn't have at any price however, was a camera inside her Playroom. 'I'm not having you record something that will one day find its way online. And believe me, it will.' It was a hard argument to counter. The week before a video clip purporting to show a sitting Member of Parliament enjoying the company of two Vietnamese women had gone viral. The tabloids were still making the most of it. 'You'll hear straightway if something's going wrong,' she said. 'Besides we'll agree a safe-word. If I think I'm in any danger, I'll give it and you can come a-running.' Despite the misgivings he knew would eat into his sleep, Carver felt he had no choice but to agree.

Now, as the details of the operation's differing stages meandered through his mind like a running stream, Carver looked forward to whatever time it would be the following night when it would all be over. By then, whatever happened, good or bad, it wouldn't be fear of

the unknown keeping him awake. That said, there was
no shortage of other candidates.

CHAPTER 43

Carver was making his way along the echoing corridor that runs past the station public reception area. He was going through the to-do list in his head when, from behind, he heard, 'MR CARVER.' He turned to see Graham Dodd, one of the Volunteer Reception Clerks, hanging out the reception-office door. 'There's someone here to see you.' Dodd nodded back over his shoulder in a conspiratorial manner.

Retracing his steps, Carver thought on who might waiting on him at this early an hour. As he squeezed between the clerk and the door, the older man whispered in his ear.

'She's been here since Three this morning. The night staff told her you wouldn't be in 'til now, but she insisted on waiting.'

Stepping through, Carver saw the slight figure, bundled up in a black parka with the hood pulled low, curled up across a couple of the metal seats that were anchored to the floor. He couldn't see her face. He didn't need to.

'Shit,' he whispered.

Ten minutes later Carver returned to his office bearing

two coffees, to find her checking out the only photograph he ever put up wherever he worked - his Initial Training Class. It helps to remember where you come from.

As she turned to take the plastic cup he held out to her, Kayleigh Lee said. 'You look funny in uniform.'

'That's why I opted for CID.'

She made a, "Ha-ha," face, but he didn't respond. She needed to know he wasn't pleased with her. Leaving his door wide open, he motioned her to the chair in front of his desk. She chose the one to his right instead. He sighed.

'Rita's on her way. She'll be here soon.'

She pulled a face.

'It's no good looking like that. I can't do anything for you.'

'You can do something about him.'

'I can't make someone be a good father. I deal with criminals'

'You think he's not a criminal? I can give you plenty of-'

'You know that's not what I mean. I'm not going to see the whole project fail because your Dad's done a bit of thieving and drugs in his time.'

'Whatever. I'm not staying there anymore. They're all doing my head in.'

'It's your home. They're your family.'

She gave a derisive snort, looked away. He let her stew.

Eventually she turned back. She gave him a defiant stare.

'I'm not going back.'

'Where else will you go?'

'Dunno. But not there.'

'You're fifteen. You can't live on your own.'

'I've been living on my own all my life. I'll be a lot better off without them all round my neck.'

Carver met her gaze, saying nothing. She was so right.

Suddenly she smiled. 'I've got an idea.'

'What?'

'I could come and live with you.'

He didn't return the smile.

He hoped Rita wouldn't be long.

'I did warn you.' The look in Rita Arogundade's face wasn't sympathetic. 'Girls her age can be really clever, and really dangerous. Now she's seeing you as the person who can take her away from all the crap in her life.'

Carver looked round. They were in the canteen, the far corner table. He kept his voice low. 'Bloody hell, Rita. You make it sound like I've been grooming her or something.'

'Have you?'

He froze, like he'd been slapped. 'What's that supposed to mean?'

'It means men like you aren't good at dealing with girls like her. That's why you get in trouble. You're all too naïve.'

'Naïve? I'm a fucking DCI for God's sake. I deal with murderers, rapists, drug-dealers. How can I be naive?'

Rita gave a self-satisfied look. 'How many of those rapists, murderers and dealers were fifteen-year old girls?'

He saw her point. 'Right. That settles it. As from now I'm off the project. You'll have to find someone else.'

'That's not the answer.'

'It is for me.'

'But not for the Lees, and not for Kayleigh. You're the only cop I've met prepared to support what we're trying to do. You're the only reason Kayleigh hasn't gone before. If you go, Kayleigh will go, and that will be that. I need you to stay on board'

'How will that work? You've more or less just said it's my fault she sees me as her white knight.'

'I didn't say it was your fault. I just said you were naïve.'

He threw his hands in the air. 'Oh, right. So I just carry on do I? And how's that supposed to work when there's a chance I walk into a room one day and find her waiting for me, naked?'

'You don't encourage her. You stay professional.'

'I haven't been encouraging her. I've never encouraged her.'

'Like I said, you might think you haven't. Sometimes all you've got to do is give the wrong sort of smile at the wrong time. Hormones do the rest. It's nothing new. Teachers deal with it all the time.'

'In that case I'm glad I'm not a bloody teacher.'

Rita almost smiled. They drank their coffee.

Eventually Carver said, 'So what do we do?'

Rita put her mug down. 'I'll speak to her. She'll go back.'

'How can you be sure? What if she refuses?'

'She won't.'

'How do you know?'

'This was just a test, that's all. When she realises it

hasn't worked she'll accept it. Deep down she loves her family and actually wants to help them, though God alone knows why.'

Carver nodded. He sat back in his chair, relieved. 'I'm glad you're involved Rita. We need someone like you.'

Rita stood up. 'Just one thing.'

'What?'

'It won't stop for a while yet. Eventually Kayleigh will get over you and grow up. Until then, be on your guard.'

'Great.'

They watched from the window as Rita's car, with Kayleigh in the passenger seat, turned out the gate. As it headed away down Arpley Street, Carver heaved a sigh of relief.

'Thank God for that. I don't know which is worse, dealing with a fifteen-year-old girl, or someone like Megan Crane.'

Jess turned to him. 'Any other time, I'd say the fifteen-year-old. In Megan's case I'm not so sure.'

Carver checked her. 'Why'd you say that?' Just for a moment, he had the idea she was about to tell him something.

'Nothing really. Just instinct.'

He waited for anything more. Nothing came. 'Well if your instincts are right, then we've got no chance. I'm struggling enough with Kayleigh.'

Jess gave a half smile. She had stayed with Kayleigh while Carver met with Rita. 'She seems like a nice kid.'

'That's the problem. She is.'

CHAPTER 44

Cosworth arrived at the Poplars at seven-fifteen, as he'd been instructed. He parked his Porsche next to Megan's Mercedes soft-top before walking up to the front door and ringing the bell. Megan kept him waiting some minutes before admitting him. Carver watched from the confines of the Control Van secreted in her over-sized garage. It nearly hadn't happened at all.

Up to thirty minutes before, Carver had been close to calling an abort on the whole operation. Late in the afternoon they'd had to abandon their plan to locate in the attic they'd agreed on earlier when the tech guys finally gave up trying to identify the source of the interference blocking the wireless signal needed to establish the vital coms link. 'Must be something in the material used in the house's construction,' the senior of the pair finally reported to a frustrated Carver. By then he'd already put out the call for an Ops Control Vehicle. He'd seen the changes in the faces of the two men as the afternoon wore on and the various bits of kit they ferried in and out of the house failed to sort the problem. It was sheer luck that a suitable vehicle came free only in the afternoon when a planned Drugs Squad op didn't run because the intended subject had got himself knifed the night before. But it was close to six when it finally rolled up the Poplars' drive. Carver breathed a sigh of relief when its roof proved just low enough to fit under the garage's up-and-over door. It meant demoting Megan's Merc to the driveway for the night, but that would mean nothing to Cosworth. The tech guys rescued some of their credibility by getting the links up and running just as Carver was beginning to think he'd have to call a halt after all. The OCV wasn't as convenient – or roomy – as the attic would have been, but it was recently refurbished, and more comfortable than many he'd sat in for hours on end. It even had a water geyser for hot drinks.

But in the few minutes to spare before Cosworth's arrival, and as the rest of the team took up their designated positions and settled themselves – Jess, Shepherd and a Coms man in the van with Carver, the rest at strategic points around the house and its approach - Carver was conscious that he'd already failed in his first objective. The attic would have meant no external doors between him and Megan which might, by some unforeseen quirk, end up locked.

An hour later, as the 'thwack' of leather on skin issued through the speaker, Carver didn't let the others' responses distract him from his mission. From the moment Cosworth crossed the threshold, he'd been focusing on maintaining a mental picture of what was happening within. If the moment came they had to act quickly, he didn't want to have to waste time thinking about the wheres and hows. Even so, their reactions still registered.

Jess was least affected. She'd heard Megan

describing how she intended to run the session and knew what to expect, more or less. Still, Carver sensed her discomfort. It couldn't be easy maintaining a dispassionate calm while listening-in to her first, 'live' D-S session in the company of three men.

Shepherd's responses on the other hand, like the night in the restaurant, were overblown. Early in the proceedings, his 'harrumphing' seemed intended to signal his low regard for what they were witnessing, as well as those involved. But when Megan moved the action to her Playroom, the tone of the session became even darker, more hard-core. Since then, Shepherd's expressions of disgust had begun to sound increasingly forced. What did he expect for God's sake? Soft music and romance?

The fourth van-dweller was a DC by the name of Owen Williams. Owen was as experienced as any Op Controller Carver knew. Yet even the normally unflappable Welshman was struggling to remain unfazed by the bizarre sounds emanating from the console in front of him. 'Bugger me,' was his earthy response to witnessing Megan Crane's transformation from wary-but-willing 'bait', to full-on paddle-wielding Dominatrix.

Carver was conscious of something else. Jess was definitely giving Shepherd the silent treatment. No eye contact either. It seemed he wasn't alone in having 'issues' with his fellow SIO. It was only the second time he'd been in Shepherd's company since he'd seen Angie, and was having to work at not giving anything away. But he didn't want anything to break until he'd heard back from the former Superintendent and ex-colleague he'd spoken with at the NCA. He hoped it would be soon. He was already wondering about his decision to not say anything to The Duke. Nevertheless, he took some pleasure from the fact that with his gangly frame, Shepherd was suffering the van's cramped confines more than the rest of them. Seeing Jess going through the scarlet-covered Operational Order for 'Operation Chaperone' prompted him to enquire again about the matter that wouldn't go away.

'You definitely told her to make sure to leave the back door unlocked?'

Jess shot him an impatient look. 'You've asked me that already. Several times. She knows. Stop worrying.'

Carver returned to his listening.

The scene being played out in Megan Crane's 'Playroom' was based around the stern headmistress/naughty schoolboy fantasy, common in the SM world. Megan was clearly familiar with it and had slipped easily into her role, dispensing verbal humiliations and chastisements that fitted perfectly. She had a way of making even the most mundane transgression sound like a capital offence.

'Look at my floor, you miserable worm. You've scuffed it. When I told you to crawl to me I didn't tell you to ruin my floor did I?'

'No Mistress. I'm sorry Mistress. Would Mistress like me to clean it up?'

'You'll clean it up alright, but first you need to be punished. Bend over. Drop your trousers.'

'Yes Mistress.' The clink of a belt-buckle spoke of Cosworth's compliance.

Over the next few minutes, as Megan had continued to verbally abuse her 'pupil' Carver struggled to interpret the string of background noises that accompanied her admonishments. Shuffles, footsteps, bangs, heavy breathing, groans, clinks and clunks all spoke to activity taking place. Carver tried but failed to visualise what was happening. He looked across at Jess. She returned an empty shrug. *No idea!* Eventually, bit by bit, the noises died away, becoming fainter until they seemed to stop altogether. Inside the van an eerie silence descended as everyone held their breath. After several seconds a loud 'click' was followed by the sound of a door, opening, then closing.

'What's happening?' Shepherd said. Carver shook his head, frowning. Moments before, Megan Crane had been berating Cosworth, telling him it was time to step up his punishment.

'Come over here,' they'd heard her say. 'I'm going to make sure you are properly restrained.' It had been followed by the sound of buckles and straps, being made ready. But now it had gone quiet.

For a full minute the group strained to listen. But while they could still hear sounds of movement, conversation had ceased.

'What's she doing?' Jess said.

Then the noises began again. More buckles and straps. Heavy breathing. Then Megan's voice, but in the background, indistinct.

'Anyone catch that?' Carver asked. They all shook their heads.

It had now been several minutes since Megan's running commentary had stopped. Carver turned to Owen Williams. 'We're dual-recording aren't we?' Owen nodded. 'Rewind the copy to when it went quiet.'

Owen's face registered his concern. 'But it'll invalidate-.'

'Do it.'

It took Owen a couple of attempts to find the right spot, but eventually he hit the 'play' button. Megan's voice, harsh and brittle, sounded over the loudspeaker.

'...need more severe punishment. Come over here. I'm going to make sure you are properly restrained.'

'There.' Carver jabbed a finger at the point where things went quiet. After several seconds' silence he said, 'Run it through again, Owen. But turn the volume right up.'

Owen complied and they listened again. But this time they heard something, just before things went quiet. A faint squeal, like a cry of surprise, cut short. It was followed by grunting and quick and heavy breathing, followed by something that sounded like the thud of something hitting the floor. Carver rose out of his seat.

'Come forward, to where we hear her again.'

Owen cued the tape. For a moment, there was the noise they'd listened to, movement and heavy breathing. Then Megan's voice, slurred, but recognisable.

'Wha... What are you doing?' It was followed by a muffled, 'Mmmphhgghh.'

'Oh Jesus,' Jess said, realising. But before she could do anything, Carver's arm shot out and his finger hit the 'transmit' button.

'FROM GOLD. ABORT-CODE-RED. STRIKE-STRIKE-STRIKE.'

Then he turned, kicked the van doors open, and leaped out into the darkness.

CHAPTER 45

Jess was last out of the van. By the time she exited the garage through the back door, Carver and Shepherd were already out of sight. About her, shouts echoed through the trees. shadowy figures crashed through the undergrowth. It was too dark to make anyone out, but she knew the other teams would be rushing to take up their containment positions. House Entry was the Van Team's responsibility.

At the back of the house she found the kitchen door wide open, light spilling into the garden. Two men she recognised as Blue Team hovered by the far corner of the house. One raised an arm.

'What's going off?'

'Stay there,' she said.

She ran into the kitchen, and almost collided with Shepherd, coming from the passage to the Playroom. There was a panicked look in his face. Behind him came Alec Duncan.

'In there,' he shouted, indicating back over his shoulder. He disappeared through the door to the hallway, Alec following.

The Playroom door was open and she dashed in just as Carver dropped the ball-gag he had taken from

Megan Crane's mouth. He shot a glance at Jess then set to undoing the ropes binding her to the post that was set in the middle of the floor. Jess swept her gaze round the room. There was no sign of Cosworth. Megan appeared semi-conscious, head lolling from side to side. Jess rushed to support her as Carver worked on the ropes. She sniffed the air, winced.

'Chloroform,' Carver said.

One arm round Megan's shoulders, she reached out to undo the rope around her wrists that went to the hook in the ceiling from which her arms were suspended.

'Careful with her hands,' he warned. 'They've been super-glued.'

Jess was next to Megan on the sofa, when Carver and Alec came back through into the lounge. She was helping the still-drowsy Megan sip tea from the mug she was holding to her mouth. Megan's hands, still joined, rested in the bowl of soapy water on her lap. As they entered, Alec was radioing Carver's instructions back to Owen, still in the van. Carver looked across to see how she was doing, which was when she saw something in his face she'd never seen before, anguish.

Setting the mug down, Jess drew Megan's gown around her some more. Her corset wasn't made for sofa-sitting, and she was in danger of spilling out. But she was too drowsy to be concerned and Jess was glad she was on hand to preserve her dignity. She had seen the way Shepherd kept sneaking sly looks as he'd offered advice on how to work the glue apart. *When did he become an expert?*

She threw Carver a questioning look, but he shook his head, glumly.

'Not a sign,' he said. 'The dog-handlers have done a sweep round the house but the only tracks they're picking up are ours. Nothing heading away yet.'

She checked with Alec. 'What about Nine-Nine?' Hotel-Victor-Nine-Nine was the call-sign for the force helicopter.

Moving the radio from his ear, Alec shook his head.

'They got halfway here but had to turn back. Cloud cover's too low.'

'Fuck,' Carver said. Not only was luck against them this night, so was the weather. The helicopter's infra-red camera would have been their best chance of locating a heat source. Without it, or a track, the chances of finding someone in the dark were next to non-existent.

'I'll go see how they're getting on outside,' Alec said, and left the room.

'How's she doing?' Carver said.

'Coming round. Give her a minute.'

As he stood with his hands on his hips, staring at the carpet. Jess could tell that beneath the calm exterior, he was beside himself. Not only had they nearly lost Megan, but Cosworth had somehow, unbelievably, got away. She'd seen the anxiety in him as they were untying her and she'd had to shout at him to stop slapping her face, telling him that she would come out of it on her own. It was the closest she'd ever seen him to panicking, as if he thought she wasn't going to wake up. Eventually she told him to leave Megan to her and to go and help the others. He'd done so reluctantly, turning at the door, a tortured look on his face, before disappearing.

She assumed it was because he'd have to explain how, and why, things had gone so wrong. In particular, how they'd missed Cosworth. She still couldn't understand it. He must have been in the act of tying Megan when the abort was given. Even if he'd heard their approach – unlikely, given that the room was pretty much soundproof – she couldn't see how he'd-.

Megan took a deep breath and sat up, signalling her reviving. Carver pulled a chair over and waited as Jess helped her take more coffee. When he spoke his voice was full of concern.

'How are you feeling? Can you tell us what happened?'

She lifted her head. 'I… I'm not sure. I turned away from him for a moment, then suddenly I felt something over my face and there was this horrible smell.'

'Chloroform,' Jess said.

Megan nodded. 'The next thing I couldn't move and my hands were… were…' She looked down. 'My God, he was going to kill me.' Her shoulders racked and she fell against Jess. Carver looked anguished.

But almost at once, she rallied, fighting to re-establish her trademark self-control. Carver gave her a few minutes.

She pulled at her hands and after a couple of tries and with Jess's help, winced as they came apart. Jess handed her a towel.

'Was there any sign of it coming?' Carver said. 'Any change in behaviour?'

She shook her head, at the same time checking out the fiery marks to her palms. 'He was a classic submissive. No aggression. No anger. Before he turned, I'd have said you were on the wrong track, completely. I can't believe I didn't see through him.'

'I guess this knocks the blonde woman theory into a

cocked hat then?'

They turned. Shepherd was standing by the door, wearing a superior look. Carver tensed and stood up.

'Blonde woman?' Megan said. 'Jess mentioned something about a woman the other day.' She looked at Carver. 'What does he mean?'

'Just a possible lead we were following up,' he said, glaring at Shepherd. 'It looks now like it may have been a red-herring.'

Jess thought that if he were a cockerel he'd be crowing.

'Well, I've no time for red-herrings. I've got a killer to catch.' He threw Carver a loaded look. 'I'll leave you to look after Ms Crane. We wouldn't want anything else to happen to our prime witness now would we?' He flashed a last, smug smile, then left.

Conceited prick, Jess thought.

'What happens now?' Megan said, turning to Carver.

'We're putting everything into finding Cosworth. We've got his car and his flat's being watched. He'll surface.'

'And what do I do?'

'Tomorrow, Jess will take a full statement from you. In the meantime, you need a good night's sleep.' He hesitated before adding, 'I'm putting a guard on your house until Cosworth's caught.' The way he said it, Jess could tell that he was ready to rebuff any objection from Megan. But for once she didn't argue.

'Alright. But I don't feel like staying here tonight. I'll have to-.'

'You can stay with me,' Jess said. 'I've got a spare room in my flat.'

'Thanks Jess. I'd like that.'

Carver checked his watch. 'I need to see how things are going.' He turned to Jess. 'If there're no other developments, I'll catch up with you tomorrow.' He bid them goodnight and left.

But as he was making his way through the kitchen he heard her call.

'Jamie?'

He stopped, turned to see her coming up on him. She stopped in front of him, close. In her boots, her face was level with his.

'Jess said it was you who realised… If it had been any later…' She gave a shudder.

He started to say something, but she put a finger to his lips.

'You saved my life Jamie. Thank you.'

Before he could do or say anything, she leaned forward and pressed her lips to his, closing her eyes and pressing her hands to his chest. Her tongue found his, flicked it, lightly. Caught off guard, his hands rose, instinctively, to the level of her shoulders. His head swam as he took in her beauty, breathed in the musky fragrance that was still tainted by the chemical that had rendered her unconscious. Then as suddenly as the kiss had come, she broke it.

Throwing him one last smile of thanks she turned and, without another word, headed back to Jess.

It took him a minute to recover his composure. When he did, he turned towards the back door. It was still wide open, light spilling out into the garden. At its far edge, he just caught the tall figure as it stepped back into the bushes, out of sight. From where he'd been standing he'd have had an uninterrupted view into the kitchen.

Carver stood in the doorway and drew a deep lungful

of clear, night air.

'Fuck You, Gary,' he muttered, and went in search of his team.

CHAPTER 46

Julie Millar stopped outside Carver's office, checked both ways – no one in sight – then put her ear to the door. She thought she could hear voices, but they were low, tinny, like a recording. She knew the closed door meant, 'Keep Out', but there was no chance. Something was wrong. She needed to know what. He'd looked awful when she'd caught a glimpse of him early that morning heading up the back stairs. His face and her instincts told her that Operation Chaperone had not gone to plan. Within the hour she was proved right. She'd heard more since. None of it sounded good.

Julie was the station's Admin. Support Unit Manager. An efficient, well-groomed woman in her fifties, she was the nearest thing Carver had to a PA, though she provided similar support to the other senior detectives who made up the hierarchy of the Northern Area CID. The arrangement suited her. It took her away from the dross most days and meant she was better informed about things than most of the station's forty-odd support staff. But of the half dozen who relied on her to keep their schedules up to date and tidy up their reports, Carver was her favourite.

She'd never quite worked out why. He could be a

grumpy sod at times, and she knew him enough to suspect he wasn't easy to live with. She'd heard people speak of a 'dark side', mentions of 'traits' that some women might find objectionable. But he'd always treated her with respect, and for a detective he was disarmingly polite. Unlike the others he never patronised her, and she enjoyed the sense of humour that was often so subtle her staff missed it. Like the occasions she knew he was flirting with her, but only because she could see his eyes. It helped that he always seemed to fall for the most interesting cases. The last few weeks she'd been preparing the Orders for the Chaperone Operations. The one for last night had been particularly enlightening. The clincher was that, again unlike the others, he demonstrated his thanks every now and then. And she was a sucker for chocolate. It was for these reasons she had never breached any of the confidences he sometimes shared with her. She wondered if he needed to share any now.

The word was Chaperone had gone down the toilet. According to the rumours, the Crane woman – the operation's 'Principle' - had nearly died, while the 'Subject' - Cosworth - had done a runner. In the last half-hour she'd heard talk it was Carver's fault. Julie was well-versed in office politics. It hadn't escaped her that the rumours began circulating only after Gary Shepherd booked on. As astute as any detective, she had sensed the antipathy between the pair long ago, though she suspected it was housed more in Shepherd, than Carver. But while her inclination was to spring to his defence, she didn't know enough to deny any of the whispers that were spreading.

Straightening herself she took one last look around.

As was her habit, she rapped once on the door and walked straight in.

He was sitting at his desk, staring at his computer screen. It looked like he was watching something – a video - which explained the voices. His head was resting in the palm of one hand. He looked pissed off, and like he hadn't slept. As she approached he did something with the mouse so that whatever was playing stopped. He also turned the screen slightly so she couldn't see it. Leaning across, she placed the morning post she'd made a point of going looking for, in his in-tray.

'Thanks Jules.' He was as distant as she'd ever seen him.

'Bad night?' She tried to make it sound casual.

A rueful look crossed his face. 'What's the word?'

'Oh… Just that last night's op went tits-up. Your man got away. You were i/c.'

He nodded, not denying it. But she saw the simmering anger, and wondered who it was directed against. *Himself?*

'Anything I can do?'

For the first time he looked up at her.

God, you look awful.

'You can keep me informed about what the jungle drums are saying, if you like.'

'Will do… boss.' As she added the redundant reference that defined their relationship, she made sure he saw the playful half-smile. He looked like he could do with something to cheer him up. She made to leave.

'Jules.'

She turned.

'Thanks.'

This time she made sure the smile was as sparkly as she could make it, before closing the door behind her.

Out in the corridor, Julie hung onto the door's handle, thinking about what, if anything, she could do. She looked down the corridor towards the main CID office. It was unusually quiet for that time of the morning. That alone spoke volumes. But she didn't want to go there. Shepherd would be around. If she showed herself, he would guess what she was about. Arrogant bastard or not, he was sharp as a razor. With a sigh, she realised she couldn't do anything until she knew more. Trouble was, who was around that could tell her? The Duke wasn't in, so no point 'dropping' into his office. She thought of Jess, but she hadn't seen her yet either.

'Bugger.'

Reluctantly, she set off back to her office. She had been away no more than ten minutes, but was sure there would be more news by the time she got there.

Carver listened as Julie's footsteps receded down the corridor, then re-started the audio recording. He'd paused it at the point where Megan was starting to berate Cosworth, the point where it all began to go wrong. At the same time, he ran the video of Corinne Anderson's cellar. Pushing away from the desk, he settled back in his chair, listening and watching. It was what he'd been doing since he'd arrived. Searching for the spark that would shed light on what had kept him awake all night.

It wasn't just that the operation had been a disaster, nor that he would have to explain why. And it wasn't last night's argument with Rosanna, though his stomach tied itself in knots each time he thought on how he'd snapped at her when she'd asked what was wrong. The forlorn look on her face as he'd left for work that morning still lingered. They both knew that his promise he would be more himself when he got home that evening was a lie. Even the sure knowledge of what Gary was doing didn't particularly concern him. Right now his 'colleague' would be making it known to anyone who would listen that he had been right all along. That it was *his* suspect who had been revealed as the Worshipper Killer. And that Jamie Carver, the so-called sex-crime expert, the man who had been openly sceptical about Cosworth's involvement, had been proved wrong.

All these things were disquieting. But what bothered him most was that, even as the hunt for Cosworth was gearing up, he still couldn't put it together. Red herrings or not, the blonde hairs, the woman on the CCTV tape, they had to add up to something. But whichever way he did the sums – and he'd been doing them all night – he couldn't get the answer to come out as William Cosworth. But Julie's interruption had disturbed his concentration. After several minutes he paused both recordings and turned to look out of the window.

'Bollocks.'

He checked his watch. The Duke should be back from his early HQ meeting any time. He might even be in his office right now. As he reached for the phone there was a rap on the door. Before he could say anything, it opened. Shepherd popped his head round. Seeing Carver alone, he slipped inside and closed the door before settling himself in the chair next to the desk.

For several seconds the two men stared at each other, then Shepherd began.

He started with a firm, 'So,' then tried to make it sound casual when he continued, 'where do we think last night leaves us?'

Carver wasn't fooled. They'd gone over things before leaving Megan's – after waiting for the dog handlers to confirm that Cosworth wasn't going to be found hiding in any ditches or thickets. He knew an agenda when he saw it. He said, 'With work to do.'

He rose, intending to go in search of The Duke. He was in no mood for buggering about.

'Hang on,' Shepherd snapped. 'I want a word.'

Carver stopped, took a deep breath. *What the hell.* He returned to his chair.

'I've put out the All Ports on Cosworth.'

Carver nodded.

'And I'm meeting Forensic at his flat in an hour.'

Carver didn't respond. They'd agreed it all the night before. He gave Shepherd a look. *Get on with it.*

'I want to get one thing clear.'

Here it comes.

'When he turns up, he's mine, agreed?'

Carver let out a weary sigh. 'Gary, I couldn't give a shit whose he is. But I'm not the SIO. Speak to The Duke.'

'Don't give me that bullshit,' Shepherd said. He leaned forward. 'You've blown this one and you know it. I was right all along, and you were wrong.'

Carver checked himself. He would rather avoid an argument, but he wasn't going to be browbeaten. 'If you feel that last night vindicates you in some way, Gary, then I'm pleased for you. I just want the bastard caught, that's all.'

Shepherd made no attempt to hide his bitterness. 'So

you can get your face in the papers again?'

'Grow up Gary. This isn't a game. I couldn't give a monkey's fuck about faces in papers.'

'In that case you won't have any qualms about leaving Cosworth to me then, will you?'

Carver sighed again, stared at the man facing him. He'd never seen anyone so anxious about getting his name on a collar. 'What's this all about Gary?'

For several seconds Shepherd said nothing. Then the dam broke.

'Cosworth was *my* man, and has been from the start. While you and Miss Prim and Proper were wasting time taking tea with perverts, I was sussing out the killer. I've worked on him. I should have him. And anything that comes after.'

Carver nodded. 'Ah.' He sat back. 'I see.' Shepherd bit his lip. 'You think that whoever nails this guy is going to get, what? Promotion? Or maybe you think it's your turn for a bit of media exposure?'

'Whatever I get, I'll deserve.' Shepherd spat the words back.

'I'm sure you will. Now, if you've made your point, I need to be somewhere.' Rising, Carver headed for the door a second time.

'I *know*, Carver.'

Carver stopped, his hand halfway to the handle. He turned back to the man in the chair.

'Know what?

'About you. What you used to, *get up to*.' Carver stared at him. 'You're sick Carver. I'm just surprised no one's ever twigged. You've managed to fool all those people who wrote you up as 'Ace Detective', but you don't fool me. What're you and the Crane woman up to?

Played any games yet? I'll bet you'd love to. Maybe even involve that nice sergeant of yours. She'd be a–.'

Shepherd managed to gain his feet a split-second before Carver's hand closed round his windpipe and he found himself pushed up against the wall. His fingers clawed at Carver's wrist, trying to relieve the pressure. But Carver was strong - and riled. As Shepherd gasped and twisted, he found himself nose-to-nose with the man he'd been tormenting.

'Listen to me you piece of shit. First of all, you don't have a clue what you're talking about. Secondly, unauthorised use of NCA Source files is a serious matter and as soon as I've got what I need, your feet won't touch the ground.' As the meaning behind the words sank in, Shepherd stopped struggling. His face paled. 'Thirdly, if I hear any more stupid remarks about Jess *or* Megan Crane, you'll have my fist to deal with along with all the other crap that's coming your way. Clear?' Shepherd pulled at Carver's wrist. He tightened his grip. 'I said is that *clear?*'

Shepherd grimaced, managed a nod.

Letting go, Carver pushed him towards the door. He slunk away, massaging his throat and gulping air. But at the door he turned, wounded but far from finished.

'You try and finger me for anything Carver and I'll drag up so much crap on you you'll smell like a shit-house. I know enough to make it sound good. That ex-girlfriend of yours, the one in Leeds with her new life and nice little boy? I'm sure she'd love to be involved in a discipline investigation. And that singer you're shagging? I'm sure she'll enjoy hearing what you used to get up to. As will all the papers that wrote you up. Don't fuck with me Carver. I've got as much on you as you've got on me.'

Carver had had enough, bollocks to the consequences. His hands balled as he started forward. But Shepherd had said his piece and was out the door before Carver could get near. His steps receded, quickly, down the corridor. Carver stopped himself from following. Not here.

Ten minutes later, Carver had calmed enough to go looking for The Duke. But as he rose from the chair a third time, the door opened and the man himself appeared.

'I've just seen Gary. Told him I was coming to see you and we should talk. He didn't seem keen.' He gave Carver a look. 'You don't seem surprised.'

Carver shrugged. All he had to do was mention the Angie thing, and Shepherd would be history. But that would also mean having to deal with the fallout that would follow. The Duke closed the door and gave him a pointed stare.

'Whatever's going on between you two it stops right now. I can't afford to have my two ASIOs at each other's throats.'

If you only knew, Carver thought. But he said nothing and returned The Duke's gaze. He wasn't sure if the older man sensed it wasn't the right time to delve, but Carver was glad when his expression changed and he dropped into the chair Shepherd had not long vacated.

'I've seen your e-mail. It seems Megan Crane's a lucky woman.'

Carver said, 'I still don't know how he caught her out. I thought she was sharper than that.'

'What I'd like to know is how the hell he got away?

The way your report reads, he just vanished. Or am I missing something?'

Carver shook his head. He couldn't blame The Duke for being sceptical.

'It was dark John. Once I gave the abort there were a lot of people running about. You've been there. You know how it is.'

It was The Duke's turn to nod. 'But the way it went down, it sounds almost like he knew you were coming before you did.'

'That's the bit I don't understand. It was almost like he was monitoring us, rather than the other way round.'

'Any theories?'

'None that make any sense.'

For several minutes they considered the 'what-ifs' and 'maybes'. It led nowhere. The Duke changed tack.

'So Gary was right after all.' He sounded almost disappointed.

'Looks that way.'

'You've still got doubts?'

Carver hesitated, knowing how it would sound. 'There are things I can't put together yet.' He recounted his concerns.

'Maybe things won't fall into place until he's caught,' The Duke offered.

'Maybe.'

Carver lapsed into silence, deciding. The idea had come during the night but until his spat with Shepherd, he hadn't been sure. He was now. He pitched it.

'Look John, everything's going to focus on Cosworth now.'

'So?'

'So why don't I take the Holland end of things? We

288

need to find the Mertens girl, the one in Cosworth's photos. Whatever she says is going to be relevant, one way or another. Any trial judge will want to know we've tried, at the very least.'

He waited, letting The Duke think on it. The girl's story could be an important link in the evidence chain. On the other hand, the defence might seek to use her to confuse the jury. Either way they needed to know. He saw The Duke's eyes narrow.

'If we find Cosworth while you're away, Gary would have to take the lead. Even when you got back, it would stay with him.'

For the first time, Carver let his weariness show. 'It doesn't matter. I just want to know how it all fits. And now we know it's Cosworth, Gary will be like a fox after a rabbit, especially if I'm not around. It's probably what's needed.'

Carver could see that The Duke was in two minds. But he was reluctant to go against his deputy.

'Okay. If that's what you want.'

The Duke rose to leave, just as a knock came on the door. It opened and Alec poked his head around.

'Something interesting,' he said.

They beckoned him in.

He approached the desk. He was carrying his mobile and he placed it down. It was showing a photograph. Carver and The Duke both leaned in to peer at the picture of a flat, black object, similar to a mobile, but with a smaller screen. They both turned questioning looks back at the D.S.

'When we were searching for Cosworth, I did the first floor bedrooms.'

Carver nodded. Their first action after rescuing

Megan, had been to search the house, top to bottom. He'd half-expected they would find Cosworth hiding in a cupboard or under a bed. 'Go on,' he said.

'I saw this on a dresser in the middle spare bedroom, the one directly beneath the attic we had planned to use. I wasn't sure what it was, so I snapped it.'

'And?'

'I've just shown it to one of the surveillance team. He says he thinks it's a blocker.'

'What sort of blocker?' The Duke said.

'One that stops wireless signals.'

Carver stared at him. For several seconds he said nothing, letting the implications of Alec's news settle. 'You're right. That is interesting.'

Carver lay in bed, cursing himself. It was two in the morning.

The evening had started well enough. Rosanna had baked some sea bass, and looked ready to forget about the previous night and morning. But she took the news about him going to Holland badly, as he'd feared.

'Why you? Why can't someone else go?'

His explanation - that the enquiry was sensitive and needed someone senior - hadn't sounded convincing, even to him. And though he thought about telling her the truth - not just about Shepherd - he'd chickened out, not sure how she would react.

So dinner had become a sullen, silent affair. She picked at her fish, waiting for him to offer something that would explain his recent behaviour. Why he'd stopped confiding in her. Where he was at night. Something other than the obvious. For his part, he kept getting to the point of saying something, then backed

290

off. He wasn't sure why. After dinner she drifted off upstairs, leaving him staring into his wine.

Now, as his arm stretched out, confirming the emptiness next to him, he admonished himself - again. Of course he'd *wanted* to tell her everything. He wanted to be able to say that it was all in the past, that he was over it. But somewhere deep down was the feeling, the fear that it *wasn't* in the past. That he *wasn't* over it. And as he dwelt on it, the inevitable happened.

He tried to stop himself, but the draw was too strong.

Suddenly he was standing in the doorway to Megan Crane's Playroom, looking at her, bound to the post, helpless. And as the memory flooded back, he screwed himself into a ball, and turned his face to the pillow.

CHAPTER 47

Carver arrived at Jess's flat on the Saturday morning just as Megan Crane was making ready to leave. It was the first time he'd seen her since they'd nearly lost her. He hadn't been avoiding, it was just that he'd spent most of the past two days accounting for what happened. It seemed everyone wanted to know how Chaperone had come so close to disaster, how Cosworth had managed to get away. The Duke, the ACC, the Force's Solicitors, they all wanted to hear it first-hand - as well as demanding a copy of the file report he was trying to work on between phone calls, 'ASAP.'

He still wasn't sure why Megan had stayed another night on top of the two she'd already spent at Jess's. He knew she'd been back to The Poplars a couple of times in the interim, but only to pick up clothes it seemed. The round-the-clock police guard on the Poplars had been organised and ready since the afternoon after. Carver only learned Megan still wasn't back staying there when the team sent to watch over her rang to enquire when she would be home. A phone call to Jess told him. 'She's still a little shaken. Another night here and she'll be fine.'

Carver was surprised. Okay, she'd been through a

frightening experience. But from what he'd come to know of Megan Crane, he wouldn't expect she would need three days to get over it.

There was a moment's awkwardness when Jess left them alone while she retired to her bedroom to take an, 'urgent', call on her mobile. Jess had told him several times that Megan wasn't blaming him. or anyone for what happened. She'd even acknowledged to Jess that she was partially to blame for not letting them use video. It wasn't how Carver saw it.

He sought to cover his embarrassment by asking how she was.

'Much better now, thanks. Jess has been a great help. No news yet I assume?'

He shook his head. 'Don't worry. We'll find him.'

'I'm not worried. Just curious.'

'You and me both.'

In the silence that followed, he thought about apologising, but remembered his conversation with the woman from the Force Solicitor's Office. 'I'd suggest you be careful about saying anything to her that may infer acceptance of liability.' Carver expected he would hear soon if she'd lodged a complaint over the way he'd framed his response.

'There's a team on your house,' he told her. 'I'll let them know you're on your way back. Don't worry, they won't intrude any more than necessary.'

She didn't argue. 'Thanks Jamie.' Then surprised him again by giving him a chaste hug as she left. As Jess walked her down to the front door, he made the call, then waited for Jess to return. He'd seen her face when she came out of the bedroom, and was concerned enough to ask if she was alright.

Her response, 'A bit tired is all,' wasn't convincing.

He probed. 'How's Martin? When's he due back?'

Her pained expression told him that, responsible for the Cosworth debacle or not, his instincts were still working.

'Want to talk about it?' He remembered Megan extended stay. 'Or have you already done that?'

With a sigh, she dropped into the couch before shaking her head, answering another unspoken question. She gave him a long look, as if debating whether to unburden herself. Then she gave a, what-the-hell, sort of shrug.

'Martin rang last night. He was due back this weekend but said there'd been a problem and he was having to stay out another couple of weeks.' Carver waited, saying nothing. 'He was ringing from his hotel room.' He waited some more. 'I heard someone in the background.'

Oh-oh.

Her eyes glistened as she said, 'I heard him "shush" her.'

Carver said, 'Oh dear,' then realised how inadequate it was. He tried bolstering her by offering alternative explanations. But he knew he was wasting his time, deceiving her in a way she didn't deserve. 'I'm sorry, Jess.'

She shook her head again. 'There were things we were going to have to sort out anyway when he got back. Now there's only one.' She turned to the kitchen. 'Coffee?'

He nodded.

When she returned she seemed brighter. He briefed her about how he thought she should play things during his absence. It was her turn to read between the lines.

'You told me most of this the last time we spoke. Why are you here when you've got a plane to catch?'

He gave her a long look, then told her about his spat with Shepherd. Not all of it, but enough.

'You need to know, Jess. Just be careful of him. And I need someone to watch my back while I'm away'.

What she did next took him by surprise. She pressed her hand over his. 'You can rely on me.'

He looked up, held her gaze. 'I know.'

Over the seconds that followed, they communicated their understanding of each other's problems. In her case, Martin. In his, Rosanna, Shepherd - and other things.

About to leave, he hesitated.

She saw it. 'What?'

'If you feel like you need to talk to someone… about Martin, and such.'

'Yes?'

'Rosanna's on her own. I think you'd find her… understanding.'

'Oh.' She looked surprised. 'Okay.'

Minutes later, driving away, Carver wondered whether he'd just made a big mistake.

CHAPTER 48

The two doors were separated by a strip of wall, three bricks wide. In the dim glow of the bare bulb overhead, their flaking paintwork still showed traces of the original olive green. On a hook set in the mortar between the bricks were two mortise keys. Old and rusted, they bore plastic fobs, one yellow, one red. The yellow one bore a black, 'L', the other, 'R'.

Megan Crane was staring at the left-hand door as if she had x-ray vision and was seeing through to the room beyond. Her jaw was working from side-to-side, the red lips set in as thin a line as they were capable of making. She had been like that for several minutes. Eventually, she reached up and took the key with the yellow fob, inserted it in the lock, and turned it. The click of the mechanism echoed in the confined space. Grasping the knob, she opened the door a fraction, held it there a second, then pushed it hard so it flew open and banged against the dividing wall.

The room within was pitch black, the light from the bulb barely penetrating. She felt a cool draught as the air from within mingled with that outside. The stale smell carried on it contained a trace of something akin to ammonia. She ignored it, used to it. Reaching round to her left, her fingers groped over the rough surface until they found a square of smooth plastic. She flicked the switch in its centre. In the middle of the room, a strip light hanging on chains flickered, buzzed and clicked, before flooding the room with cold, white light.

Within the room, the walls were mainly bare brick, though some areas still showed the original reddy-brown brick-paint that had once covered them. It was simply furnished, with a toilet in the far corner, a sink and, next to it, a plain wooden table. In the middle of the floor, was an iron bed with a bare mattress. On it, the figure of a man lay spread-eagled, wrists and ankles shackled to the corners. A grey, wool blanket covered his torso down to his knees. His head was sheathed in a leather hood, a cloth gag stuffed in his mouth, held in place by a leather strap. But light or noise must have penetrated through because as Megan stepped forward, the figure responded, pulling at his shackles and grunting through his gag. The bed springs creaked, loudly.

Megan stood just inside the doorway for several seconds, before approaching to stand looking down at him. Reaching out, she took hold of the blanket and, in one swift motion, flung it away. The man jerked, as if he had been struck with a crop. A half-smile came to Megan's lips. Bending down, she undid the hood's buckles and slipped it off.

The strip-light was directly above. He squinted in pain, turning his head from side to side as he pulled at his shackles. Eventually, slowly, as his eyes adjusted, his struggles calmed and he became still, though breathing heavily, cheeks blowing in and out. He gazed up at her, still squinting until eventually his eyes focused enough for him to realise who - what - he was seeing. He froze, and stopped struggling.

Through all this, Megan Crane stood, still and silent. After a further minute's silence, she lowered herself to sit next to him. Reaching across, she brushed a stray lock of hair back off his forehead, the way a mother might tend a sick child. And when she spoke, her voice was similarly soothing.

'Now then William Cosworth, you and I have a lot to talk about.'

PART III

All that glisters..

CHAPTER 49

Carver was snaking his way towards Schiphol Airport's passport control when his mobile rang. He checked the screen, saw it was Jess.

'I've just landed. What's up?'

'Alec's just rung me. Thought you'd want to know. They've found Cosworth's last girlfriend, the one called Petra. He and Gary are with her now. Apparently she's saying some interesting things about her ex.'

'About the murders?'

'She's not fingering him for them, yet. But she's confirming he's big into SM and gets off on frightening women. He likes the rough stuff. Used to slap her around a lot. She's got a habit and only put up with it 'cause he kept her supplied.'

'So why'd she leave?'

'It's not clear yet if she did, or whether he kicked her out. Bit of both maybe.'

'Okay. Let me know if she comes up with anything interesting.'

'She has mentioned one thing.'

'Go on.'

'It seems he's obsessed with taking a particular photograph. Something he calls, 'The Perfect Picture'. She says she doesn't know what it is, but it's definitely fetish. He keeps trying it on different models, but reckons he hasn't found the right one yet.'

'Dead models or live ones?'

'She's not said.'

'Hmm... Did he try it on her?'

'No. She's too skinny, apparently. Seems he likes curvy women.'

Jesus Christ. 'Well that would cover our victims, I suppose?'

'I'd say so.'

'Anything else?'

'Not yet. I'll keep you posted.' About to ring off, she added, 'And Jamie?'

'What?'

'Behave yourself. You know what they say about Amsterdam?'

'What's that?'

But she was gone.

He put his phone away as he reached the control booths. He looked for the line with mostly UK Passports and a minute later was nodded through. On the other side he scouted around. Over by the exit from the baggage area, under the 'Nothing To Declare' sign, a shaven-headed man in a dark suit was waving. Carver headed over. As he neared, the man thrust out a hand which Carver took. It felt like a vice. The man followed it up with an amiable hug.

'Good to see you again, Jamie. Good flight?'

'Not bad, Erik. Nice to see you too. Thanks for

meeting me.'

'Better than sitting round a couple of days while you try and find your way out, I thought.'

'As I remember, it was you went missing at Heathrow that time.'

'That was because of the shit way you English run your airports. Here, we don't have those problems.'

'Right. Well let's see how long it takes you to get us to a decent bar. I need a drink.'

'Don't worry, our table is already booked.

Taking Carver's carry-case, Erik Van Tulp, Head of the Vice Division of the *Politie Amsterdam*, marched them to the nearest exit onto the Plaza. His car was right outside, parked on the yellow-hash markings. A young woman in the bright green uniform of the Airport Police was making sure it wasn't about to be towed away. As they got in, Erik called to her in Dutch and winked. Carver thought the smile she flashed back was more than a simple, 'Thank you,' from Erik would have warranted.

The Dutchman checked once over his shoulder, then swung out to join the never-ending stream of traffic, ignoring the loud horn blast behind. Carver settled back. The guidebooks put the city thirty minutes away by car. Remembering Erik's driving and disdain for parking restrictions, he expected he would have a glass in his hand sooner than that. Over the next few minutes the man Carver had first met on a European Crime Investigators' Course several years before took a series of calls on his mobile whilst also concentrating on getting them out onto the A4 without hitting anything. Carver used the time to reflect on Jess's call. Something she'd said had resonated with him, but he wasn't sure what. He groped for it, running back over the brief conversation. Then it came. Cosworth's obsession. *'The Perfect Picture.'* Now where had he heard that phrase before? As he mused on it, his thoughts returned to where they'd been as his plane had landed.

He had no idea how long he'd be away. No more than two or three days, he hoped. He had things to do. Stuff to sort out. First priority was Rosanna. When she'd dropped him off at the airport, he'd tried to reassure her, telling her that things would be coming to an end soon. That once he was back and Cosworth was in custody, things would be as they had been. She made out like she believed him, though he knew better. As he'd waited in the departure lounge, staring into his Macallan, he'd made a decision. As soon as work and her engagements allowed for it, he would take her off somewhere. They needed time together, without the telephone ringing, without him having to leap out of bed in the middle of the night to attend some bizarre murder scene. 'And fuck Shepherd too,' he murmured as his thoughts turned to the man who, next to Cosworth, was troubling him most.

As if Rosanna, Cosworth and Shepherd weren't enough, he was also starting to wonder about Jess. Nothing to do with her boyfriend problem. He'd seen signs before that. A subtle change in attitude, small alterations in her routines. It used to be she'd tell him her plans for what was left of the evening as they finished work; 'Meeting the girls.' 'Speaking to my mum.' 'Catching up on Eastenders.' She'd stopped doing that recently. It bothered him. An inquiry like Kerry could suck you in before you know it, especially if you were new at it. If anyone could testify to that, it was him. His concerns had crystallised when he'd bumped into Megan at her flat. He hoped to God he was wrong, that it wouldn't happen to her the way it had him. He'd seen them growing close the past few weeks. And Jess's trouble was, she was so assured of herself she wouldn't even see the danger. Worse, was the suspicion that he'd actually seen signs weeks ago and ignored them, maybe even encouraged it, knowing they needed Megan and that if one of them could get close it would work in their favour. He hoped he hadn't miscalculated. He was still thinking on it when Erik finally put his phone away and turned to him.

'So then, Jamie. Tell me all about this strange case you are involved in. But first, I need to know. Are you and the beautiful Rosanna still…? He cast a leery glance at Carver. 'Or has she dumped you? In which case I will need her address so I can show her what it is like to be with a real man.'

Carver shook his head. Someone listening might have assumed Erik was taking the piss, the way policemen do. He knew better. Erik was married to a stunningly beautiful architect named Vanessa. She'd accompanied Erik on his last trip to the UK. The four of them had gone out together for a meal. The head cold that had been ruining Rosanna's sleep for more than a week gave them a genuine excuse to turn down the other couple's invitation to return to their hotel room, 'for a nightcap.' Carver had heard Erik speak of how he and Vanessa had an 'open' marriage. Carver still sometimes wondered where the 'nightcap' might have led.

Without turning to look at the man he was hoping would help him find the woman he was looking for,

Carver said, 'Piss off and just drive.'

CHAPTER 50

Jess woke in the chair to the sound of her mobile ringing. Checking it, she saw it was the same number as earlier that evening. Then, she'd had neither the energy nor inclination to answer it. But with everything that was going on, she supposed she ought to. She brought the phone to her ear, and waited.

'Jess? Hello? Jess, are you there?'

A woman's voice. Familiar. *Tearful?*

'Jess, it's Rosanna. Please talk to me.'

'I'm here Rosanna. What's wrong?' *She sounds worse than I feel.*

'I'm sorry if I'm- I don't like to bother you, but-'

'What is it, Rosanna?'

'The last time we spoke. You told me to call, if I was worried about Jamie?'

Jess remembered. The day he got the call from 'Angie'. When Rosanna spoke of his nightmares.

'When he left, he said something about you perhaps needing company?'

'He did?' *The last thing I need right now is company.* But the woman was clearly upset. She remembered his last words to her. *Rosanna's on her own... you'd find her understanding.* Had he been trying to tell her something?

'Did he give you my address?'

'Yes.'

'Bring a bag. You're staying the night.'

CHAPTER 51

As Shepherd settled into the sofa that was every bit as comfortable as he remembered, he wondered how many times Carver had sat there. Not that it mattered. Tonight it was his turn to make the play. About to place his mug down on the coffee table, he noticed its sparklingly-clear surface. He hesitated, and cast about for something to put it on. But nothing was to hand and the woman didn't move to offer him a coaster. He had no option but to cradle it in his hands. *Whatever*. He cleared his throat to speak. She beat him to it.

'So what's so important you needed to see me so urgently, Gary?'

He wasn't sure if there was a hint of mockery in her tone. If there was, he would soon change it. 'Jamie asked me to check on you while he was away. To make sure you weren't worrying about Cosworth, or anything.'

She looked surprised. 'That's odd. I told Jamie I was fine. Especially with two policemen guarding me.' She turned, slightly, in the general direction of the front gates where the nondescript silver-grey Ford hadn't moved since she'd returned home.

Shepherd shifted in his seat, feeling the first stirrings of a slight unease. 'Yes, well… He also wanted me to check in case you've remembered anything else about what happened. Anything he said, or…?' Though he'd rehearsed the words several times, he was conscious that for some reason they suddenly seemed rather hollow.

'Or… what? Something other than the twelve-page statement I gave to Jess you mean?' The corner of her mouth turned up just enough to register.

'Umm… well you might have remembered something new since then.'

'I might… But I haven't.' Her gaze settled on him. She waited.

Shepherd felt himself beginning to redden - *Damn the bitch* - and sought refuge in his coffee. When he looked up, she was still waiting, only now there was no mistaking the thin smile. The two dark pools bored into him and the confidence that had driven him to come drained away as surely as if she'd pulled a plug. In that moment, as he rummaged for something – anything - he might use to justify his visit, Gary Shepherd saw, with absolute certainty that things would never go the way he'd envisaged. Not for the first time, the compulsion that drove him to follow in the footsteps of the man he both revered and hated had led him to miscalculate. But even as the seeds of panic began to sow themselves, he remembered. At the end of the day, Megan Crane was just a witness. And as ASIO to the Kerry Inquiry, he had every right to call on a witness. He relaxed. He even managed to return her smile, safe in in the knowledge that even if the imaginings that had brought him were based on a misconception – as it was beginning to look like they may have been- there was never any harm in trying.

CHAPTER 52

Jess glanced over at Rosanna, curled up on the couch in front of the fire, the empty wine glass dangling from her fingers. She wished sleep would come to her as easily, but their long conversation still resounded, pushing the prospect of sleep way out of reach.

Nothing Rosanna had said had come as much of a surprise. She'd seen most of the changes Rosanna described in Jamie herself of late. The tension, the moodiness, the uncharacteristic reluctance to share his thoughts. But as Rosanna made clear, whatever was gnawing away at him had been there for weeks, rather than days. And it was getting worse. Not only were the two barely speaking, it seemed Jamie had told Rosanna remarkably little about the inquiry, even less about Megan Crane. Instead he'd been staying up late or coming home in the early hours, saying only that he'd been, 'working late.'

Jess was sure that Rosanna's worst fears - she didn't actually voice them, but Jess could tell they were there – were groundless. But when she tried to reassure her, she struggled.

Clearly, there were things Jamie preferred Rosanna not to know, both about Kerry and his work in general.

She'd wondered how much she knew about his previous cases. Not much, it turned out. She worried that if she said the wrong thing, she might reveal something he wanted kept locked away, perhaps for good reason. Even so, there were things she thought Rosanna could know that might help. Things such as that the Kerry murders were not, 'just another series of murders,' as he'd said, but involved bizarre sexual practices most people would find disturbing. And that Megan Crane - Rosanna had heard the name but little else - knew about such things and was working with them to help catch the killer. But as Rosanna pressed her, again, about, 'This Megan Crane,' Jess realised she was leaving bits out. Bits she felt she couldn't talk about without giving the wrong impression. Such as Megan's ability to draw people in, to ensnare them. She still wasn't sure why she hadn't actually been more open about her being a dominatrix. Presumably Rosanna would have guessed as much - wouldn't she? But it was when Jess referred back to the Hart case that she slipped up and mentioned Angie.

'Angie?' Rosanna said.

Jess kicked herself. Trying to explain about Megan had been bad enough. She tried her best.

'He has seen this Angie recently,' Rosanna said when Jess finished. It was a statement, not a question.

Jess didn't know how she knew, but put it down to a worried lover's intuition.

'The day I phoned you,' she said. 'But I was there when he took her call. I'm sure he hadn't heard from her in a long time.' But she couldn't say why he'd had to drop everything to rush off and see her.

Which was where it all broke down.

For all that Jess tried to reassure Rosanna - putting Jamie's behaviour down to the pressures of the investigation - there was a gap in her knowledge. Eventually she ran out of things to say, at least in terms Rosanna might understand.

They sat in silence for a while, then Rosanna reached out and squeezed Jess's hand.

'Thank you,' she said. A minute or so later, she added a whispered, 'I'm sorry, Jess.'

Jess wasn't sure what she meant, but when she turned to ask Rosanna was asleep. After staring into the flames for a long time, Jess decided. Rosanna had raised questions for which she had no answers. But she knew where she might find some.

Detective Constable Tony Turner roused himself as the sound of a car engine firing up echoed down the drive. He looked up towards the house. Shepherd's Saab was turning round, making ready to leave. He nudged the man dozing next to him. 'Dan. Wake up. He's off.'

Dan Hewitt jerked himself upright and shook himself awake. The last thing they needed was for Shepherd to catch them sleeping on the job. He checked the time. 'Quarter-past two? Fuck me.' The Saab started down towards them. 'Five hours? He's had a good fucking night.'

As the Saab stopped just before the gate, the detectives shielded their eyes from the glare of its headlights but waved to signal they were alert and awake. The Saab's lights flashed an acknowledging signal, then he was through the gates and heading down the private track that led to the main road through the village. As the tail-lights disappeared they both turned to look back up at the house. All was in darkness.

'That's a tenner,' Tony said, holding out a hand.

Dan shook his head, ruefully, and rummaged in his wallet.

'All I can say is, she's gone right down in my estimation. I didn't think she'd give him the time of fucking day. Just goes to show doesn't it?' He passed the note to his partner, took a last look up at the house, then settled back in his seat and closed his eyes.

'Now, where was I?'

CHAPTER 53

The houses were the sort the Dutch call, 'Merchant's Houses'. Like many of their type, they overlooked one of Amsterdam's many canals. Carver couldn't remember which one. He'd lost his bearings within a minute of them leaving the car on the meter into which Erik had actually fed coins. 'Bastards at Headquarters are clamping down,' he growled, seeing Carver's surprise.

As they crossed yet another ornate footbridge with intricate ironwork, Erik pointed across at a house which, apart from being bright blue - the others were mostly yellows and oranges - was indistinguishable from the rest. 'There,' he said, as if he were one of the country's famous circum-navigators spotting landfall. Given what Erik had told him about the place they were heading for, Carver wondered how Erik knew which building it was before they were close enough to make out numbers.

Carver remembered visiting a 'preserved example' of such a 'Merchant's House,' during a leisure-break weekend with Gill, years before. He was surprised, therefore, when he stepped through the open front door and discovered that the two properties could not have been more different. At some stage in its recent history, the house had been gutted and re-built from the ground up. Open staircases connected what looked like a series of mezzanines constructed from a range of wooden, glass and metal materials. The arrangement meant it was possible to see up as far as the roof – which was also partly glass. The design allowed light to flood in and reach areas which, before the rebuild, would never have seen any. Carver thought it looked stunning, the sort of thing you might see in a Bond film. It wasn't the only similarity.

Amongst the spotlights, reflectors and cameras littering the various levels, floated several men and women. Most of the men were dark, muscular, and swarthy - villains' henchmen types. The woman on the other hand were toned, tanned, very attractive and, in most cases, not wearing much.

As Erik turned to check Carver's reactions, Carver tried to look as if porn-sets were ten-a-penny in Warrington. Erik wasn't fooled. Turning, he addressed the slim young man dressed all in black and sporting a full beard who came rushing over to intercept them. Erik spoke in English, explaining who they were and showing his identification, before informing him they were there to see Oscar Werner. If the young man was fazed by the police arriving on set wanting to see the director, he didn't show it. Looking up, he shouted.

'HEY, OSCAR.'

A couple of mezzanines up, a shaven-headed black man lent over a metal railing to gaze down on them. The way his muscles bulged under his black tee-shirt, Carver wondered if he also had a performing role. The young man jerked a thumb at Erik and Carver.

'Police. They want to talk to you.'

Oscar looked somewhere between annoyed and

intrigued. 'What about?'

'Katelijne Mertens,' Erik called up.

Oscar hesitated, then nodded. 'Come up. Mind the cables.'

As they passed the various levels, Carver took in what he assumed were the normal trappings of such productions. Beds in various states of disarray. Bare flesh. Sex paraphernalia. He wondered what went on there when it wasn't being used as today. He was also conscious that some of the actors – both sexes – were eyeing them, - maybe just Erik - in a way that suggested that bagging a police officer still carries a certain cache in some quarters.

They reached Oscar's level as he finished telling everyone to, 'take five,' and that he would call them when he was ready to go again. Turning to them he said, 'Coffee?'

'Five minutes later, they were sitting on a corner-couch arrangement on one of the upper levels. Below, cast and crew had gathered to smoke, drink coffee, and speculate over what the police were after. Mixed with the cigarette smoke drifting up was a pungent smell Carver had no difficulty recognising.

'So tell me,' Oscar said, sipping from his steaming Styrofoam cup. 'What's your interest in Katelijne?'

Erik turned to Carver. *Over to you.* He took his cue.

Carver told the former porn-star how he was investigating Katelijne's involvement in a modelling shoot that might have a bearing on a murder inquiry. He didn't mention fetish and skipped over the details of the killings themselves. Oscar listened in silence, staring at him as if he were weighing him for a part, though it would have to have been someone's father. Carver

316

ended with, 'I'm hoping Katelijne may be able to tell me something that would point towards our murderer. She might even have an idea where he's gone to ground.'

Oscar looked at Erik. 'Gone to ground?'

'Where he's hiding,' Erik said. Oscar nodded.

Carver waited. Oscar finished his coffee. Carver prompted him. 'Do you know where I can find Katelijne?'

As Oscar took a deep breath, his chest expanded and his muscles rippled in way that hinted at his former, career. 'You won't find Katelijne Mertens in Amsterdam. Or anywhere for that matter.'

Carver's stomach sank. *She's dead?*

'Why not?' Erik said.

Oscar shrugged, like it was no big deal. 'She doesn't go by that name anymore.' Carver's depression lifted. 'She calls herself Franky, now. She runs *Jeux*.'

In the silence that followed, Carver wondered what he was missing. Oscar's face read, *Conversation over.* He turned to Erik. His colleague's face was a mix of surprise, amusement, and admiration. He passed Carver the knowing look Carver was beginning to find irritating.

'What's *Jeux*?' Carver said.

CHAPTER 54

Megan Crane dialled the number on the piece of paper. A woman answered.

'Hello?'

'Anna Kirkham?'

'Who is this?'

'My name's Megan Crane, Anna. Please don't hang up, I mean you no harm, but I know you used to go by the name Angela Kendrick. I'm sorry to contact you like this, but someone we both know is in trouble and I'm ringing because I think that you, I, *we*, may be able to help him.' On the other end there was only silence. Eventually, Megan said, 'Are you still there?'

'Who do we both know?'

'Jamie Carver.'

There was another pause. 'Who are you? How do you know Jamie? Did he give you my number?'

'No, he didn't. I'm happy to explain everything, including how I got your number, but I'd rather not do it over the telephone, if you get my meaning? I'm helping him with a case much the way I think you once did. I'm not out to cause trouble and I know how you are probably feeling right now, but I-'

'Are you a reporter? Because if you are I'll-'

'No, I'm not a reporter. Please believe me, Angie, I'm just someone who's in a similar position to one you once were.'

'How do you mean?'

'I mean that we share similar, shall we say, personal interests?'

'Are you in the business?'

'Not exactly. But I'm close enough to understand some things.'

Another pause. 'Do you know someone called Jess?'

'Jess Greylake? The sergeant who works with Jamie? Yes, I know her very well. In fact, she and I-'

'Is this coming from her? Did she ask you to contact me?'

'No, she doesn't know anything about this. What makes you think that?'

'It doesn't matter. When you say he's in trouble, what are you talking about? And what makes you think I can help him?'

'I know he had some, problems, in the past. I think you'll know what I'm talking about. If I'm right, you'll also know he doesn't like to talk about such things. I'm worried it may be happening again, maybe worse this time. I thought that if you and I could meet, swap notes as it were, it might give me a better idea of what, if anything, I ought to do. Of course it might all just be in my imagination and I could be wrong, but at the very least you can probably say if it's the same as before. I'm sure you know him a lot better than I do.'

'What makes you think I'd know him any better than you?

'I'm sorry, I didn't mean to infer anything. I understand you worked with him a couple of times? I've only been involved a few weeks so I assumed-'

'What do you want? It's not easy for me. I have a little boy and I've had enough disruption here lately. If you want to meet, I'd have to arrange for my mother to come over to look after him.'

'That's fine. Like I say, I don't want to cause trouble, especially with a little one. Whatever works best for you. Where do you live? I've only got your mobile number.'

'I'm in Leeds.'

'That's not too far. I'm just the other side of the Pennines. What about a pub somewhere? I don't mind driving over if it would help?'

There was another silence. Eventually she said, 'There's a pub called The Oak On The Hill. It's on the old road over the Pennines, the A268. Just this side of Hebden Bridge. I could meet you there.'

'That would be fine. When do you think you could manage?'

Carver tossed his mobile on the bed and poured a larger measure from the bottle of Jameson he'd bought from the kiosk opposite the hotel. Whatever Rosanna said, it was obvious there was something she wasn't telling him. He didn't think it was anything to do with the problems they'd been having. This was something else. She'd sounded strange, like she was reluctant to talk, almost as if she was afraid someone might hear. It made him wonder what was going on. She'd blamed it on her being unsettled by the prowler she'd thought she'd spotted a couple of times recently, but he suspected that was just an excuse. Twice over the past fortnight, she thought she'd seen a figure in the garden at night. He'd checked around but found nothing. The back of the house looked out over bare fields, a footpath running along the back fence. He'd put it down to her mistaking walkers for prowlers. That said, he had found an area of flattened grass by the tree that stood at the corner of the garden where someone could have lingered, though when and for how long it was impossible to tell. It could just be a walker pausing for a rest, or waiting for a partner to catch up. He'd promised to mention it to the local PC and ask him to give the path some passing attention, but hadn't got round to it. There hadn't been any burglaries in their area for years, and all the houses around were alarmed, including his. 'I'll call Josh and ask him to call round and see you tomorrow,' he told her. 'Don't worry. I'm sure it's nothing.'

'Just hurry back, Jamie,' she said just before she hung up. The way she said it, it sounded as if something was riding on it.

He spent the next thirty minutes replaying the conversation in his mind, looking for clues. There weren't any. He rang Erik.

'Can we do *Jeux* tonight?' he said when Erik answered.

'No reason why not. But what happened to our reunion night out?'

'Maybe next time. I think I ought to get back.'

'Worrying about how they're managing without you eh, Jamie?'

'Something like that.'

'They say an inability to let go is a sign of insecurity, did you know that?'

'Fuck off. What time will you pick me up?'

CHAPTER 55

The entrance to *'Jeux'* lies in an alleyway just off Muiderstraat in the Docklands district of Amsterdam. It sits on the edge of the Entrepotdok, the complex of sought-after converted-warehouse apartments in the heart of the city. It was still early for Amsterdam - before ten - and as Carver and Erik approached the nondescript black door with the dim orange light above, there was only one other couple heading in the same direction. They were dressed outlandishly and disappeared inside as the two men arrived. Erik spoke briefly to the black-clad Asian doorman and flashed his I.D. He directed them inside and they made their way up the stairs.

At the top, the young Goth-Girl in charge of the cloakroom gave them a distasteful look, as if she thought anyone who didn't take the trouble to dress properly lacked respect. They moved through into the main lounge.

The room was 'L'-shaped. At the far end a bar ran the length of one wall. At first glance, it looked no different to the average nightclub, though the chains and shackles hanging from hooks around the walls gave some hint. Carver couldn't tell if they were real, or plastic props.

He suspected the former. Tables and chairs were dotted around with upholstered, semi-circular, bench seats around the perimeter. Mirrors and reflecting surfaces were everywhere and the lighting was subdued with an over-emphasis on red. Around the corner of the 'L' was a dance floor with a raised stage at the far end. There, two men and a woman were busy assembling, noisily, some sort of metal-framed apparatus. Jazzy music was playing, but it was easy enough on the eardrums to signal that the night hadn't started yet.

But what marked the place from other venues, were the outfits. Oscar Werner had said that that the club operated a strict dress-code - which meant fetish, though men, apparently, could get away with black tie. Carver and Erik had chosen not to comply. Being early, there were only a few groups in the place. For the most part they were dressed in striking outfits of leather, rubber or similar, shiny materials. Buckles and straps were in abundance. Eyes followed as Carver and Erik crossed the floor to the door next to the bar. Carver reflected on the irony that it was he and Erik attracting the strange looks.

Erik knocked on the door. As they waited, Carver studied the two young women sitting a few feet away at the bar. They were sipping exotic-looking drinks through straws. The taller, black-spiky-haired one was holding a length of chain, the other end of which was attached to her blonde friend's collar. Both had far-away looks in their eyes as they regarded the two detectives. Erik flashed Carver a smile and a wink. 'I think we should have dressed to come here Jamie.'

Carver didn't respond. He was surprised how uncomfortable he was feeling, conscious that the surroundings were triggering disquieting associations.

The door opened to reveal a grossly overweight man wearing evening dress. He had thinning hair, a florid face and was holding a cigarette at chest height, pointing it at them as if it were a gun. He was expecting them - the door guy had obviously rung ahead - and ushered them in without a word. He closed the door behind them and locked it, before turning to address them. Erik spoke with him, in Dutch this time. The only word Carver recognised was, 'Franky'. When the conversation finished, the man left. After he'd gone Erik turned to Carver.

'You okay Jamie? You seem a bit quiet.'

Carver pulled a face. 'Not my sort of place, Erik'

A couple of minutes later the door opened and a woman came in. She had striking platinum hair that was ruler-straight and fell to just below her shoulders.

'I'm Franky. Sorry to keep you. I was setting up my equipment.'

Carver didn't ask what type of equipment. It took him a few moments to place her as the woman in the Skin-Tight photo-shoot. Several years had passed and despite the makeup, they all showed. Her body, however, was as trim as it had been. Her eyes were bright blue, her nose a bit on the large side. She wore a low-cut, shiny-black blouse, a knee-length, red-leather pencil skirt and carried herself with the confidence of someone who feels she doesn't have to explain herself. As they shook hands, Carver thought she looked like someone who smiled a lot, though right now her expression was serious.

'Oscar told me to expect you,' she said to Erik.

'Then you know what we want to speak to you about,

Mevrouw,' Carver interjected, remembering to use the formal Dutch term of address.

She turned to him, taking him in for the first time, as if debating whether she was going to deal with him or Erik. As she was making up her mind the fat man returned. He walked over to the desk, picked up the phone and pretended to speak to someone.

Whatever questions may have been in Franky's mind they seemed to resolve themselves as she answered Carver directly. 'Yes, I do.' She threw a glance at the man at the desk and said, 'Come. Let's go somewhere we can talk.'

They followed her out of the room and she led them to a table at the back of the club.

'Peter is okay,' she said, 'but sometimes he's too nosey for his own good.' She asked what they were drinking, then went to the bar and spoke with one of the young waitresses.

Erik turned to Carver. 'An interesting woman Jamie, yes?'

'We're working Erik, remember?'

'I might have to ask her to show me her equipment!'

Carver shook his head.

Franky returned and offered them cigarettes. Erik took one and held out his lighter for her. Carver noted it as just one more example of Amsterdammers playing by their own rules. But he spotted the look that passed between her and Erik as she leaned into his flame.

She turned to Carver. 'I understand you are investigating some murders?' He nodded. 'And you are interested in a photo-shoot I once did?' He nodded again. The waitress arrived with their drinks. Franky waited until she'd gone before continuing. 'Let me guess. I am tied in this position-' She put her hands and wrists together and held them up in the way Carver recognised. '-while a man threatens me with a ribbon?' 'Carver gave her a hard stare. 'What makes you think it's that one?'

'Because in all the time I was doing that sort of work, it was the only time I felt scared. And when I say scared I mean terrified, as in, for my life. It wouldn't surprise me in the least if he's killed someone.'

Carver glanced to his right. Erik was suddenly quiet, all his attention on her.

'What was it, exactly, that terrified you?' Carver said.

'Right from the start, there was something about him that just wasn't right. I've met people who are into all kinds of weird shit in my time, but not like him. He was into the scene we were shooting in a really deep way. He was so intense, I had the feeling that if I'd just been some trick off the street-' A shudder rippled through her. 'Well, I don't like to think what might have happened. And the phone calls after didn't help.'

'Phone calls?'

'About a week later, he started ringing me. He said some of the shots hadn't come out right. He wanted me to do a re-shoot. I kept putting him off, but I was working through an agent at the time and contracts for commissioned shoots usually contain a re-shoot clause. I was worried I could get myself blacklisted or something if I didn't cooperate. Then one night I found him lurking around outside my flat. I asked him what he was doing and he gave me some bullshit excuse. It was only then I realised he must have followed me to get my address. It freaked me out. I told everyone my mother was ill and came back here to get away from him. I was only going to stay a month. I thought he'd forget about me and maybe, you know, find someone else to stalk? Then I heard from a friend he'd been making enquiries, trying to track me down, so that was it. I decided to stay here. Just to be on the safe side I dropped my old name and started again as, 'Franky.' I've been here since.'

Carver sipped his drink. 'It must have been bad, to scare you out of the country like that.'

'Believe me, it was. But then, she was just as scary'

Carver started, looked across at Erik, then back at her. 'She? She who?'

'The woman. His girlfriend, or whoever, whatever, she was. She was into it as much as he was, maybe more.'

Carver held up a hand. 'Hold on. There was another woman there?'

'Like I'm telling you. They were both into it. That was what scared me so much. As it went on, they both got involved in setting the scene, doing the rigging, setting up the poses. They were getting off on it. I could tell. It was almost like they were practising. It all had to be just right. Made me wonder what they got up to on their own. Well I wasn't going to find out.'

'This woman, what did she look like?'

Franky blew her cheeks out. 'I didn't get to see her face much. She was wearing one of those kitten masks. She was blonde, I remember that.'

'Why was she wearing a mask? Wasn't that kind of odd?'

Franky gave a snorting laugh. 'Odd? Listen, my friend. You get used to odd in this business. No it wasn't odd. People often sit in on shoots, especially if it involves fetish. It's not unusual some of them like to keep who they are secret. I remember one time there was a man, I'm sure he was a member of your parl-'

Carver stayed focused. 'You mentioned she was blonde. Long or short?'

'A bit longer than mine is now.'

'Can you remember a name, anything about her?'

She screwed her face, summoning memories. 'I'm not sure. I remember *his* name alright…' She closed her eyes, as if trying to visualise the scene. 'He was Eddie, and her name was…'

'What?'

She opened her eyes. 'What?'

'You said his name was Eddie.'

'Yes, it's her name I'm trying to remember.'

'Don't you mean William?'

'No, William was the photographer, though I knew him as Willy. The man's name was Eddie, or Ed, or something like that.'

Carver froze. He stared at her, blinking. 'I thought we *were* talking about Willy. William Cosworth?'

'No, like I say, he was the photographer. I'm talking about Eddie, the scary one. I thought he's the one you are interested in?'

Carver held up his hand again. 'I'm confused. Go back. Tell me again. Exactly who was there?'

Franky looked impatient, as if she had made it all plainly clear and it was his fault for not listening. She took a deep breath, but then did as asked. 'There were three people. Four if you count me.'

'Right.' Carver said. He raised a thumb. 'William Cosworth, the photographer.'

'Yes, like I said.' She glanced at Erik as if saying, *Who is this idiot?* 'Then there was the couple I've told

328

you about. The man I heard Willy call Eddie, and the woman… I've just remembered. I think her name might have been Trish, or Tricia. Something like that.'

'Why were they there? What was their part in it?'

'It was their shoot. They'd commissioned it. They were paying Willy. Or I assumed they were.'

Carver dug inside his jacket, produced the copies of the photos he'd brought with him, laid them out on the table. 'We're talking about this shoot, yes?'

Franky examined them, nodded. 'That's the one.' Her face changed, showing distaste at the memories.

'I thought it was for the magazine, Skin-Tight?'

'Yes, for them as well. But it was the couple's commission. I don't know what the deal was. I never get involved in those things. I just got paid by Willy, as always.'

'You'd worked with him before?'

'A couple of times.'

'How was he? What was he like?'

She frowned. 'What do you mean?'

'I mean was he weird and scary as well?'

She gave a wry look. 'They're all weird, in their different ways. But I wouldn't have said, 'scary', particularly. Willy could be a bit creepy sometimes. And pushy. He liked to try his hand now and then, so you had to make sure he knew you were just there to pose.'

'I heard he got into some trouble once with one of his models. Did you hear about that?'

'Yes, I heard about it.'

'Was it true, what she accused him of doing?'

'I've no idea.'

'Might it have been?'

She thought on it. 'Maybe, who knows? But then

329

some girls, when they start they don't know what to expect. If they're on drugs, and most of them are, they can come out with all sorts of stories. I took most of what I heard with, what do you call it, a pinch of salt?'

'Did Cosworth- Willy, did he seem particularly interested in this scene, the putting the hands together thing, the threatening you with the ribbon?'

'Only as much as he needed to take the pictures and video. Like I said, it was their scene, not his.'

'It was videoed as well?'

'Of course. Always is these days.'

Carver noticed her gaze beginning to wander. She was losing patience. 'I'm sorry Franky, but it's important that I understand the part everyone was playing.'

'I understand. But maybe you need to find this Eddie, rather than Willy.'

'Maybe. Had you seen him before, or since?'

She shook her head. 'Only that once, and the night I found him hanging around outside my flat.'

'Is there anything else you can tell me about him? Height, age, what he looked like?'

'He was quite tall, slim. Fortyish? He had a bit of a beard, not too bushy though. I remember he had very deep voice and a strange…' She groped for the word.

'Accent?'

'Yes, a strange accent. I think it was what you would call, Northern'

Carver froze again. His mind started racing, stringing thoughts together. *Not possible.*

As his face took on a blank look, Franky turned to Erik. 'Is he alright?'

'Jamie?' Erik said. 'What is it?'

Carver took out his mobile. 'Just a minute.' He began

navigating.

Franky and Erik waited. After a few moments, Carver found what he was looking for. It was a PDF file of a magazine article that had come attached to an email one time and which he'd downloaded for no reason other than someone had showed him how. He brought it up and scrolled through it. One of the pages showed two photographs, both men. He zoomed in, turned the phone to show it to Franky. She leaned forward.

'You look younger.'

'It's a few years old.'

She squinted, focusing in on the other picture.

'Imagine him with a beard,' he said.

She took her time. 'Hmm… It was a long time ago but, yes, it could be him.'

Carver stared at her. Something cold started crawling through his gut.

Holy Mother of God.

Carver pressed the phone to his ear as the group that had followed him outside to smoke erupted into laughter again. Turning away, he moved to the edge of the dock, looking out across the black water and the city lights reflected in its stillness.

'Sorry John, I missed that. Say again.'

'I said, 'Was she certain'?' The Duke sounded sceptical. Carver didn't blame him.

'Not a hundred per cent, but close enough.'

'Fuuuck,' The Duke said. Carver waited while he digested it. 'So what does it mean? What can it mean? And where does it leave us with friend Cosworth?'

'I'm not sure yet. I'm still trying to get my head around it. Could be he and Hart got together after the shoot. Maybe he's the missing accomplice some said never existed.'

'Jesus, that would shake a few up.' He let out a frustrated sigh. 'Hellfire, Jamie, how much weirder can all this get?'

But Carver was still thinking it through. 'There's the blonde to think about it as well. Remember the CCTV Alec turned up? Plus the hairs from the scene. It could all fit.'

They batted it back and forth for a couple more minutes, then The Duke switched tack.

'Whatever it means, wherever it takes us, I need you on the first flight back tomorrow.'

Carver sensed something. 'Why? What's happened?'

'Gary Shepherd's gone missing.'

CHAPTER 56

The Duke slid the copy of Tony Turner's Observations Log towards Carver so he could read the entry.

'Two fifteen in the morning?' Carver said. 'What the hell was he doing there 'til that time?'

The Duke raised a quizzical eyebrow, the inference clear.

No way. Even so…

The Duke spread his huge hands. 'She *says* he wanted to go through her statement with her.'

Carver checked the log again. 'It doesn't take five hours to go through a statement.'

'I'm only telling you what she said. She says he went through it paragraph by paragraph, almost like he thought she was making it all up. He kept challenging her on the details. Go see her. Ask her yourself.'

'Don't worry, I intend to.'

'Good. Either way, she was the last person to see him, apart from Tony and his mate clocking him out. After that-' He blew on his fingers, the way a magician does when he makes something disappear.

'Cosworth?' Carver asked, though doubtfully.

The Duke shrugged. 'We can't rule it out. But I can't see him taking Gary. Not on his own. Why would he?'

Carver crossed to the window, looked out onto Arpley Street. He had his own ideas as to why Shepherd might have called on Megan Crane as soon as his back was turned. They didn't include going over statements. But he could think of nothing that would account for him disappearing soon after. Like he couldn't account for the long-dead Edmund Hart being the originator of the Worshipper Scenario. *What the hell's going on?* He remembered his last conversation with Shepherd. Time to get another monkey off his back.

'There's something I need to tell you.'

The Duke's hand came up. 'If it's about this NCA informant thing, I already know.'

Carver's surprise turned quickly to guilt.

'Danny Roberts came to see me.'

Carver waited. Roberts was a Superintendent with Professional Standards.

'He had a bloke from the NCA with him. They've suspended one of their Senior Agents for passing information to Gary about this source of yours, Angela Kendrick? Carver nodded. 'Turns out he and Gary were old mates. We found a printout when we searched Gary's office.'

'I'm sorry John. I should've-.'

The hand again. 'I know. You wanted to wait until you had the evidence. I can live with it. But just so you know. If you'd told me? I'd have sat on it.'

Carver nodded, feeling even guiltier. The Duke deserved better. Another lesson learned. But it prompted a thought.

'Maybe that's something to do with him dis-.' But the Duke was already shaking his head.

'It didn't break until the day after he disappeared. He

couldn't have known.'

Carver fell silent again. Shepherd disappearing just didn't make sense.

'It's with Professional Standards now,' The Duke said. 'They'll want a statement.' Then he added, 'Which reminds me. Danny rang me yesterday. They're trying to get hold of this Angela, but she's not at home and isn't returning calls. He thinks she's gone to ground and wants you to ring him. He wants your help to get her to cooperate.'

Carver nodded. 'Right.' He chided himself for not thinking of Angie sooner. The internal discipline inquiry that would now kick in would involve her, big time. He needed to speak with her before he contacted Roberts, let her know what to expect. She wouldn't be happy. But The Duke was still talking.

'…also mentioned something about some log-in failures under your user-name on their Intelligence Database a few days ago. They wanted to know if it could have been Gary. I said I couldn't see you giving Gary your user-name and that it was probably just you forgetting your password.'

Carver's mind raced. He nodded. 'It's been a while since I logged in. Took me a few goes to remember.'

The Duke tutted. 'Bloody computers. They do my head in.'

Carver's gave a sympathetic smile. But behind it he thanked God that The Duke's renowned technophobia meant he wouldn't dwell on how an ex-NCA Intelligence Officer could 'forget' a Personal Source File password. He was already moving on.

'I've spoken to the ACC about a replacement for Gary. He's seeing what he can do. But it'll take a few days.'

'I'll manage,' Carver said. 'What else has been happening?'

He thought he should ask, but his mind was already elsewhere.

Carver had to wait to see Jess. She was out helping Alec gather statements over CCTV recordings. In the meantime he tried Angie, but the message said the number was unavailable. He made a mental note to try again later, then went and left a note on Jess's desk.

It was late in the afternoon when she appeared in his doorway. He beckoned her in. She looked puzzled when he came round his desk, pointed to a chair, and closed the door behind her.

'How was Amsterdam?' she said as he returned to his seat.

'I'll tell you about it. First, what's everyone saying about Gary?'

She shrugged. 'There's all sorts of rumours. Something about Professional Standards being involved? The Duke's been keeping it tight. Do you know what's happening?'

Carver sighed. 'He's got himself in some trouble.'

'How so?'

'Remember I told you about our little fall out?' She nodded. As he told her about Shepherd approaching an old informant of his, a woman called Angie, she listened in silence. When he got to the part about Shepherd accessing Angie's Source Record, she started to redden. She reddened further when he told her that a Senior NCA Agent had been suspended, and Professional Standards had launched an investigation.

'So he's going to be in the shit when he surfaces?' There was a catch in her voice as she spoke.

He nodded. 'But there's something I can't work out,' he said.

'What's that?'

'Remember that day I took a call and had to leave. The day I asked you to phone Rosanna?'

'Yes?'

'The call came from Angie. After I left, someone accessed her Source File Record from my computer. I can't understand how Gary-.'

'Alright.' She dropped her head so that her hair fell forward, a cascade of guilt. 'No need to piss about.' She looked up, met his stare.

'Tell me.'

She told him how, after speaking to Rosanna, she remembered seeing Angie's name in Megan's file and that it was she who hacked his computer.

'How did you know the password?'

She lifted a finger, pointing to the corner of his white board.

He turned to look. 'Ah.'

But he was beginning to understand. He'd sensed something was different when he'd got home from Amsterdam the night before. He and Rosanna hadn't had long together, but she'd seemed more… patient. But Angie's NCI record was fairly bland, so how would she know-. He looked at Jess. The look on her face told him. *There's more.* He felt a panic stirring, deep in his gut.

'After you left, Rosanna came to see me. She said she was worried about you.' She bit her lip. 'I went to see Angie.'

CHAPTER 57

Carver felt her admission like a hammer blow to his stomach. He stared at her. 'You did what?

'I went to see Angie.'

For seconds he couldn't move. While waiting for her to get back, he'd worked out most of it. She was the only one who knew his user-logon. The hacker had to be her. After thinking on it, he'd come to accept that her snooping was probably well-intentioned. His plan when he saw her was, to get her to cough, give her suitable 'words of advice', and leave it at that. The thought she may have taken things further, as far as actually going to see Angie, never entered his head. His defence mechanisms kicked in.

'What the FUCK are you doing Jess? These are things that don't concern you. Christ, I thought we were supposed to be working together.'

Her eyes took on a glassiness, but when she spoke it wasn't to apologise.

'Yes, we are supposed to be working together, but that cuts both ways. You haven't been prepared to tell Rosanna, or me, what's wrong, so we… I, had to find out for myself.'

Carver fought to stay calm. 'Did Rosanna go with you?'

'No.'

Thank Christ. 'What did you talk about? What did she tell you?'

She hesitated, then began. At first, Angie had refused to see her. It was only when Jess spoke of her and Rosanna's worries she agreed to her calling round. Jess had told her about the Kerry Inquiry, more than he had it seemed. And about Megan Crane, and how she'd had come close to becoming a victim. She described Angie's horror on hearing of it. But it got her talking.

Carver nodded. 'It would. So what did she say?' He was resigned to the inevitable, like a candidate at an election who knows he's lost his seat, but has to stay to hear the result.

'She told me about how she met you during the Ancoats case, then again during the Escort Murders Inquiry and you became close. That a stake-out went wrong and Hart attacked her. How you blamed yourself. The trouble you had with it after.'

She didn't mention about the counselling, but he assumed she knew. If Angie had told her so much, she'd have mentioned that as well.

Jess continued. 'She told me about Shepherd coming to see her. What he said to her. What he wanted her to do. Like you, I was mad as hell, but she said you were sorting it. She didn't know how but it didn't matter. It was enough to give me some idea of what you've probably been going through.'

Carver felt the blood rushing into his face. He'd never felt so exposed in his life.

'Have you spoken to Rosanna since?'

She nodded.

'You told her?'

'Most of it.'

He turned away, 'Fucking JESUS.'

From nowhere, Carver's worst fear had become reality. He wondered what the effect would be, especially on Rosanna. It didn't matter how much Angie had told her. It had started and it would all come out. Everything. He let out a heavy sigh.

'Thanks, Jess.'

She rounded on him again, her stare fierce. 'Don't start going all self-righteous on me.' She jabbed a finger. 'It was *you* kept things hidden. Rosanna at least deserved to know. You should have faced up to it before now. You're supposed to know about these things. Work it out, but don't blame me for asking questions. I'm on your side, remember?'

Carver stared at her. Up to now, he'd only ever seen Jess as his DS, their relationship defined in terms of their rank difference. Suddenly, she was no longer his junior, but a determined woman with a point to make. Not criticising, nor judging, just saying it the way she saw it. But he was still angry. The root of it, of course, was shame. And embarrassment. Knowing that didn't help.

As if sensing it, she softened her tone. 'It doesn't matter, you know? It's in the past. Rosanna just wants you back. You and Angie were in a crazy situation, even she realises that.' Then she added, 'Angie said you shouldn't let it ruin things.'

He could see the sense in what she was saying. But it didn't excuse anything.

'What I… What we did was...' He groped for the words, struggling to express what he'd never talked about before, to anyone. He was even finding it hard to look at her. 'It was unprofessional.'

'Rubbish. It was just two people caught up in the situation they were in. Simple as that. If you ask her, Rosanna will tell you the same. Don't dwell on it Jamie. We've both seen some crazy stuff the past weeks. You've heard what Megan Crane says. It doesn't make you a bad person.'

He gave a deprecating snort. He'd said it himself, many times, but had never really believed it. But this time it was Jess saying it. Sensible, rock-steady, Jess. Had he been wrong all this time?

He sighed. 'Maybe. If you say so.'

'I do.'

He nodded. It was time to move on. Other matters demanded his attention. But she had one last question.

'I suppose Professional Standards will want to see me?' She sounded resigned.

For the first time, he realised. She would be worrying about her job. Prosecution even. He shook his head.

'They don't know it wasn't me who accessed Angie's file.'

'But won't it come out if-'

'It won't. Trust me.'

She gave a wan smile, stole his line. 'If you say so.'

'I do,' he said, likewise.

For a long while they said nothing, letting the silence draw a line under the subject. She asked what he'd discovered on his trip.

'Just a minute.' He pulled his bottom drawer, moved

a couple of manila folders, took out the bottle of Macallan. There was dust on it. From another drawer he produced two glasses. He passed them across to her and she ran a tissue round them. He poured a measure in each, offered one to her. To his surprise, she took it, more so when she knocked it back in one. He couldn't remember the last time he'd shared a drink in his office before dark. Those days were long gone. He showed her the bottle again but she shook her head, the sensible one back on. He re-ran the briefing he'd given The Duke, telling her about what he'd learned from Franky.

Her eyes widened as the surprises kept coming.

The Worshipper scenario wasn't Cosworth's?

Two others present?

A blonde woman, and a man called Eddie?

Edmund Hart?

'Oh. My. God.'

She threw him the same questions as The Duke. How could it be? What does it mean? What then about Cosworth? As before, he had no answers. He fell silent, giving her time to get used to it – whatever 'it' was. Then her face changed. 'Tell me again about this woman. What did Franky say her name was?'

'Trish, or Tricia, or something like that. She wore a mask so there's no way we're going to be able to- Jess?' As he'd talked, her attention had shifted, eyes glazing over.

'What? I'm sorry, I was just thinking of… something….'

She's going again. 'What is it?'

She hesitated for a moment, checking herself. 'You're probably going to hate me for this. Especially after the Angie thing.'

342

He made a wry face. *What could be worse than Angie?*

'There's something I never told you. I didn't think it was important because… well it just didn't seem to matter. But… this thing about a blonde woman, and the hairs? And now there's a blonde whose name could be Trish or Tricia? And we've talked about maybe looking for someone who presents as sub, but may actually be dom?'

'Christ Jess, just tell me will you?'

She focused. And told him about the night Megan had introduced her to her house-slave, Tracy. Tracy with the blonde ponytail. Tracy whose name isn't so far away from Trish, or Tricia.

Not for the first time since they'd started talking, Carver found he had no words. He'd known she and Megan had grown close, but never *that* close. He stared at her, trying to grasp it.

'Nah. It would be too much of a coincidence.'

'Not if Tracy is targeting Doms. Don't forget, *we* chose Megan because she fits the victim profile.'

'That's true….' He wondered if the twists and turns in the case were making them see shadows. Whether his scepticism about Cosworth being a lone killer was making him susceptible to fanciful theories. He weighed it, decided it wasn't.

'Who is she? What do you know about her?'

Jess shook her head. 'All I know is, she sees her fairly regularly.'

Carver cast his mind back. Megan had once given them a list of occasional 'acquaintances', as a 'just in case' contingency. He tried to remember a Tracy. He mentioned it to Jess. 'Was she on it?'

Jess looked abashed. 'She said it was one relationship she absolutely had to keep private, for Tracy's sake. We weren't interested in women then and were still in the game of building trust, so I gave her some slack. She left her off it.'

Carver bit his lip. But after not telling The Duke about Shepherd, he was in no position to criticise. He was already feeling the rush that comes when a potentially promising lead suddenly presents itself. In his head, he began running what-ifs.

After a couple of minutes he stood up so suddenly Jess jumped. She had gone back into herself. She looked up at him. She seemed confused, mouth hanging open. His keys lay on the side of the desk. He snatched them up.

'Where are you going?'

'To see Megan.'

'Do you want me to come with you?'

'Not this time. I think she and I need a private chat.'

CHAPTER 58

'Tracy?' Megan said. She sounded scornful. 'Don't be ridiculous Jamie. I've never heard anything so absurd.'

Her reaction was as he'd anticipated, but he wasn't going to push too hard - yet. He didn't want the barriers to come up.

'How do you know about Tracy anyway?'

He waited, letting her work it out.

'Jess.'

He nodded.

She gave an apologetic look. 'It was a bit of silliness. It shouldn't have happened.'

'It doesn't matter. Tell me about Tracy.'

She went quiet, thinking on it, then began. 'Her name's Tracy Redmond. She lives somewhere over in the Cheadle area.' Over the next few minutes she told him what she knew. It wasn't much. Tracy had been coming to see her for around eighteen months. She was into the fantasy of enforced, sexual-slavery. Every now and then, she liked to play the part of Megan's house-slave for a few days, a good deal of it spent chained up in the Playroom. She left her off the list she'd given Jess because Tracy was sensitive about her position. She was a barrister, or so she'd told Megan.

He asked if she ever showed interest in switching.

'Never,' she said, but then caught herself.

'What?'

'Did Jess mention, Arthur?' His bewildered look was answer enough. 'He's another… special friend. He was there the same night I introduced her to Jess.' Carver sighed, wondering what else they hadn't told him. 'Sometimes I make Tracy top Arthur. It's part of the game.' Carver waited, saying nothing. 'I think she enjoys it.'

He asked for Tracy's address. She said she didn't know it. Seeing his sceptical look she said, 'Honestly, Jamie. She's never given me her address. She's quite paranoid about being found out. She says it would ruin her.' Megan brightened. 'But I've got her mobile number.' She left the room and came back with her mobile, brought up a number, showed it to him. He rang it through to the MIR, telling the duty DS to run an urgent subscriber check. When he came off the phone he saw her confused look.

'You've not told me what this is all about yet. Why are you suddenly so interested in Tracy? And what's happening about Cosworth?'

He thought about how much to tell her. For her safety, it was time to fill in some of the gaps. He told her about the blonde hairs, the CCTV footage Alec had found, what he'd learned from Franky, though he left out the bit about Edmund Hart. As he spoke her eyes widened, As Jess's had done.

He spread his hands. 'It could all be coincidence. But you can see why we're interested.'

She nodded, but still looked doubtful. 'If… if somehow Tracy was involved in some way, why hasn't she done anything to me before now? She's had plenty of opportunities.'

He told her about Cleeves's theory that the killer could be leading up to something. 'Maybe you're part of the killer's Grand Plan.' She shuddered, and the thought he'd frightened her gave him a strange feeling. He lowered his tone. 'There's something else.' She sat up, gave him her full attention. 'Gary Shepherd's disappeared.' Her brow furrowed. 'He's not been seen since he came to see you.'

For long seconds she did a good job of not giving anything away. But her silence and too-calm reaction spoke volumes. She lifted a hand to her mouth.

'What?' he said.

She hesitated. Once before when he'd caught her out, she'd looked abashed. He saw the same look now. She took a deep breath.

'The night Gary came to see me, he was being… I didn't like the way he was. I thought he needed teaching a lesson.'

'What sort of lesson?' *Surely not-*

'He was being… superior. Acting like a prick. I decided to show him how foolish he was.' She avoided his gaze, bowed her head.

'You didn't…?'

She nodded quickly, her hair bouncing and shimmering. 'I took him into the Playroom. Tracy was there.'

'Ohhh Shit.' Carver said. He hardly dared ask. 'Spare me the details, but what happened?'

'I shouldn't have done it, but he was being such an arse.' She actually looked contrite. 'I played with them. I made sure he knew I don't like being treated like an idiot.'

He couldn't believe it. 'You and Gary? And this Tracy?' He slumped back in the sofa, not sure whether to laugh or cry. But Gary disappearing afterwards left no room for humour. 'What happened after?'

'Tracy was planning to go home that evening. I was supposed to drive her. Because she was late, Gary offered to take her.'

'She left with him? Oh, Christ.'

She tried to sound reassuring. 'Believe me, Jamie. I know her. I'm sure his disappearing isn't anything to do with her.' But there was less confidence in her voice than there had been.

'Are you sure you don't have her address? Gary's life might depend on it.'

But she seemed in earnest when she said, 'Honestly, Jamie. You can search the house. If I had it, I would give it to you, if only so you can rule her out. I'm sure when Gary turns up, you'll find it's nothing to do with her.'

His phone rang. He listened for a few moments, then said, 'No, thanks. I'll get back to you.' He put it away, frustrated. 'Tracy's mobile's a pay-as-you-go. We can't trace the subscriber just off the number.'

'What if I ring her?' she said. 'I could make an excuse to see her.'

'Good idea.' They agreed a story and she called the number. The voice said that the phone wasn't in use or may be switched off.

'Damn,' he said. 'I'll get our tech people onto it. They may come up with something.'

Drained by the day's succession of revelations, he rubbed at his forehead. A dull pain was starting.

'Let me get you something,' she said.

She poured him a Jameson's and came and sat next to him on the sofa. He remembered her fragrance. Shalimar.

'This must be so difficult for you all,' she said. 'I know you and Gary don't see eye-to-eye, but I'm sure you wouldn't wish him any harm.'

He shook his head. She was right. Whatever his thoughts about Shepherd, he didn't like to ponder the possibilities if the last person to see him alive was this Tracy, and it turned out she was connected with the killings. Glancing at Megan, he could see guilt in her face. He tried to reassure her.

'It isn't your fault. You were just giving him what you thought he deserved. Any other time it would be amusing.' His curiosity got the better of him. 'As a matter of interest, how did he...?'

She flashed a wicked smile. 'Putty in my hands.'

'I can believe that,' he said. Again, he stifled the impulse that nearly made him chuckle. She slapped his knee, playfully, but left her hand resting on it. He drank his whiskey.

'It must be especially hard, for a man like you.' She rubbed his knee, the top of his leg.

'What does that mean?' He came on guard. But her face showed only sympathy.

'I know what goes on inside that head of yours, Jamie Carver.'

She lifted a hand to his left ear and combed some hair back.

He moved back. 'I don't think so.'

She sat forward on the edge of the sofa, took his hand.

'I've been part of the scene for a long time, Jamie. I know what men like. What they want.'

He made to get up, but she placed a hand on his chest and pushed him, gently, back. He thought about resisting but the way she was sitting, she might end up on the floor. He didn't want to overreact and risk embarrassing her.

'It's alright,' she said, 'Don't be embarrassed. I knew that first day. I could see the struggle within you.'

'Megan, I'm not-'

'Shhh.' She pressed a finger to his lips. She spoke softly, almost a whisper. 'You saved my life, Jamie. I'd never hurt you. I just want you to know, that I know.' She leaned into him. Her lips took the place of her finger. Not a kiss, an invitation.

Carver felt his heart thumping. There was a drumming in his ears. But she seemed calm, utterly in control. Her dreamy eyes played with his, burning into his brain, delving. Her breath mingled with his own.

'I can help, Jamie. If you want me to.'

He didn't answer. *So beautiful.*

'*Do* you want me to?'

Somewhere deep inside, a voice he'd listened to before, in another life, cried, *YES*' He wrestled with it, trying to ignore it. He'd known this moment would one day come. He'd steeled himself for it. But it was harder than he'd ever imagined. She pressed her lips to his again, but harder this time. Her tongue began playing with his, as it had, briefly, the night they almost lost her. The memory of it had never left him. But this time it stayed, She cupped a hand to the back of his head, pulling him to her. His head swam. Her scent was all around him. He let go.

Suddenly she was in his arms and they were kissing, urgently. His hands roamed over and under her dress, now holding her face, running through her hair. He lifted her and she slid, easily, into his lap as they took each other's tongues, deep. She began to fall backwards, pulling him with her, down into the sofa. He went to follow, but sitting up the way he was, he could only go so far. He pulled back a little to adjust his position, scrabbling at his collar, tearing at his tie. Their mouths separated and as he yanked his tie off she fell away from him, arms reaching out, eager to keep the separation brief.

In that moment, as he looked down at her, and from where he would never know, Rosanna's face, sad with tears, swam before him. Suddenly he saw the chasm into which he was about to disappear. He hesitated. As if sensing what was in his head, she tried to claw him back. Too late.

He stepped away from the edge.

In one fluid movement, he lifted her off him, stood up and deposited her gently back on the sofa, dropping his head and shoulders to slip from under her grasping arms. He moved quickly to the other side of the room.

'Jamie?' A hurt whimper.

'I'm sorry Megan. It's not going to happen. And if you know me as well as you say you do, you know why.'

She propped herself on an elbow, waves of glossy-black hair falling, provocatively, over her face. She was heart-achingly desirable. He had to get out, fast. Grabbing his jacket, he headed for the door. Without stopping he shouted back over his shoulder. "I'll let you know if we get anything on Tracy.' He slammed the front door behind him.

On the doorstep he gulped a lungful of cool, night air, just as he'd done after the last time she'd kissed him. He let it out slowly, then headed for his Golf.

Megan Crane remained sprawled across the sofa long after Carver had gone. She was smiling, but also berating herself. She'd underestimated him. But she knew now she had been right. She had seen it in his eyes. The hunger. The fear. If she'd played it a bit longer, she'd have had him.

She gave a throaty chuckle. 'Next time it'll be different.'

God, she loved this game.

The two detectives watched as the Golf turned, wheels spinning in the gravel, and came down the driveway. Dan Hewitt returned Carver's quick wave, then he was gone, accelerating down the track rather quicker, Dan thought, than was good for the car's sump.

'Bugger.' he said.

Tony Turner logged his DCI's departure, then held out a hand.

'You're not very good at this, are you, Danny-me-old-mate?'

Dan fished inside his jacket. 'Only an hour?. He must have had a knock-back.'

'Not our Jamie Carver,' Tony said. 'I told you, he's straight as a die. There's no way he would get involved with someone like her.'

Dan Hewitt handed the tenner across to his colleague. 'Well someone ought to tell him he needs to lighten up a bit.'

Carver banged his hand against the steering wheel. He was furious with himself for forgetting - again - the oldest rule in CID. *Beware beautiful victims and witnesses.* He hadn't intended it would happen. That was all in the past. The present belonged to Rosanna. But as he put the miles between him and his narrow escape, his thoughts came round to Shepherd. They needed to find this Tracy, and quickly. One thing was clear. Megan had kept things from them. What else was she holding back? It was time to do what he should have done a long time ago.

He rang the duty DS again on hands-free. After briefing him up, he issued three instructions. The first was to arrange a search warrant for The Poplars. 'Tell whoever it is she's withholding personal details of a suspect, and that there's no privilege involved. Two. I want a POLSA Team briefed and ready to go at six tomorrow morning. Third, call out the duty Intelligence Officer. I want a full search and trace on a Tracy Redmond living in the Cheadle Area. Give it a ten-mile radius. She may be a barrister, in which case it should be easy.' He waited as the DS wrote it down and listened as he read it all back, then rang off. It meant another early start. But at least they would have a few hours together. He remembered Jess's words. 'Rosanna just wants you back.' Well it was time to come back. And to tell her. Everything.

Half an hour later as he locked the Golf, he heard the plaintive tones of Amalia Rodrigues, Rosanna's inspiration, coming from the cottage's open window. He couldn't remember the last time she'd played it. As he came through the door, her voice called from the front room.

'Jamie?'

He went through. Open on her lap was the bulky biography of Maria Callas he'd given her for her last birthday. She let it slip to the floor as she rose, smiling, to come round the sofa. As they embraced, a weight lifted off his shoulders. He wasn't sure when they would talk, but it didn't matter now.

'I got back as soon as I could. Things are happening and I'll need to be out early tomorrow. But it's nice to be-.' He felt her stiffen. 'I know. I'm sorry. It can't be helped. But we have the rest of the evening to ourselves. Let me see you. You look gorgeous.'

He held her at arm's length, but her face was cold, the smile gone.

'You smell of *her*,' she said.

CHAPTER 59

It was late evening when Jess finally stopped re-running the CCTV footage from the garage near Corinne Anderson's home. After hearing Jamie's story, she'd wanted to judge how close the blonde woman was to Tracy. But after watching the grainy sequence over and over and slowing it right down, the best she could come up with was, Maybe. It was the problem they'd faced since the inquiry began. Too many, 'maybes'. She'd just logged out of her computer when her mobile rang. It was Megan. She took a deep breath.

'Hi Megan. What's up?'

'Sorry to bother you Jess, I'm-. Are you alright? You sound strange.'

'I'm fine. Tired, but fine.'

'You work too hard. You need to take some time off now and again.'

'I wish. Go on?'

'Jamie came to see me this evening.'

'I know.'

'He was asking about Tracy.'

Jess bit her lip. Why did she feel like a snitch? She'd done nothing wrong. 'I know.'

After a longish pause, Megan told how they'd tried

Tracy's mobile, but without success. 'The thing is, since he left, I've thought of another way I may be able to contact her. I've been trying his mobile but he's not answering. If you hear from him could you tell him? I'll ring him to let him know how I get on.'

Jess sat up. 'Hold up, Megan. Don't be doing anything until you've spoken to Jamie. It could be dangerous.'

'Nonsense. You saw what Tracy is like. She wouldn't hurt a fly. I just need to convince him, that's all. Besides, if I don't catch her tonight I might not get another chance. I'll let you know.'

'Wait Megan, we-' But she was gone. 'Damn'. She rang her back. It went straight to voicemail. She waited for the beep. 'Whatever you do, Megan, do NOT, attempt to contact Tracy. I'll try and get hold of Jamie. Don't do *anything* until you've heard back from me. That's an order.' She rang Carver. Also voicemail. 'Whhaaaat?' She left a message telling him to ring her back. 'It's *urgent*.' Then she dropped the phone on the desk and held her head in her hands.

'Aaargghhh.'

Carver awoke with a start, and realised that the banging noise wasn't a dream, but real. The bedroom was filled with a flickering, blue light. Together with what he'd put away before coming to bed, it made his head spin. He swung his legs out of bed, blinking himself awake just as Rosanna appeared in the doorway. She looked scared.

'What is it?'

'It's alright. It's work.'

As he stood up he glanced at the alarm clock. It read 02.23. By the time he got downstairs the adrenalin had kicked in and he was awake.

He opened the door. It was raining, heavily. Looming in the doorway, the dark figure of a traffic cop was silhouetted against the lights of the Range Rover halfway up the track. In the drizzle, its flashing lights lent the scene a surreal quality, like something from a science fiction film. Carver was glad they had no immediate neighbours.

'DCI Carver?' the PC said.

'Yes?'

'Sorry to disturb you sir, but Control Room's been trying to get hold of you.'

Typical, Carver thought. The night you disconnect your landline so you can get some sleep is the night they need you.

'And they've tried your mobile but it seems not to be working.'

That's right sonny, don't dare suggest I might have switched it off.

The PC completed his message. 'They've asked me to tell you. They've found DCI Shepherd.'

CHAPTER 60

Megan Crane gazed down on the woman's sleeping form, thinking about how best to accomplish her next step, knowing how dangerous it could be. The blonde hair formed a yellow gauze over the pillow's white cotton and, as she'd gone about her preparations, she'd taken a moment to reflect on the woman's beauty, unadorned by shackles or chains. Now, as she listened to her soft breathing, Megan's expression changed with the emotions running through her; tenderness, pain, regret and, especially, resolve.

Careful not to disturb the sleeping woman, she slipped a handcuff round the slim white wrist next to the pillow. Then, reaching under, she flipped her onto her back and in one quick motion dragged her other arm behind her, locking the wrists together.

'Wh-, What are you doing?' the woman said, waking to her predicament. She tried to twist round and sit up. But Megan's gloved hand gripped her jaw, pulling her round so she could see her face.

'You've been a naughty girl, Tracy. It's time for a little chat.'

'You BITCH,' Tracy screamed. But before she could say anything else, Megan swept the bedclothes back, grabbed a handful of blonde hair and pulled her to her feet.

'OWW! You're hurting.'

'Now, now,' Megan said, pulling her towards the door. 'Be a good girl, or I'll have to punish you.'

As Megan dragged her through the door, the woman stopped struggling to concentrate on the handcuffs. Hair in one hand, wrists in the other, Megan led her up some stairs. They ended at a plain, white door.

'Now don't struggle, or you'll fall,' Megan said, releasing her hair to turn the handle.

She pushed her prisoner through the door and, still holding her wrists, reached back to close it behind them. Then she turned so they both faced the man standing in the middle of the room.

Keeping a firm grip on Tracy she said, 'William, this is Tracy. Tracy this is William. Or am I right in thinking you've already met?'

CHAPTER 61

Howard Gladding stood up and flexed his knees before turning to the watching detectives. 'It's not what I'd call, 'Classic Worshipper Pattern.' But I don't think there's any doubt, do you?'

Carver glanced at The Duke next to him. His gaze was rooted to the bed, more especially, the body arranged on top of it. It was the first time he'd known his boss ignore the banned 'Worshipper' tag. But right now he suspected the other man's thoughts were less on how Gary Shepherd had come to meet his death, as the fact he'd lost one of his team, and in the most horrible way imaginable. And for all the ill-feeling that had lain between him and his colleague, Carver was finding it hard not to give in to the twin tugs of rage and grief – he could barely believe it *was* grief – that kept threatening to overwhelm him. He'd once heard a Merseyside Chief-Super speak about the time they'd lost a PC during a summer street riot. He described the impact on himself and the force as a whole as, 'Like a small nuclear device going off.' Carver was already getting a sense of what he'd meant.

As for the way Shepherd had died, Howard was right. There wasn't any doubt.

Apart from the dining chair which had been turned upside down on the middle of his bed and over which Shepherd was tied - his bachelor-semi being without the regulation post - the familiar trademarks were there. The closely-wound ropes. The super-glued fingertips - the way his arms were tied to the chair legs, the killer hadn't quite been able to get the palms to meet, but the effect was the same. The ligature - one of Gary's brightly-patterned ties - that bit deep into his neck. The only departure was the red boxer shorts, stuffed roughly into Shepherd's mouth and which prevented what Carver regarded as the series' most gruesome trademark - the swollen, blue-black tongue - from showing. And it was no good speculating about how the killer had managed it. It was way too early for that. Even so he couldn't stop thinking about Tracy. Had Gary invited her back here after leaving Megan's instead of taking her home? Howard was yet to pronounce on an estimated time of death. But given the state of the body – and the smell – they were clearly looking at days rather than hours.

They'd already established that the ex-girlfriend who'd found him - she'd called to collect some old clothes and let herself in with her key thinking he was out – hadn't been there for weeks. For all anyone knew, he could have been here since the night he'd left Megan's. On the other hand, the fact that the unopened ready-meal on the counter in the kitchen hadn't rotted, spoke of someone being here more recently.

A noise behind made him turn. Jess was framed in the doorway. She'd put on a paper suit to join them. Carver suspected she would wish she hadn't. The way she was staring at the bed, he guessed the tableaux was already burning itself into her memory like nothing she'd witnessed before.

As if sensing his stare, she turned to him. 'Claire and her team are just arriving.'

Carver nodded. The call for Forensics had gone out even before he'd arrived. He gave The Duke a nudge. When he turned, Carver was surprised to see wetness on his cheeks.

Carver nodded towards the door. 'We need to talk.'

The Duke took one more lingering look towards the bed. Then he turned and without saying a word, marched out of the room.

They gathered on the small, paved patio at the back, out of the way of Claire and her team. The Duke had already been on-scene when Carver arrived and this was the first opportunity he'd had to bring his boss up-to-date about Tracy and her meeting Shepherd at Megan's. The big man's face was grave as he listened.

When Carver was finished The Duke said, 'How sure are we he left with this Tracy?'

'That's what Megan says.'

'And we don't know where she lives?'

'Not yet, I was going to-' Carver stopped, feeling Jess's hand on his arm.

She said, 'Did you get my message?'

'I've not had time to-'

'Has Megan spoken to you since you saw her last night?'

'No, why?'

Jess described Megan's call, about her trying to contact Tracy.

'You told her not to, I hope.'

'I did, but I'm not sure she was listening. That's why I rang you.'

Carver checked his watch. Five fifteen. At Macclesfield nick the POLSA team would soon be assembling. Stepping away from the others, he dug out his phone and rang the number of the duty watch at the Poplars. Tony Turner answered. During the minute the conversation lasted, Carver's voice rose several levels. He finished with, 'I don't care if you are due off at six. Neither of you go anywhere until I've got there.' He reported back.

'*Someone* left the house late last night. They *think* it was Megan.'

'They *THINK*?' The Duke said, his face darkening.

 Carver shook his head, but said nothing. He would deal with Tony and his mate later. He dialled Megan's mobile, then held it up so they could hear the steady, 'unobtainable' tone.

'Fuck,' The Duke said.

Jess said, 'Oh, Christ.'

Carver turned to The Duke. 'I need to go.'

The Duke nodded. 'Go. Find her.'

But as Carver made to leave, Jess following, The Duke called after them and they both turned. He looked at them, square.

'Whoever this fucker is, find 'em before anyone else dies.'

Carver and Jess exchanged glances, then left.

CHAPTER 62

'Bloody Hell, Tony,' Carver snapped. 'How can you not be sure?' He was furious, and didn't care who knew it.

Looking like a man who feared his days on CID may be numbered, Tony Turner shuffled his feet in the gravel at the bottom of Megan Crane's drive. The sound echoed under the trees. Next to him, Dan Hewitt, the junior of the pair, was keeping schtum. On this occasion he was happy to let his partner do the talking. Parked just beyond the gateway, a blue van containing the search team waited. Leaning against the bonnet, a tall, gangly man in dark blue fatigues with the legend, 'POLSA' on a breast pocket was drawing on a roll-up. Inspector Brian Bennett, the duty POLSA Search Advisor, was working hard at not letting Carver see him taking amusement from the detectives' discomfort. The DCI was pissed-off enough as it was. Jess stood off to the side, observing.

'We just assumed it was her,' Tony answered to Carver's question.

'You *assumed?* You were supposed to be watching. What the hell were you doing?'

Tony did his best, but knew he was on a loser. His explanation about them not expecting her to be on the move so late sounded weak, even to him. By the time they'd come to, the car was already through the gates and behind them, half way down the track. 'I'm sorry Boss. We've done four straight shifts. You know what nights do to you.'

'It's nothing to what I'll be doing to you if we've lost her. I *assume* you didn't see if she had anyone with her?'

'Like who?'

'LIKE ANYONE. Does it matter?'

'Er, no, we, er, didn't see. Was someone with her when you left last night, then?'

Carver sighed, and shook his head. He gave Tony a last, disappointed look, then dropped it. He called to Bennett. 'We're going in Brian.'

Bennett took a last pull on his cigarette, squeezed the tip out between finger and thumb, and put it in his top pocket. He banged, twice, on the side of the van. Eight men and women wearing blue overalls spilled out through the back doors, draining coke cans and flicking away stubs as they eased life back into cramped limbs.

At the front door, the rest of the team hung back as Carver spent some minutes ringing the bell, banging on the knocker, shouting through the letter box. It drew no response.

As Carver turned back to them, Tony Turner spoke up. 'It *must* have been her,' as if hoping it mitigated their error.

Carver was in no mood to let anyone off hooks. 'Unless she's already lying in there, dead.'

Tony reddened and clamped his mouth shut. Next to him, Dan Hewitt glared at his partner.

Carver turned to Bennett. 'Let's get inside.'

Five minutes later, Carver stepped over the shattered

and twisted remains of what had been Megan Crane's kitchen-door and frame. As with most modern doors with good locks, the Entry Team had had to more or less knock the frame out of the brickwork before it gave. The thought went through his mind that if Megan could see the mess, she would have a fit. Right now, he would be more than happy to witness it.

He made straight for the Playroom, Jess right behind. When he saw it empty, he heaved a sigh of relief. Jess pointed to rings set in the wall to the right. 'That's where Tracy was.' He nodded.

They returned to the kitchen where Bennett was waiting for his team to reassemble following their initial sweep. Open on the table was the copy of the house-plan they'd used to plan the Op the night Cosworth went missing. This time Bennett would use it as their search plan. As the last of his team returned he turned to Carver.

'Confirmed the house is empty, Mr Carver. She's not here.'

Carver nodded, 'Come with me.' He led him through to the Playroom.

'Fuck me,' Bennett said, taking it in.

'Keep everyone out of here. I'm going to call Forensic in to do it. We don't know yet it isn't a murder-scene.'

They returned to the kitchen and Carver left them to do their stuff. He wasn't POLSA-trained and knew better than to interfere. The team knew what they were looking for. If there was anything in the house that could tell him who, or where, Tracy was – or Megan for that matter - they would find it. Jess stayed with the team. She would act as 'interpreter', to give pointers on anything they found. Carver headed to the front living room where they'd all met that first time.

Without Megan's illuminating presence it seemed colder, less welcoming than he remembered, even allowing for what had happened the night before. He stared out of the window, wondering where she was. His feeling of foreboding was growing. He wished she would walk in right then. He would happily take a bollocking over the mess in the kitchen.

He rang The Duke, gave him an update and told him he would keep him appraised. Then he rang Claire Trevor, still at Shepherd's, and told her he had another potential scene he needed her to do. 'Just one room, mainly.' From her response, he could tell she wasn't pleased to have scenes queueing up.

Morning dragged into afternoon. With the house, garage and out-buildings there was a lot to cover. The Forensic team turned up around two. Claire had left the Shepherd scene in the hands of her deputy and called in another team for the Poplars. She'd showered and changed, and was in a different vehicle with new kits. He showed her the Playroom, ignored her reaction.

'I need to identify anyone and everyone who has been in here.' He paused. 'You may find traces of Gary Shepherd.' She swung round, shocked. 'There may also be blonde hairs that match those from the other scenes.'

'It's a big room. There's a lot of equipment that will need to be done.'

'Take as long as you need.' he said.

As time passed without any word on Megan and nothing coming from the search, Carver's anxiety rose, steadily. He kept checking his voicemail and with the

MIR, but there was no news. The only message was from a DCI from Professional Standards wanting to speak to him urgently about Angie. Stuff him, he thought. His discipline inquiry could wait.

He rang Rosanna. She was calm, but sounded a little off-hand. He told her where he was, what was happening.

'How long will it take?'

'The rate it's going, all day.'

They talked about when he might be home. She told him to make sure he ate something. Bennett had already arranged a fish and chip run to the shop in the village. She changed the subject.

'I checked the shed this morning. I think someone's been in there again.'

'Really?' He thought on it. 'I'll arrange to get it alarmed. I'll get our CPO on it. Nothing missing?'

'Not that I can see.'

'Good. I'll ring later, let you know how it's going.' By the time he hung up he thought – hoped - she'd thawed a bit. He went to see where everyone was and how they were doing.

The House Team had started at the top and were working their way down. They'd done the second floor, were just finishing the first, and would soon start downstairs. He returned to the kitchen and picked his way through the meagre collection of plastic bags and envelopes containing the bits that had been deemed, 'promising'. Nothing jumped out, though he took a long look at the notepad from the side of Megan's bed. On it was the impression of whatever she'd written on the previous sheet before she ripped it off. An Ezda or a light test would reveal what it said. He wandered out to the front just in time to see two more of Bennett's team, a PC called Darren, and his partner, Judy, coming out of the garage. Judy pointed something at the up-and-over door and it started to lower.

He diverted in their direction. 'Wait.'

'There's nothing there boss,' Darren said. The door closed as Carver arrived. 'We've been right through it.'

'Open it up again.'

Judy pointed the remote and the door rolled up. Megan's gleaming Mercedes convertible stood next to the empty second bay. He stared at it.

'How's this here?' He turned on Darren and Judy.

Darren was immediately defensive. They'd all witnessed the interrogation at the gate earlier.

'No idea. We were just told to do the garage. It's clean.'

But Carver was out and already heading back down the drive, fast. As he reached the gate, Dan and Tony were pouring coffee from a thermos. Dan held it up.

'Want one Boss?'

Carver went straight to Tony. 'I thought you said she drove out in her car?'

Tony stiffened. 'She did.'

'So how come her Merc's still in the garage?'

Tony relaxed, a question he could answer.

'She didn't take the Merc. She used the four-by-four.'

Carver blinked. 'What four-by-four?'

'The one she keeps in the garage, next to the Merc.'

He blinked again. 'How long has she had a four-by-four?'

Tony looked at his partner. 'Dunno. Far as I know it's always been there. I think she uses it sometimes instead of the Merc.'

Carver's mind raced. He'd seen her Merc many times, but never a four-by-four.

'It's here all the time?'

Tony became wary. 'Like I said, she must just use it now and again.'

'It's definitely not used by anyone else? Someone who comes and goes?'

'No,' Tony said, sure of his facts.

'Who's it registered to?'

Tony's newfound confidence disappeared in a flash. 'Er… her I assume.'

Carver's voice took on an edge. 'You did check it when you logged it out?' Standard protocol. All vehicles entering or leaving an O.P. are owner-checked.

Tony began to redden, again. 'Er, well with it not being a visitor, I didn't think there was much point.'

Carver's hand shot out. 'Show me the log.'

Dan Hewitt, who had been following every word, dropped his beaker of coffee and dived into the car. He came out holding a clipboard which he handed to his grim-faced boss, at the same time exchanging a nervous look with his partner. Tony shrugged, like he was in the shit already, so WTF.

Carver scanned down the log sheet showing the past Twenty-Four hours' comings and goings. He pointed to an entry timed at 2320 the previous evening. It read, "MC out of OP. Driving Toyota 4X4" followed by a registration number.

'Is the number right?' Carver asked.

Tony looked to Dan.

'Yes,' Dan said. He sounded more hopeful than sure.

Carver passed the sheet to Tony. 'Run it.'

While Tony made the call, Carver paced. Dan

watched, nervously. When Tony emerged from the car, his face was even redder. He read from his notes.

'It's registered to a Tracy Redmond, 18 Oakfield Avenue, Heaton Chapel.'

Carver froze. Then he turned and started running back towards the house. As he ran he shouted, 'JESS. WE'VE GOT HER.'

CHAPTER 63

Heaton Chapel is one of Stockport's smarter suburbs. Oakfield Avenue comprises solidly-built, mainly detached houses with decent sized gardens to front and rear. They got there just as dusk was falling, Carver, Jess and Alec Duncan. Carver had reasoned that Tracy Redmond wouldn't recognise Alec the way she would Jess and, possibly, himself. As they cruised down the avenue, checking house numbers, Carver noted that most of the cars had German Marques, with the odd Jag for good measure.

Jess pointed ahead and to the right. 'That's it.'

Fronted by a low wall, number eighteen's front garden had been block-paved to provide an open parking space, which was empty. To the right was a garage with a metal up-and-over door. Next to it, a wooden gate into the rear garden was set in a high wall. Carver drove past, parked up then twisted round in his seat. 'Suss it out, Alec.'

Alec was gone five minutes. When he returned he said, 'No sign of anyone. No lights. I knocked next door. They're an Asian family. Only Mum in at present.

The way she describes her neighbour, it sounds like our Tracy, and her Toyota, but they don't see much of her. She keeps herself to herself and is out most of the time. She thinks the car was here around nine this morning, when she went out. It definitely wasn't here when she came back about two this afternoon.'

Carver checked around. It was now early evening. The occasional car drove past, a few pedestrians as well. Commuters returning home.

Jess said, 'What about a warrant?'

Carver looked at her. Most times with a case like this, he would be careful to follow the book. But right now lost time could mean the difference between life and death. He shook his head. 'A warrant would take hours. Besides-,' He turned to Alec. 'We don't need one if we're in pursuit of a suspect.'

It took Alec only a moment to pick up. 'Now that you mention it, I think I did see a blonde woman through the window, though it might turn out to have been just a reflection.'

'Carver nodded. 'In that case...'

They all got out. Before Carver locked the car he delved in the boot.

Jess rang the bell while Alec checked the gate. It was locked. When no one came, Jess rang again. Still no answer, Carver slipped the crowbar from under his jacket and passed it to Alec. Seconds later, the back gate was open. They slipped through and around the back. Along the back wall, the windows and doors were in good order. Metal-framed and hard to force without noise and effort, like Megan's back door. Around the other side they found another door in a recessed porch. It was older, with separate top and bottom glass panels.

The recess meant sound wouldn't carry. Carver wasn't overly fussed, but there was no point drawing attention if it could be avoided. Alec made use of the crowbar again and they were in in less than a minute, with only the bottom panel smashed.

They found themselves in a utility room off the kitchen. There was a strong smell of take-away. They soon saw why. The kitchen sink was piled with discarded oriental-style food containers and half-eaten remains. The ripe smell told Carver some of it had to be days old. From what he could see, the mess was at odds with the rest of the house. Whoever had been there recently had other things on their mind than clearing away supper. Carver went through into the hall, stopped and listened. The house was silent. If anyone was in, they'd have heard them entering.

He called out. 'Hello? We're the police. Anyone home?' No answer.

Several doors led off the kitchen and hallway. He nodded to Jess and Alec. 'Check down here. I'll look upstairs.'

On the first floor landing he counted seven doors. Towards the back of the house there was another flight of stairs going up. The two front rooms were bedrooms. One had a double bed that had been slept in but not re-made. A woman's room, items of clothing hung off wardrobe doors and handles. The dressing table was crammed with make-up items and traces of a perfume he didn't recognise lingered. The other front room had twin beds, both made-up, both unslept in. A third door opened onto an airing cupboard containing bedding and towels. Next to it was a bathroom, and next to that a separate toilet. He noticed that the water in the toilet bowl carried a reddish tinge. He checked out the bathroom. It was dusty and looked like it hadn't been properly cleaned in a long while. In the combination bath/shower were some blue towels, some of which were marked with dark, reddy-brown stains. A foul smell emanated and he stepped back. 'Phwoar.' About to leave, he glanced in the hand-basin. Lying across the plug-hole was a vicious-looking hunting knife, the sort with a serrated edge towards the end of the blade, which was clean. His heart started thumping. The sixth room was piled with junk against one wall. Bags of clothes, cardboard boxes, bits of furniture. The seventh, overlooking the back, was kitted out as a gym. There was a runner, a cross trainer, weights, benches and assorted fitness equipment. Whatever else Tracy was, she liked to keep fit.

He was about to mount the back stairs when Jess called up. 'Jamie?'

He retraced his steps and looked down into the hall. Jess was at the foot of the stairs.

'Anything?' she said.

'Not yet.'

'There's something down here you need to see.' There was a strange tone to her voice.

She waited while he came down, then led him back through the kitchen, into a living room then another room off which looked like some sort of den. A long table was pushed up against the wall. It was covered in papers, some loose, some bound, and piles of folders. There were also photographs, bound together in booklets in a way that looked familiar. Jess indicated a pile of papers she'd pulled out. He could see why. They were also bound, but with pink ribbon, as court documents often are. Trial depositions.

'Take a look.'

He moved closer. Tracy Redmond was, or had been, a barrister. Court papers weren't particularly significant. But two items drew his eye. One was a list of criminal indictments. Before he'd read a word something in his sub-conscious marked them as familiar. But it was the second item, a sheet of paper with the name of the case emblazoned across the top in stark, neat, court script that took his breath away and sent his senses reeling. REGINA - V - HART. The reference to the court circuit – 'In the County of Chester' - sealed it. These were Edmund Hart's defence documents.

'What the-?'

She touched his arm. 'And there's this.' She handed him a photograph.

It looked like it had been taken at some formal social event. The washed-out colour and hair styles suggested it was several years old. It showed an attractive, blonde woman in a revealing red dress and with a thin, black collar about her throat.

'That's Tracy,' Jess said.

It took Carver less than a second's study to realise that the man whose face he recognised at once, and in whose arm Tracy was entwined was not her client, as the presence of the court papers could have suggested, but rather, her boyfriend, lover and, no doubt, Master.

Carver felt a chill run through him. He turned to Jess. She was wearing a grim expression. 'We were right.' He said.

She nodded.

Carver's mind raced. Tracy being connected to Edmund Hart raised all sorts of questions, and implications. The most obvious was, is she the much-argued-about missing accomplice? But even as the several trains of thought occurring threatened to carry him away, he remembered. He hadn't finished upstairs yet. Instinctively, he looked up, as if seeing through to what lay two floors above them. A feeling of dread crept into him. Turning away sharply, he headed back the way he had come, leaving a surprised Jess staring after him.

'Jamie?'

'There's another floor yet,' he called back.

She hurried after him.

He went straight to the back stairs and started up. Near to the top, a stout door barred his way. He tried the handle. It was locked, no sign of a key. He called back over his shoulder and passed Jess who was right behind him.

'ALEC, I NEED THAT BAR.'

Moments later, Alec appeared and handed it up.

Carver jammed the flat end between the door and the frame and heaved back. Some of the frame splintered but the door sprang open. He went up and in, Jess and Alec following.

Outside, darkness was falling. But twin skylights in the roof let in enough of the fading light for Carver to see it was another dungeon-type playroom of the Megan Crane variety. It covered the entire roof space and contained the sorts of 'furniture' with which they were all now familiar. Behind him someone threw a light switch.

He didn't need to turn to see her. As the room lit up, she was there right in front of him, hanging by the neck from a rope anchored to a roof-beam. She was naked, hands tied behind her back. Scattered around, were items of clothing that looked like they had been cut, or torn from her body. She was hanging at an angle facing away from them, towards the front of the house. Her head had fallen forward so that her dark hair hid the face he didn't need to see to know would be blotched and bloated.

'Ahh, Christ.'

Behind him, Jess whispered, 'Oh my God.'

'Fuck-ing Jesus,' Alec said.

Directly under her, the killer had piled some sheets. Once white, they were now stained a dark crimson-brown. Her legs and torso were streaked with blood. Carver remembered the knife in the sink in the bathroom.

For several moments none of them moved. There was no immediate need. Urgent action of the life-saving variety was not going to be called for.

Eventually, on shaking legs, Carver started forward. As he stepped, carefully, around her, he was surprised to realise he was actually crying. Real tears. When he stopped in front, his heart was beating faster than he could ever remember. Already, feelings of guilt - and failure - that would outweigh anything he had experienced in the past were threatening to overwhelm him.

I'm sorry Megan. I'm so sorry. He looked up at the horror before him. 'I'm sorry.' The only words that would come.

He made to reach up to her, but it was as if his arm was stuck to his side so that he had to make a conscious effort to get it to move. His hand shook as his fingers neared the cascade of hair obscuring the face that had once been so beautiful.

I'm sorry...

He felt its silkiness against his skin as he brushed it aside. He didn't particularly want to gaze on the features that would bear no resemblance to how they once were, but he knew he must. He owed her that much. He focused through his tears, parted the dark curtain, and gazed upon her – and leaped back several feet.

'FUUUCK.'

Wide-eyed, he stared at her for several seconds, before sinking to his knees. Then he tipped his head back, and let out a howl of anguish that echoed round the room and made Jess clamp her hands to her ears.

It wasn't Megan.

It was Angie.

CHAPTER 64

During Edmund Hart's trial for the murders of seven, High Class Female Escorts, Carver learned much about himself. In the weeks and months following, he learned a great deal more.

Up to that time, Carver's understanding of what it feels like to suffer what is often referred to as a 'breakdown', or to experience real, debilitating 'stress', was sketchy, at best. He knew, vaguely, that 'stress' is something people suffer when work or personal pressures become more than they can cope with. But he had little personal experience of it. He didn't know what it felt like to be properly 'stressed'. He wouldn't. He loved his job. He was lucky in that his personal life had never derailed in any of the ways some people's do - the single exception being his divorce. His health was good, and his finances were okay - more or less. Work-wise, he'd always coped with whatever the job threw at him, including the responsibilities that come with running a Major Crime Investigation. What he'd never realised however, was the extent to which that coping ability was linked to his own self-image. Carver had always viewed himself, and took pride in doing so, as someone who always sought to, 'do the right thing'. As someone once pointed out, it would have been during his formative years that he developed a strong sense of 'right', 'wrong', and 'justice'. As he grew into adulthood this understanding became his moral compass, though it didn't necessarily follow that meant being a slave to, 'the rules'. If serving 'justice' meant bending them, or even subverting them all together, then so be it. Given his job, it was as well that this tendency was balanced by a strong sense of professionalism. And though a band of grey often separated white from black, he was clear about when and where to draw the line. As his career progressed, these attributes served him well. By the age of thirty, he'd made Detective Inspector, occasionally filling the SIO role in respect of, if not yet first tier, then certainly second tier, major crime. At no time did he give any thought to what influence his father may, or may not, have had on his career progression.

Then he met Angela Kendrick.

By then, Carver was already experienced at cultivating and running informants, his attachment to NCIS - later to become the National Crime Agency - had seen to that. He was well versed in Informant Handling, and knew well the practical and moral dilemmas it brings. It had never been a problem. As he liked to instruct his team, 'Stay on the right side of the track, keep it business-like, don't get personally involved, and you'll be fine. Ignore those rules, and you'll find yourself on the slippery slope.'

Which is exactly what happened with Angie.

Before Hart, Carver had never had a case before the court where he wasn't one-hundred-percent confident that whatever crap the defence might throw at him, none of it would stick. His moral compass had always seen to that. In that respect, Regina –v- Hart was a whole new experience. And six weeks waiting to see if today was the day the defence would drop a bombshell that would blow a good part of the prosecution case apart, and maybe lead to the worst serial killer the country had seen since the Yorkshire Ripper walk free, was a long time to be under the cosh. Day by day, week by week, it took its toll. It began with sleepless nights. Then came the sweats. Soon it was the racing heart-beat, the shakes, an inability to concentrate on anything apart from what might happen. By the last week of the trial, Carver arrived in court every day convinced that the case was on the point of collapse – and that his relationship with a key prosecution witness would be the cause of it.

The reality was that the weight of evidence against Hart - the sightings, the forensic, the DNA, the stuff found in his house – meant that Carver's evidence was almost immaterial. The only way Hart wasn't going to get convicted was if evidence emerged that the jury had been got at, and there was never any need for that. But Carver didn't see it that way.

Even after Hart's conviction, Carver remained convinced his relationship with Angie would come out and the case would be called for re-trial. By this time, it was obvious to many that something was wrong. Things got worse when the documentary aired, followed soon after by the Sunday Times Magazine feature. They both focused, though to differing degrees, on the, 'young/intuitive/inspirational' Detective Inspector reported to have led the investigation. Which was wrong to start with. Carver was actually one of three ASIOs to what was the largest man-hunt the country had seen for years. But the way the Times journalist, Jackson, presented it, The Escort Killer investigation was going nowhere until Carver joined it and brought his particular skills and experience to bear. According to Jackson, it was Carver and Carver alone people should thank for seeing Edmund Hart put where he could do no more harm. It was bollocks, of course. Carver knew it. The media people knew it. Everyone close to the investigation knew it. It didn't matter. That was the way it was told and it was the way it stayed. Unsurprisingly, some weren't happy. The fact that Carver tried at every opportunity to make clear that he had only ever answered, truthfully, the questions asked of him during several, on-the-spot talking-head shots and interviews made no difference. The seeds were planted and the rumours grew. And while those closest to him knew the truth, there were plenty prepared to believe that Carver really was the grandstanding, self-promoting, stand-on-anyone's-shoulders-to-get-himself-noticed egotist the rumours painted. A man whose sole aim was to fulfil the ambitions set for him by his soon-to-retire Chief Constable father. And nothing Carver did or said, made a blind bit of difference.

Through it all, there was Angie.

And the fact she was pregnant.

And that the date of conception worked out to when she and Carver dined alone in her apartment while 'going over a few last things' before her meeting with a suspect known as 'Eddie' – or the day following, when Edmund Hart carried on raping her, even while the police outside were doing their best to find a way of breaking down the steel-reinforced door that, ironically, was meant to ensure her safety. Angie came from a

Catholic background. Despite her chosen profession, she remained close to, and respected, her mother. Abortion was not an option. She refused a DNA test. She remained steadfast in her belief that Carver was the father.

Carver didn't handle it well. It was only in the weeks and months following, after finally realising that if he was ever going to return to work he needed to listen to what people were telling him, that he sought help. Which was when he began to understand what had happened to him, and why. It was dressed up in all sorts of flowery psycho-babble of course, most of which sounded, to him, like bullshit. But the basics were clear enough. He'd let his guard down and erred in a way that threatened to undermine not just the most important case in years, but also everything he thought he stood for - the strong, always-do-the-right-thing individual he - and his father - wanted him to be. He also learned that when it comes to the human mind, everyone is different, but also the same. The threshold where people are so conflicted their cognitive abilities cease to function is different for everyone. Some people never reach it. But when it happens, what you need to be able to do is switch off, and walk away.

Right now, Carver was thinking of doing exactly that. After the initial, terrible, shock of discovering that the woman he once loved had been murdered in the most brutal, horrific way, he managed, just, to hold things together. Two things helped.

The first was Jess and Alec who between them dragged him out and back downstairs and badgered him so he stayed focused on what he needed to do. 'You need to call The Duke.' 'Shall we report it to

Manchester, or our Control Room?' 'Do you know the local DI?'

The second was that professionalism again. The realisation that right now he was the man in charge. And that if he wanted to ensure that whoever had murdered Angie – whether Tracy Redmond or someone else - was brought to book, then instead of giving in to the grief and horror that made him want to find some warm, dark place and curl up into a ball, he needed to make sure that things were done properly. Like contacting the right people, in the right order. Like making sure that the scene was properly preserved. Like making sure that Tracy Redmond's details and those of her car were circulated to those who needed them.

When the local police began to arrive – it was Greater Manchester's patch – he continued to hold it together enough to tell them what they needed to know, before passing them to Jess and Alec while he did the same with the DCI from the force's Serious Crime Squad. The DCI was a man called Peter Rigby. Carver had heard of him, though the two had never met When, instead of getting on and managing it as the murder scene it so clearly was, Rigby began demanding to be told the ins and outs of the whole Kerry Investigation, the inner demons Carver was battling against started to show. 'Just deal with the fucking scene,' he urged the other, 'We'll do the rest.'

Rigby was a thirty-year serving Manchester Jack, ten of them spent with the force's Serious Crime Squad. He probably had more experience investigating murders than Carver, The Duke and the whole of the Cheshire CID hierarchy put together. The suggestion, from an outside-force detective, on *his* patch, that he should just, 'deal with the fucking scene' and not ask questions, did not go down well. Things were about to blow when Jess stepped in.

Taking light hold of the DCI's elbow, she smiled at him. 'Can I just have a quick word Sir?' She didn't wait for a reply but guided him to the other side of the room where she spoke with him, quietly, but firmly. While they were consulting, Carver made more phone calls. Across the room he was conscious of the looks, glances and nods being aimed in his direction. More than once he heard Rigby declare, 'Fuck me.'

When Rigby returned, he was calmer, and more disposed to cooperate than he had been. 'I'll see to things here, mate. Don't worry.'

Carver nodded his thanks, to Jess also.

But once all the immediate stuff had been seen to, Carver began to recognise what was happening in his head. Random thoughts kept popping into his brain. Some needed thinking about, like the fact they still needed to find Megan. Others didn't. What the hell did it matter whether or not Rosanna had anything in for supper that evening – assuming he ever got home in any time to eat? He thought about ringing her and letting her know what had happened, but decided against. It was such a horrendous thing to have to share, he should do it face-to-face. Besides, if he told her over the telephone, she would only worry about him - maybe with good reason. Then something occurred to him that *was* important. In fact, it was the most important thing of all. 'Fuck,' he said. And immediately felt bad for not thinking of it sooner.

He dug out his phone, went into voicemail, brought up the message from the DCI in Professional Standards he had ignored earlier and hit ring back. It rang several times before a voice said, 'DCI Braithwaite.'

Carver told him who he was, where he was - and what had happened.

Braithwaite's gasp sounded clear in his ear. 'Angela Kendrick? Dead? Christ.'

It took a few minutes, but once he got his head round the facts, he told Carver how Angie's boyfriend, Rob, had reported her missing two days earlier. Knowing her history, as well as what had happened with Shepherd, he thought Carver might know something and had been trying to get hold of him.

Realising that had he taken Braithwaite's call he may have been alerted to the danger Angie was in earlier, Carver froze, and closed his eyes. *If I'd only known...* But then he wouldn't have known where to look for her. She'd have died anyway... he thought.

The DCI was thanking him for letting him know.

'She's got a son,' Carver said.

'That's right.'

'Where is he?'

'With his Gran, I believe. The boyfriend's a lorry driver.'

Carver nodded. He'd met Angie's mother, Sue, twice. Once at the hospital where her daughter was fighting to hold onto her life and, unknowingly at that point, the one just starting inside her, and again during the trial. They were frosty meetings. But he knew that since that time she'd grown devoted to her grandson. He remembered she lived somewhere near Oldham. He asked the DCI if he had her address. He didn't but his partner did.

'He's at the City game right now. I can ring him and

get him to phone you?'

Carver thanked him, and rang off.

He stared out at the back garden they'd broken into two hours before. It seemed ages ago now. *Jason...* He squeezed his eyes shut. As tight as possible. Wetness still seeped through. He felt himself beginning to shake, muscles going into spasm. It had happened before. He tried not to hold himself rigid – the instinctive response – and worked at slowing his breathing down. *Long and deep....* It helped, a little.

'Jamie?'

He turned. Jess was staring at him, wearing a worried look.

'You okay?'

He steeled himself. Nodded. 'I think we ought to-'

'Jamie.' Her hand came up in a 'stop' signal.

'What?'

'There's nothing more we can do here. We should go. Rigby's got things in hand.'

'Okay. In that case, we'll head back to-'

'No.' The hand again. 'The only place you're heading is home. You need a time out. We'll pick it all up with The Duke in the morning. You need to get some sleep.'

'Oh yeah, like I'm going to sleep.'

'Whatever, you need to be home.' She closed on him, stared up at him. 'You know what I'm talking about.'

He thought to come back at her, but then realised. She was right. If he stayed here any longer he would start to lose it. Fuck, he was *already* starting to lose it. 'Megan's still out there somewhere. She-'

'We don't know where she is and until Tracy turns up, there's nothing else we can do. It's no good running round in circles.'

He gave in. Nodded. 'Okay.'

'Give me your keys. I'll drive.'

'Like hell.'

'Give me your keys.'

In the end they compromised. Jess sat up front while he drove them back to the Poplars where Alec had left a car. She wanted to make sure he was fit to drive. He was, just. When they got there, Claire and her team were just finishing up their examination of Megan's Playroom. The search team had gone long ago. He told Claire about what they'd found at Oakfield Avenue, and gave her the name of the Forensic she would need to liaise with in the morning. Now going on eight o'clock, Tony Turner and Dan Hewitt had finally been allowed to go off shift to be relieved by another crew. Carver made sure they knew to ring him at once if Megan, or anyone else, showed.

'You sure you're okay?' Jess said as he made ready to leave. She and Alec were going to wait while Claire finished and left.

'I'm fine,' he said.

'No, you're not. Take it easy going home. Do you want me to ring Rosanna and let her know you're on your way?'

He thought about it. 'Okay, but just that. I'll fill her in when I get home.'

'Okay. Drive safe.'

As he headed down the drive, Carver's thoughts were around how, one day, Jess would make someone a good wife and mother. And though he took her advice and drove, 'safely', he would never remember anything about the journey.

CHAPTER 65

Jess watched as Carver drove out through the gates and waited until the Golf's lights passed out of view down the track. Then she took out her phone and called Rosanna. It rang several times before dropping into voicemail. She left a brief message telling her he was on his way and giving enough detail so she would have some idea what to expect. She finished with, 'Some TLC I think, Rosanna, if you know what I mean?' She said she would ring again in thirty minutes, just to make sure she'd got the message. She left Alec talking with the gate team while she went to see how long Claire would be.

Claire was in the kitchen with her two assistants. They were labelling samples, organising and packing away kits and steel cases. Before he left, Brian Bennett had called someone to do a temporary repair on the back door. Most of the mess had been cleared away.

'Finished?' Jess said.

'Just about. The room was actually pretty clean but we've got hairs and we've taken swabs off everything. I suspect we'll have traces from several sources. Hopefully, what you need will be amongst them.'

As Claire's team started ferrying kit out to their van,

Jess mooched about, going from room to room, remembering the times they'd spent there with Megan, preparing for 'meetings', pumping her for information that might lead them to the killer. Like Carver, she was worried. *Where are you Megan?*

Claire called from the back. 'We're going Jess.'

Returning to the kitchen, Jess thanked her for her efforts, and waved her out. About to leave, Claire remembered she hadn't closed up the Playroom.

'Don't worry,' Jess said. 'I'll see to it. You get off.'

The Playroom door was standing open, lights still on. As she peered in, she realised it no longer spooked her the way it once had. She cast her eyes over the fittings and equipment, remembering the night Megan had led her there, the night she first met Tracy. *If I'd known then what I do now…*

She reached round the door and flicked the light switch. There were no windows so the room went totally black. Turning, she was about to close the door when she saw something, and stopped.

Across the room, a vertical sliver of light seemed to be showing on the far wall. Her first thought was that light from the kitchen must be filtering through and catching on a piece of equipment. But she couldn't think what it might be. She flicked the lights back on. A padded bench-affair fitted with straps and restraints rested at waist height against the wall, but nothing else. She stepped into the room, closed the door and switched off the lights again. The sliver of light still showed, only this time it seemed to be joined at the top by another, this one horizontal so it formed an upside down 'L'. She flicked the switch. The lines disappeared. Off again. They returned. 'What the-?'

Leaving the lights on, she crossed for a closer look. That part of the room was kitted out as a mock-dungeon, the wall covered in a stone-effect paper. Leaning over the bench, she ran her hand over it. It seemed smooth. But something caught her eye and she leaned in, closer. It took her a while, but then she saw it. A thin gap in the wall followed the line of the light she'd seen. She put her eye close to it. The light was coming from behind. She stood back, looked up. A slight mismatch in the stone-pattern above spoke of a similar gap running horizontal to the first.

'It's a bloody door.'

CHAPTER 66

Carver spent the first twenty minutes of his drive home re-ordering the to-do list he'd started on the moment they'd all left Oakfield Avenue. He needed a distraction from the grief and pain threatening to overwhelm him.

He was still going over it when he rounded a left-hand bend and had to stand on the brakes to avoid running into a trailer full of potatoes being pulled by a tractor waiting to turn right. The jolt of the near-miss brought him back to reality long enough for him to realise. It was exactly the sort of obsessive behaviour someone had once warned him about. 'It's as if your brain gets stuck in a loop,' the woman had said. 'Unless something happens to break you out of it, it can go on for hours.' As he swerved around the tractor, he nodded to the farmer who'd nearly killed him. He owed him one. But if he wasn't careful, he'd end up back in that place he'd found himself following the Hart trial, and which he'd sworn to never visit again. He needed something - anything - that would take his mind off things.

He pressed a button on the steering wheel. The dash-menu screen lit up. 'Music,' he said. 'Music,' the car's voice acknowledged. 'Amalia.' An album cover showed.

'Play.' Then he settled back and let the voice of the woman who was Rosanna's inspiration wash over him.

By now Jess would have spoken with Rosanna. She would know he was on his way. He imagined her, waiting for him. She would be shocked, naturally, when he told her about Angie. But in some way he couldn't explain, he was looking forward to it. It would be the start of a long conversation, one they should have had long ago. And once it was over, they could start rebuilding what they'd once had. He shook his head, realising how close he'd come.

'Never again,' he said, and gave himself to the music.

CHAPTER 67

'Hang on,' Alec said.

Jess stopped tugging at the bench as he bent double, peering beneath.

'I think there's... Yeah, there's a catch here. His shoulders heaved. There was a click.

Jess pulled at the bench again, only this time it moved smoothly outwards – as did the door in the wall it was attached to.

'Bugger me,' Alec said.

Jess moved around to peer through the gap. Stone steps led down into darkness. A dim bulb fixed inside and above the door's frame – the source of the mysterious light – lit only the top few.

'Look at this,' Alec said.

As she turned he pointed at the back of the door. It was covered in the sort of baffling she was familiar with from interview rooms.

'Soundproofing,' he said.

She was about to start down, but he pulled her back.

'Not so fast, lassie. Uncle Alec first.'

Another time, she may have thought to challenge such obvious sexism. But Alec was bigger, and heftier. If there was something...

The steps were steep. Alec took them slow and steady. As she followed, she tried not to think of all the films she'd seen were someone descends into a dimly lit cellar and something horrible happens. It was dark at the bottom and as she stepped off the last step she found herself up against Alec's back as he cast about for another light switch. Hearing his heavy breathing, she realised her heart was also racing.

'Aha,' Alec said.

Another bulb came on, as dim as the one above. There were two doors on their left, side by side. Keys hung on a hook between them. To the right was an alcove. Jess peered round and saw it was set up as a home-office, complete with desk, chair, computer and printer. Shelves fixed to the wall held an assortment of storage boxes and ring-binders. Next to the desk was a metal filing cabinet, four drawers high.

'Good God,' Jess said.

Jess had never really believed Megan's claim that she didn't keep records or correspondence. But during all their visits, particularly when they'd surveyed the house to prepare for her meeting with Cosworth, she'd never seen anywhere she might do so. Now she knew why. Curious, she slipped around Alec as he reached for the keys.

On the desk was an angle-poised desk-lamp. She switched it on. On the wall above was a pin board, covered in photographs. About to check them out, she spotted a sheet of paper in the print-tray. She picked it up and scanned the text. A description of an SM scene - two women and a man she gleaned - it read like an extract from the sort of erotica that has become popular in recent years. But her instincts told her it wasn't fiction. It seemed Megan was also a diarist.

Behind her, Alec muttered oaths as he tried keys in locks. 'Bastard.'

Dropping the paper, she leaned forward to inspect the photographs. They were in shadow and she couldn't see them clearly so she turned the desk-lamp up and round. At once she realised they were surveillance-type photographs. Taken at distance using zoom, some showed a man, others a woman, caught in random poses, going in and out of buildings, getting in and out of cars. The detail was still fuzzy in the dim light and she was having difficulty making out the faces clearly. She leaned in, closer.

Behind her, Alec said, 'That's the one.'

There was a click and one of the door handles rattled. She glanced round. He had one of the doors open, the room beyond was pitch black. He muttered something about a light switch. She turned back to the photos. It took a moment, then she realised what she was looking at. She gasped and stepped back just as a light came on behind.

'Oh, fuck.' she said.

At the same time Alec cried out, 'FUCKING JESUS.'

CHAPTER 68

It was past nine when Carver pulled onto the driveway. He drove past the house and parked in front of the garage next to Rosanna's SUV. He cut the engine, but instead of getting out, he waited, giving himself a few moments, steeling himself for what was to come. *Deep breaths...* The music had worked as he'd hoped. He was ready.

He reached for the door lever. But even as he pulled it, his phone rang. His first thought was to ignore it. But there was too much happening. He checked the screen. It was Jess.

'I'm okay, Jess. I've just got home. I'm fine.'

'You're there? Is everything okay?'

'Sure. I told you not to worry.'

'You've seen Rosanna?' She sounded breathless, like she'd been running.

'I'm about to, if you'll let me.' He heard something, in her voice. 'What's up?' He opened the door, stepped out onto the drive.

'We've found Tracy. And Cosworth.'

He froze. 'WHAT? Where?'

'There's a cellar under Megan's Playroom, with a hidden door and everything. She's been keeping them there.'

'WHAT?' His head swam. *'Keeping them there?'* 'What are you saying? They're dead?'

'No. They're alive. Not too good, but they'll make it.'

'What the hell…? What about Megan? Have you found her?'

'No. But there's something else.' For the first time he heard the fear in her voice. His heart started pounding. 'There're   photographs here. Surveillance-type stuff. They're of you, and Rosanna. They-'

'Me? And.. ROSANNA?' He tried to digest it. He couldn't. 'Whose are they?'

As he spoke he looked up at the house. Lights showed through gaps in the curtains and blinds. But something was missing. Then he realised. He couldn't hear anything. No music playing. He started towards the house.

'They're hers, Jamie. Megan's. She's been following you. Both of you. Some of them of are of you and Rosanna, *AT YOUR HOUSE* .'

'Here? *She's been here*?' His pace increased. 'Why would she be following us?'

'It's her, Jamie. Not Tracy. Or Cosworth. It's her. She killed Angie. Now she's after you, and Rosanna.'

In that moment he saw it. Like the final piece in a jigsaw that he'd been holding the wrong way round. Suddenly everything fitted. A feeling of horror, ten times worse than when he realised he was looking at Angie, filled him.

He started running.

'Alec's ringing Control Room now Jamie. They'll send someone. They- Jamie?'

But Carver wasn't listening. He'd dropped his phone

the moment he realised. It was no good to him now.

The back door was unlocked. He burst through, into the kitchen. Empty. He ran through into the living room, and stopped dead in his tracks. In front of him was the most terrifying thing he'd ever seen.

CHAPTER 69

Across the room, Rosanna was sat on one of the kitchen chairs. She was swathed in rope, a strip of silver duct-tape across her mouth. Her face was streaked with tears. Carver recognised the handiwork at once. Megan Crane, wearing a long, blonde wig, stood over her. Dressed in her classiest, dominatrix attire she was pressing the point of a knife like the one he'd seen in the sink that afternoon into the skin above Rosanna's jugular.

'What sort of time do you call this, Jamie? Wherever have you been?'

For long seconds he could only look between the two faces. Rosanna's, pleading; Megan's, taunting.

'Oh Jamie,' Megan said. 'Your face. You should see yourself.' She made a play of realising something. 'But of course. You haven't seen my blonde look have you? I only wear it when I'm working. Do you like it?' She swung her head round, like a girlfriend showing off a new hairstyle.

Carver swallowed, fought to maintain control. 'It's over Megan.' He held out a hand. 'Just give me the knife.'

As he made to take a step forward, Megan gave an, 'Ah-ah,' and pressed the point deeper into Rosanna's flesh. A speck of blood appeared, trickled down her neck. Rosanna squealed and squirmed. He eased back.

'Now, Jamie,' Megan said. Her motherly voice. 'Don't do anything silly.'

His mind raced, weighing his chances. A gap of several yards separated them. There was nothing to stop him launching himself across the room. But in the second or so it would take to reach her, she would have time to use the knife. He opted for reason.

'It's too late Megan. We've found Angie, and Tracy and Cosworth. My people know you're here. They're on their way. They'll be here soon. Don't make matters worse than they already are.'

She tried to mask it, but he could tell she was unprepared for the news. There was no way she could know of the day's events. He wondered how long she had been there. A good while he judged. He saw her eyes narrow, as if she was trying to work out how much of what he'd said was true, and how much guesswork.

'You know jack shit, Jamie. You're all bullshit. You always were.'

'It's true. We've found your cellar, the photographs, the court papers at Tracy's, everything. You were Edmund Hart's lover, like Tracy used to be. This is all about revenge.'

'Well that's very fucking clever of you then, isn't it?' She grabbed a handful of Rosanna's hair, yanked her head back. Rosanna screamed into her gag. 'But who's in control here, Mr Ace-Fucking-Detective? Me, that's who.'

Her tone was bitter and Carver knew he needed to be careful. He scrambled for options. None came. Alec would have told control room by now. Help would be on its way. But Pickmere was pretty isolated. How long? Ten, twelve minutes? And what happens when they get here? Just keep her talking. He checked Rosanna. Her eyes were beginning to roll. Megan continued.

'I suppose I ought to be impressed, not that it matters. By the time anyone finds you and your-' She brought her face close to Rosanna's, licked her tongue all the way up her cheek, '-lover, I'll be long gone. And unlike you, I'll have kept my promise.'

'Promise?' Carver thought he knew, but he needed her to talk. She smiled an evil smile. 'Come on, Jamie. You know what I'm talking about. To kill you and that other bitch of course. For spoiling everything. If it wasn't for you Edmund would still be alive, and we'd still be together'

'Still killing you mean?'

She gave an obstinate look. 'Maybe, maybe not. That was always more Edmund's thing than mine, though I have to say-' She cast her eyes down at Rosanna in a way that made his skin crawl. 'It has its attractions.'

'If it's about me and Angie, then there's no need to hurt Rosanna. You can let her go.'

She feigned sympathy. 'Oh Jamie, that's so, *gallant.* But that's the whole point. It was because of you the man I loved died. So now I'm going to kill the woman, or should I say *women*, you love. First, Angie. Now her.'

He didn't even try logic. He needed to unsettle her more. He tried a different tack.

'So why all the window dressing? The whole Worshipper thing. Killing all those women. What was that all about?'

'Well, I had to make it interesting, Jamie. Or you would never have got involved. And without you I wouldn't have been able to find Angie. A simple murder wouldn't have done it. It had to be especially challenging to attract a man of your... experience?'

As it all became clear, his blood ran even colder. Five women murdered? Shepherd as well? Just so she could get close to him?

'I admit I was stuck on how to do it at first. Then I remembered the little scenario Edmund came up with years ago with Tracy. The one he got William to photograph. And I thought, that would be perfect. Right up your street as it were. And I was right, wasn't I?'

Carver sensed another brick falling into place. 'The magazine. DOM. You sent it to me.'

'Of course. You were taking so long to make the connections, I decided you needed a little shove in the right direction.' As if amused by her own cleverness, she threw her head back and laughed. For a split-second he thought he saw half a chance and girded himself. But she must have seen him tense and before he could move she focused again.

'Don't Jamie. You're not dealing with a novice. I know what I'm doing.'

The chance gone, he checked Rosanna again. Her head was lolling from side to side now, almost out of it. He needed to do something. Anything.

Having reinforced her command of the situation, Megan seemed happy to gloat. 'Once I had you, I knew it would just be a matter of time before you led me to Angie. As it happened, our friend Gary was most helpful in that regard. So talkative, once he got going.' The smile came back. 'Once I *made* him get going.'

'And Tracy was going to take the fall, I take it? The hairs you left at the scenes were hers?' She smiled a self-satisfied smile. 'I had a nice little suicide pact planned for her, and Cosworth. It would have looked like they were both in it together. But it seems you've ruined my plan. Never mind. Another time perhaps.'

He shook his head, tried to inject confidence in his words. 'There's not going to be another time, Megan. Whatever you do here, you can't get away. There's nowhere you can hide.'

She gave a sly look. 'Oh, don't worry about me, Jamie. I know *lots* of well-connected people who will be more than willing to help me disappear.' She gathered herself, as if renewing her resolve. 'But before all that, I have to keep my promise to Edmund.'

On the arm of the sofa, next to Rosanna's chair, was a set of handcuffs. She picked them up, tossed them to him.

'On your wrist. Just one for now.'

Puzzled, he did as ordered. *Now what?* He still couldn't work out how she thought she was going to kill them both. Rosanna was her shield. If she did something to her, he'd be on her in a flash. Knife or no knife, he'd make sure she didn't get up again.

Her next move provided the answer.

She nodded to his right. 'Now, up on the chair.'

At that moment, Carver was as scared as he thought possible. But when he turned to follow her direction and saw what she'd pointed at, he realised he was wrong. A second chair was set up under one of the room's exposed cross-beams. From it, a noose of thick hemp dangled. His stomach flipped a terrified somersault as he realised her intention. He turned back to her, trying to control the panic that was threatening to engulf him.

'Megan, I-.'

'DO IT.' she screamed, and pulled Rosanna's head back again, pressing the blade's edge to her exposed throat. 'Do as you're told and I might let her live.'

She's lying, he thought. *But what choice do I have?* 'ALRIGHT. Don't hurt her. I'm doing it.'

He stepped up.

'Now, you know the drill. Over your head.'

Out of options, all he could think of was to beg.

'For God's sake, Megan, please. You can't…'

'I can Jamie. I am.' The coldness in her voice told him pleading would do no good. 'Do as you're told, or your Rosanna dies.'

He slipped the noose over his head. Its coarse fibres itched his skin.

'Pull it tight.'

He did so, feeling it close round his neck.

'Show me.'

He held the rope high, so she could see it was snug.

'Good. Now, hands behind your back.'

He did as told.

'Cuff the other wrist.'

The chair wobbled as he wrestled with the cold steel. He stopped and steadied himself before continuing. The noise of the ratchet was like distant thunder, heralding a storm. A precursor to death.

'Let me see.'

He half-turned to show her his wrists. She examined them, then approached and made sure they were tight, closing the ratchets a couple more notches. Satisfied, she relaxed. 'You're such a good boy, Jamie. If I had more time, I'd give you a nice reward.'

The lascivious look she threw him fell on cold ground. Panicking to the point of despair, Carver was finding it hard to think straight. *I should have gone for her.*

'There now.' She dropped the knife onto the sofa. 'We're all ready. Time to get on with it, Jamie.'

Standing before him, she held up a length of black ribbon for his inspection. 'Recognise this?' She smiled up at him. 'Can you guess what I'm going to do with it?'

His eyes widened as he realised, helpless to stop it.

Turning, she stepped behind Rosanna and looped the ribbon around her throat.

'NO MEGAN.'

As she pulled it tight, Rosanna tried to scream, but couldn't. Her face began to redden, eyes bulging as she twisted from side to side, trying to escape the suffocating pressure on her throat. But it was no good. Megan was practised at her art, and strong.

Carver pulled at the cuffs, but, desperate not to lose balance, didn't dare struggle too much. And as he watched, he felt his mind going. It was like falling asleep knowing he was slipping into some nightmare from which he would never waken.

Suddenly Megan let go and Rosanna fell forward, sucking air, noisily, through her nose. She smiled at him again, torturing him. "How was that Jamie?' she said, innocently. 'Was that okay for a practice?'

He glared at her, chest heaving, nostrils flaring. 'You twisted, fucking bitch. You're going to rot in hell.'

'Maybe. We all have to die sometime. But at least I'll have had my fun. Speaking of which. It's time for you to experience what Edmund experienced. What he *wanted* you to experience. Time to say goodbye, Jamie.'

Taking up the ends of the ribbon, she pulled them tight again. But this time, as Rosanna started choking again she played out the ends enough so she was able to step closer to the chair, while still keeping the ribbon taught. As she placed her booted foot up onto the edge of the chair, Carver saw her intention. She was going to make them watch each other die. He saw her thigh muscles tense and he just had time to stiffen himself, before she kicked the chair away and he fell.

The drop was less than twelve inches, but it was enough that it could have snapped his neck. That it didn't, was only because he'd made sure the knot was to the back of his neck, rather than the side. And by keeping himself rigid as he dropped, he let his upper body absorb some of the impact that his neck alone would otherwise have had to bear. But he could do nothing to prevent the rope tightening round his throat, choking off his air.

But even as he fought against the constricting tightness something happened that, had he not been fighting for air, would have grabbed his full attention.

A noise like a bomb going off rocked the room. At the same time, the front window crashed inwards, showering glass everywhere. Something large and black came through to land on the floor in a tangle of horizontal blinds and curtaining, rolling into the space between him and Megan.

Dangling on the end of the rope, legs kicking in desperate search for the purchase that wasn't there but which was his only possible hope, Carver could only be dimly aware of what was happening. He was already becoming light-headed. He knew he had less than twenty seconds before the blackness took him, after which… Still, he managed to register the look of astonishment on Megan Crane's face as she stared at the object that rose from the midst of the debris, straightening up to reveal itself as a figure dressed in black motorcycle gear and a full-face crash helmet.

Before Megan could react, the figure's head went down and it charged forward like a bull in the ring to bury its head in her midriff with enough force that Carver heard the, 'whoosh' as the air was forced out of her lungs. At the same time the figure wrapped its arms round her and used the momentum to carry her back several feet where they crashed into the sideboard. Megan screamed in pain as she took the brunt of the collision, before they both fell to the floor.

Carver was still with it enough to fear that Megan would recover first and in some way reassert herself. But even as she raised herself onto an elbow, the intruder rolled up onto its knees and kicked her arm away so she fell heavily again. As she lay on her back, the figure dragged itself up to sit astride her chest. Taking hold of Megan's shoulders, it pulled her up so her head was off the ground several inches.

By now, Carver's eyes were flickering so he could barely see. He didn't need to. He knew what was going to happen. The figure leaned back, then snapped its head forward in a full-on butt, smashing the helmet into the middle of Megan's face. There was a crunch of breaking cartilage and bone, and blood splashed. Then the figure let go of Megan's shoulders so her head fell back to hit the floor with a crack and she lay still.

As the blackness closed in, the last thing Carver saw was the figure dragging itself off Megan Crane's still form and turning towards him. Somewhere far away, a voice called, 'HANG ON, JAMIE.'

There was a roaring in Carver's ears and he began to panic as he realised his lungs were empty. He gasped for air, swallowed, gasped again, then it was there, rushing into the empty spaces, bringing him back. He spluttered, gasped one last time, then opened his eyes just as the mouth that had been clamped over his disengaged and drew back. There was a film over his eyes so he couldn't yet make out the features that hovered over him but he could hear the creak of the motorcycle leathers next to his ear and was aware of two things. One, he was on his back, on the floor. Two, he was alive. As his breathing steadied and some but not all the panic began to subside, his eyes focused enough for him to make out the face staring down at him.

To begin with, it was etched only with worry. But then, as he blinked himself back to consciousness, the lips formed into a smile and Kayleigh Lee said, 'You alright, Jamie?'

Epilogue

Carver stared at the two women and the man across the desk. Their expressions ranged through expectant, to hopeful, to challenging. They were waiting for him to tell them how, if he were an Area Commander, he would set about drafting his Annual Policing Plan. He knew what they needed to hear. He'd read the latest Home Office Memorandum on the subject, full of phrases such as, 'Community Involvement', 'Police-Public Partnerships', 'Stakeholders'. But they weren't going to hear them. Not from him. Not today. Instead, he was going to do what the voice inside his head had been telling him he should be doing during the thirty minutes he'd been answering their questions. What he wasn't sure of, was how to tell them. Then he realised. It didn't matter. However he put it, the result would be the same.

Fuck it.

He stood up.

As he did so, the trio comprising the Superintendent's Promotion Interview Panel – more commonly known as, 'The Board' - rocked back in their chairs, thrown by the sudden change in the man they'd been expecting to impress them with his grasp of the subject of their enquiry. Their reactions almost made Carver smile. They looked like they thought he was about to attack them, or something. He didn't. What he did, was make eye-contact with each in turn, before saying, 'I'm sorry Ladies, Sir. I shouldn't be here.'

As his words registered, shock and apprehension gave way to puzzled surprise. The middle of the three

411

and the Board Chairman, Deputy Chief Constable, Derek Riley, was first to recover. Leaning forward, he pinned Carver with a look Carver read as, *I hope you're not serious.*

'I'm sorry? What do you mean, you shouldn't be here?'

Carver took a deep breath, already resigned to whatever fallout his decision would trigger. 'I mean that right now, I ought to be somewhere else. I'm sorry if I've wasted your time.'

Riley checked the woman on his right. Alison Roebuck, the force's ACC Operations, appeared to be still grappling with the unexpected turn the interview had taken. Her mouth was opening and closing, but no words came. To his left, Rachel Spencer, the force's Human Resource Director was showing the first signs of concern. She would be wondering if they'd unwittingly done something to prejudice Carver's chances, prompting him to throw in the towel and, perhaps later, raise a grievance. Riley returned his gaze to Carver.

'Is it anything to do with what happened? Your voice, throat or anything?'

Carver shook his head. 'Nothing to do with any of that.' True, there were still days when, by the time he finished work, talking felt like someone was sticking pins through his windpipe. But it was nowhere near as bad as it had been. There'd been mornings recently when he woke up feeling almost normal.

'I take it then, you know what you are doing?'

Carver nodded. 'I do.' He was tempted to say more, but resisted. It would serve no purpose, and besides, right now he wasn't really interested. He just needed to get out. 'If you'll excuse me?' Turning, he headed for the door.

As he grasped the handle, Riley called, 'Mr Carver.'

Carver turned. He couldn't read the look on his DCC's face. Riley had a reputation for being fair, but ruthless when he needed to be.

'You're sure about this?'

Carver met the scrutinising gaze. 'Yes.'

Riley gave it a moment, then said, 'In case you were wondering, you were doing alright.'

Carver nodded an acknowledgement, but said nothing. What happened next was up to them. They would either understand, or they wouldn't. As he left the room he didn't look back, nor did he linger outside to hear anything he may pick up. He could imagine. Walking out on a Promotion Board, particularly when it was going well, would be seen as evidence of either a loose screw, a career death-wish, or both. Carver thought that neither applied in his case, though he could be wrong.

As he headed down the corridor that would take him to the back stairs and a hopefully low-key exit from Headquarters, he wondered how long it would be before his phone started ringing. He needed to get his calls in first.

Five minutes later, he turned left out of the main gates, towards Chester. He travelled less than two miles before turning off onto the car park of the Shrewsbury Arms and parking at the back. He dug out his mobile. Rosanna was first.

'How did it go?' she said. Even through the hoarse croak, he could hear the eagerness in her voice. It triggered an acute feeling of guilt. She deserved better.

'Let's put it this way, I don't think they'll be fitting me for a uniform any time soon.' *Actually, that could be exactly what will happen.*

'Why? What happened?'

'Mmm, I'll tell you later. It was… interesting.'

There was a pause, then a note of suspicion entered as she said, 'What have you done?'

He sighed. 'Like I said. Later.'

'Are you alright?'

'Yeah. Just some things I need to do, then I'll be coming home. I'll tell you about it then.'

'So.. we won't be opening the champagne?'

'We might, if you're allowed. What did the consultant say?'

'He says the x-rays show definite signs of improvement. He thinks now that the damage may not be permanent after all, but I have to rest my voice for another month then they will have another look.'

'That's good.'

'That they'll do another X-ray?'

'That you can't talk for a month.'

As she reverted to her native language and the expletives she reserved just for him, he threw in a, 'Speak later,' and hung up.

He rang another number. A woman answered. They spoke briefly, agreed a time. He rang off, got on the road again. He called Jess on hands-free.

She tried to sound upbeat. 'How did it go?'

Word's not out yet then. For a second, he thought about dodging it, but then remembered. Whatever their difference in rank, she was as close to a real partner he'd had for a long time. He took a deep breath. 'You'll hear soon. They'll say I bottled it.'

He heard her suck air. 'Did you?'

'No. I walked.'

'You *what*?'

'I'll explain when I see you.'

'Hmm. Maybe you don't need to. I can probably guess.'

'That helps. How was the case meeting?'

'Okay, I think. Everyone seems happy enough. The Duke reckons its coming together.'

'And Craig?'

'He's got his head round most of it. I help him out now and then.'

'I can imagine.'

Even now, three weeks after, Carver still wasn't sure how he felt being replaced as Case Officer in the case of The Crown versus Megan Crane. He understood the reasoning. The fact that everything revolved, in some way, around him, raised obvious conflict of interest issues. The defence would have a field day if it came to trial with him still at the helm. But he was surprised just how far he'd been cut out of things, and by The Duke of all people. He had nothing against his replacement. He and Craig McDonagh had come up through CID together. Not friends exactly, but solid colleagues, McDonagh was an able investigator. But he didn't know the territory like Carver. In his idle moments he worried what his replacement might be missing. But that was where Jess came in. And once the trial began, there would be opportunities to make sure everything got laid out the way it should. Especially the stuff about Angie. Besides, it wasn't as if he had nothing to do.

'What about Merfyn? What's his take on it?' Merfyn David QC, was lead Counsel for the prosecution.

Having worked Carver's cases before, their respect was mutual.

'He wants to talk to you. He said he'd welcome-' Jess affected a passable Welsh accent. '"Some, clarrr-if-ic-ation over a couple of matters."'

Carver allowed himself a half smile. 'Right.'

'One thing. He's not going to pursue the little fingers angle.'

'He's not?'

'Too remote, he reckons.'

Carver wasn't altogether surprised. He'd wondered himself if, come the trial, the judge may rule it spurious.

It was during the one follow-up interview with Megan Crane he'd managed to sit in on before they barred him, when he spotted the significance of Corinne Anderson's bent-over little fingers. As she'd sat alongside her solicitor, saying nothing to every question McDonagh put to her, while all the time giving Carver the Mona Lisa smile he already knew would haunt him the rest of his life, he noticed her hands, resting flat on the table. Both of her little fingers were deformed. Kinked, so they wouldn't lie flat, the left one quite markedly. He cursed himself for not noticing before, but then reasoned, it only showed when her hand rested on a flat surface. And the only real chance he'd had to notice was that night her hand had found its way onto his thigh - and he'd had other things on his mind at the time. Perhaps if he'd spent more time with her, he might have seen it sooner and things would have been different. Then again, things might have been different in ways he didn't want to think about. He still saw it as a potential link in the evidence chain. But Merfyn David knew his trade, and if he thought otherwise... We'll see, Carver thought.

'One other thing,' Jess said.

'Go on.'

'After the meeting, Merfyn pulled me aside. He asked me how I think you'll hold up in the box.'

'And you said?'

'You won't have a problem.'

'Right.'

She waited, giving him the opportunity to say more. He didn't.

'So what will you do? About the Board thing, I mean?'

'Nothing. There's more important stuff to worry about.'

'Like…?'

'Like… I'll tell you when I see you.'

'When will that be?'

He thought about it.

'Soon.'

'You're a mine of information.'

'I know. Watch my back Jess.'

'I will. And Jamie?'

'Yes?'

'When it all starts… I mean… If you need someone to talk to...?'

'Thanks. I'll remember that.' He hung up. He knew what she'd meant. They'd spoken about it.

The past week or so, the media frenzy that had been running flat out since that night had calmed, a little. His last, direct approach from the press had been almost two weeks ago. Even the tabloids had finally stopped speculating about what actually happened. But once the trial started, it would begin again. One thing was already clear. Some media elements were lining up to use his past profile as a launch-pad for what they would no-doubt seek to portray as another instalment in the 'exciting career' of - as one had, horrifically, put it – 'Britain's foremost, serial-sex-crime detective'. It made him sick, and he'd told the Force's Marketing Manager he wanted no part in it, even if the Chief did see it as an opportunity to present the force more positively than in most of the stories showing up in the press these days. He still couldn't believe how they'd talked about it at the 'Media Strategy' meeting he'd attended with The Duke. At one point he'd wondered if they were discussing some Hollywood film script. He even called a time-out to remind them that people had actually died and others – Rosanna, Tracy, himself? - had been damaged by the events surrounding what he only ever heard referred to now as, 'The Worshipper Murders'. It made little difference.

The trouble was, only he knew the truth. That mistakes had been made. That some on the team had acted unprofessionally, putting themselves and others, at risk. That far from a professional investigation leading to the unmasking of the killer, the investigators had become 'involved', with disastrous consequences. And what will that do to their precious, 'Media Strategy' if it comes out? No, *when* it comes out.

It wasn't all.

Only now, after detailed analysis of her banking and phone records – those they knew about – and especially the explosive contents of the filing cabinet from her cellar-office, was it becoming clear just how extensive Megan Crane's network of 'friends' really was. It included people in positions of power, and authority.

People whose interests lay in not having their unconventional leanings aired in public. Which was why someone, maybe more than one, had arranged for Butler's, the most renowned Chambers in Criminal Practice, to provide silk for Megan Crane. So that matters other than the salacious details of the murders and her lifestyle, may be on offer to slake the media's unquenchable thirst. Even now, Solicitor's Enquiring Agents, - retired detectives mostly– were digging into every aspect of the case. Sniffing out things that might divert a Jury's – and the press's – attention, away from those who might otherwise find themselves in the spotlight. And Jamie Carver was their number one target.

Lawyers can sometimes be fickle, but they're not stupid. No DCI worth his salt could be as clean as the way the media had, up to now, presented Carver. He had to have made mistakes. He'd already had a telephone call from a friend on the Manchester Evening News telling him that someone was enquiring about a key witness in the Edmund Hart case. Someone who might have gotten involved with one of the investigators. And if they knew that then… He stopped, recognising the signs. Sleep was hard enough to come by as it was. He shook his head, trying to clear it of the diverting shadows.

He rang Rita.

'How are you, Jamie?'

Why does everyone ask the same question? His first thought was she sounded strange, then he realised. She was trying to sound sympathetic, recognising what he'd been through. It wasn't her strong point. 'I'm getting there. How's Kayleigh?'

She gave one of her customary snorts. 'Kayleigh's Kayleigh. She'll be okay.'

'Is she… er… how is she…?'

'If you're asking if she's over you yet, then the answer's 'no', but she's listening at any rate. She's one hell of a girl, I'll say that for her.'

'Tell me about it. Has she said much? About what she'd been doing?'

'Some. Apparently she followed you home a few times, hung around a bit, did a bit of stalking, spent a few nights in your shed. You know, the usual girl-with-a-crush-on-an-older-man type of stuff. You should be glad you don't do social media. She'd have been all over you.'

As he listened, Carver made a mental note to brush up on his Surveillance Awareness Skills. *Mike Frayne would love her.*

'She'll be okay though, won't she?'

'I think so. Eventually.'

'Have you talked to her about what'll happen after the trial? The papers, all that stuff?'

'I told her the court will give her protection to begin with, but it'll come out anyway. There's too much of a story there for it not to.'

'Will she cope with it?'

'Our Kayleigh? You must be joking. She'll be in her element. You watch, she'll be on daytime TV before you know it.'

'You think so?'

'She's a heroine, Jamie. How many fifteen-year olds do you know can throw themselves through a window, take out a serial killer, then save the would-be victims by giving them CPR?'

'Fair point.' Reassured a little, he switched subject. 'What's the news on the project?'

'It's carrying on, but we're having to revamp some of the TOR. Whatever happens to Kayleigh, the rest of the family still need to be protected. They aren't as robust as her. It could do them a lot of damage.'

'If there's anything I can do..?'

'Thanks, but right now you're best staying out of it. There's bound to be some reporter prepared to spin things so some will wonder what the hell was going on, if you know what I mean?'

'I do. Do me a favour, Rita. Tell Kayleigh I was asking after her and that I'll see her after the trial.'

'I'll make sure she understands.'

As he hung up, Carver's phone beeped. He checked his log. It showed two missed calls. The first was The Duke, the second his father. He may be retired, but some of his old network still worked. He ignored the return-call option and turned off the in-car connection. There would be time enough for all that. He had no idea what The Duke would make of it, but he thought he'd understand. And in a way he was even looking forward to speaking to his father. It was time he understood some things also.

In the twenty minutes following, his mobile rang several times. He didn't answer and he didn't check to see who was calling.

After driving anticlockwise round the M60, he took the Oldham exit, then made his way to the neat housing development two miles outside the city centre. He found it no trouble. He'd been there two weeks before. After the funeral.

He parked on the road across the bottom of the drive

and waited, gathering his thoughts. Turning to his left, he found he could see through the front window into the room beyond. A woman was standing there, looking out at him. Also waiting.

Right.

He got out and walked up the path. The door opened before he could ring the bell.

The expression on Susan Kendrick's haggard face was neither welcoming, nor accusing. He didn't try to read it. Whatever her thoughts - about him, her daughter, what had happened - there was nothing he could do to change them. Not yet.

She nodded a greeting of sorts, and stood back to let him in. He stepped past her and turned left into the front room. Paul Kendrick was sitting in the same armchair where Carver had seen him last. On his lap was that morning's edition of the Sun. For all Carver could tell, he might never have moved. He glanced up as Carver entered. His face was even more unreadable than his wife's.

Carver nodded. 'Hello Paul.'

The man nodded back, but said nothing and turned his gaze back to his paper. Sue harrumphed, but he ignored her. Carver looked at her, shook his head. *It doesn't matter.*

She pointed at the door leading through to the back room from where the noises Carver had heard the moment she opened the front door were coming. She nodded. She even tried a smile. He couldn't begin to imagine how hard all this must be for her.

He nodded back, smiled a, *Thanks*, and went through.

The boy was sitting in the middle of the floor,

surrounded by bits of Lego and half-built starships. He looked up as Carver came in. He didn't exactly smile, but later, on his way home, Carver would convince himself there'd been some recognition there.

'Hello Jason,' he said.

As he settled himself on the floor next to the lad, thoughts of bloodline, and parentage never entered his head.

The end

A Word from Robert

Thank you for reading LAST GASP. I hope you enjoyed meeting Jamie Carver, Jess and the rest of his team. The events portrayed here are set to impact on Jamie's personal and professional lives for some time to come - as becomes apparent as the series progresses. In particular, whilst the next two books, FINAL BREATH and OUT OF AIR, are complete stories in themselves, some of the themes, subplots and characters introduced in LAST GASP are developed further so that together, the stories form a cohesive trilogy - *The Worshipper Trilogy* - which many readers have been kind enough to comment on as being amongst the best they have come across in the crime/detective genre. I hope you may come to feel the same. They are all available now in e-book, paperback and audio format. For more information visit my Amazon Author Page or my website, robertfbarker.co.uk.

Enjoyed LAST GASP? Please consider posting a review. Reviews are the lifeblood of authors as they help to keep our books visible to new readers, and give us a better understanding of what you like in a story. You can post a review by visiting the book page and clicking on, "xxx customer reviews" HERE.

Read on to learn what happens next…

Megan Crane has unfinished business with Jamie Carver.

Find out what happens next in, FINAL BREATH - Book Two of The Worshipper Trilogy

A monstrous killer, safe behind bars.
But how safe is 'safe'?

An archive of debauchery and murder, poised to
ruin reputations, careers, lives.

A detective running out of time to find what he seeks.

For more information, click HERE or on
the image, above; or visit your favoured on-line
book store and search for FINAL BREATH
by Robert F Barker

Read on for a preview, a FREE download, and to
register for updates about future new releases, and
special offers

FINAL BREATH

Eighteen months on from the case that nearly cost him his life, only DCI Jamie Carver knows the full extent of Megan Crane's network of depravity – and the storm that will hit when others learn of it. It includes people in high places, including Whitehall's corridors of power, and maybe even the upper echelons of the Police Service itself. When members of her former network start meeting with mysterious deaths, Carver suspects that someone is out to make sure that their involvement with the deadly dominatrix stays hidden and will stop at nothing to make sure that happens. Desperate for information, but right now chained to a desk, Carver's only recourse is the one person he vowed to never have contact with again – Megan Crane herself.

The second in the *DCI Jamie Carver Series,* and **Book Two of The Worshipper Trilogy,** FINAL BREATH is a compelling story of intrigue, conspiracy, and brutal, bloody murder – one in which Jamie Carver finds himself up against people in high places, while forced to renew his acquaintance with the woman who, despite all his efforts, continues to haunt his dreams.

FINAL BREATH

Prologue

As has become his habit, the man waits until late evening when most have gone, to progress the work that plays on his mind more and more these days. Soon, he will have to make others aware of the time-bomb on which he is sitting. Before then, he needs to know how far the fall-out will spread, more importantly, who he can trust.

Tonight, he is working his way through more of the video files stored on the hard drive they recovered from the bottom drawer of the filing cabinet that now stands over in the corner. In doing so, his focus is less on the *what,* than the, *who*. Some he has identified so far - those who like to see themselves in the gossip mags for example - may not be overly-concerned about aspects of their lifestyle being revealed. They may even revel in it. For others, it would spell disaster, personal *and* professional.

As he finishes typing-up the file note on the clip he has just watched and clicks 'save', he checks the time. It is coming on ten o'clock, the limit he set himself for that evening. The hours he devotes to the work have expanded in recent weeks. In part, it is due to his desire to just get on and be done with it. But he is also conscious of the urgency of the task. When the shit hits the fan, he doesn't want to be the one accused of feet-dragging. He is also mindful of the effect it is having on other areas.

The woman with whom he shares his life for instance.

Like him, she still bears the scars of what they went through. He knows how she feels his absences. Once before he lost someone because he failed to pay attention to things that matter. He is determined that it will not happen again.

About to close-down and clear away, he pauses. He still has ten minutes. Provided the next clip isn't too long, he should still be home in good time. He hesitates, then clicks on the icon. Almost at once, he realises his mistake. The telling factor is the quality. Most of the stuff he has seen is amateurish, filmed on hand-held devices, the sort of thing people put up on social media every day.

Not this.

The stillness of the frame suggests a mounted camera of some sort. And the first edit, a few seconds in, shows at least one other is being used. Lit, staged and, by the look of it, maybe even scripted, it is of a different order to the others he has seen. A couple of the others are almost, but not quite, of this standard, the activities depicted, the sort that cater to a very narrow range of tastes. As he waits to see what the focus of this particular scene will be, he holds his breath, gaze locked on the screen. It doesn't take long for things to become clear, and when they do, his stomach starts to churn the way it does when he knows he is about to witness something it will take him a long time to forget.

It starts with the girl being led into the room. It is not so much her nakedness and the blindfold that worry him - it is a common motif in such productions - but her hesitancy, and age. The first could be down to good acting. But whilst her figure suggests someone of at least consenting years, it is clear she is not yet fully mature. His guess is late-teens, which means that regardless of whether she works in the industry or not, she is exploitable. Such exploitation takes many forms. Money, drugs, physical coercion, even the sex. His instincts tell him that in this case, the middle two are most likely.

It is when the camera pans and he sees the wooden beam with the noose hanging from it, the low stool set up beneath, that real fear starts to replace the churning. He knows how these days, visual trickery, clever editing, even CGI, can achieve the desired effects. But something tells him that what he is about to see may not involve such techniques.

For the next few minutes he sits and watches the scene play out. In many aspects, it mirrors the sort of 'edge play' that those whose tastes run in such directions can access on-line any time they wish. Only the girl's reactions, and the clip's provenance, tell him that what he is witnessing is not, in any sense of the word, 'play'. Tears of fear are hard to achieve in such circumstances, especially in one so young.

The end, when it comes, is not so much an anti-climax, as a confirmation of expectation. He has seen it coming, pictured it in his mind, from the moment he saw the noose. His own experiences of many months before helps in this regard, and he is far from unaffected. In this case, familiarity does not lead to immunity, the reverse in fact. Having seen it before, experienced it, he is uniquely placed to empathise with the girl's terror, to feel her pain. And though he closes his eyes, tight, towards the end, it does not lessen in any way the overall impact. The shaking that began in his arms early on before spreading through the rest of his body, continues throughout. And when, after a period of silence, he opens his eyes and sees the blank screen signalling the clip has ended, he knows that he does not have to wait until he can steel himself to watch it all the way through, to know *how* it ends. The same for its significance.

To this point, he has been comfortable responding to queries about his evening activities by referring to it as, 'research'. He has done so in the belief that the case that almost cost him his life - others were not so lucky - is now closed, that the matters he is 'researching' are historical. He knows now he was wrong.

The case is not closed.

In reality, it never was.

It merely continues.

And it is all going to happen again.

CHAPTER ONE

'I'm Xena,' the dark-haired girl says.

'I see,' the man says. *Zeena? What the Hell sort of a name is Zeena?*

'And I'm Gabrielle,' her blonde companion says, giggling.

'Of course.' *I'm missing something.*

"Xena" steps back to give the man to whom she is talking a better look. 'Is this okay?'

His eyes slide down to her boots and back again. *You've got to be joking.* But when he sees the hopeful look in her eyes, he chickens out. 'It's er… very original.'

Gerald Hawthorn has a vague notion that the girls' outfits - all gold bracelets and dangling fronds of leather and suede - are inspired by an old TV series. One that achieved cult status way back. Some swords-and-sandals romp about a mythical warrior-princess. But he and Barbara have never really done TV, and he doesn't like to ask, in case the girls think their attempts to comply with the club's strict dress-code aren't up to scratch. It was why he opted for a polite-but-neutral, 'Interesting outfits, ladies,' when he'd approached to introduce himself and welcome them to, Josephine's.

In truth, Gerald thinks the pair have missed the mark. Whilst his carefully-worded guidance allows for some interpretation, it doesn't run to any form of 'fancy dress'. Especially as the range of interests catered for at the venue he and Barbara have worked hard to establish as the foremost of its kind outside London, are quite narrow.

But it is the girls' first visit, and so he doesn't say anything. They will see for themselves as the evening wears on. And if they become regulars, they will soon pick things up. So he keeps conversation light and, whilst the older couple they came with chat to friends at the bar, he goes about making sure they don't have any wrong ideas, as he likes to do with first-timers.

Eventually, conscious he is nearing the point at which a couple of twenty-somethings may start to misconstrue the attentions of a man old enough to be their father - *grandfather?* - he decides it is time to move on. He hasn't sought to discover what they are into, other than themselves, but he suspects he'll know before the night is over. Wishing them a pleasant evening, he excuses himself.

As he moves away, they huddle into each other. And before passing out of ear-shot, he just catches the word, 'cutey', which brings on a smile. Gerald Hawthorn knows he is wearing well for fifty-five, and that women half Barbara's age still admire his combination of boyish good-looks, healthy tan and still thick, steel-grey hair. But he never tries to capitalise on his good fortune. He learned that lesson years ago. Nevertheless, as he heads off, the girls' murmurings lend his saunter an easy confidence that falls just the right side of arrogant swagger.

As he nears the club's newest feature, a faithful reproduction of the stocks on display in the Tower of

London's Black Museum - it cost an absolute *fortune* - Gerald's nose tells him the evening is starting to get underway and that it is time to check for, 'spoilers'. Many years in the club business, Gerald lets his sense of smell, as much as his other senses, tell him when things are livening up. Usually an hour or so after opening, it is when the lingering odours of furniture polish, disinfectant and Carpet Fresh give way to a heady cocktail of perfume, alcohol and pheromones. Loitering next to the stocks, he lets his practised gaze roam the room, seeking out anyone who looks like they don't belong. A lesser man may have difficulty completing the task. But though Gerald isn't blind to the sights on offer, he is professional enough not to let himself be distracted -an immunity built up during their Soho years.

It being a second Friday – Intermediates' Night - he takes his time. With so many new faces, the chances of someone out to cause trouble, or worse, a reporter working on an exposé, are raised. But they have several journalists on the books now, and they assure him that these days, the tabloids won't look twice at a place like Josephine's, not unless it involves a 'celeb', and he and Barbara are always careful about those.

As he completes his sweep, he relaxes. Apart from some new couples gathered in the middle of the room, already sharing excited introductions, he recognises most of the faces. And those he doesn't, seem sufficiently at ease to suggest it is not their first visit.

It is a good crowd for a Friday. In fact, the place is as full as it has been since Christmas. People finally seem to be getting over the brooh-ha of, The Trial, and all that followed. He hasn't heard *Her* name mentioned for months. Tonight there is even something of the old buzz in the air. It is mixed with outraged and, in some cases, embarrassed laughter as people compare outfits, or out themselves for the first time. As usual, the majority are second, or even third-timers testing things out one last time before graduating up to first and third Saturdays - 'Seniors' Nights.' He glances across at the bar where Greg and Nichole are only just coping. A couple of minibuses have arrived together, and for several minutes the reception area is chaos as everyone seeks to get in out of the cold. Most of the women's outfits - some of the men's also – do not lend themselves to standing outside on wintry February evenings while the door staff check IDs. It makes Gerald think about the design for the new reception area lying on his desk. Barbara could be right, maybe it should be bigger. Across the room, Carmen, their accomplished Meeter-And-Greeter, is doing her thing. A willowy red-head, she looks stunning, as always, in her green bustier. About to join her, a touch on his elbow stays him. He turns.

A blonde woman, hair coiffured and back-combed into a golden mane, is at his shoulder. She is wearing a white halter-neck dress, the front and sides of which plunge over her still-ample cleavage to her waist, where they are nipped by a thin, gold belt. Below it, the dress flares open from just below her crotch, allowing glimpses of well-toned leg sheathed in glossy, white hose. In her strappy-heels she stands an inch or so above him - a Goddess - and he feels the familiar stirrings. She kisses him, lightly, on the cheek before draping a tanned arm over his shoulder. Her gold bangle sparkles under the lights, and the five-diamond ring he bought for their tenth anniversary twinkles blues and yellows.

'How're things looking?' she says, as she casts her gaze over the assembling guests, as he had been doing.

'Should be in for a good night,' he says. 'Or we will be, once Alison shows up.' He checks the bar again where Greg and Nicole, are earning their pay. 'This is the third time this month she's been late. I'm going to have to have words with her when she gets here.'

Barbara Hawthorn gives her husband a sideways glance. 'I'll do it,' she says. 'You'll have her in tears.'

Staring into the lively blue eyes, he feigns surprise. 'Who? Me?' But he cannot keep it up. She knows him too well.

'I see Arthur's back,' she says. 'We've not seen him in a long time. Who's the girl?'

'Where?' He turns in the direction she is looking, which is when he sees her.

Leaning with her back against the far wall, near to the entrance to the Theme Rooms, she is talking to the sixty-plus corporate accountant they haven't seen since the scandal broke. He wonders how he missed her. He'd seen Arthur earlier as he'd circulated, and spoken to him, though only briefly. She must have been in the ladies. Wearing a shiny black dress which seems moulded to her, she is tall, even allowing for her heels. And the glossy, sandy bob looks real, rather than a wig, as many like to wear. As she and Arthur lean in to each other, conspiratorially, her gaze sweeps the room, falling on groups of guests, drinking them in, before moving on. Her undisguised surveillance, coupled with her confident manner - she looks as at home as a Saturday-Nighter - sparks Gerald's interest.

'I don't know her,' he says, staring across. 'He must have found himself someone new. Looks interesting, wouldn't you say?'

The hand on his shoulder flicks his cheek. 'Down Rover. You go help Carmen. *I'll* say hello to Arthur.'

She sets off across the room, exchanging nods of recognition and words of greeting with those she passes. As heads turn to follow her progress, Gerald takes pleasure from witnessing the effect she has on people - of all ages. At fifty-three, Barbara is even better preserved than he is.

As he joins Carmen and the newbies, now arranged on the sofas in the middle of the lounge, some of Gerald's attention stays on the trio across the room. Arthur's partner smiles as Barbara says something to her, then passes comment to Arthur, at which he laughs, heartily. Barbara turns, seeking him out, and points. The girl sights along the outstretched arm and for a split second there is eye contact. Gerald's pulse quickens. But then he hears Carmen saying, 'And this is Gerald,' and he turns to give his guests his full attention. There will be time for eye-games later.

'Gerald is one of the club's co-owners,' Carmen says. 'I'll introduce you to Barbara later.'

For the next few minutes he goes through the drill. Being welcoming - it isn't an act. Showing just the right amount of relaxed charm to put the women at ease, without alienating their partners. Mirroring the firmness, or lack of it, in the men's handshakes.

He asks how they have come to hear of Josephine's.

'Through your web-site,' says a woman with jet black hair and fingernails to match.

'From a guy I work with,' the male half of a younger couple says. 'He's been coming for years. I didn't believe him at first.'

'We saw your advert in Skin Two' a middle-aged man says, nervously. Then he remembers, and looks up, sheepishly, at the older woman perched on the chair's arm above him. Already in role, she glares at him. But it is early in the proceedings, and she lets it go.

Through it all, part of Gerald's interest stays on what is happening across the room. And though he cannot see their faces - Barbara's back is to him – his built-in antenna tells him that the mood has changed. Huddled into each other, the jokey chatter and smiles seem to have disappeared, replaced by earnest expressions and hand gestures. At one stage, as Carmen is explaining to her group the rules governing how to go about checking whether a scene is 'open' or 'closed', Gerald turns, to see how they are doing. He just catches the quick glance Barbara casts in his direction, before turning back to hear whatever it is the girl is saying. He isn't sure, but he thinks Barbara looked rather tense.

A few minutes later, Barbara breaks away and he sees her mouth to the couple her usual, 'Enjoy your evening.'

But the smile that goes with it isn't her normal one. And instead of coming back to him, she makes her way to the office next to the bar. As she opens the door, she turns, sending him a look he reads as, *'We need to talk'.* A feeling of disquiet begins to make itself felt in his stomach. A minute later, Gerald excuses himself to go join her.

As he enters, she is pouring herself a Glenfiddich. Usually, she is even stricter than he is about sticking to their, 'No Alcohol While Working' rule.

'What is it?' he says.

She tosses the drink back, then turns to him. Her face

is flushed, but it is too soon for it to be the whiskey.

'You won't believe it.'

'Who is she?'

She re-fills her glass, then turns to him once more. 'She's Arthur's niece.'

'And?'

'And she's police.'

He waits. It isn't as if she's the first.

'And she's asking about, *Her*.'

As the reason for his wife's early imbibing finally becomes clear, Gerald Hawthorn feels the world around closing in on him once more, just as it did all those months ago.

The call came in the early afternoon. It interrupted Q's dictation, and lasted only seconds.

'Tell me where, tell me when,' the man said.

Q thought he sounded weary, as if resigned to the inevitable. His podgy features broke into a sly smile as he made his reply, which was equally short. But despite its brevity, the exchange was enough to ensure that for the rest of that afternoon, Quentin Quinlan had to fight even harder than usual to keep his mind on his work.

As luck would have it, it was Wednesday, the day, 'Q', as he was universally known, liked to keep free of his more important engagements, just in case he needed to take some mid-week time-out to indulge his other interests. That particular afternoon he had scheduled only two appointments. The first was with a naive but not-bad looking middle-ranking oil company executive. Recently come out, the man was convinced that his Chairman's failure to grant him a place on the board was clear evidence of, 'blatant homophobia.'

Q's second client was a titled Cotswolds landowner. Six months earlier he had sold several acres of paddock to a couple of thirty-something, city re-locators. For no good reason Q could discern, the landowner had taken a belated dislike to the couple, and was now looking for Q to find a legal means through which he could steal his land back.

One thing Q was good at – the bedrock upon which his firm's reputation as one of the South West's leading litigators was built – was his ability to make his clients believe he shared their problems. That he was as committed - no, more committed - to righting the wrong they have suffered as themselves. In reality, he found most of the problems his clients brought him boring in the extreme. As he listened to them droning on about whatever 'grievous injustice' they believe themselves to have suffered, he often liked to imagine throwing them from the window of his executive office on the third floor of Cheltenham's historic Corn Exchange Building. Unless they were particularly interesting, when he imagined other things.

This afternoon, Q's eloquence was such that by the time both meetings ended - sooner than either client had been expecting - both left satisfied that their particular case was top of Q's High Priority List. They also believed that their cause was being pursued with all the vigour Quinlan and Quinlan's considerable resources could muster, and that they could look forward to early resolution.

In both cases Q waited until the door was firmly closed, before returning the papers to the, 'Special Attention' pile on the shelf behind him, and from where he had retrieved them only minutes before the clients had entered.

It meant that by four o clock he was free. Remembering to transfer the documents and other items upon which his future now depended, from his safe to his briefcase, he left the office, locking the door behind him. As he passed the temp with the yellow hair and dark roots, who had been his PA for the past month, he dropped his voice recorder onto her desk. He barely looked at her as he said, 'I'm heading over to Wilding's for a pre-meet before tomorrow's hearing. I won't be back today.'

Abi Forshaw watched her boss's overweight frame as it waddled its way through towards the Reception Suite. The way Q was leaning to his left, she wondered what could be in his briefcase that was so heavy. She didn't believe his story about going to Wilding's for a second. In the short few weeks she had worked at Quinlan's, Abi had come to understand why Q had had to make do with agency PAs for so long. And like those before her, she had come to decide that she'd had enough of his complete lack of consideration for those he employed. She had already set a mental reminder to not miss the following day's Evening News, the one with the jobs supplement. With her experience, she didn't need to work for someone to whom the word 'ethics' was a shorthand reference to an inappropriate joke he had circulated on the office e-mail concerning a lisping prostitute and a punter from Clacton-On-Sea.

In mellow mood following the telephone call, and with the rush-hour traffic yet to build, Q took the back road through the countryside to the Gloucestershire village of Newent. It was going on five when he swung his Merc onto the parking area in front of the former vicarage on the village outskirts which, twelve months earlier, had been redeveloped into three, single-floor Executive-Apartments. Driving home, he had been buoyed by the thought that soon, he would no longer have to worry about the exorbitant lease payments.

Q's apartment was on the first floor which, as there was no lift, and given his physical condition, was as well. Nevertheless, he was breathing heavily by the time he reached his front door at the top of the stairs. Unlocking it, he stepped inside, dropped his briefcase, and turned to the keypad on the wall. As he punched in the alarm-code, he called, 'I'm home Jezebel. Come to Daddy.'

He turned towards the kitchen but stopped as the keypad gave out a series of beeps. Thinking he must have entered a wrong number, he tried again. About to turn away, the beeps returned.

'Now what?'

Three times in the past month he'd had to call out the engineer to rectify faults in the supposedly, 'state-of-the-art', alarm system. He checked the panel, and was surprised to see the orange light blinking. Hadn't the man said that meant the system was in standby-mode? Puzzled, he stared at the display, but could not make sense of it. He was certain he'd set it when he left home that morning, and Mrs Rogers didn't clean on a Wednesday. Something else. Jezebel hadn't appeared to greet him, either.

Beginning to feel something wasn't quite right, but unable to put a finger on what, Q decided to leave sorting the alarm out until later. If he had to call the company out again, he would be giving them a piece of his mind. Switching the system to, 'disabled', he went in search of her.

He headed through into the kitchen, expecting to see her lurking under the table, but there was no sign. Calling her name in the sing-song she always liked, he shuffled through the chintzy lounge and into the master bedroom. But her welcoming voice and silky caress remained absent. Lifting the bed's counterpane, he bent to check underneath - one of her favourite hideaways.

'*There* you are,' he said. '*Whatever* are you doing you silly girl?' He reached for her, but to his surprise she recoiled, backing towards the wall, mouth wide, as if about to give one of her hisses. He was shocked. She never reacted to him that way. She loved him.

'Goodness, Jezebel. Whatever's the matter?' As he reached further under the bed, his large head and shoulders disappeared beneath the counterpane. And as he stretched towards the frightened animal, labouring from the exertion, he wondered about what could possibly have made her so nervous.

A noise from behind made him stiffen. A light bang, like a cupboard door closing, followed by soft footfalls on carpet. A voice he'd heard once already that day, though only briefly, said, 'You did say your place didn't you Q? About five?'

Panic rose within him. He forgot all about Jezebel.

And as Quentin Quinlan began to back his considerable frame out from under the bed, the thought came that he may have miscalculated. Badly.

Want more? - Click **HERE** or visit your on-line
Amazon store and search for
FINAL BREATH by Robert F Barker

In case you missed it earlier..

FREE DOWNLOAD

Get the inside
story on what
started it all...

Get a free copy of, *THE CARVER PAPERS* - The
inside story of the hunt for a Serial Killer - as
feature in LAST GASP

Click on the link below to find out more and get
started
http://robertfbarker.co.uk/

A quick word about Reviews

Enjoy reading? Do you know that reviews are the life-blood of e-book authors as they ensure books stay visible to new readers and bookstore 'browsers'? If you enjoy an author's books, let others know by posting a review and help him or her keep writing. If you enjoyed LAST GASP, please spare a moment to post a review as indicated below. Thank you.

If you purchased through:-
Amazon go - here
Amazon.co.uk (UK) go - here
Kobo - here
iTunes/iBooks - here
Barnes & Noble (Nook) - here

Ready for more and want to know what happens next? Go here

About The Author

Robert F Barker was born in Liverpool, England. During a thirty-year police career, he worked in and around some of the Northwest UK's grittiest towns and cities. As a senior detective, he led investigations into all kinds of major crime, including murder, armed robbery, serious sex crime and people/drug trafficking. Whilst commanding firearms and disorder incidents, he learned what it means to have to make life-and-death decisions in the heat of live operations. His stories are grounded in the reality of police work, but remain exciting, suspenseful, and with the sort of twists and turns crime-fiction readers love.

For updates about new releases, as well as information about promotions and special offers, visit the author's website and sign up for the VIP Mailing List at:- http://robertfbarker.co.uk/

Printed in Great Britain
by Amazon

48990917R00255